Ann Granger has worked in British embassies in various parts of the world. She met her husband, who was also working for the British Embassy, in Prague, and together they received postings to places as far apart as Munich and Lusaka. They are now permanently based in Bicester, near Oxford.

Ann Granger's Mitchell and Markby novels are also available from Headline, as are those featuring Fran Varady, a youthful private investigator living on her wits in inner-city London. *A Rare Interest in Corpses*, set in Victorian times, is the first in a brand-new series.

ANN GRANGER

A
RARE INTEREST
IN CORPSES

headline

First published in 2006
by HEADLINE BOOK PUBLISHING

First published in paperback in 2006
by HEADLINE BOOK PUBLISHING

4

978 0 7553 2044 8 (ISBN)

Typeset in Plantin by Avon DataSet Ltd,
Bidford-on-Avon, Warwickshire

Printed and bound in Great Britain by
Mackays of Chatham plc, Chatham, Kent

Headline's policy is to use papers that are natural, renewable and
recyclable products and made from wood grown in sustainable
forests. The logging and manufacturing processes are expected to
conform to the environmental regulations of the country of origin.

HEADLINE PUBLISHING GROUP
A division of Hodder Headline
338 Euston Road
London NW1 3BH

www.headline.co.uk
www.hodderheadline.com

This book, which is set in the past, is for my grand-children, William and Josie Hulme, who are the future . . .

I should like to thank all those who helped me in researching the background to this book and in particular (and in alphabetical order!) Catherine Aird, David Bell, Joe Burrows and Joan Lock.

Chapter One

Elizabeth Martin

THE ENGINE emitted a long sigh rather like an elderly lady loosening her corset and enveloped everything and everyone in a sulphurous pall of smoke and steam. It swirled along the platform and upwards to be trapped beneath the station roof. The smell took me back to Mary Newling's kitchen where, as a small child, I'd been given the task of peeling hard-boiled eggs.

At unexpected intervals the smoke veil parted and a figure emerged briefly before disappearing and being replaced with another in a flickering lantern show. Here was a woman with a large bag in one hand and, with the other, towing a small boy in a sailor suit. As they vanished, in another spot appeared a man in jacket and trousers of a loud check pattern with his hat at a rakish angle. I must have appeared to his view as suddenly as he to mine. He gave me a sharp, predatory look and I just had time, before

1

the smoke curtain was drawn over him again, to see the look turn to one of dismissal.

'Come along, Lizzie Martin!' I told myself briskly. 'You're neither pretty enough nor well-dressed enough to need worry you'll be troubled.'

All the same, it bruised my vanity to be dismissed so quickly.

The smoke was thinning rapidly now and the next figure to appear before me wore, to my great relief, the uniform of a porter. A small, wiry man of uncertain age, he grinned at me and tapped his cap in a gesture meant to signal respect, but which unfortunately looked much like the conspiratorial tapping of the brow to suggest simple-mindedness in a third party.

'Take your bag, miss?'

'I've only the one,' I apologised, 'and a hatbox.'

But he was already reaching for them and I found myself setting off after him at a fair pace towards the barrier. My ticket was whisked from my hand by the grand-looking official on guard there and my escort and I arrived on the main concourse.

'Being met, miss? Or need a cab?' The porter was peering up at me.

'Oh, yes, a cab, but—'

Too late. 'Follow me, then, miss. I'll take you to the rank.'

Mrs Parry had written to me at length, regretting it would not be possible for anyone to meet me but giving detailed instructions as to what I should do on my arrival in the capital. I should entrust my belongings to a porter who must be (the next words were heavily underscored) an employee of the railway company and no other. If I handed over my bags to anyone else, I should not be surprised if I never saw them again. I had obeyed that instruction, at least.

I was well on my way to obey the second: to take a cab, selecting one drawn by a horse in good condition, and enquiring first of the driver as to the amount of the fare. I should have him bring me to her address by the most direct route. Cabmen were sometimes impertinent when dealing with single ladies and I must on no account encourage this.

A small band of ragged children appeared and ran alongside me, importuning me for pennies.

'*Go on, gerrahtovit!*' roared my porter with unexpected ferocity. As the band scattered, jeering at him, he added to me, 'You want to watch out for them brats! Don't never take out your purse in front of them.'

'No, indeed not!' I agreed breathlessly. I was a new-comer, clearly from the provinces, but I wasn't stupid and we also had child thieves where I'd come from.

A new odour was added to that of smoke, coal ash, grease and unwashed humanity: horses. We had reached a rank of four-wheeled carriages of the type known as 'growlers' from the general racket made by their wheels.

'More suitable for a lady on her own,' confided my

porter. 'You don't want to go hiring a hansom. Where do you wish to go, miss?' And before I could answer, 'Look sharp, there, Wally! Here's a lady wants a cab.'

The cabman in question had been leaning against his horse's rump, engaged in the leisurely eating of a pie. He now pushed the last of the crumbling pastry into his mouth and adopted an alert manner. It didn't make him look any the less alarming. He was stocky and brawny and his features were so battered that it gave the impression he'd collided with a particularly solid object at some point in his life. Alone, I should have hesitated to approach him.

He saw my startled expression and addressed me. 'You worried by this squashed mug of mine, miss?' He pointed a stubby finger at his nose which was particularly crooked. 'That comes of my illustrious career in the prize ring that does. Illustrious but brief, mind. It was a woman made me give it up. "Wally Slater," she said. "It's the prize ring or me." Being young and foolish at the time,' he added confidentially, 'I took her and now she's my ever-loving wife and I'm driving this cab for a living!' He fell to chortling and slapping his sides. The horse gave a sardonic snort.

'Never mind all that, Wally,' my porter reproached him. Like the horse, he had probably heard this story innumerable times before. 'Where do you want to go, miss?'

I gave him the address, Dorset Square, adding, 'It's in Marylebone.'

'And very nice, too,' observed the cabman, taking my bag from the porter.

'How much?' I asked quickly, mindful of my instructions.

He squinted at me, which made him look even more frightening, and named his fare. I caught the porter's eye and he gave me an encouraging nod which I took to mean the price was a fair one. Or he might just have been in league with the cabbie. I had no way of knowing. They were obviously old acquaintances.

My suspicions were further aroused when the cabbie went on, 'It might turn out sixpence extra, miss, if we have to go the long way round on account of all the carts.'

'I want to go straight there!' I said sternly.

'Nah, you don't understand, miss,' said Mr Slater earnestly. 'They're clearing the site for the new station, see? Pulling down the houses and taking all the rubble away. It's blocking the streets all around and giving us cabbies no end of trouble. Ain't that right?' he appealed to the porter.

The latter's head bobbed like a nodding automaton. ' 'Sright, miss. The Midland Railway is going to get its own terminus, see, instead of sharing others? St Pancras it'll be called. The railway company has bought up all the houses and turned out all the people as lived there, and now they're pulling everything down and making it nice and flat. Why, even the church will have to go.'

'They're going to build that up again somewhere else, that's what I heard,' said the cabbie.

'Are they going to build houses for people to live in somewhere else, that's what I want to know,' countered the porter.

'It's the graveyard,' confided the cabbie with lugubrious relish, 'as they reckon will give them trouble. They've tried digging under it by way of an hexperiment, but they keeps finding *yooman remains*, as I've heard.'

They bent their joint gaze upon me to make sure I appreciated this gruesome fact. It was, I fully realised, a means of putting a stop to my objections.

'Very well,' I said, attempting to sound businesslike. I pressed a coin into the porter's hand and he gave me another of his peculiar salutes before scurrying away.

I just had time before allowing myself to be handed up (or rather, bundled) into the cab, to take a look at the horse. It seemed sound enough to my inexperienced eye, although had it been the most pitiful, overworked, broken-kneed nag on the streets of London, it would have been too late to quibble about it. We were off.

I have to admit I was curious to have my first sight of London and peered out as we rumbled and bounced along. I hoped too for a breath of fresher air as the inside of the growler smelled stale and sweaty although it was clean enough. But I soon decided against putting my face through the opened window. The noise was deafening and there was an alarming press of other vehicles around us heading this way and that, the drivers all shouting at one another to give way and watch out. There seemed only a notional respect for the requirement to keep to the left, most preferring to go straight down the middle of the road if they could, often to avoid a slow-moving omnibus drawn by its weary sweating horses. As for the other requirement, that cabs give way to private carriages, that too seemed honoured more in the breach than the observance.

All this was to say nothing of pedestrians who put life and limb at risk to dart between unforgiving wheels which at the least spattered them with mud and worse and would have bemired me had I been fool enough to put my head right out. Here and there crossing sweepers did their best to clear a path for the better dressed but most passers-by seemed resigned to the dirt. So I contented myself with observing from within as a bewildering parade of images flickered by, hardly glimpsed before gone.

With the pedestrians mingled sellers of every kind of small item from penny news-sheets to ribbons and matches while costermongers had set up stalls or parked barrows from which to sell fruit and vegetables. A strong smell of fish which briefly invaded the cab suggested a woman seated by a large barrel was selling herrings. A more enticing smell came from a stall on which stood two large copper urns dispensing hot coffee.

We were passing the site of the new station, apparently. I could see little of it but its existence was represented in the numerous carts laden with debris mingling with the other traffic. A swirl of dust-laden air invaded the growler causing me to cough. I had been warned of the nuisance these carts were causing, but even if I hadn't been, their lack of popularity was clear. Pedestrians expressed vehement frustration and cabmen hurled abuse as the creaking vehicles lumbered slowly along causing queues to form behind them. For my own part, I found these wagons and their loads singularly pathetic. Clinging to the heaps of broken bricks and shattered tiles were scraps of fabric which once had been a window curtain or a cheap carpet; occasionally a broken chair or a mangled piece of iron bedstead perched insecurely atop the lot. The remains of a straggling rose bush bore witness to some inhabitant's desire to have a garden of a sort. Broken planks, door and window frames poked up skeletal fingers, as if they would climb out of their rubble tombs. We jolted abruptly to a halt and I wondered if we'd arrived.

Some telepathy was at work, as a small trap window flew open above my head and opposite. Wally Slater's eyes peered through it down at me. 'Just another cart, miss. There's a bobby stopping us to let it through.'

'Bobby?'

'Peeler, miss, a hofficer of the law, what has made it his business to take charge. They're very good at doing that, the police, taking charge and interfering in an honest citizen's daily business,' concluded the cabman resentfully.

Now I did venture to put my head out of the window to see what was so different about this cart that the law had stepped in to aid its progress. A fresh cloud of dust assailed my nostrils and I sneezed. I was about to pull my head back inside when the new vehicle appeared approaching from a turning to our right. It was another wagon, much like those carrying rubble, but this carried only a single mysterious object covered by a tarpaulin. Unlike the whistling and catcalls which had greeted the other carts, a curious, uneasy silence fell as this one rumbled into view. Nearby an oldish man pulled off his cap.

The cab rocked and I saw that my driver had clambered down from his perch and approached a burly man in workman's clothes whom he appeared to know. They began a whispered conversation.

'Is it an accident?' I called out.

They both turned towards me. The workman opened his mouth but the cabman answered quickly, 'Nothing to worry you, miss.'

'But it is a dead body they are transporting there, is it not?' I persisted. 'Has there been some kind of fatal accident where they are working at the site of the new terminus?' I remembered then that some of the excavations being carried out involved a graveyard. 'Or is it a coffin from the churchyard?'

Walter Slater, ex-prizefighter, was looking at me in a way both shocked and disapproving. Whether he thought me bluntly practical or morbidly fascinated, either way it wasn't in his view how respectable young ladies should behave in the face of death. A little more distress was called for. However, I was never one for wailing and fainting. Nevertheless, perhaps he deserved an explanation.

'I am a doctor's daughter,' I told him. 'And my father was often called to accidents at the—'

Here I broke off. I had been going to say 'at the mines' but this was London, not Derbyshire, and what would these men know of coal mines?

So I completed my sentence, 'At the request of the authorities.'

The cabbie said, 'Yes, miss, I dare say.' But I saw my lapse of taste was not to be overlooked.

Now, Lizzie! I told myself again severely. You must watch your tongue! This is London and provincial frankness probably isn't the done thing. If you scandalise even this cabbie, what dreadful social gaffes do you risk making with the more sensitive class of person?

The workman, however, seemed amused by the exchange. 'Bless you, miss,' he said cheerfully. 'This ain't an old one, this is a fresh one.'

Slater growled at him to hold his tongue, but as I was already marked down by Wally as a person given to improper interest in the event, I might as well be hanged for a sheep as a lamb.

'What do you mean, a fresh one? It is an accident, then?' I demanded of the workman.

'They found a woman's body,' he returned with relish. ' 'Orribly murdered. She was in one of the 'ouses they're pulling down. They found 'er body hid under an old bedstead as was in there. She'd been there a few weeks, they reckon. She was as green as a cabbage and the rats—'

I felt myself blanch as the cabbie snapped, 'That's enough!' and cut short any further unwelcome details.

But I think he was well satisfied that the few provided had proved too much even for my composure. He gave me a look which clearly added, 'And serve you right, miss, for showing such an unladylike acquaintance with matters you ought to know nothing of!'

My loss of face was saved by the police constable who had been holding back the traffic. 'Come along, there!' he shouted at us.

The delay was over. Mr Slater scrambled back on to his perch and whistled to his horse and we went on our way.

I settled back, replacing on the seat beside me my hatbox which had fallen to the floor, and tried to put the workman's grisly description from my mind. But in its place came the image of that other body I'd seen carted away in a similar rough and ready fashion, all those years ago. That, of course, had not been murder. Or perhaps it depended on how you looked at it. As far as my father was concerned it might as well have been.

I forced both memories away, although I couldn't but reflect it was a violent introduction to London. I thought again of the scraps of curtain material fluttering in the breeze atop the bricks and the broken woodwork. Where had all the people gone? I wondered. Those who had lived in the demolished houses? Had they been given any say in their eviction? Probably not. They had been cleared away in the name of the unstoppable progress of the

Railway Age and they had left behind something dreadful indeed.

The horse had broken into a brisk trot. The traffic was thinner and we were in a much smarter part of town, passing down residential streets fronted with elegant dwellings and turning at last into a quadrangle lined by town houses looking out over a grassed area. It was as though we had stepped aside from the hustle and bustle into a world where life moved at an altogether more manageable pace. We drew up before one of the houses.

Mr Slater appeared to open the door and assist me to alight. 'This is the house, is it?' he enquired as if I might have misdirected him. 'Very smart. If ever I come into a fortune, which is not very likely, I should live in an 'ouse like this one. But, as they say, the probability of that is not very.'

His tone was philosophical. The horse blew gustily through its nostrils.

'And what might you be going to do here, then?' asked Mr Slater.

It seemed Mrs Parry had been right to warn me that London cabmen could be impertinent with single ladies. I opened my mouth to tell him it was none of his business, but I caught such a quizzical look in his eye that I burst out laughing instead.

'I am to be paid companion to the lady of the house, Mr Slater.'

He sucked his yellow teeth and the horse stamped

impatiently on the cobbles, striking a spark from its iron shoe.

'I hope it may suit,' said the cabman gravely.

'Thank you, Mr Slater. Now, could you bring my bag, please?'

'Very prettily put,' he returned. 'You're a young lady what takes the trouble to be polite to a cabbie. That shows a very pleasant nature, to my mind, even if you do take a funny sort of interest in the lately departed. You know what?' he concluded. 'You're a rare one, you are. That's my opinion. You're a rare one.'

He seized my bag, stomped over to the front door and rapped loudly with the knocker.

As footsteps approached across a tiled floor on the other side, the cabman suddenly added in a hoarse whisper, 'Seems to me you're all alone in London, miss. If you ever need help, you send a message to Wally Slater at King's Cross cabstand. Anyone there will pass it on.'

I was so surprised by this offer that I had no answer and no time to wonder what had prompted it before the door opened.

Chapter Two

THE GUARDIAN of the door was a butler of daunting impassivity. He received the news of who I was without comment and cast the barest glance at my plain walking dress and sensible laced Balmoral boots before directing me into the hall, there to wait one moment while he paid the cabman.

I could not see them from inside the house but I heard Wally Slater's cheery, 'That'll do it!' and, as the door was closed again, his whistle to his horse and the clatter and rumble of the growler's departure. I felt that although I had been so short a time in London I had made – and been parted from – a friend.

I had taken the few minutes alone to look about me with a lively curiosity. The house appeared expensively furnished in the latest taste, as far as I could tell. My knowledge of such things was limited. There was a good deal of Turkey carpeting which I knew to cost a pretty penny. I'd struggled to find money to replace our parlour carpet at home and been obliged to settle for something much more modest. A profusion of plants grew in ornate jardinières. The walls were crowded with some, to my mind, out-of-place paintings of Highland cattle incongruously jostling watercolours of the Italian Lakes. Mingled scents of beeswax and pot-pourri combined with a lingering background presence which I identified when I saw the gas jet projecting from the wall. This was modernity indeed. We'd had nothing but candles and lamps at home. A long-case clock ticked quietly in a corner.

'If you would follow me, miss?' The butler was back, staring at me still without a flicker of any emotion. 'Mrs Parry will receive you in her private sitting room.'

This sounded immensely grand. I was by now on the way to being a little overawed as well as tired from my journey.

I would afterwards go up and down that staircase many times and know it to be a short journey, but following the butler on the afternoon of my arrival in Dorset Square it seemed in the nature of a lengthy progress. He took his time and I was obliged to fit my step to match his. I wondered whether he always moved at such a snail's pace and if it was due only to the seniority of his position on the staff or if, indeed, he was giving me time to observe my surroundings and be impressed. We abandoned my luggage in the hall; how pathetic and worn my bag and hatbox looked seen from above! I averted my eyes in embarrassment.

I had leisure to take in a gallery of more paintings on the walls. One or two were quite nice sketches of Italian scenes but, as below in the hall, they were inappropriately interspersed with moody Highland cattle and blue hills in a purple mist. There were no family portraits. Perhaps they were elsewhere. More jardinières littered the landing with more leafy fronds sprouting from them; and a statue on a pedestal reaching as tall as I was. It was the figure of a turbaned youth holding aloft a branch of candles with a graceful arm. The candelabrum-bearer's sightless eyes were fixed on me, his full lips curved in a crescent. I felt quite grateful for that bronze smile.

The butler's ploy had worked and by the time we reached the door of the first-floor sitting room I can't say I had the impulse to flee – I had, after all, nowhere to run to – but I was apprehensive as to what I'd find. But as soon as I entered the room there was a rustle of silk and a small, stout but very lively woman scurried to meet me and embrace me warmly.

'There you are, dear Elizabeth! Did you have a good journey? Was the railway carriage clean? There is always such a risk of smuts from the engine to say nothing of having holes burned in your clothing by flying cinders.'

She looked me up and down anxiously for signs of damage.

She was a good deal younger than I had imagined she would be, scarcely three or four and forty. As I knew her husband had been a contemporary of my father's, I had

17

expected her to be much of an age with him. Her skin was very smooth, unlined and of that creamy quality which is sometimes found among country girls. Her hair was smoothed to either side of the central parting and mostly hidden beneath a frilled lace cap, just a glimpse of chestnut curls escaping at the nape of her neck. Though her figure was far from fashionable, her clothing came from the hand of an excellent dressmaker and, taken altogether, the impression was of an attractive woman of a certain age.

'I am quite all right, ma'am, and thank you for your kind enquiry.'

My apprehension on the staircase had vanished. I did however feel as though I was being assailed on all sides. The sitting room was as cluttered with knick-knacks and pictures as the hall and stair walls. It was a bright day in late May and, though cool, not really cold. Yet a coal fire crackled in the hearth making the room, to my mind, overheated. Coming from a household where the decision to light the fire was taken daily on the basis of first assessing the temperature outside and the likelihood of being chilled to the bone inside, this seemed wasteful to me. But the sight of the coals was cheery. They also made me wonder where they had been mined and if by some chance they, like me, had made the journey from Derbyshire.

'First we shall have some tea,' Mrs Parry said as she urged me towards a chair. 'I have told Simms to bring the tray as soon as you arrived. You must be very thirsty and very hungry. We dine at eight. Can you wait until eight?'

She peered at me. 'Shall I ask Simms to bring some light meal as well as cake? Say, a pair of poached eggs?'

I assured her I could wait until eight and a slice of cake was all I needed.

She seemed rather doubtful about it, but cheered up when the butler reappeared, greeting the appearance of the tea tray with cries of delight and clapping of her podgy hands. For all the tray was a monster of its kind laden with two kinds of cake, seed and sponge, and a dish covered with a silver lid, Simms, still without flickering a muscle of his face, managed it dexterously. When he had set it down, he swept off the silver lid to reveal a stack of hot muffins dripping butter.

'Only a plain tea,' confided Mrs Parry. 'But after your journey I dare say you are ready for almost anything.'

I was beginning to suspect I would need to be ready for almost anything in this house, and that food and the associated meals played rather an important role in Mrs Parry's day. She certainly ate more of the muffins and cake than I did, all the time urging me not to be shy and dabbing her chin with her napkin to catch the trickles of melted butter. At last she sat back with a satisfied sigh and I saw that she was going to turn to business.

'Now, Elizabeth, as my late husband's god-daughter you are quite a member of the family already and not just a paid companion like—' She broke off for a merest second before going on smoothly, 'Some young women.'

I was sure that she had been about to say something

else and wondered what it was that some prudence had made her decide to keep from me, at least for the time being. But I realised this was the moment to express my very real gratitude to her in offering me a home at a time when my situation had become desperate.

'Now, now, my dear,' said Mrs Parry, patting my hand. 'I could not do less. Mr Parry always spoke well of your late papa – although lamenting his lack of a sound head for money. He was sorry, I know, that your father having set up as a medical man in such an out-of-the-way part of the country prevented him from visiting.'

I was not sure whether she meant that my father should have visited or that the late Mr Parry should have done so. Either way, I didn't consider that Derbyshire was so very far out of the way, but Mr Parry's business would have given him as little time to travel as my father's calling gave him no time at all. Mr Parry, I knew because my father had told me, had made a good deal of money importing exotic fabrics from all corners of the world and also by some subsequent shrewd if unspecific investments. He had certainly left his widow comfortable.

'I have given some thought,' said Mrs Parry now, 'to what you are to call me. In the circumstances, I have decided on Aunt Parry.' She beamed.

I was embarrassed but thanked her.

'Naturally,' she went on, 'you shall live here as a member of the family. But because you will need to keep up appearances, I realise you will require pin money and besides, you will also hold the position of my companion. You have no money of your own, do you, my dear?' she added sympathetically.

I could only shake my head.

'Then, shall we say . . .' She ran a skilled eye over me. 'Forty pounds a year?'

It was no fortune but I had not to pay for my food and lodging and I should be able to manage if I practised a little thrift. Although, if I was to 'keep up appearances', it might involve a good deal of thrift.

I thanked her again and asked a little nervously what my duties would entail.

'Well, my dear,' said Aunt Parry vaguely, 'to read to me and make up a four at whist. You do play whist?' She leaned forward to await my answer.

'I know how to play,' I said cautiously.

'Good, good! I see from your letters to me that you have a neat hand. I am in need of someone to write my letters, a secretary. I find the keeping up of correspondence very wearisome. You shall accompany me whenever necessary and be in this house when I receive visitors; perhaps run a few little errands, that sort of thing.'

Mrs Parry stopped, eyed the remains of the sponge cake and appeared to enter into an inward struggle.

It occurred to me that I was going to earn my forty pounds a year. It sounded as if I would have little time to myself.

'And talk to me,' said Mrs Parry suddenly. 'I do hope you are a good conversationalist, Elizabeth.'

I was immediately struck dumb but nodded, I hoped convincingly.

'Now, I expect you would like to rest. Are your gowns quite hopelessly crushed in your trunks? Have you one that Nugent can iron out before dinner? I'll tell her to go along to your room and collect it directly.'

'Is there to be company at dinner, Mrs— Aunt Parry?' I was beginning to worry, conscious of the meagre contents of my one bag.

'It's Tuesday,' said Mrs Parry. 'So Dr Tibbett will be with us. Tuesdays and Thursdays are the dear doctor's evenings to dine here. He is not a medical doctor like your papa but a man of the cloth and most distinguished. Frank is still in town so he'll be there, too. He knows I don't like his choosing Tuesdays or Thursdays to dine with his friends. Poor boy, he is at the Foreign Office, you know.'

'I didn't – I mean, is Frank your son, Aunt Parry? Forgive my ignorance.'

'No, dear, Frank is my nephew, my unfortunate sister Lucy's boy. She married a Major Carterton who suffered a sad addiction to the gaming tables. Frank, like you, was left with nothing but, as I said, he's making his way at the Foreign Office and there is talk that he will shortly be going abroad. If so, I do hope it will not be anywhere too hot or too cold, or anywhere dangerous. Besides, the food, you know, is very strange in far-flung corners of the world. They eat quite disgusting things and season it all with peculiar condiments. While in London he generally makes his home here where he is at least able to enjoy a good English table.'

Aunt Parry heaved a sigh and, giving way to temptation, helped herself to a final slice of cake.

Simms, the butler, had reappeared silently at some point during the latter part of the conversation.

He said, 'If you would follow me, miss?'

He led me up to the next floor, along a corridor and indicated a door. 'Your room, miss.'

That was to be it. He left me there and I opened the door. Someone was already there ahead of me, a sharp-faced woman in a drab dark grey gown of intimidating respectability. She had taken my clothes from the bag and laid them all out flat on the bed. She straightened up from this task as I entered and turned to face me.

'I'm Nugent, miss, Mrs Parry's personal maid.'

'Thank you, Nugent,' I said, 'for unpacking my things. That's very kind of you.'

It was also extremely embarrassing. She could hardly have missed the darns in my stockings, the scorch mark on one gown resulting from an instance of carelessness when a rapid movement had caused the crinoline supporting the fabric to swing too close to the fire, to say nothing of the fact that a tartan cotton gown had been painstakingly unpicked, the material turned, and the whole reassembled to serve another day. But if Nugent thought my wardrobe scanty and well worn she didn't show it.

'Shall I press this one, miss?' She held up my best gown which I had intended keeping for special occasions.

'Yes, please do,' I said meekly.

Nugent whisked away with my gown over her arm. She had left in the bottom of the bag my few personal possessions. I took out my hairbrush and comb and a little ivory-backed hand mirror and set them out on the dressing table. The table itself was of old-fashioned style dating, I guessed, from the middle of the previous century. It had originally been a pretty piece with marquetry inlay but several pieces of the pattern of flowers in a cornucopia were missing. I guessed that its dated look and dilapidated state had led to its being banished to this room for use by the companion. I put out next the little japanned box which contained my few trinkets; I could hardly call them jewels. I had only an amber necklace and a little ruby ring, both of which had belonged to my mother.

She was the last thing I took from the bag, or at least her likeness was. I held it in my hand and studied it. It was a little watercolour, oval in shape and measuring about six inches top to bottom and four at its widest. It was set in a frame of black velvet and I guessed it had been mounted in this way at her death. It had hung by my father's bed. I had little memory of her. Not for the first time I wondered if I resembled her. The painter had made her eyes appear blue or grey. Mine were grey. Her hair was of a chestnut hue, but mine was quite dark brown. Mary Newling, our housekeeper, had told me that my father had never 'got over losing the dear lady'. I quite believed it. Although he had been a man of even temper and kindly disposition, I had always sensed a sadness lurking behind every smile. I placed the portrait flat on the dressing table until such time as I should be able to hang it on the wall.

There were plenty of pictures hanging there already, as elsewhere in the house. At least I was spared hairy, long-horned Highland cattle, gazing at me in a purple mist. Instead there were more Italian views and a particularly dislikeable oil of a weeping figure, heavily draped, surrounded by dark trees and what appeared to be tombstones. At the first opportunity I would take that down and hide it.

I opened the japanned box and saw among my simple jewellery a small piece of grey shale. This was my talisman, given to me long ago to bring me luck. It was in its way a curiosity. Impressed in its surface was the delicate and exact outline of a tiny spray of fern. I picked it out and turned it this way and that so that it caught the light, then I put it gently back. From now on, I would need to make my own luck to overcome any future obstacles. The first of these would be that very evening when I met the rest of the household.

I sighed. I was so full of cake and muffins that I couldn't imagine eating any more food that day. At home we had eaten our main meal of the day in the old-fashioned way at noon. This suited my father, who saw patients at his surgery in the mornings and drove out to visit his housebound patients in the afternoon, often not returning until late. We then ate a simple supper before the fire, generally toast and perhaps, if it were winter, some of Mary Newling's robust soups of root vegetables in a beef stock. The thought of the 'good English table' which awaited tonight filled me with dread.

I also feared I'd appear a bumpkin, even in my best gown. But I was still wearing half-mourning for my father and that surely meant no one expected me to turn out looking like a fashion plate.

I took myself downstairs a little after seven. I had twisted my hair into a simple knot and draped a shawl of Nottingham lace around my shoulders over the bodice of the gown Nugent had returned beautifully pressed. For good or ill, I'd have to do. Early though I was, the other company was already assembled.

I found them in the main drawing room; of grander proportions than the small sitting room I'd seen earlier and finely furnished. Again, a splendid fire roared in the marble fireplace. Aunt Parry greeted me effusively. She was what Mary Newling would have described as a sight for sore eyes. Her silk gown was in one of the still-new colours, magenta. Her lace cap had been abandoned and her chestnut hair was dressed in an extraordinary style, a tribute to Nugent's skills. It curled in a fat roll like a sausage

to either side of her head above her temples, with a bunch
of false ringlets hanging down behind. From her earlobes
dangled earrings with large green stones in them. A
matching necklace and several bracelets added further
decoration. I hoped all of these were paste and thought
they must be. An Indian rajah would have been hard put
to find so many emeralds if they were real.

There were two gentlemen standing before the fireplace.
They were deep in conversation as I entered but immediately turned to stare at me. The older one, on the right,
stood with his foot on the brass fender and his right arm
resting on the mantelshelf with its velvet and lace trim.
The younger one, on the left, reflected his pose in reverse.
It was impossible not to compare them with the pair of
china King Charles spaniels on the mantelshelf behind
them. The one on the right had been expounding some
point and the other listening attentively. But now they fell
silent as Aunt Parry presented me to them with:

'Now, here is Elizabeth Martin, come to keep me
company. She was Mr Parry's god-daughter and her late
father and Josiah were boyhood friends.'

There was no similarity between the two men now they
had abandoned their pose at the fireplace. The older man
was, I supposed, about sixty and must be Dr Tibbett. His
thick silver-grey hair curled on his collar and with his
luxuriant side-whiskers he made an imposing leonine
figure. His dress was severely black and I remembered he
was a clergyman.

The other, therefore, was Frank Carterton, the rising star of the Foreign Office. I reflected wryly that despite Mrs Parry's statement that Frank, like me, had been left with nothing, our situations had turned out very different. I depended on the charity of Mrs Parry to employ me. Frank was able to make a career. I suspected, too, his aunt made him a generous allowance. He was dressed in a well-tailored black cutaway coat with swallowtails and a brocade waistcoat of exotic appearance. His black silk neckcloth was tied in a large bohemian bow. His hair was curled, I suspected with the aid of tongs, and he was undeniably a good-looking young man. He ran his eye over me and I was unpleasantly reminded of the man at the railway terminus, who had appeared so briefly in the smoke and given me such a dismissive glance. It set me against him. Besides, I had never been able to abide dandies.

Dr Tibbett, the clerical gentleman, was also studying me closely from top to toe and now spoke. 'I hope you are a Christian young lady, Miss Martin.'

'Yes, sir, to the best of my ability.'

Frank Carterton passed his hand over his mouth and turned his head aside.

'Strong principles, Miss Martin, strong principles are what support us in times of need. You have lost your father, I believe. I hope you appreciate Mrs Parry's good nature in offering you such a comfortable home.'

I did appreciate it and I'd already said so, to the lady herself. So I merely said, 'Yes, of course I do!'

It came out sounding rather sharper than I'd have wished. Frank Carterton raised his eyebrows and favoured me with another and closer look.

'And a humble spirit!' said Dr Tibbett sternly.

'Now then, Frank,' interposed Mrs Parry a little nervously, 'tell us what you have been doing today.'

'Toiling at my desk, Aunt Julia. I have been responsible for the spoiling of large amounts of paper and the wasting of a great deal of ink.'

'I'm sure you work very hard, Frank. You must not let them take advantage of your honest nature.'

'The work is hardly strenuous, Aunt. I write a memo and send it to the next department, which writes another and sends it back to me. So we go on, back and forth, for the best part of the day, like a party game of forfeits. The amusing part of it is, the departments lie adjacent to one another and any one of the clerks has but to leave his desk and put his head round the door of the next room to make his enquiry. But that is not how government does things. I do have some news, as it happens,' Frank added a little too carelessly.

Aha! I thought. Whatever it is, his aunt will not like it.

'As I've been explaining to Dr Tibbett, I have been told today that I am shortly to be sent to St Petersburg to join the staff of our embassy there.'

'To Russia!' cried Mrs Parry. Magenta silk rustled and green earrings bobbed, the light glittering on them and on the bracelets as she raised her plump white arms. The

29

gesture might have looked theatrical if her horror had not been so obviously real.

'It's impossible. The climate is quite dreadful, months of snow, and the countryside full of wolves and bears and desperate Cossacks such as those who slaughtered our soldiers in the Crimea. The peasants are uncouth and drunken, disease is rife, and whatever will you do for entertainment?'

Carterton bent reassuringly over her. 'I'll do my best to keep clear of all of those. Don't worry, Aunt, I do believe I shall be quite happily employed there. St Petersburg is a fine city with theatres and balls. I shan't be put in the way of any peasants. The Russian gentry are most cultivated and, to a man and woman, all speak excellent French, or so I'm told.'

But Mrs Parry was not to be persuaded and although Dr Tibbett lent a hand to support Frank she was still bewailing his fate when Simms appeared to announce dinner. Dr Tibbett offered his arm to Mrs Parry and that meant that I, perforce, had to accept the arm Frank offered me.

'Funny old stick, ain't he?' whispered Frank, nodding at Tibbett's back, as the clergyman and Mrs Parry preceded us into the dining room. 'Dines here twice a week, plays whist another two days and generally finds an excuse to call on the remaining days. You know what that means, don't you?'

'He is a friend of Mrs Parry,' I muttered, wishing he

would not speak in this way, especially as there was a fair possibility he might be overheard.

'Don't take fright,' he returned, guessing what was in my mind. 'Old Tibbett never hears any voice but his own. It's my belief he is courting Aunt Julia. Good luck to him!' And Frank chuckled though quite what was so funny I had no way of knowing.

'When do you leave for Russia, Mr Carterton?'

'Ouch! Not yet awhile. Sorry. Have I offended you? I hoped you'd be a much better sport than Maddie. When you practically bit off Tibbett's head back there I had the highest hopes of you. Don't let me down, Miss Martin, please!'

He rolled his eyes at me comically.

I was not amused but I was intrigued. Who was Maddie? Annoyingly, now that I had a question to put to him, we had reached the dining room and I would have to wait.

It was soon apparent that Dr Tibbett's booming voice would dominate the dinner table as he began to give us his opinions on every topic of the day. Frank had the knack of saying just enough to keep Tibbett going and Mrs Parry accepted every word with rapt respect. Remembering Frank had told me the gentleman dined here twice a week and visited frequently, my heart sank. As Mrs Parry had expressed the hope I would be a good conversationalist, I took the first opportunity offered to enter the talk myself and asked Dr Tibbett if, by chance, he held a living in the area.

But I learned Dr Tibbett, apart from a brief stint as an assistant curate after he had been ordained, had never been a parish priest. He had spent almost his entire life as a schoolmaster, indeed as a distinguished headmaster. If he'd had no influential patron to further his career as a parson, then to turn to another calling had probably been wise. An ill-paid curate without hope of a living was little better than a poor relation like me. But a headmaster in a good school is a person of standing, requiring of respect. It certainly explained one thing: where he had acquired his hectoring manner. He addressed us as he would have done a captive audience of small boys.

He now set about putting me in my place for having dared to interrupt his flow. 'I hope, Miss Martin, that you will adapt to the ways of this household and be everything that Mrs Parry requires of you.'

'I shall do my very best,' I promised.

'You will be aware,' he went on, bending a ferocious eye on me, 'that the dear lady has already suffered one great disappointment.'

I was alarmed because I couldn't think what I had done, in the short time I had been in the house, to offend my benefactress.

But Frank spoke up quickly, saying, 'Dr Tibbett doesn't mean in your respect, Miss Martin.'

Mrs Parry was looking confused. She dropped the fork with which she had been dissecting a piece of turbot and mopped her mouth with her napkin. 'I had not actually mentioned the wretched business to Miss Martin, I'm afraid. I thought tomorrow . . .'

'Ah,' said Dr Tibbett, not a whit discountenanced at having put his foot in it, in the common parlance. 'Awkward explanations are never easier for being delayed.'

'No, indeed,' stammered poor Mrs Parry.

Frank moved in to take charge of the conversation. From his look I guessed he was displeased at Dr Tibbett's reproachful tone towards his aunt.

'See here,' he said. 'It's not a secret and, well, not such a scandal. It's like this, Miss Martin. There was someone before you who held the post of companion to Aunt Julia. Her name was Maddie Hexham.'

'Miss Madeleine Hexham,' said Dr Tibbett testily. He was taking badly to having his thunder stolen. 'A young person from the provinces, from the North, as are you, Miss Martin.'

'She came excellently recommended,' said Mrs Parry rather pathetically, I thought. 'With references from a friend of Mrs Belling.'

'Living in London,' said Dr Tibbett, fixing a direct gaze on me, 'was not what she was used to. To her inexperience of a large city and its temptations were added her own lamentable weakness of character and, we have to say, a certain talent to deceive. No doubt that is how she gained her excellent references. By dissembling, ma'am! By dissembling!'

'The fact of the matter is,' Frank said loudly, 'Miss Hexham disappeared from this house without a word of warning and no one has seen her since. Didn't take a thing with her and at first we all thought she had met with some accident. We informed the local police. Much they did about it. However, as things turned out, we needn't have bothered.'

'She wrote,' Mrs Parry explained. 'About ten days later, Elizabeth, I had a letter from her. Not a long letter but sufficient to – I cannot say to set our minds at rest – but at least sufficient to tell us what had happened. I was very surprised. But at least I suppose she felt she had to inform us of her actions.'

'And what were those, ma'am?' growled Dr Tibbett, his eyes alight with triumph. 'She had fallen into sin and debauchery, that is what her letter told us!'

'Run away with a man,' translated Frank.

'She wrote she was sorry to put me to any inconvenience,' Mrs Parry said sadly. 'She had not taken her belongings, her clothes, as to have been seen leaving the house with a bag would have occasioned questions. She begged me to dispose of them as I saw fit.'

'No sense of her responsibilities,' pronounced Dr Tibbett. 'Moral weakness, ma'am, moral weakness, sadly seen so much now in Young Persons!'

'When was this?' I ventured to ask.

'Oh, let's see, six or eight weeks ago,' Frank said. 'It will be nearer two months than not. I must say I was surprised, too. She always appeared something of a little mouse. Who'd have guessed it?'

'A dissembler!' snapped Dr Tibbett.

The conversation was interrupted at this point by the departure of the remains of the turbot and the arrival of a roast leg of veal. When it restarted, the topic of my predecessor had been dropped by common consent.

After dinner Dr Tibbett and Frank Carterton took themselves to the library to smoke cigars and Mrs Parry and I returned to the drawing room. I was by now very tired after a long day and it was a great effort to stay awake, let alone make much conversation.

Mrs Parry took the opportunity to return to the subject of Frank's proposed departure for Russia.

'I knew, of course, that Frank would be sent away somewhere. But I had hoped it would be somewhere congenial, say Italy. Mr Parry and I travelled to Italy on our wedding journey. The climate was so gentle and the scenery so beautiful, I quite fell in love with the country. We stayed in a delightful villa on the shores of a glorious lake surrounded by mountains. From time to time there would be spectacular electric storms and the lightning would bounce from peak to peak. But Russia, whatever will he do there? To think that only about ten years ago we fought them in that terrible war around the Black Sea. Frank's father was a cavalry officer, too, and might well have been present at some engagement there had he not blown out his own brains some years earlier.'

I was at a loss how to comfort her on any of these accounts, but soon the gentlemen returned and I was relieved of the necessity to try. I thought, as they came into the room, that Frank looked a little flushed and out of countenance. I wondered if there had been some argument. If so, it had not affected Dr Tibbett who seated himself with a practised flick of his coat-tails and effortlessly took charge of the conversation as before.

We were now treated to his views on the current situation in the Church of England. This, if he was to be believed, was beset by enemies on all sides. The forces of Disestablishmentarianism were marshalling their troops and infiltrating Parliament. Moreover, he informed us, the Church was undermined by the growing influence of the Methodists without and the sinister intentions of the Tractarians within, to say nothing of the assaults of Darwinism and its pernicious theories.

'I have read Mr Darwin's book on the origin of species,' I said brightly, seeing an opportunity both to prove myself a good conversationalist and to stop Dr Tibbett's seamless diatribe for a moment or two. His booming tones were making my head ache. Mrs Parry sat nodding like an automaton and Frank stared up at the ceiling, murmuring assent from time to time although he probably had no idea to what. I suspected his mind was elsewhere.

A stunned silence followed my words. Mrs Parry looked puzzled. Frank took his gaze from the ceiling, raised his eyebrows and grinned. Dr Tibbett steepled his fingertips.

'Not a suitable work to place in the hands of a lady,' he observed.

'My father bought it shortly before he died. He was reading it, in fact, on his last evening.'

'Ah!' exclaimed Dr Tibbett as though that explained everything.

'Oh well,' said Frank entering the conversation and with a gleam of mischief in his eyes. 'I have not read it as Miss Martin has, but I understand Darwin and his fellow naturalists have it all worked out that Creation as the Bible tells it is all bunkum. The world wasn't created in six days and there were all kinds of weird and wonderful animals about before the likes of you and me set foot upon the earth, is that not so, Miss Martin?'

Dr Tibbett cleared his throat. 'I myself agree that we must interpret what the Old Testament tells us. It speaks of six days when, possibly, what is meant is six epochs. But as to monsters roaming the earth? We must class the majority of those with the mermen and maids and giant sea reptiles of the ignorant mariner's fantasy.'

'Even so, the world must once have been a very different place,' I said. 'They say where there are now seams of coal there were once great forests and I have a piece of shale—'

I was not allowed to finish.

'My dear,' said Dr Tibbett, 'such things can be explained by the Great Flood in which the world was destroyed and then recreated. You clearly suffer from the confusion that can so easily be caused by placing such a work as Mr Darwin's in the hands of Young People. My advice to you, Miss Martin, is when you have finished your daily chapter of Scripture, to read suitable works of fiction of an improving nature. There are some, I believe.'

'James Belling has a collection of fossils,' said Frank. 'He goes off to Dorset and such places and digs them up. There are some pretty queer creatures among them. There's nothing like them around today. Darwin has surely discovered something.'

'I do not deny the existence of these bones,' conceded Dr Tibbett. 'I have viewed some myself. They are very curious. But that they are as old as claimed I doubt. The most extravagant calculation cannot make the world more than a few thousand years old. Nor can I agree that so many different creatures can arise from so few ancestors. Young Belling may well have found some interesting specimens and I accept that some species may have died out before the coming of the Great Flood.'

'One does wonder what our own ancestors—' Frank began.

He was not allowed to finish. Dr Tibbett, who had been arguing in quite a reasonable tone of voice until that moment, became red in the face and launched into a tirade.

'I will not allow these things to be said! Man must be a superior being to the rest of Creation. It is inconceivable that he is an animal like – like an ape! If, indeed, he were, he would have created nothing himself. What of music, art, literature and philosophy? Will you count every civilisation the world has ever seen as mere chance? Did an ape build the pyramids? Did an ape cause Rome to rise? Were the immortal words of Homer penned by a chimpanzee? Different species of animal and fish may have come and gone but Man himself has always been of superior intellect and ability. Man alone has a sense of the spiritual. Man alone can conceive of things beyond his immediate experience, which no mere beast can ever do.'

'Well, sir, I confess I don't understand it myself,' admitted Frank, retreating before the fire in Dr Tibbett's eye and the manner of his delivery. 'The notion that our ancestors shambled about, barely upright, covered in hair, devoid of speech and – forgive me, ladies – any vestige of clothing, does seem a trifle far-fetched.'

'Far-fetched?' thundered Dr Tibbett. 'It is more than that. That, if anything, sir, is bunkum!'

'Have we not time,' put in our hostess, 'for a hand of whist before you go, dear doctor?' Her manner, as we had argued, had been growing increasingly restive. Darwinism was of no interest to her and valuable time was being lost which might be employed in her favourite occupation.

It seemed we did. Frank set up the card table and although I was no expert card player, my earlier tiredness had abated and I'd acquired my 'second wind'. I managed to acquit myself fairly well. The rest of the evening passed in quite a jolly way. Even Dr Tibbett relaxed his formal manner a little, although once or twice I caught him studying me when he thought my mind on my hand of cards. His look was neither antagonistic nor friendly, merely blandly neutral. Sharp though, for all that. I felt I was being slotted neatly into some scale of humanity. Dr Tibbett might not support the theories of Darwinism, but he had his own notions of mankind and womankind.

The visitor left the house around eleven. Frank went downstairs with him but returned immediately. He threw himself moodily into one of the chairs around the card table and picking up some cards at random began to deal them out in meticulously straight rows for no purpose I could see. Mrs Parry had gone up to her room where Nugent patiently waited to undress her mistress and take down the extraordinary edifice which crowned her head. This meant I could also retire. I opened my mouth to say good night to Frank but he didn't look up and appeared unaware I was still present. I made to slip out of the room. But unexpectedly Carterton spoke.

'Wait,' he said, 'you will need a candle.' He got to his feet, took a candlestick from a nearby side table, lifted it to light it at the gas jet and handed it to me.

I thanked him but my thanks were acknowledged only with a nod. 'Good night,' I added.

This at least brought forth a muttered 'good night.'

As I passed along the upper landing a gust of chill night air made my candle flame flicker and I realised the front door was still open. I leaned over to see why. Dr Tibbett was still there, talking to Simms. But the conversation ended even as I looked. Simms handed him his hat and cane. I thought Tibbett was unaware of my observation but he must have sensed it for he suddenly looked up and I caught the full force of his stare. Automatically I retreated into the shelter of the turbaned boy candle-bearer. I was embarrassed; he would believe I was spying. I went up to my room annoyed by the whole silly little incident. I did wonder what he had been chatting to Simms about.

I was now dropping with exhaustion. Nevertheless there were some thoughts which buzzed around my brain and wouldn't be dislodged as I climbed unaided from my clothes into my nightgown and unpinned my knot of hair.

There were no gas jets to be seen on this floor. The expensive convenience was restricted to the reception rooms. I sat before the rococo dressing table and began to brush my hair in regular long strokes as I had been taught by my one-time governess, Madame Leblanc. The amber glow of my candle was comforting and far nicer, I thought, than the hissing gas and its unrelenting hard bright glare.

In the corners of the room the shadows cast velvety veils. It would not be too difficult to imagine someone who stood there and watched. I thought of Madeleine Hexham whose name had come up at dinner, not to everyone's wish. I glanced around me. It was likely that I'd been given my predecessor's room and that it was here she had planned her flight into the arms of her mysterious lover. Who had he been and where had she met him? How long had she been in this house before her abrupt quitting of it?

Had Tibbett and Frank Carterton had some exchange of words on her account in the library later? Had Frank been given some kind of dressing-down resulting in his returning so out of sorts after seeing Tibbett as far as the street door and delivering him there to Simms? It was unsettling to learn that Miss Hexham's memory aroused strong feeling. She had probably come to this house just as grateful as I was to be offered the position of companion. She had left her modest baggage in the hall as I'd done and followed Simms up the staircase, wondering about her future. Had she not been happy here? My employer seemed very kind but Madeleine had not confided in her. I resolved to ask Frank who was, I suspected, something of a gossip when not sulking.

There had been at least a practical result of these events for me. Madeleine's sudden departure had left Mrs Parry unexpectedly without a companion and, when she heard of my need to find such a situation, it must have appeared a gift. It did not make it less kind of her to have taken me in. But on the other hand, I was a little relieved of the burden of gratitude. A fair exchange was much more to my liking.

Finally my thoughts returned again to Frank Carterton, of whom I had received a mixed impression. He could be, if he set himself to it, quite charming and entertaining. He was also not above stirring up mischief.

To take matters a step further, was Frank right in his whispered suggestion that Dr Tibbett was paying court to my employer? I could well believe it possible. Mrs Parry was an attractive and wealthy widow. The clergyman–schoolmaster obviously stood high in her esteem. Was that why Frank looked forward so enthusiastically to departing for Russia? He had no wish to be here on the day when he could call Dr Tibbett 'uncle'?

I put down the hairbrush with relief and rose to go to my bed. I extinguished the candle and a kind of darkness fell yet unlike the total darkness of night I was accustomed to. My eyes adjusted to the gloom and I found I could clearly distinguish the shapes, if not the details, of the furniture. The glow came through the windows from the gas lamps placed outside at intervals around the square. Mrs Parry's room was, I'd learned, on the opposite side of the house and overlooked the quiet green privacy of a pocket-handkerchief-sized garden. For me, the companion, it would be the noise of London astir from early morning onward and a view, albeit of the grass and trees in the middle of the square, yet obscured by the coming and going of vehicles and pedestrians. I pulled the curtain a little aside and peered out and down. At the moment it was deserted, the sulphurous yellow of the gas lamps below shining on the cobblestones. But even as I watched, I heard the click of a street door and a figure appeared from the house, threw a cloak round his shoulders with a debonair gesture and walked off briskly, swinging a stout cane.

Frank Carterton, having done his duty by his aunt that evening, had overcome his fit of pique and was setting off about Town and his own pleasures.

Chapter Three

Inspector Benjamin Ross

'HERE WE are, sir,' said Sergeant Morris hoarsely.

We had picked our way between piles of rubble stacked in some places as high as slag heaps. These roads had never been paved and over time had become rutted and potholed, the walls of the ruts set like stone, even before the present onslaught which was leaving Agar Town razed and deserted as if the object of some Biblical wrath.

Broken bricks littered our path and made each footstep treacherous. Between lumps of masonry and fallen rafters sticking up like the shattered spars of a shipwreck, the ground was further churned by the wheels of the wagons and pitted with abominable-smelling potholes marking the site of demolished privies and open sewers. I kicked aside the mummified corpse of a rat. Another nearby, still decomposing, was a mass of writhing maggots.

Though the weather was cool, it had not rained in

several days and this morning the wind swirled around us. The air was full of dust, forcing itself into our nostrils and throats, so that we coughed and were forced to cover our faces with our handkerchiefs. Even the bony flanks of the dejected nags waiting to haul the wagons were dressed with pinkish-grey powder. In this setting the poor beasts suggested the spectral horses of some apocalyptic nightmare.

I saw that some sporadic activity had started again at the point furthest from the spot towards which we were headed. Men were busy at a shell of a house, its roof, windows, and doors all gone together with part of the upper brickwork. My eye was caught by two or three fellows perched insecurely at first-floor level. They were knocking out the front wall with regular swings of sledgehammers so that great chunks of brickwork fell in slabs to the ground beneath. As each crashed down, a fresh cloud of mortar and brick dust billowed into the air and the navvies above, caught in the upflow, were covered in a thick coating. They reminded me of the colliers I knew in my youth with their mantle of coal dust. I wondered whether the men who worked here would also suffer in later years, as so many colliers including my own poor father did, with lung troubles.

As soon as these navvies on their lofty eyrie spotted Morris and me, they gave a warning shout and all work ceased again. The men on the half-demolished façade let their tools hang from their brawny arms and stood as still as grey statues. Those below removing already demolished masonry leaned on shovels and pickaxes to watch us go by, their faces sullen. One man, his woollen cap, features and clothing all grey with dust, turned his head and spat to one side. It surprised me he had enough spittle left.

'She should not have been moved,' I muttered, more to myself than to poor Morris. He had already borne the brunt of my frustration as well as the brooding resentment of the labourers and the outright hostility of those in charge.

'Yes, sir, I do recognise it, sir. But the foreman, a downy bird if ever I saw one, and the fellow from the railway company kicked up a devil of a fuss, begging your pardon. The labourers themselves, they were turning very nasty. I couldn't expect a pair of constables to handle it.'

The figure of a constable appeared as he spoke. He was a youngster, clearly nervous, who looked relieved when he recognised Morris and then, when he spotted me, apprehensive again.

'Biddle,' Morris informed me. 'He's a good lad but he's not been long in the force.'

I thought privately that Biddle scarcely looked the minimum age to enrol, eighteen. Moreover, he was wearing one of the tall helmets which had recently replaced the familiar glazed top hats such as I had worn when I had first entered the police force. The new headgear still attracted much comment. To be honest, the helmet perched atop Biddle's round skull in a way which I was afraid would make it a natural target for small boys with catapults.

Morris, too, seemed struck by the sight. 'I don't know about these helmets, sir,' he murmured to me. 'I know the old hats were always likely to fall off at the first bit of action and they made your head like a furnace when the weather was hot. But they at least lent a man a bit of dignity.' More loudly, he enquired, 'Where's Jenkins, Biddle?'

'Round the back, Sergeant, arguing with that foreman. I think the gentleman from the railway company has come back, too. They're not happy that the work hasn't restarted in this area now the dead woman's been taken away.'

'Are they not, indeed?' I allowed myself to say sarcastically, and then added, making the effort to sound more matter-of-fact, 'So, this is the scene of the crime, eh?'

It wasn't the wretched Biddle's fault any more than it was Morris's. Biddle, pink and sweating in his high-buttoned uniform and with the helmet looking even more insecure, said earnestly, 'There's no one gone in, sir. I've been here, or Jenkins has, all the time.'

The other houses in the row had been pulled down but these three at the end still stood, leaning against one another like a trio of drunken men. If one moved, they'd all fall. The body had been found by workmen entering the first of them to make preparations for the demolition.

They were narrow houses, cheaply and shoddily constructed of inferior materials, deemed fit for the poor and designed chiefly in order to make a quick fortune for the builder. I had just seen how they crumbled before the blows of the sledgehammers like a child's castle built of wooden bricks. This was – or had been – Agar Town, notorious even in a city with more than its fair share of slums. Here a whole family had lived in one room and, in the worst cases, shared the room with other tenants. All the residents had shared the communal privies in the yards at the back where some also kept pigs. Sewage would have overflowed from the latrines and the pigs devoured the waste. A pig will eat anything. It's a useful beast. Nearby the pump from which they all drew their water still stood. I hoped the navvies were not tempted to drink from it. Cholera had paid regular visits to Agar Town. The newspapers were saying Mr Bazalgette's ingenious sewer system would deliver London from that plague, although those same journals reported numerous new cases in the East End at that very moment.

In any case, there were other plagues: typhoid, diphtheria, consumption and those maladies which affect the poor alone and spring from despair. No one lives long in such conditions. Men are lucky to live forty years, women often less. Children die like flies and those who survive emerge from the hovels of their homes deformed and pale as ghosts, little old men and women themselves by ten years of age. I know such places and I knew Agar Town. When a man, or woman, is starving and has nothing to lose, what is there to stop either of them turning to crime?

Perhaps the sweeping away of Agar Town to make way for the new railway terminus and yards might even be argued a blessing in disguise. Were it not for the fact that I suspected it had simply served to move the area's problems elsewhere.

'Mind how you go, sir,' advised Morris, leading the way. 'That outer wall is unsafe. Don't go leaning on anything, will you? The whole lot could come down around our ears. Fact is, it's one of the reasons the foreman gave for moving her out. "Don't blame me," he said, "if by the time your inspector gets here, the whole lot has tumbled and your dead woman is buried good and proper!" Only his language wasn't near as decent as that. But he had a point, sir, as I could see. Best be quick, sir.'

'All right, all right!' I said testily. I could see for myself how shaky the whole structure was. 'You've spoken to the men who found her?'

'Yes, sir, I took statements and they made their marks to them. Irish fellers, the pair of them, crossing themselves and hoping as the poor woman would rest in peace.'

We had made our way down a narrow hallway stinking of mould and generations of unwashed bodies. There was another insidious miasma seeping from the walls: poverty. It has its own smell; despair an odour all its own. I felt it now creep into my nostrils and pulled out my handkerchief again to press to my nose.

'Whiffs a bit, don't it?' observed Morris kindly, noticing my distress.

I was ashamed of my weakness and put the handkerchief away.

We had reached a back room. Here there was a new smell, the sweetly rotten stench of death. *She* had been taken away but nothing would remove the foulness until the whole place came down. I looked around, trying to envisage the room as a home. Someone, probably in an attempt to keep the draughts out, had lined the walls with old newspapers. Advertisements for exhibitions of water-colours by 'a lady', good-quality imported French soap and antiquarian books formed an incongruous background to a life in which any of those things would have been totally meaningless. The floorboards were bare, rotten in parts, and all furniture had been removed but for a broken bedstead against a wall.

'She was under there,' said Morris, pointing at it. 'Half pushed underneath but not hidden although whoever put her there had thrown a bit of old carpet over her. Her feet stuck out. You could have seen what it was straight off, the minute you came in here, even if you hadn't smelled her first. The men who found her knew it at once for a corpse and yelled for the foreman to come. Then, according to the foreman, they all downed tools. None of 'em would touch a brick, not anywhere on the site, not while she stayed. He panicked because the railway company would blame him for the delay. He would have it that she must be moved. I told him regulations said, the inspector must see her for himself, but he sent off someone to fetch the

Ann Granger

gentleman from the railway company and *he* sent off somewhere else. In the end, word come down from the superintendent, we could move her out to the nearest mortuary. But I got a bit of chalk and drew round the spot, see?'

Morris pointed proudly to a roughly scrawled shape on the floorboards half under the old bedstead.

'I took a good look round, Biddle and Jenkins too. We went upstairs and everything. We didn't find anything of interest.'

Morris had done his best to prevent removal of the body but, in the end, the railway company had called on friends in higher places. As the men pulling down the houses to clear the whole area for the building of the new railway terminus would not work while the body lay *in situ*, *ergo* the body had been removed. It now lay in the mortuary which is where we would go when I'd seen what was left to be seen here. You see I have learned my Latin phrases. I am an ambitious man and I've worked hard. I've spent long hours by candlelight making good the shortcomings in my education and now I'm an inspector of the Metropolitan Police Force based at Scotland Yard. But when I look in the shaving mirror of a morning I often observe aloud, 'You fool nobody, Ben Ross. A collier's son you were and a collier's son you remain.'

I looked down at the dusty floor and Morris's effort to preserve the evidence and sighed. The workmen who had found the body had tramped all over the place, followed by the original constable called to the scene and then Morris and his helpers. If there had been any small clue to be found, it had long been demolished.

There was a shout from outside. Heavy footsteps echoed in the hall and Biddle put his pink shiny face and wobbly headgear through the doorway. 'Gentleman from the railway company is here and that foreman feller, as well – sir.'

I was not sorry to have the excuse to get out of this claustrophobic place of death. But I remembered to say, 'Well done!' to Morris because, in the trying circumstances, he had done well.

He looked mightily relieved. As we moved back down the hall, he whispered in his hoarse undertone, 'Her clothes was very good, sir, no old rubbish. Whoever she was, she didn't live round here.'

Stepping out of that place into the dusty sunshine was like stepping out of a tomb. Two men were waiting for me. One was clearly the foreman, a burly fellow with a drinker's nose and an expression of cultivated blankness. I recognised the expression well enough. He did not intend to assist the police. This was probably not because he had anything to hide but simply because, like every other man working here, he disliked us – and that even before we, in his view, had caused a problem. It sometimes puzzles me, when I take the trouble to think about it, that the population at large has so little to say in our favour. The poor claim we harass them. The wealthy claim we don't do enough. Between the two the vast majority see us as an expense upon the public purse and another burden on the honest citizen.

Speaking of honest citizens, I turned my attention to the man from the railway company who probably claimed this distinction. He was a pale-faced young fellow in a frock coat, wearing spectacles with oval lenses. His air was one of irritated self-importance. He held his silk hat in one hand and was mopping his brow with the other using a large spotted handkerchief. He tucked this away as he saw me.

'Fletcher,' he said briefly. 'I am clerk of the works here and, as such, I represent the railway company.'

'I am Inspector Ross,' I replied. 'I represent Scotland Yard.'

The sunlight glinted on the oval lenses as he gave me a sharp look to see if I meant any facetiousness. But he saw in my face that what I had meant him to understand was that his credentials did not outweigh mine.

'Quite so,' he said. 'I'm hoping, Inspector, that now you've visited the place where the unfortunate female was discovered, we may be allowed to begin work here again. Time is money.'

'And death is inconvenient,' I said.

This time he didn't trouble to give me that sharp look. He just pursed his mouth before countering with, 'You can see for yourself the unstable nature of the buildings behind you. We must proceed to bring them down in the approved manner. If not, they will fall by themselves and there is great risk of injury if not further death.'

This was true. But I ignored him to turn to the foreman. 'What is your name?'

'Adams, sir.' He was chewing on something as he spoke, probably a piece of tobacco. He shifted it to the other cheek and continued to stare at me in that bovine way.

'Before the workmen entered the property this morning and found the dead woman, who last entered it and when?'

'How should I know?' he retorted. 'Before we started work on this row of houses, no one went in there. Why should they? Everything was taken out of them weeks ago.'

'And when did you start to demolish this row of houses?'

'Two days ago. They came down easy. We had no trouble until we got here and found her.'

'The men are superstitious,' put in Fletcher fretfully. 'When word spread that a body had been found, they all stopped work on the entire site.'

Unexpectedly Adams took a different view. 'They showed respect, gentlemen. Respect for the dead. It wasn't decent to work on and her lying there.'

Also, I thought to myself, they feared one of them might be accused of the deed. In the face of this they had closed ranks.

'So the workmen found her. They sent for you and you sent for the police, is that it?' I kept my tone matter-of-fact. It wouldn't do to let Adams see I was affected by the atmosphere.

'That's it,' Adams returned. 'And there's been one of your fellows standing guard on the place since, that one there with the pudding basin on his head, mostly.' He nodded towards poor Biddle. For all his expressed scorn, wariness had entered his otherwise stolid expression. Ours was a silent duel. We were like chess players.

'And then I received word,' Fletcher put in, determined to have his version of events heard and oblivious of my unexpressed tussle with the foreman. 'I hurried here immediately. Not a brick was being moved. Not a cart. I saw at once that she must be removed so I sent word to my superiors. Besides,' he added, realising that I cared nothing for delays to his schedule, 'to preserve the body for your inspection it was necessary to bring it out. The unsafe condition—'

'I know all that!' I interrupted him, wearied at having the same tale dinned into my ears over and over again. Morris, Adams, Fletcher and any other Tom, Dick or Harry who might have anything to say would sing the same tune. The fact was, the body had been moved. I could do nothing about it and they all knew it. 'Well, as far as I'm concerned you can start work here again,' I said.

Fletcher looked relieved and took out his pocket watch to calculate just how much time had been lost. Adams turned and trudged off to summon back his workmen, I assumed. I sensed he was glad to be free of me.

'What about Biddle and Jenkins, sir?' Morris asked.

'They can begin by questioning everyone working here,

beginning with Mr Fletcher and Adams. I want to know the pattern the work here follows.'

'But there are hundreds of them, sir!' burst out Biddle, indicating the workmen around us.

'I will see every available constable is sent down to help you.'

Biddle and Jenkins looked resigned and glum.

'You and I, Sergeant, have an appointment at a mortuary. The coroner has given the order for the body to be investigated by a surgeon.'

Biddle and Jenkins cheered up and exchanged glances of satisfaction. Rather their tedious job than ours.

I have seen death many times but few times when it moved me to such pity. There had been one occasion to equal it, long ago when I'd been a boy. Now I was a police officer and all of us fancied we were hardened to the sight of what fellow men could do. Yet Morris, experienced man that he was, also seemed moved by the sight, shaking his grizzled head sadly.

Dr Carmichael stood to one side waiting patiently for us so that he could be about his grisly work. He at least showed a proper medical detachment. He was a tall, angular man with faded red hair and sharp little blue eyes. Like any surgeon working upon the living, he wore a dirty frock coat soiled with ancient blood and smears of viscera. This was his dissecting coat, to be donned when he went about his professional duties. He would change before he left and leave here smart as a pin with no passer-by guessing what he had been at.

I have read there is some medical man in Glasgow who is claiming a greater rate of success in his operating theatre through dousing everything and everyone there, including the unfortunate on the table, with a carbolic spray. This is because he believes infections spread by some kind of organism invisible to the naked eye. The idea of the existence of these organisms originates, so I understand, in the work of some Frenchman or other. But doughty Carmichael was of the old generation and I couldn't imagine him fooling around with carbolic sprays. Anyway, all his patients were already dead.

The mortuary to which the body had been taken was the nearest available to the scene and was located in a cramped extension to the rear of an undertaker's premises. The mortal remains of the undertaker's more respectable customers lay in superior surroundings next door.

Our unknown woman lay on the chipped porcelain tray well away from any chance sighting by the bereaved visiting those other dead. She had been stripped naked and revealed to be a tiny little thing although an adult female, not five feet in height and slender in build. Her flesh also resembled marble, the multicoloured sort in which purples and pinks and reds all mingled like a crazy piece of patchwork, except above her stomach which was a uniform grey-green. There was a deep wound at her left temple and her features were so distorted that it was impossible to tell if she had once been pretty. But her long flaxen hair was spread out around her head in a glorious halo, untouched by the ravages of decay. Her small even teeth glimpsed through her parted lips looked perfect. I looked at her hands. She wore no wedding ring but that might have been stolen or removed to prevent identification. Such rings are sometimes engraved with personal messages. The fingers themselves were already marked by the onset of decomposition but the nails were neat. She had not been a working woman, in my opinion, or she'd have had roughened hands and missing or rotten teeth even at such an age.

'How old?' I asked Carmichael.

'I'd say she was in her middle twenties,' he returned.

We all spoke quietly as if we'd been in a church.

'And how long dead?'

He hunched his shoulders. 'That is difficult to say in the circumstances. Longer than a week but less than two? Let us say two weeks at the most.'

'Is that the cause of death, would you say?' I pointed to the head wound which showed fragments of skull protruding through the peeling skin.

'You hardly need me to point that out to you,' Carmichael returned in his dry, precise way. 'I doubt the internal organs are still in good enough state to tell us very much. I shall conduct a thorough examination, of course. But that head wound would certainly seem sufficient cause of death. She was severely battered with some heavy instrument.'

'We found no weapon at the scene, sir,' said Morris. 'I had a proper search round made.'

He had contrived to find a corner into which to tuck himself but was still too near to the deceased for his liking. Morris sometimes displayed a prudishness unexpected in an officer of his many years' service. I had noticed it before. He was genuinely embarrassed not just by the sight of her but at the thought of the desecration male hands were about to inflict on the young female's body. Every line of his form and every crease of his face revealed his unhappiness.

'That demolition site is full of potential weapons,' I said. 'Every man working there has a shovel or axe.'

Carmichael cleared his throat. 'In my opinion the weapon was not of that sort. Judging by an examination of the wounds with a magnifying glass, they were caused by something long and fairly narrow.' He produced the glass from his pocket and handed it to me. 'See here, you may look for yourself.'

Morris pulled himself together, put aside his natural instincts, and edged forward to join me in closer examination. Given a specific task he was able to view the remains simply as a puzzle.

'A poker?' he suggested brightly after we had both peered through the glass at the wound.

'Too narrow, more likely a walking stick or cane with a metal head to it,' I gave as my opinion.

Behind us, Carmichael said, 'It was wielded with

considerable force. Her attacker meant to kill her. There are marks of at least five distinct blows.'

'He was angry,' I murmured. 'Perhaps he was jealous.'

'I can't help you with his motivation,' Carmichael observed, 'only with the results of it.'

'Quite so, Doctor. What do you say, Morris? He stood before her – so . . .' I raised my arm. 'And struck her thus . . .' I brought my arm down but stopped short of the body. 'He is right-handed, along with the vast majority of the population. Where are her garments?'

Carmichael, who had been watching my play-acting impassively, nodded towards the far side of the room. 'On yon table.'

The woman's clothing had been carefully removed and tidily folded and set out. Morris had been right in his judgement of them. A gown of lavender striped poplin of good quality. Petticoat, corset, a cotton chemise and drawers, stockings, kid boots; all these of good quality also and all of them were puzzling to me. They were grimy but of a superficial grubbiness. These were not clothes which were seldom if ever washed and in which the grime was engrained. The outer wear, that is to say the poplin gown, was the most dirtied, smeared with mud and something greenish. I peered at it more closely. It was mould of some sort and had got there when the garment was rubbed against some surface which had mould upon it. The material itself was not mouldy. The underwear was cleaner, only the cotton chemise much sweat-stained. I guessed the unfortunate soiling of the drawers had taken place on death.

I picked up the little boots and turned them over. The soles had not been mended. But the uppers were well moulded to the shape of her foot, so not new. A pair of good boots had lasted her a long time. That, together with the modest nature of her dress, suggested she had not belonged to that class of young women who walked the streets a great deal in search of custom. So, she had not done a lot of tramping on cobbles, just the occasional outing to shop or church, to pay a visit or two in the neighbourhood.

'No bonnet or hat,' I observed to Morris. 'Nor any shawl. But these are not a poor woman's clothes. Not a rich woman's, either, but a respectable one's. This is no ladybird.'

'Who found her?' called Carmichael. On being told that workmen had done so, gave his opinion that, 'they probably first took any bonnet or purse or shawl or indeed anything they might sell on. Then they raised the alarm.'

Morris ventured to contradict Carmichael's jaundiced view of working men. 'They struck me as both of them too distressed to think of it, sir.'

'Whatever happened,' I said, 'we have only what we see here and these things tell us this is a young woman who in normal circumstances took some care over her appearance. The stockings are carefully darned although there is a small hole in one toe. I think, Sergeant, she did not die in that room. She died elsewhere, nearby perhaps, and the body was taken there. She's of small build. There are handcarts and wheelbarrows all over that site. To have packed her into one and thrown something over her would not have been difficult.'

'Someone would have seen something, sir.'

'At night? I doubt the area is secured. There is nothing there worth stealing unless someone had a mind to take away a few doors or window frames and I don't suppose the company would be worried about that. In fact, if you or I were walking by after dark and saw someone trundling along a barrow in a way suggesting he didn't want to be too closely observed, wouldn't we assume just that? He was making off with a few door locks or a chimney piece he might sell on?'

'True, sir, but then, who is she? A decent young woman, well, she'd be missed.'

'Exactly, and someone has missed her, I'll be bound. We'll have to check all reports of missing women received in the past six months. We'll start with central London and, if necessary, spread outwards.'

'She'll not have been dead as long as that!' Carmichael reminded us from the far side of the room.

'Indeed, Doctor! But she may not have been killed at once. The clothing bothers me. Why did she wear the under-bodice for such a long time that it became so stained with sweat? And look, the feet of the stockings are also quite stiff with sweat and wear. Why did she not darn the hole in the toe? This, I am sure, was someone who was normally neat and tidy, in the habit of mending her stockings, and would certainly have changed soiled linen. I wonder if she may have been held prisoner somewhere.'

'Poor little lady,' said Morris, looking shocked.

'First things first!' I said briskly to him. This was not the time to become maudlin. 'Perhaps her skirt has pockets in it. You try that side and I'll try this.'

I felt along the seam and sure enough, there was a pocket. I thought at first it was empty but when I pushed my fingers into it they encountered something. I pulled out a small white handkerchief, unused, neatly folded and pressed flat. 'Here we are, Sergeant. Let's have a look at this. Why, I do believe we're in luck!'

I spread out the tiny cambric square. It was embroidered in blue silk thread with the initials M.H.

'Well, Miss M. H.,' I said. 'You have spoken to us from beyond!'

Carmichael gave a disapproving cough. He was of Presbyterian persuasion and took exception to any light-ness of reference to religious matters.

Morris had been scowling at the handkerchief. 'See here, Inspector sir,' he said suddenly. 'Why not lure her to somewhere near the river and then tip the body in? More than likely it would have gone down as a suicide. In that house, he should have known she'd be found.'

'It's a good question, Sergeant, and I suspect the

answer is that the site in Agar Town was handy for him. He may not have thought men would go into the house before it was demolished. The houses had already been cleared. Perhaps he expected a ball and chain to be swung against the whole lot and everything brought down, like Samson brought down the temple on his tormentors.'

(I put that in to tease Carmichael. Unworthy of me but there it is.)

'He expected the body to be thoroughly crushed and when the fabric of the place was loaded up to be carted away, why yes, she'd be found, but in such a state that it would not be possible to say how she died.'

I stepped back and Morris, looking his relief, edged towards the door.

'We'll leave you to it, Doctor,' I said to Carmichael.

There was a movement behind me and a young man with a waxy complexion and lank dark hair, wearing what looked much like a butcher's apron, joined us. I'd seen Carmichael's assistant before. I had not liked him then and I didn't like him now. There was a glow in the fellow's eyes as their gaze rested on the dead woman which sent a tremor up my spine. But it wasn't a job, I supposed, for which there were many volunteers.

It was an hour and a half later in my office where, divested of my coat and my shirtsleeves rolled up, I had my head over a bowl of water, sluicing away the dust and the smell of that morning's work, when I received Carmichael's preliminary report. I raised my dripping face and mopped at it with a towel before taking the note a constable proffered me.

Carmichael's opinion as to cause of death had not changed. He was puzzled that although the body was that of a woman who had been generally well nourished, yet the stomach and digestive tract were completely empty of food in any stage of digestion. She had not eaten for some forty-eight hours before her death. But a far more significant discovery he had kept for the last sentence of his report. It might well indicate a motive for her murder.

Chapter Four

Elizabeth Martin

NOT SURPRISINGLY after a long and busy day I slept soundly. I didn't hear Frank return. However, I've always been an early riser and found myself awake at six as usual.

My instinct was to jump out of bed and it was a strange feeling to know that I hadn't to be about household duties as someone else would be taking care of those. I turned over and tried to go back to sleep but it was no good at all. Not only habit urged me to get up but through the window, which I had left a little open at the bottom, I could hear the sounds of a great city astir. Carts rolled noisily over the cobbles and workers on their way to their employment exchanged greetings. No one, it seemed, spoke quietly. Then I heard a cry of 'Milk-o! Fresh from the cow-o!' To my astonishment this was followed by a plaintive low. A cow, here in the middle of fashionable London? I scrambled out of the sheets, ran to the window and, flinging up the sash as far as it would go, leaned out.

Sure enough, there below was the cow and a boy holding it by a headstall. It was a dispirited beast with a dull coat and ribs like a toast-rack. As I watched, a girl in an overlarge mob cap and apron came scurrying up the basement steps from this house carrying a pot-bellied pitcher. She spoke to a woman who stood by the cow, holding in her hand a small three-legged milking stool. The woman set down the stool, settled herself on it and began milking the cow into a metal pot which looked like some kind of measure. When it was full she stood up and poured the contents into the pitcher the kitchen maid held out. A coin changed hands. The maid carried the pitcher carefully back down to the basement and the cow and its attendants moved on. After some minutes, the cry of 'Milk-o!' was audible from the next street followed by the lugubrious lowing of the poor brute which was required to plod around in this way.

I turned from the window and looked round the room. There was a wash-stand in one corner and I expected hot water would be brought up, but when, I had no idea. To return to bed now was out of the question. I decided I could at least go down and explore the house. I dressed hurriedly and let myself out into the passageway.

There was no one about upstairs or, as far as I could see, on the ground floor. The servants must all be down in the basement from which I'd seen the girl with the pitcher issue. They were probably having their breakfast. Drawing room and dining room were empty. Another smallish room at the rear of the building suggested breakfast might be served there later. Meat salvers, stands for hot dishes and a bain-marie basin stood on a long oak sideboard. The remaining ground-floor room was on the right immediately one entered the house through the front door and I had not been inside it. I turned the handle and pushed.

Two instantly recognisable odours assailed my nose: book leather and stale cigar smoke. This must be the library to which Dr Tibbett and Frank had retired after dinner. It was in darkness, so I made free to draw back the heavy curtains and let the morning sunlight flood in. It was a small room with bookcases on all sides and a big leather-topped desk in the middle with a chair before it. A pair of more comfortable leather-covered winged chairs stood either side of the fireplace. I longed to take a close look at the books and imagined myself happily settled in a wing chair to read, if ever Mrs Parry released me for long enough.

Above the hearth hung a portrait of a handsome man with thick dark hair and an air of prosperity. There was something familiar about his face and I dragged from memory a visitor to our house when I had been very young, perhaps only six or so.

I knew that a visitor was coming long before he arrived because of the amount of cooking going on in Mary Newling's kitchen. Pots of soup were reboiled up daily to prevent them going 'off'. There was a wonderful cake, a monster of its kind, packed with dried fruits and decorated with toasted nuts which I was not allowed to pick at, under threat of not being allowed a single slice later when it should be cut. Flies buzzed before the meat safe in which a large pink leg of pork sat in a pool of its own pale blood awaiting the great day of the newcomer's arrival when it would be sent down to the baker's to be put in his oven when the bread-baking was over. It was like Christmas, even though that festival wouldn't be for weeks yet.

I was confined to my nursery during his arrival and all I saw of him was the top of his hat as he alighted from the pony-trap sent to meet him. Molly Darby, my nurse, leaning out of the window beside me, saw no more than I did much to her great disappointment. But later I was called down to our cramped drawing room to meet him. Molly straightened my skirts, smoothed my hair and instructed me, 'Do behave like a lady, miss!'

This was good advice but impossible to follow as I hadn't the slightest notion how to behave in company, never having been taught.

I jumped down the wooden staircase making a great racket and burst into the room, eaten up by curiosity. But I stopped short on being confronted by a tall man with a sad face, dressed all in black. For a moment I was in confusion. But his eyes twinkled at me kindly and I lost my brief and sudden bashfulness.

'Why,' he said, 'so you are Miss Martin. I am honoured to make your acquaintance.'

'I am Miss Martin,' I informed him, taking the hand he held out and shaking it firmly. 'But mostly I am called Lizzie, you know. When I am older I shall be Miss Martin and I shall wear a bonnet with cherries on it to church.'

My father, seated by the hearth, uttered a small groan but the visitor chuckled.

'You must forgive her and me, Josh,' said my father. 'She is a wild little thing and a complete ignoramus, but it is my fault.'

I saw that there was a cut-glass decanter, with glasses, on a small table. I knew it to contain some sort of expensive wine and only to be produced on very special occasions. I thought my father's complexion rather rosier than usual but perhaps that was because he was sat by the fire.

'What is there to forgive? She seems a bright child to me and certainly favours Charlotte in looks.'

'Yes,' said my father curtly. I thought that even if he agreed with the visitor's remark he had rather it had not been made. I saw a flicker of pain cross his face and I understood that he grieved for my dead mother. I went to him and took his hand and he kissed the top of my head.

I wondered now at the visitor's words because my own opinion, as I have written, taken from my mother's likeness upstairs in my bedroom, was that I didn't favour her much. But then, I had not known her and the visitor presumably had.

He must have been my godfather, Josiah Parry, here immortalised in oils. I suppose I was told his name at the time but I hadn't remembered it. What I did remember was that, on leaving, he presented me with a shilling, whispering, 'Put it safely by, Lizzie, and save up for the cherry bonnet!'

I thought the shilling a small fortune. Sadly it was spent not saved and I have never owned a bonnet with cherries on it. I frowned now before his portrait. Mrs Parry had remarked that her husband had not visited us in Derbyshire. But he had certainly done so at least once. Had she forgotten this or not known of it?

There was a small ebony and ormolu clock on the mantelshelf and a box of safety matches. At home Mary Newling had always bought the old-style lucifers and I had continued to do so when it had fallen to me to make this purchase. They were a little cheaper.

Without warning, I heard a click of the door behind me and a gasp. I turned and saw a surprised housemaid with a pan and brush.

'Sorry, miss,' she said. 'I didn't expect to see anyone yet.'

'I'm about to go,' I said awkwardly. 'I only came down because I thought I might see someone to ask if I might have some hot water in my room.'

'Yes, miss, I'll see it's sent up directly.' She was still looking at me in a perplexed way.

'I am Miss Martin, Mrs Parry's new companion,' I told her.

'Yes, miss, I guessed as you must be.'

On impulse I asked, 'Were you employed here when Miss Hexham was Mrs Parry's companion?'

'Yes, miss.'

'You must all have been very surprised when she left so suddenly.'

'Yes, miss. But Mrs Parry gave us her clothes what she left behind her.'

By 'us' I assumed she meant all the servants. The picture of them dividing up the belongings of my predecessor was not a pretty one.

'Shall I get on then?' The maid held up her dustpan and brush.

I should not have asked the girl questions. She would certainly report my interest below stairs. Besides, I was holding her up. So I simply asked her what her name was. She told me it was Wilkins. I thanked her and left her to her work, taking myself back to my room. People wandering around under the servants' feet first thing in the day were obviously a nuisance. I should have to learn to get up later.

Wilkins did not forget my request, however. I had not been back in my room above ten minutes when a knock at the door heralded the kitchen girl in the mob cap I'd seen earlier, this time staggering under a can of hot water. Seen close at hand, the girl looked no more than twelve years of age but might have been thirteen. She was of scrawny build with the pinched look of children who have grown up ill-nourished and probably born to mothers themselves half-starved. To tell the age of such a child is difficult.

'Why, what is your name?' I asked.

'Bessie, miss,' she replied, pushing up the mob cap which had worked its way down over her eyes.

'Oh,' I said, taking the can from her before she spilled it. It was very heavy and difficult to imagine how her thin little arms had managed to haul it up three flights of stairs from the basement. 'So you are called Elizabeth, as I am.'

At this I got a similar perplexed look to the one I'd had from Wilkins earlier. Bessie frowned and said she didn't think she'd ever been called Elizabeth. As far as she knew, her name had always been Bessie. They'd called her that at the orphanage.

So, a charity child. At least the institution had kept her from the streets and trained her well enough to go into service.

'I saw you earlier,' I said, 'from my window. You were buying milk.'

Bessie sniffed. 'I don't reckon much to that milk. Mrs Simms, she will buy it because, she says, if you see it come from the cow you know it hasn't been watered. There is a feller comes round with a cart and milk churns, but Mrs Simms, she don't trust him.'

'Why don't you, er, reckon to the cow's milk, Bessie?'

'It stinks,' said Bessie. 'It's what they feeds them poor animals on, cabbage stalks and rubbish from the markets mostly. I don't never drink milk.'

I managed not to laugh as I didn't want to offend her. She seemed such a sturdily independent little soul, for all her waif-like appearance.

'Do you remember your parents, Bessie? Before you went to the orphanage?'

'No,' said Bessie briefly.

'I'm sorry,' I told her.

Bessie brightened. 'I was left in a church, in a box with *Newman's Pork Pies* written on it. So they give me the name Newman because I didn't have no other and I don't know why they called me Bessie. Still, could've been worse, couldn't it?'

On that philosophical note she vanished through the door.

When I finally found my way downstairs for the second time it was gone eight o'clock. Breakfast was set out in the smaller dining room as I had guessed it would be. Frank Carterton was already there, eating heartily and apparently none the worse for his night on the tiles. Indeed his mood seemed markedly improved since we had parted company the previous evening, his fit of the sulks quite forgotten.

'Good morning!' he greeted me cheerfully. 'You're an early bird. You won't see Aunt Julia downstairs before midday, believe me.' He gestured at the meat salvers now laden with a couple of cold joints. 'I'm afraid I've finished the best of the beef and you'll find what's left rather scrappy.

75

But there is plenty of boiled ham on the bone there. Or I recommend Mrs Simms' excellent omelettes.'

'The ham will be enough,' I told him.

'I'll cut you some,' he offered, leaping to his feet, grabbing the carving knife and beginning to hack copious amounts of meat from the bone until I begged him to stop.

'I am beginning to learn something about the running of the household,' I told him, when we were both seated and he began to eat again. 'So the Simmses, husband and wife, hold the position of butler and cook—'

'Mrs Simms is cook–housekeeper,' said Frank indistinctly. 'She's a stickler for being called that. She runs the place and she runs poor old Simms. Veritable dragon, our Mrs Simms.'

The thought of the impassive and hugely dignified butler being organised by a virago of a wife amused me. I was curious to meet Mrs Simms and wondered if she ever left her kitchen lair.

'There are also a couple of housemaids,' said Frank vaguely, 'couldn't tell you their names.'

'I have met one called Wilkins.'

'Then you have discovered more than I have. Wilkins, is it? I'll wager a pound to a penny the other one is called Perkins. Those are housemaids' names, in my experience.'

'And a little scullery maid called Bessie, a charity child.'

'The mushroom!' declared Frank, setting down his knife and fork. 'You must mean the skinny urchin I see scurrying in and out of the basement; wears an overlarge bonnet and a white apron. The creature looks just like a mushroom that has acquired a pair of feet, something even Mr Darwin didn't think of. So it's called Bessie, the mushroom, is it?'

'Is *she* . . .' I corrected him. 'Are those all?'

'All except Nugent, that's another formidable woman. Not a bad old girl, though.'

I was a little annoyed by Frank's cavalier way of talking of the staff who cared for him and his aunt. But I gave him the benefit of supposing he had been taught no better and meant no unkindness by it.

The door opened and an enticing aroma of coffee heralded Simms who having put down the silver pot enquired if I wished a hot dish from the kitchen.

'Thank you,' I said. 'But the ham is quite sufficient for me this morning.'

It was more than sufficient. I was struggling to get through it. Frank had served a generous helping and I had not quite recovered from last night's dinner. To watch Frank eat, one would have believed he'd starved himself for a week.

'No kidneys, I suppose, Simms?' he asked the butler wistfully.

'I shall enquire of Mrs Simms, sir.'

When the butler had left us, I glanced at the long-case clock in the corner of the room. 'What time do you have to be at your Foreign Office desk, Mr Carterton?'

'Oh, see here,' he said. 'You will call me Frank, won't you? You are my Uncle Josiah's god-daughter and so we are almost cousins, of a sort.'

'All right,' I agreed.

'As to my desk, I have been given the morning to allow me to visit my tailor.'

'Visit your tailor?' I couldn't help sounding startled.

'Yes, to order a set of clothes for Russia, you know. Followed by a visit to my shoemaker. I have been advised to wait until I get there to buy winter boots. If one goes hunting in the winter snows, it seems one needs felt boots. Sounds odd, don't it? But leather soles stick to the ice. That's what they tell me, at any rate.'

'I shall be sorry not to see you in the Russian snow in your felt boots, Mr— I mean, Frank,' I said drily. I couldn't help it. The image was quite out of keeping with the spoiled young man-about-town sitting across the table from me.

'One can hunt bears,' Frank informed me. 'I'm looking forward to that.'

'Bears? What would you do with a bear if you shot one?'

'Why, eat it. They tell me bear steaks are very good eating. So is bear soup, but I don't fancy that. Bear steaks might be jolly.'

I put down my knife and fork, partly because I could eat no more and partly because I could not put up with any more of this nonsense.

'Frank,' I said. 'You will allow me to make a request, I hope?'

'Certainly, I am at your command.' I thought he looked at me a little warily for all his debonair tone.

'Thank you. It's this. I realise it amuses you to tease Dr

Tibbett and sometimes your Aunt Julia, but do leave off this ridiculous way of prattling on with me. You are perfectly sensible, I'm sure.'

He leaned back and eyed me. 'You are very sharp, Elizabeth Martin.'

'I am a plain speaker, that's all.'

I decided, since I'd declared myself to be forthright, to plunge on. 'I have been wondering, for example, just how long you have known you will be going to St Petersburg? It seemed a little odd to me that you should decide to tell your aunt about it before two other people, one of them a stranger. I should have thought you'd tell her in private. Or did you plan, by so doing, to avoid her first, let's say, rather emotional response?'

I wondered if I'd been too daring. He would be right to take offence, but he only smiled.

'Ah, you've got a good head on your shoulders, a good-looking one, too.'

'Stop that!' I ordered immediately. 'I am not pretty. I can see that for myself in any mirror.'

'I didn't say you were pretty,' he retorted. 'No, you are not, nothing so vapid. You are handsome; I think that's the word. You have an intelligent and very expressive face. As to the last, may I offer a word of warning? Keep your feelings to yourself around here. I may act the fool occasionally, but it's a very good mask, you know.'

Before I could reply to this, Simms returned with the

dish of devilled kidneys. Frank promptly set about these as if he'd only just started his first meal of the day.

When we were alone again, I asked, 'Why should I need to be so careful of letting my feelings show? Or would that make me look a provincial?' Before he could reply, I asked on impulse, 'Or has it anything to do with Madeleine Hexham?'

Frank left off eating to lean back in his chair again. His expression became thoughtful. 'Between us, one never knew what Maddie Hexham was thinking. She never offered an opinion about anything. She played an entirely predictable game of cards. I never saw her read a book except some nonsense from the circulating library. I suspect Aunt Julia found her rather dull.'

'So, were you surprised when she disappeared?'

'I was annoyed because Aunt Julia sent me haring down to the local police station to inform the stalwart minion of the law there of Maddie's unexplained absence. I wasn't entirely surprised when Aunt Julia received the letter telling us she had eloped. I put it down to her reading those books. They were all about that sort of thing. She was quite a pretty woman or would have been with a little animation in her features, but as I said, if she had a brain, she showed no sign of being about to overuse it. Even the letter told us precious little. Not where she'd gone nor with whom. Perhaps she feared we'd seek to make her return, but we'd hardly do that. Aunt Julia felt betrayed and Dr Tibbett was in his element promising her eternal damnation.'

Frank pushed a piece of kidney round his plate. Perhaps even he had reached his gastronomic limit. 'See here,' he said. 'One can't help but rag old Tibbett occasionally in a gentle sort of way. He's no fool and one mustn't overdo it. I don't mean to tease Aunt Julia, who has been very good to me.'

'And do you really think Dr Tibbett a suitor for your aunt's hand, as you suggested? Or was that just another tease? You seemed to find the idea amusing.'

Frank burst out laughing. 'Here,' he said. 'Allow me to pour you a cup of coffee. There's milk there in the jug.'

I remembered what Bessie had had to say about the milk and peered at the jug with some misgiving. The contents certainly looked a curious blue-grey colour but I couldn't smell any odour, not without putting my nose right to it and I couldn't do that in front of Frank. I resolved to drink my coffee black.

Frank put his elbows on the table, folded his hands beneath his chin and fixed me with, for him, quite a serious look.

'You probably know Aunt Julia was Uncle Josiah's second wife.'

'I didn't know for sure, but I wondered about that,' I said. 'There is the difference in age, of course. But also, she told me Josiah Parry never visited my father. Yet I remember one visit, when I was very young. So I think Aunt Parry did not know about it, or had perhaps forgotten. At any rate, my godfather came alone. I remember he was very sad and never smiled, though he spoke to me very kindly. So possibly he was in mourning, perhaps for his first wife?'

'I say,' said Frank in admiration. 'You *are* sharp! I was right. I shall have to watch what I say. You remember everything and you puzzle it out.'

'I am a stranger. It's natural I should listen carefully and puzzle things out if I can,' I defended myself.

'Well then, let me tell you about my Aunt Julia. You will see from it that things are not always quite as they seem here. My mother and her sister were daughters of a country clergyman. I think that is one reason Aunt Julia likes to have Tibbett around; it refreshes memories of a clerical childhood. My grandfather had nothing but his living to support his family and they were as poor, if you'll excuse the pun, as church mice. My mother eloped with my father and I am sorry to say he was no great provider. Aunt Julia did not intend to fall into a similar trap. I'm not sure how she met Uncle Josiah, but he was a widower and wealthy and she didn't mean to let him escape. Don't mistake me. She made him an excellent wife. She took an interest in his business affairs, possibly because she realised she might outlive him. Aunt Julia is another who dons a mask, Elizabeth. She pretends she has no interest in anything but whist and her own comfort. But her greatest interest is in making sure that comfort will always be provided for. That is why the idea she would marry Tibbett is so amusing. He thinks she will. I know she won't. She will not hand over control of her money to anyone else, you see. Tibbett will find he has to settle for dining here regularly, playing a hand of whist and being treated as the Dispenser of All Wisdom. I believe when he realises that, he will accept the role. As I said, Tibbett is no fool.'

'But is my godfather's business still continuing the import of cloth from the Far East?'

Frank shook his head. 'That stopped with his death. But he had made many other shrewd investments. He bought a great deal of property before he died. The rents brought him a steady income. My aunt has added to it. In fact, she owns a fair amount now, houses mostly. She has recently done very well out of some of it. They are to build a new railway terminus, you know.'

'I do know,' I admitted. 'I – we, that is to say the cab, passed by the site on my way here yesterday.'

'She owned some property on the site. The railway company came wanting to buy every standing structure in the area and offered a good price, all in order to pull them down,' said Frank confidentially. 'I think Aunt Julia was more than satisfied with the bargain she drove for her part of it.'

I felt startled to hear this news and recalled the creaking wagon with its sad load. I wondered if I should mention it. But perhaps Frank would think me ghoulish, as I suspected the cabbie had thought me, so I kept silent.

Frank rose to his feet and tossed his crumpled napkin on the table. 'I must be off. Busy day, you know.'

He left me alone and very thoughtful.

Chapter Five

AS FRANK had warned me, Mrs Parry, or Aunt Parry as I must learn to call her, did not appear until almost noon, just in time for a light luncheon to which I did little justice. If this was indeed to be her habit, then it meant I would have the mornings free for my own interests and that was very encouraging.

I had remained in the house after breakfast in case she had come downstairs earlier, despite Frank's information. I spent most of the time in the library. I found writing paper and ink there and took some of the time to write to Mrs Neale, the kind neighbour who had given me a temporary home after I had sold the Derbyshire house. She had expressed some concern at my leaving for London, a strange city, to be among strange folk. Mrs Neale, who had never set foot outside her home town, meant 'strange' in both senses of the word. In my letter I told her I had met with no problems on the journey and my prospects looked very good. I was sure this news would soon be passed around the entire community and talk would be of nothing else. I sealed it up using a scrap of wax in a tray on the desk, and took it out into the hall where I had noticed a small wooden box for the receipt of post leaving the house. I put my letter in it but resolved that once I had found out where the post office was, I would take my letters there myself. If, of course, I wrote any more on my own account.

Later in the afternoon a Mrs Belling called. I remembered the name as that of the woman who had 'found' Madeleine Hexham and introduced her into the household. I was curious to see her but my first impression of her was not favourable. She was smartly dressed wearing one of the new-style crinolines, far less exaggerated than the sort that had previously been the height of desirability. It gave her skirts a conical shape. On her head above a chignon of what was certainly false hair (it was blacker than her own) was perched a modish little casquette. Her features were sharp and her nose in particular long and pointed. I thought she looked like some kind of bird, perhaps a jackdaw, inquisitive and artful. She asked me a great many questions about myself, my father, my place of birth and anything else she could find to ask of me, all in a very direct way. I thought this ill-mannered of her. I had not come to London to be employed by her, after all! Even Aunt Parry seemed to find her friend's quizzing of me went a little too far and interrupted her after some minutes with a question about the visitor's son, James.

This name I had also heard. Frank had mentioned that James Belling was a collector of fossils. Mrs Belling lost interest in me and began to expound on the virtues and amazing intelligence of James and her other offspring. There was, I gathered, in addition to James, a daughter who was married and currently in an interesting condition. There was another younger daughter who was certainly bound to be married before long and a young son away at school. He, too, was destined for a brilliant future. Quite where James came in this list of siblings, I was not sure. I guessed he might be a contemporary of Frank Carterton and so either the eldest Belling or the second eldest (after the married daughter). I was relieved to see Mrs Belling depart and had the impression that Mrs Parry was not sorry to see her friend go, at least on this occasion.

We were not, however, to be without a visitor for long. Minutes later Simms appeared in the doorway, his impassive countenance for once quite animated, and announced, 'I beg your pardon, madam, but there is a police officer here and he wishes to speak with you.'

'Whatever for?' asked Aunt Parry. 'Tell him I am otherwise engaged, Simms.'

'I am sorry, madam, he wishes to speak with you personally, most particularly. He has sent up his card . . .'

I wish I could describe the manner in which Simms said this and the way in which he advanced across the room and held out a silver tray on which lay a modestly printed rectangle with the legend *Inspector Benjamin Ross*.

Metropolitan Police. Scotland Yard. It was obvious the butler believed a police officer had no business possessing a card nor presenting it in a respectable household, thus requiring Simms himself to carry it upstairs.

'How very odd,' said Aunt Parry, picking up the card cautiously and turning it this way and that. 'Where is he, Simms? What does he want?'

'I put him in the library, madam. He came just before Mrs Belling left and I thought perhaps you might not wish her to see him. As to what he wants, madam, I have been unable to ascertain. He won't say.' Emotion vibrated briefly in the butler's stately tones.

'Yes, of course, that was wise of you, Simms. Oh dear, how very peculiar. What about his boots?'

'His boots are quite clean, madam. He is not in uniform.'

'Well, then, I suppose he may come up. No, wait. Elizabeth, go down and see what he wants. See if he will be content with talking to you. If he won't, then you must bring him up here, I dare say. Only do check his boots.'

I followed Simms downstairs. The butler opened the library door and stood aside to allow me to enter. He then shut the door smartly on me and the visitor, no doubt fearing that some other person might pass by and see us.

Inspector Benjamin Ross was standing at the far side of the room before the hearth, looking up at the portrait of Josiah Parry. I could only see that he had thick black hair, was soberly dressed in street clothes and held his hat in his hand. He turned now and could be seen to be a surprisingly young man for his rank. He was clean shaven with an alert intelligence about his features and dark eyes.

However, any surprise I might have felt at his appearance was far outweighed by the effect the sight of me had on him. I didn't know what he had expected: whether he'd thought Mrs Parry herself might have come down or some male figure. When he saw me, though, he looked quite thunderstruck. He opened his mouth, closed it again and then managed a faint 'Ah . . .'

'Inspector Ross?' I asked, holding up the little visiting card which I had brought down with me.

'Yes,' he said, still staring at me.

'I am Elizabeth Martin, Mrs Parry's companion,' I said sternly so that he should know it wouldn't do to try and fool *me*.

'Yes,' he said again, most strangely. 'Of course you are.' He then fell silent again and continued to stare at me in that same astonished way.

I began to lose patience, a commodity rather in short supply with me at the best of times. Was there some oddity in my appearance? Had my hair tumbled loose? Was there a spot on the end of my nose?

'I beg your pardon?' I prompted sharply. His peculiar manner was beginning to unsettle me. I wondered if it might have been better to arm myself with something more formidable than a small oblong of stiff paper or at least to have asked Simms to accompany me into the library.

Anyone may have a visiting card printed and it was all we had to support his claim to be a police officer.

He seemed to pull himself together and began to speak very quickly, 'Forgive me. I was hoping to speak to Mrs Parry who, I understand, is the owner of the house. Is she at home?'

'She is at home,' I admitted. 'But to be open with you, she is rather puzzled as to the reason for your calling here. Could you tell me something about it?'

I was still trying for sternness but my ear had caught a familiar intonation in his voice. I thought, He is not a Londoner. One might almost believe he hails from my part of the country. This idea was disarming. I felt myself thaw.

He gestured apologetically with his hat. 'I am sorry, Miss Martin, I can only discuss the details with Mrs Parry.'

I frowned. 'But can you not give me at least some indication of the – the nature of your call?'

He hesitated. 'It is possible I have some unwelcome news for her.'

'Frank!' I exclaimed. 'Have you come to tell us some accident has befallen him?'

'Frank?' he asked sharply and frowned. 'That would be Mr Francis Carterton, would it?'

'Yes, Mrs Parry's nephew. He is currently living here. Is there something wrong?'

The inspector looked at me strangely again. 'No, as far as I'm aware, Mr Carterton is safe and sound. He's not at home, then, obviously.'

'He is employed at the Foreign Office,' I told him. 'Although I understand that this morning he was—'

There was no reason why I should shield Frank Carterton from any criticism but still, I thought it best not to tell the visitor that Frank had spent the morning at his tailor's.

'I believe this morning he had some other engagement. But he should be at the Foreign Office now.'

'Well, then, I can track him down there later,' said Ross briskly.

This only served to deepen the mystery. I was now curious to know what it was all about and it seemed there was only one way to find out. I glanced, I hoped not too obviously, at his boots. They appeared to present no threat to the carpets.

'If you will follow me,' I said, 'I'll take you to Mrs Parry. She is in her private sitting room, upstairs. You may leave your hat on the hall table if you wish.'

I turned to lead the way. I was conscious as I walked upstairs that the inspector followed behind and I could feel his eyes upon me. Perhaps the police studied everyone like that, I thought. But I do hope he'll soon be satisfied and lose interest in me!

I introduced him to Aunt Parry who appeared pleasantly surprised at his appearance and unbent to the extent of inviting him to sit down, which I didn't think she had been planning to do.

'I am sorry to trouble you, madam,' he began.

'It is not my nephew?' she interrupted anxiously.

'No, ma'am, it is not about Mr Carterton. It is about a young woman by the name of Madeleine Hexham. I understand she was employed here as your companion.'

Aunt Parry's alarm increased. 'Oh, dear . . .' she exclaimed, throwing up her podgy hands. 'Don't tell me she has come back? I don't want to see her.'

'You will not see her, ma'am, and I fear she will not be coming back.'

He said this very soberly and the hairs prickled on the back of my neck.

'Some harm has befallen her,' I said before I could stop myself.

'Sadly, yes.' He nodded. 'A body has been found and we believe it to be hers.'

'A body?' cried Aunt Parry, starting up and then falling back in her chair.

I jumped up ready to render assistance and Inspector Ross half rose to his feet. But she waved us both away as we loomed over her.

'Do you mean a dead body? I suppose you do. How very— My good man, you have a very brusque way of announcing such a shocking piece of news.' Her face had reddened alarmingly and her plump fingers gripped the arms of her chair so tightly the knuckles stood out through the skin.

'I apologise, ma'am,' said our visitor, 'I'm afraid it's in the nature of my duties that I'm often the bearer of distressing news and there's really no other way of telling it than bluntly.'

Aunt Parry pulled out her handkerchief and began to wave the small lace-edged square up and down before her face in lieu of a fan. It struck me that there was more irritation than grief in her manner and that the fluttering handkerchief served very well to hide her features until she could compose them.

She let her hand fall to her lap. She certainly appeared more in control. 'When – where – how?' she demanded, adding pettishly, 'Oh dear, if only Frank were here or Dr Tibbett. I repeat, Inspector, you might have waited until this evening when there would be a man in the house.'

'If I could first ask you about the circumstances of her disappearance,' Ross said firmly.

He clearly had no more time to spend on her protests and considered her well up to being questioned. I think she recognised it because she blinked once and then stared at him very hard.

'It was reported at Marylebone police station on the eighth of March last that she had left the house the previous day and not returned that night. She was described at the time as being of slight build, not tall, fair-haired and wearing a lavender-striped poplin gown. She was also reported as probably having worn a paisley shawl and a small bonnet, but those last items are missing. That is to say, we have not yet recovered them.'

Aunt Parry waved her hands at him to stop his speech.

Her plump chin had set obstinately and I fancied she was becoming angered again. 'This is quite impossible. Yes, she left here in a very odd way, just walked out one morning without a word to anyone and taking not a thing with her. But we had, that is to say, I received a letter from her a week or so later. I'm sure there is some mistake, Inspector, and the unfortunate woman you are talking of is not Madeleine.'

'A letter?' Ross sounded excited. 'Do you still have it? May I see it?'

But Aunt Parry shook her head. 'No, I don't have it. I was so angry with her. She wrote that she had eloped! We had no idea! We had never suspected! I tore it up.'

Ross looked dismayed but rallied. 'There is no doubt, ma'am, it was in her handwriting?'

'Should it not be?' She gazed at him in bewilderment. 'It looked like her hand. I showed it to Mrs Belling, the friend who introduced Madeleine to me. She had had some previous correspondence with her. Madeleine came from the North. She was not personally known to Mrs Belling, but to a friend of hers in Durham, if you follow me. But Mrs Belling did not question it being her hand-writing!' Aunt Parry shook her head. 'I really cannot take this in.'

'I am truly sorry,' Ross said. 'Then can you tell me, as exactly as possible, what she wrote? The very words, if you can.'

With something of the dexterity of a magician, as he

spoke he produced a pocketbook together with a pencil, and sat ready to take any reply down. I was astonished by this and so, I fancy, was Aunt Parry.

I opened my mouth to tell him how impressed I was by his efficiency but managed to close it again before any word escaped.

Aunt Parry gazed at him and the pocketbook in despair. 'But I don't remember exactly. She wrote only that she was sorry to have caused any inconvenience. Yes! Those were her words. I remember thinking that it was a remarkable understatement. We had been quite frantic with worry about her and now she wrote and said she had left with a man! "The gentleman to whom I am engaged to be married," she wrote, the first we knew of it. Dr Tibbett said he did not believe there was any such engagement. Oh, my goodness me, are you writing it *all* down, Inspector?'

Ross's pencil had been fairly flying over the page but he paused in his scribbling to ask, 'Dr Tibbett?'

'A friend whom I am accustomed to consult,' explained Aunt Parry. 'Dr Tibbett is a man of the cloth. He spoke very harshly of Madeleine. He believes her to have behaved in a thoroughly depraved way. But now you tell us she may be dead? How did she die?'

Ross put away his pocketbook, which seemed to relieve Aunt Parry. But her respite was to be short-lived. He studied my employer briefly before he said, 'I am afraid she died violently.'

Mrs Parry raised her hands and then let them fall limply into her lap. She said nothing.

'Can you tell us, Inspector,' I asked, 'where Miss Hexham's body was found? Was it far from here?'

He turned his steady scrutinising gaze on me. 'It was in Agar Town,' he said eventually. 'In a house scheduled for demolition. They are building a new railway terminus as you probably know. All the houses have been coming down and the house where she was found is among the last section to be levelled.'

'In Agar Town, oh no!' gasped Aunt Parry. 'Surely not.'

'It is not a place you would have expected her to be found,' Ross said. 'I understand that.'

My employer and I were silent but for different reasons. Mrs Parry, I guessed, was horrified because she had not long since sold her property in that area for the purpose of that very demolition. I was frozen with horror. It had been Madeleine Hexham's corpse that had crossed my path the previous day on my way to this house. Whatever had happened to her? Who could have done it? By what whim of malicious Fate had I been passing in the growler at that very instant? I was not superstitious but it couldn't appear save as some terrible omen.

Ross obviously took our lengthy silence as a dismissal. He rose to his feet. 'I am very sorry, ladies, to have been the cause of such distress. I'll leave you now. You will need time to recover. I may need to return and speak to you again, Mrs Parry. If you can remember anything at all . . .

or if any member of your household has any idea as to the identity of the man with whom Miss Hexham ran away, please let me know at once.'

Aunt Parry whispered, 'Of course.'

'And an officer will call to question the servants, with your permission.'

The last words were a formality. An officer would come and quiz the staff whether Aunt Parry gave her permission or not. She knew it and again I saw that flicker of annoyance in her face. She signalled faintly at me which I took to mean I should escort the inspector out.

When we reached the hallway downstairs, Ross paused by the hall table but didn't pick up his hat. Instead he gestured towards the library. 'Could I have a few words more, Miss Martin? I do understand you are deeply shocked.'

'I did not know her,' I said. 'I came here only yesterday to replace her.' But I led the way into the library and closed the door. I did not want any of the servants overhearing. Ross had warned they would be questioned and before that they would all have heard the news. But half-heard scraps of conversation were not the way for them to do it.

'I am sorry to ask anything of you,' Ross said. 'But if I could see Miss Hexham's belongings? Mrs Parry said she took nothing with her when she left. I presume they are still here, perhaps put away somewhere? Possibly that butler will know where.'

'I'm sorry,' I said. 'But I understand there was nothing but her clothing and Mrs Parry gave that to the servants. I believe there was something in the letter to the effect that the clothes were to be disposed of as Mrs Parry saw fit.'

He looked exasperated but then resigned. 'Well, it was a vain hope, perhaps. After such a long time, it's not surprising her belongings were cleared out. But she left nothing else? No letters? No diary?'

'To my knowledge, no. But I was not here at the time, as I told you.'

'Left nothing, wrote that her clothing should be disposed of, that does not seem strange to you, Miss Martin?' he asked abruptly.

'I suppose she did not intend to come back.'

'Or someone wrote the letter in her hand to make it seem so,' he said quietly, watching me to see how I took this suggestion.

I replied as calmly as I could, 'The thought occurred to me when you were speaking to Mrs Parry. If she was murdered, and by violence I take it you mean murder, then her murderer would wish the search which had been started for her to be called off.'

'Except that it was not called off,' Ross said. 'No one went back to Marylebone police station to report that news had been received of her. She remained a missing person as far as we were concerned.'

Well, that will be Frank, I thought crossly to myself but did not say it. He probably forgot or couldn't be bothered.

Aloud, I said, 'I wish I could help you. I didn't know her but it's a terrible thing to have happened.'

'A great shock for Mrs Parry,' Ross said. He fixed his dark intelligent eyes on me. 'And although you say you did not know her, yet I can see it has upset you.'

'I should explain,' I said awkwardly. 'Yesterday, on my way here in a cab, we were held up by the passage of a wagon carrying a dead body. It was in the area where they are pulling down the houses. That body was hers, wasn't it?'

Ross muttered something. He looked angry. 'Very likely!' he said curtly. 'I am sorry you saw it. I am sorry you were there and I am sorry you are here!'

'What do you mean?' I found his last words as strange as I had found his whole manner towards me. I know I spoke quite sharply.

He sighed. 'You do not remember me,' he said. 'There is no reason why you should. But we have met before, quite twenty years ago.'

'Oh no,' I said, shaking my head. 'That's impossible. I have only just arrived in London from Derbyshire, as I explained to you. Josiah Parry,' I pointed at the portrait above the hearth, 'was my godfather. His widow, Mrs Parry, offered me the situation of companion after I wrote asking for her help, following the death of my father.'

'So Dr Martin is dead,' he said. 'I am sorry to hear it. He was a good man and I owe him everything.'

'You knew my father!' I gasped.

'And you. You are Lizzie Martin. You came with your father when he was called to a pit accident. A child died . . .'

I knew I was gaping at him. 'Yes, I do remember that! I hid in the pony-trap that morning. I was only eight years old. But how could you possibly know of that?'

'I was there but you won't remember. I gave you my lucky piece of shale with the image of a fern in it. I dare say you threw it away.'

There was a sudden flash of memory, an image, revealed as if in a shaft of lightning on a night sky, of a dark-haired boy with coal-grimed face and clothing. 'I remember you,' I said slowly. 'And as for your piece of lucky shale, I have it still. But, how . . .?'

I broke off in some embarrassment because what I'd been about to blurt out would sound so rude. But he was ahead of me.

'How did I get from that to here? Well, at the time that child died the government had already passed a law which forbade the employment of anyone under the age of ten in the mines. The little boy who died – his name was Davy Price and I mind him well – he'd been under ten years of age. Your father made a great fuss about it with the authorities. As a result, the company dismissed all of us who were under that age. Joe Lee and I were nine years of age at the time. We were neither of us sorry not to have to go back down the pit, but it was a great loss to our families not to have our wages. Your father knew it.'

The inspector's gaze drifted to the rows of packed book

spines on a shelf opposite. 'Most pitmen can do no more than make their mark. You probably realise that.'

'I suppose so,' I said a little awkwardly. 'But it's not their fault if there are no schools for them.'

His gaze shot back to engage mine with disconcerting directness. 'But why should the children of pitmen need schooling? That's what most people would say. It would only serve to fill them with ideas above their station.'

'That would seem to me a most foolish argument,' I retorted, 'and one my father wouldn't have supported for an instant! I know that he tried very hard to persuade several wealthy men of the town to band together and set up a charity school, as there are others in other towns. He was always sorry that he failed.'

I was surprised because I thought I heard Ross chuckle although there was no corresponding smile on his face. 'I'm not surprised he had no luck. My own father knew no more than to make his mark despite my mother's attempts to teach him. Oh yes, my mother knew her letters!'

I blushed because I realised I had shown my astonishment at this piece of information.

'When she was a girl,' he went on, 'the vicar of her parish set up a Sunday school for poor children. My mother learned both to read and write and was made a monitor to teach the younger ones in turn. Later she taught me and, after my father's death, earned a few pence teaching any other children in the pit village whose parents could spare the money or thought it worth the expense.

101

Dr Martin's original intention, when he knew us to be without employment, was to find us labouring work. But when he heard that both Joe and I could read well and write a fair hand he declared our education should not be wasted.'

Ross pulled a wry face. 'I remember very well how he came to our house and sat listening to both of us read aloud to him and write at his dictation. He quizzed us both at great length and eventually dismissed us. We went outside and asked one another what on earth that had all been about! We later learned he had offered to pay for our proper schooling. Joe's parents were hesitant at first but when my mother told them she meant to accept the offer for me, they agreed to it. So Joe and I, wearing new boots paid for by your father,' a smile flickered across his face, 'started our studies at the town's grammar school where we soon found out how ignorant we were! We had to work hard if we were not to sit on the younger boys' benches indefinitely and it was a powerful incentive. I admit we found those first weeks tougher going than any shift down the pit. But thanks to that, I was able to find work as a clerk for some years on leaving school. Then, when I reached eighteen, I came down to London to try my luck.'

He smiled broadly and suddenly looked quite different, relaxed and glad to escape his official duties if only for a moment. But for the second time I had a memory of having seen that grin before. 'Like Dick Whittington,' he said, 'I was persuaded that the streets were paved with gold. But they were not, being mostly mud, and the living expensive. I joined the police. They were anxious to recruit men at the time. Thanks to your father, I not only had enough education but more than most recruits. I had worked hard of an evening over my books to improve it further. I reached the rank of sergeant quickly and, last year, that of inspector, one of the youngest in the Force.' There was a modest pride in his voice to which he was in every way entitled.

The action of my father which had so benefited Ben Ross was typical of him. His charity in this and other ways had left me penniless but I did not criticise him for it.

'My father would have been both proud and happy to know you have done so well,' I said.

'It has been my determination to do well,' he said seriously, 'since Dr Martin's kindness opened the door for me.'

I had no doubt of his sincerity and of his determination. I wondered if my father had unwittingly unloosed the monster of ambition in the collier's son he had taken under his wing. But I should not criticise Inspector Ross. I had seen the awful place where he had begun his working life as a child. Who would not want to escape it for ever?

Aloud I said, 'I am glad to have met you again, though perhaps the circumstances could be pleasanter.'

He hissed in an annoyed way. 'It's the devil of a business,

begging your pardon, Miss Martin, and I wish you had nothing to do with it!'

'You will be coming back to speak to Mrs Parry again and let us know how you progress in your investigations?' I asked. 'She will want to be kept informed. I had better go now and comfort her.'

'Yes, yes, of course you must. She was angry at Miss Hexham for the way she behaved but to learn she is dead, well, that's another matter, and that she died as she did.'

'It is not only that,' I said unthinkingly. 'But she owned some property in Agar Town and sold it to the railway company. My late godfather invested in a good deal of property and I believe my Aunt Parry owns houses all over London.'

It was only when I finished speaking that I realised the full import of my words. It could not be coincidence that Madeleine Hexham had been found in Agar Town. In some manner, her death was linked to this house. I knew my sudden realisation was written on my face.

Ross said slowly, 'Did she, indeed?' and I knew he was thinking as I was. Abruptly he asked, 'Do you know what kind of houses those were in Agar Town?'

I stared at him and shook my head.

'They were some of the worst slums in London, and that is saying something.'

'Josiah was – Mrs Parry still is – a slum landlord?' I gasped. This comfortable house with its luxurious furnishings, the 'good English table' and my forty pounds a year, all this was funded by poor people living in wretched slums? The food I had eaten that day felt heavy in my stomach. Everything about me seemed tainted. I thought I would be sick.

'Please, sit down!' Ross urged me and led me to the wing chair. I was happy to collapse into it. 'I am so sorry,' he said abjectly. 'I should not have told you that on top of everything else.'

'No, it's right I should know,' I whispered. I managed to rally and got to my feet, albeit a little unsteadily. 'You must go now, Inspector.'

'Yes, yes,' he said, moving towards the door.

Simms was standing outside with the visitor's hat at the ready. I was not surprised. I wondered if he had heard anything through the panels but they were solid enough and I doubted it.

He greeted our appearance with, 'I will see the officer off the premises, Miss Martin!'

I thought Ross might be angered by the butler's words, intended as they were to put both of us in our places. But he only looked amused.

'Goodbye to you, Miss Martin,' he said with a bow.

'Goodbye, Inspector Ross.'

I managed the farewell with tolerable composure and walked to the far end of the hall. I waited there until Simms returned from having seen the intruder safely off the premises. It was to be his turn to be surprised.

'Ah, Simms,' I said. 'The inspector brought some very

sad and shocking news. It seems poor Miss Hexham has been murdered.'

I had the satisfaction of seeing Simms lose all countenance. He gaped at me. 'Murdered, miss?'

'Yes. There will be a police officer coming here to question the staff. Do prepare them for it, will you? He will be particularly anxious to know where Miss Hexham went after leaving this house, so if anyone has any idea at all, the officer should be told.'

Simms nodded, swallowed and uttered a gurgled noise which I interpreted to mean he would tell the staff.

I thanked him and added a request that he bring the Madeira wine to the sitting room as Mrs Parry was probably in need of a restorative. Simms rallied at being given this order.

'I'll do it at once, Miss Martin.'

I went back upstairs to do my duty by my employer. My mind was in turmoil and it was not only on account of Madeleine Hexham.

Chapter Six

IT WAS some little time after Inspector Ross's departure before Aunt Parry, having taken two glasses of the Madeira, retired to her bedroom, there to lie down and allow Nugent to minister to her with a cologne compress. Before that she expressed herself at great length and forcefully on the subject of Madeleine Hexham.

She was sorry, of course, to hear she had perished so horribly but what was one to expect? Dr Tibbett had been right. The girl had fallen into bad company with dire results. Whatever would Mrs Belling say? She would be highly embarrassed and would, of course, blame her friend in Durham who had found Madeleine in answer to Mrs Belling's request, made on behalf of her friend, Mrs Parry. Mrs Belling's correspondent had shown a very poor judgement in recommending the girl. To think she, Aunt Parry, had taken the girl under her roof and shown her every kindness. Now, no doubt, the lady in Durham, to cover her own shortcomings, would blame Mrs Parry for not keeping a stricter eye on Madeleine.

What Aunt Parry did not say, but what occurred to me, was that this very much resembled the game of 'musical chairs' which children play at parties. Everyone seeks a refuge and no one wishes to be caught out when the pianist stops playing. Now the music had stopped for poor Madeleine and all who knew her bolted for a position of safety.

Eventually Aunt Parry rose to her feet and observed, 'I hope I may never have such grief on your account, Elizabeth!'

'No, Aunt Parry, of course you won't.' I felt myself flush as I said this. I didn't like being warned against any course of action I'd no intention of undertaking. As if I'd be so addle-pated as to elope with some admirer who felt it so necessary to protect his identity that not a soul knew his face! Having thought this I then scolded myself mentally for falling into the trap of blaming Madeleine for her own misfortunes. Whoever the man was, he'd had the gift of persuasion. Madeleine had believed him. Who knew whether, in her situation, I might not have believed him too? But I did like to think I was sharp enough to scent a deceiver.

Aunt Parry's expression had softened and she patted my arm. 'But you are Josiah's god-daughter and your papa was a respected man, a professional medical man. The circumstances are quite different. Well, it is a lesson to us all.'

When she had gone I made my escape to the privacy of my own room and sat down to disentangle the thoughts chasing one another around my skull. Madeleine's death had resulted in a strange meeting for me. I hadn't recognised him, of course. How should I? It had all happened over twenty years before and we had both been children. But I remembered the events and the circumstances of our meeting as if they had taken place a mere week before.

Early spring that year had been a chilly damp season. It had rained heavily during that night, as I recalled. The sound of it beating on the window glass kept me from slumber as I lay tucked up in my bed with the blanket pulled well round my ears. At last I'd drifted into uneasy sleep only to be awoken by the heavy-handed *rat-tat* of our brass fox-head door knocker, followed by a couple of urgent thumps with a fist on the panels of the front door.

I sat up, thinking at first it might be thunder. But then I heard a distant voice, shouting, 'Doctor! Dr Martin! You are needed, sir!'

I scrambled on to the windowsill and peered out. The nursery was at the very top of our house which was an old narrow one with rooms stacked high upon one another like children's building blocks. It was just before dawn and far down below me I could see the bobbing light of a lantern in the gloom, casting an inadequate yellow circle. A dimly perceived figure held it. I wasn't afraid because this sort of early-morning visit happened not infrequently. My father was the most popular medical man in the town.

The other was old Dr Fray and he, it was well known, never turned out before breakfast, even for an emergency, unless it involved the gentry. In addition, my father was the designated police surgeon and was called out on all kinds of business. A messenger in the early hours was as likely to bring news concerning the already lifeless victim of a brawl in an alehouse or a dead vagrant found by the roadside as the more respectable medical summons to a woman in labour. At barely eight years of age I was already well aware of that.

If I sound a somewhat precocious child, then it's because I was. My mother had died when I was three and I had been left to the care of my father; our housekeeper Mary Newling; and my nurse Molly Darby, a plump, indolent girl. I had always roamed around our house, up and down its narrow stairs and in and out of its many hidey-holes, for a large part of the time unattended and unobserved. Thus I listened to conversations I shouldn't have been party to and acquired information by no means suited to my tender years.

So there was no fear someone would come and order me back to bed. I could hear Molly snoring peacefully in her bed across the landing. The front door could have been knocked in altogether by the caller and she wouldn't have stirred.

I struggled to push up the sash but my arms were too short and I could only make it creak open a bare inch at the bottom. Already the cold grey light of early dawn was creeping over the peaks on the horizon and through the crack in the window I could hear the voices which rose clearly on the chill crisp air. My father had gone down to open up and was talking to someone. I heard him say, 'I'll come directly. Run round to the stable, will you, and tell the boy to put the pony to the trap?'

At that moment some small devil got into me. Not a large serious one, just some imp who was twiddling his thumbs at that hour with nothing to do. I decided I'd like to accompany my father. It would be exciting. It would also be declared quite out of the question if I asked, so I wouldn't ask. I knew that it would take the stable boy quite a few minutes to harness up the pony which was newly bought as a replacement for our former pony. That one had been a placid mare who hadn't minded small girls scrambling on to her and would back into the shafts of her own accord. But old age had led to her being sent to live out her remaining days in comfort on a nice farm, or so my father had told me. I knew this wasn't true and the mare had gone to the knacker's yard. But I didn't want to distress my father by letting him see that I was upset, so I had pretended to believe the well-meant untruth.

Was it also true, I had wondered briefly, that we went to heaven when we died, or did they just take you off somewhere like the knacker's yard? I reproached myself immediately because heaven was in the Bible. I'd attended funerals and knew them to be sombre and decent affairs and where much was made of a 'sure and certain hope of resurrection'. But sadly there was nothing in scripture about ponies.

Still I nodded and said I hoped the farmer fed the pony carrots sometimes, because she liked them so. My father was relieved I hadn't burst into tears and said yes, he was sure about the carrots. It was an early example in my life of people conspiring to accept what they know is a lie, because the truth is too unpalatable. As I grew older, I saw and heard how often this is the case. It was also, in the matter of the carrots, an example of how, once you tell a lie, you have to start embellishing it. In no time at all, it becomes a real nuisance.

Just at that moment I was concerned only with scrambling into my clothes. Dressing was a complicated business and I usually had the help of Molly. Of course I couldn't call Molly now. I managed to pull on my drawers and a petticoat and a dress but my boots had been taken away by Molly to be cleaned, so I pushed my bare feet into an entirely unsuitable pair of satin party slippers, wrapped a crocheted woollen shawl round my shoulders and scurried down the back stairs.

I was now faced with the problem of actually getting out of the house. The front door had been unbolted, it was true, but there were risks in leaving that way. I could too easily be seen. The back door would still be fast and I knew my fingers weren't strong enough to draw back the heavy bolt. Then as I reached the bottom of the stair I heard a rattling sound from the kitchen at the back of the house. Someone was doing the task for me. I peeped round the door and saw that Mary Newling had been roused by the commotion and was opening the kitchen door. She presented an awesome sight in a voluminous nightgown and plaid shawl, her head a forest of rag knots. I was momentarily sidetracked by these, wondering why she tried to curl her hair, since she normally wore it hidden by a cotton bonnet.

She dragged open the door and shouted out into the yard, 'What's amiss?'

A voice called back, 'The doctor's needed at the mine!'

'God help us!' returned Mary, 'is it an explosion or a roof-fall?'

'Neither, missus, they've only found a body!'

Only *a* body? Even I understood he meant there had been only one fatality. When the pit props gave way or the firedamp caused an explosion, the bodies came up by the dozen, if they ever came up at all. Most men still worked by the light of traditional lamps with flame open to the air. Molly Darby had chilled my infant imagination with tales of men buried down there among the coal seams they worked, women and children too. Molly's father and three brothers worked in the pit and her own mother, when young, had crawled underground through cramped passages with heavy baskets of coal on her back until an accident had left her lame. It was Molly who explained the irony that where the safety lamp invented by Sir Humphrey Davy was in common use, men were required to work in even deeper and more hazardous tunnels.

Although ours was a small mining town on the Derbyshire coalfield, we seldom saw the colliers themselves in the town. They and their families lived in mine villages, cramped purpose-built housing near the pits described to me by Molly. If one person turns over in bed, she had declared cheerfully, then the fellow in the bed in the next-door house falls out! Behind each house was a pigsty and its carefully fattened occupant would be slaughtered at the beginning of the winter. Its preserved meat would supply the mainstay of the family's diet until spring. Colliers were required by their employers to buy their provisions at the mine shop, exchanging tokens there which were not acceptable in other shops in the town. These tokens were known by the nickname of 'truck', Molly told me, adding, 'It keeps them from spending their wages in the pubs.' It also increased their isolation from the town's other inhabitants who had no cause themselves to visit the collier villages.

As a result a kind of superstitious awe of them had grown up. They were acknowledged to be a hardy and self-sufficient race but a breed apart, of mythical strength and resilience, who ventured down into the dark depths where most people would have feared to go. Mary Newling would sigh from time to time when conversation led to the existence of the pit, and give her opinion that it was a dangerous life and no one should be obliged to earn a living scrabbling about like a mole in the dark.

This was generally followed by a grumble about the price of good sitting-room coal and dire reference to the fact that one of the local mine managers had just built himself a mansion on his profits.

Mary had not approved the hiring of Molly Darby as my nurse. My father had done so in an effort to help the Darby family. 'The doctor is letting his good nature make a decision his common sense would not!' sniffed Mary. 'Not for the first time. Nor, you mark my words, will it be the last.'

All this meant that I longed to visit a mine as I would any forbidden place. Not to go down into the dark, mind you, just see it from above. I didn't like the dark much and was always happy to hear Molly Darby's snores across the landing. But I was more than ever determined to smuggle myself into the trap. Mary had turned away from the back door, pushing it shut but not rebolting it. I hid in the stairwell as she stomped past, muttering to herself, and began to climb the stairs. She met my father coming down and they began a brief conversation. Now was my chance.

I ran across the kitchen, opened the door a crack and squeezed through. We had no garden, only a cobbled yard. On the far side was a primitive stable with a loft above in which the boy slept. There was a good deal of activity in the yard. It was growing lighter now. I could see how the stable boy and another man, presumably the one who had brought the message, were struggling between them to get the new pony into the shafts. It was a showy animal with white socks and an uneven temperament. It didn't like being dragged from a warm stall in the early hours and was clearly demonstrating its feelings. It kicked out as I watched and struck the visitor on the leg. He let fly a volley of abuse including several words I'd never heard before. I stored them in my memory, though I realised they were not for my use. I was a child with sharp ears.

Now was my moment. Keeping to the shadows, I scurried round the outside of the yard, along the front of the stable and scrambled into the trap unseen. Once there I pulled the rug which was always kept there over me and crouched down under the wooden seat.

The trap rocked violently as the pony was eventually partly coaxed and partly forced to back between the shafts. My father arrived in the yard and the trap rocked again as he climbed up and took the reins. I wondered if the messenger would also climb up and accompany him. If he did so, I would almost certainly be discovered. But he didn't and my father called to the pony, shook the reins and we were off.

It was very cold. I hadn't realised how chilled I would be. In my run across the yard I'd ploughed through puddles left by the overnight rain and my silly satin slippers had become soaked. My lack of stockings was soon felt. My crocheted shawl was of little use: too many holes in it. I was already shivering with cold and feared I was in a fair way to freeze. I tried to snuggle down into the rug and pull it closer around me. There was an exclamation from my father.

'What the devil?'

The rug was yanked away and I was revealed. We were still travelling at a fast clip along the rough road and the trap swayed and bounced. My father didn't draw rein but just snapped, 'What are you doing there, Lizzie?'

'I wanted to come with you,' I said.

'Pah!' I sensed that he wanted to use some of the language I'd heard earlier in the yard but he was repressing it. 'Well, you will have to stay there now,' he ordered. 'I can't turn back.'

'I'm cold,' I said unwisely.

'Then you will have to stay cold, won't you? Wrap yourself in the rug and do your best.'

I knew he was very angry. I wasn't so much frightened as sorry and said so.

'Sorry?' he said. 'What has sorry to do with it?'

I couldn't answer his question. But it worried me to think I might have done something so bad that I couldn't atone for it with an apology. Were there sins so bad you could never be forgiven, no matter how remorseful you were and tried to make it up?

Now I could wrap myself properly in the rug things weren't so bad. The wind ruffled my hair and made the tips of my ears sting, but otherwise I wasn't quite as cold as I had been. I was getting used to it.

We were already out of the town and heading along a country road. This was strange territory. In the distance were odd hills shaped like pyramids. I rubbed the tip of my nose with the back of my hand to restore some feeling to it, and saw, when I took my hand away, that it was smeared black. This could only come from something in the air. I wanted to ask some questions of my own: where exactly we were headed, what had happened to necessitate our journey and if someone was dead, who it was and how had he died?

But I decided discretion was the better part of valour and anyway, when we arrived I'd find all these things out for myself.

We drew up eventually outside a large stone building surrounded by wooden sheds. Beyond it towered a brick chimney. I gazed about me eagerly. I had never seen anything like it. It was a much bigger area than I'd imagined it would be; almost a town in itself: busy, untidy with a jumble of buildings of weird design and mysterious usage and everywhere blackened by coal dust. Behind them rose another of those pyramids, a huge man-made hill of slag. There were women and children climbing over it like so many ants, painstakingly seeking out small pieces of coal to add to the collection in buckets and bags they carried. People came and went in bewildering confusion, some hurrying, and some walking slowly and wearily. There were carts drawn by scrawny grubby ponies which were never groomed and, nearby, a group of men stood talking quietly together. Their faces were blackened with coal dust, their clothing equally soiled. I knew they were upset about something and angry too, but despite that, there was an air of helplessness about them. Whatever it was, they could do nothing about it.

My father jumped down from the trap with a curt, 'Wait there, Lizzie! Don't move, do you hear me?'

I hadn't time to promise him I would stay where I was before he had disappeared into the stone building.

I realised now that I was myself the object of some scrutiny. I looked round and saw a thin, wiry boy in tattered clothing standing nearby. He was holding the pony's bridle, a job I suppose my father had given him. He was a little older than me, as far as I could judge, and he was studying me carefully. He was taking his time about it, seeming unbothered by the fact that I could see him doing it. He had a shock of dark – or perhaps only grimy – hair but his face was reasonably clean. His eyes were also dark. There was something gipsy-like about him. If he had simply been staring at me, 'gawping' as Mary Newling would have called it, I could have borne that with equanimity. But this slow assessment was unsettling.

Perhaps I showed it because now he asked casually, 'Who are you, then?'

The casual phrasing of the question annoyed me further. I knew I must present an odd sight, sitting in the trap with the rug round me and my hair unbrushed. But I drew myself up and announced loftily, 'I am Miss Martin. Dr Martin is my papa.'

'Oh, aye,' said my interlocutor in that same easy drawl. 'And what would Miss Martin be doing here along with her papa?'

'It's none of your business!' I snapped. 'You are a very impertinent boy. Go away!'

At that he grinned outright. He had a wide smile, ear to ear, and his teeth were very white and even. This was in itself unusual. The only boys of his type I had seen before, street urchins, had generally lost a tooth or two in brawls. He made no move to leave. I decided to use his presence to acquire some knowledge. Besides, I wished to assert my authority.

'What is that building?' I asked, pointing at the large stone block into which my father had gone.

The boy looked surprised at my ignorance. 'Why, the offices.'

'Who works there?' If he thought me ignorant, so be it. I *was* ignorant of how things were done in this place.

'Fellows with nice clean hands,' said the boy drily. 'As never goes down a pit but knows all about sending others down there.'

He seemed to make a sudden decision, foraged in his pocket and withdrew a small dull grey object which he handed to me. 'Here, you can have this, if you want it. It might bring you luck.'

'It's a piece of shale,' I began, anxious to show him I did

know something, but then I saw it was more than that. There, pressed into its surface, was the image of a small fern, so distinct and so minutely perfect in every tiny detail that I gave an impetuous exclamation of delight, causing the boy to give his grin again.

'It's not shale, then?' I asked wonderingly and a little embarrassed because I had been so pleased at identifying it.

He shrugged his thin shoulders. 'It's shale. You find lots of bits like that around here. You split 'em open and if you're lucky, there's something like that inside.'

Just then, my father came out of the stone building, accompanied by a stocky man who seemed almost as broad as he was tall. The stranger wore a creased frock coat and, possibly to give the impression of increased height, a very tall silk hat which looked singularly out of place. He also had a clay pipe stuck in his mouth but it didn't seem to be lit. He chewed on it as if that was its purpose, which added an extra grimness to his pugnacious features. I didn't know who this man was, but I did think I didn't much like the look of him. However, I realised he was clearly a force to be reckoned with. The coal-grimed colliers, who had been talking together, stopped whispering to stare at him and then they moved slowly and silently away, their backs turned to the scene.

'I'm off!' said my companion and promptly disappeared, too, abandoning the pony and me.

I hoped Inspector Ross would prove more tenacious

now in his task of tracking down the murderer of Madeleine Hexham and not scuttle for cover as that coal-grimed urchin had done then!

They are all afraid of that man, I thought to myself at the time. He must be very important. And also, I realised, very powerful. Somehow this made me like him even less.

My father, I noted with pride, was not afraid of the man in the tall hat. He walked briskly beside him and both went into a shed. After a while, they came out. Now I could see that it was my father who was angry.

His voice rose clearly on the early-morning air. 'That child is nowhere near ten years of age. You know as well as I do that it's been unlawful for almost two years to employ a boy under the age of ten to work underground.'

There was so much rage in my father's voice that I thought it would affect Tall Hat but he just stared insolently at my father and shrugged his broad shoulders. When he took the pipe from his mouth to reply, his voice was aggressive.

'The boy's parents told me he was ten years old, but small for his age. I believed them. You know what runts these collier brats are.'

I was surprised at his tone because my father was normally treated by everyone with great respect. How dare he? I thought crossly. How dare he speak to my papa like that?

I waited confidently for my father to put the fellow in his place. But although I could see how angry he was, when he spoke his voice was very steady and cold. Somehow it was more terrifying than if he had shouted.

'Yes,' he said. 'I know that these children are born to malnourished mothers, that they are themselves ill fed and are accustomed to do heavy, unsuitable work from the earliest age. Little wonder that they suffer from rickets and other damage and their frames are stunted. But there is no way that child back there –' here my father gestured towards the shed behind them – 'there is no way that child could be taken for anything more than six or seven.'

Before Tall Hat could answer, there was a disturbance and two men backed out of the shed door, carrying a stretcher between them. On it lay a small heap covered with a blanket. As one of the men stumbled on the uneven ground, the stretcher tilted and the blanket moved. A hand slipped out from beneath it and dangled over the edge, a tiny hand.

My father removed his hat but Tall Hat only snorted and kept his ridiculous headgear firmly in place.

A cart had been brought up to the door and the men began to load the stretcher on to it. Suddenly a hideous scream split the air. I had never heard anything like it and I started up in fear. The pony was alarmed, too, and started forward without the boy to hold her head and steady her. The trap lurched and I had a vision of being bolted away with. I grasped the reins and hauled on them with all my strength and to my great relief the pony stopped.

A woman had appeared running towards my father, Tall

Hat, and the cart with the stretcher on it. She waved her arms as she ran and shouted incoherently like a madwoman, her mouth working and forming gargoyle-like shapes. The shawl she wore as working women did, over her head and pinned beneath her chin, became loose, slipped and fell down into the dirt. But she was heedless of her loss although her clothing was poor and scanty. Her face was lined like an old woman's but from the way she ran she had to be quite young. Reaching the cart, she scrambled into it and threw herself over the small body on the stretcher, wailing and clawing at the blanket to pull it away from the face of the corpse. I realised this was the little boy's mother and watched in horror.

'Davy, Davy!' she was crying. 'It's Mam! Do wake up and speak to me!'

Tall Hat turned aside with an expression of disgust. The men who had carried the stretcher stepped back and looked discomfited and awkward. My father went forward and tried to speak to her soothingly but she only screeched the more. At last three other shawled women who resembled the child's mother appeared, and managed to drag her from the cart. The men now picked up the shafts of the cart and began to manhandle it away and the group of women followed it, the bereaved mother supported between them.

When they were out of sight, but not out of earshot, my father replaced his hat on his head and turned to Tall Hat.

'There will be an inquest,' he said curtly. 'You have my

word on it. I'll see to it. There will be no covering this up.'

Tall Hat still seemed unimpressed by my father's words or manner. 'Do as you please,' he said. 'The boy's own mother, that one who was wailing and carrying on there, she herself told me the boy was ten years of age. I believed her. There's no coroner can prove I didn't.'

With that, he turned and walked back into the mine offices. My father came towards the trap. He climbed up into it, took up the reins and whistled to the pony. I knew he was still angry but I also knew his anger was not directed against me for my naughtiness in hiding in the trap. It was directed elsewhere to bigger and more serious targets. I sensed he was probably unaware of me sitting on the wooden seat beside him. I fancied, as we passed through the gates, that I glimpsed the boy who had given me the good luck token, but I was not sure, though I twisted on my perch to look back. If he'd been there, he'd already vanished.

We were halfway home before I ventured to speak. 'It was a little boy who died,' I said. 'A very little boy, wasn't it, Papa?'

My father glanced down at me and I think he only then remembered I was there. 'Why, Lizzie . . .' he said. Then, giving his head a shake, 'Yes, indeed, a very little child. I think hardly as old as you are.'

'What was he doing in the mine?' I asked. 'He wasn't big enough to dig coal, surely?'

My father pulled on the reins and we came to a halt.

The sun was up now and shone with gentle welcome warmth on my shoulders. We had left the area of the mine behind us and not yet reached the outskirts of the town. We found ourselves in a pleasantly green rolling landscape, the slag pyramids just small shapes on the horizon. It looked so clean and peaceful; the filth of the place we had just left and the awful scene I had just witnessed there hardly seemed real now, as if it had all been a bad dream.

'He worked as a trapper,' my father said. 'Do you know what that is, Lizzie?'

I shook my head.

'Well, now,' said my father. 'How shall I explain it to you? Let's see. The air underground is very foul. Fresh air must be brought into the workings. So they dig two big ventilation shafts.' My father gestured with his hands to indicate two long narrow tubes. 'The fresh air is drawn in through the one, and along the mine tunnels, and the bad air is drawn out through the other. To control all this there exists a system of wooden trapdoors. They are operated by children, little boys, who sit there all day for that purpose.'

'In the dark?' I asked, appalled.

'Yes, Lizzie, in the darkness.'

'All alone?'

'Quite alone.'

I thought of the little boy, younger than myself, who had been forced to sit long hours alone in the darkness underground. I tried to imagine how frightened he must have been, and how lonely. I wondered if there had been any rats down there.

'Why did he die?' I whispered.

My father sighed. 'I wrote on the certificate "exhaustion". That didn't please Harrison.'

'Harrison is the man with the tall hat and the pipe?'

'Yes. He has overall charge there. He was at pains to point out to me that the work the child did was not arduous and that "exhaustion" was, in his view, an inappropriate choice for cause of death. I pointed out to him that exhaustion comes from many sources, hunger and fear among them. Harder to prove but just as real is the loss of all hope. I believe the child died because there was no longer any reason to live. But that is my private opinion and not a medical one. I shall explain it to the coroner as lack of food and general debility.'

Suddenly he struck his clenched fist on the rail to which the reins were hitched. 'And it should not have been! For two years now it has been unlawful to employ a boy under the age of ten – or a woman or girl of any age – to work underground! Harrison knows that full well.'

'So,' I asked, 'will Mr Harrison be punished?'

'What?' My father sounded amused but in a curiously mirthless way. 'No, my dear, no one will be punished. Harrison will say he was unaware the child was so young. The parents will be frightened or bribed into confirming that they lied about their son's age. I doubt anyone will even be fined. Or if the mine owners are fined, it will be a paltry sum. But it won't happen again. I shall see to that. I shall make such a fuss that Harrison, for all his obstinacy and lack of any moral sense, will not dare to allow another child so young down the pit!'

He untangled the reins and shook them and we moved on again. The good luck token was in my pocket. I thought I would show it to my father when a suitable moment came. That would not be for a while yet. The pony, sensing it was on its way back to its comfortable stable, trotted swiftly with ears pricked and we were soon home again.

As my father led me indoors, we were again greeted with the sounds of a woman in tears. Molly Darby sat on the stairs with her pinafore pressed to her face, and was howling her eyes out because I was not to be found and she was blamed. She was being berated energetically by Mary Newling who stood over her accusing her of being an idle sleepyhead who would be turned out of the house by the doctor when he got back, see if she wasn't, and without a reference. Why, Miss Elizabeth might be anywhere and never seen again by any of them! The poor innocent could have been taken away by gipsies or fallen into a drain or run down by the carrier's cart. The driver of that was nearly always drunk, as everyone knew.

'Why, here she is,' said my father, pushing me forward to prove none of these calamities had befallen me.

Molly screeched and leapt up, folding me to her capacious bosom.

'Oh, sir! Oh, Miss Elizabeth! Wherever have you been? I

swear, sir, I looked in on her at seven sharp and she was gone! I never heard a sound!'

'Take her upstairs and clean her up,' my father said wearily. 'Mary, be so kind as to make me some tea.'

I looked down and saw that my hands and clothes were covered in a thin layer of the coal dust which hung always in the air above the mine workings. Presumably my face was equally begrimed.

As I was hauled up the stairs by Molly, my father called out again.

'Wait!'

We stopped. Molly said fearfully, 'Yes, sir?'

'Lizzie,' said my father to me.

'Yes, Papa?' I sounded as nervous as Molly, afraid I was now to receive some punishment for my escapade.

'Always remember what you saw today,' my father said. 'Remember, if you will, that it represents the true price of coal.'

As soon as I was able, I put my coal fern with my other childish 'treasures' in a battered japanned box. I knew I would never forget what I had witnessed that morning. I didn't fully understand my father's last remark. But after that day I never again heard Mary Newling complain about the price of sitting-room or any other coal.

My father was a good man and an affectionate parent. But he had a great deal on his mind. As long as I appeared happy and in good health, he didn't worry about me.

Nevertheless, my hiding in the trap that morning must have given him food for thought. He realised I was in a fair way to grow up a complete little savage. Shortly after the episode at the mine, Molly Darby left our house to marry a farmer and was replaced by a governess, Madame Leblanc. It was typical of my father that he engaged this person chiefly because she was in desperate need of a situation and could start at once. Once again his good nature overcame his common sense.

I soon decided that there had never been a Monsieur Leblanc and the 'Madame' was a courtesy title. But she was really French and claimed to have come to England many years before as governess to a very good family. Unfortunately, this family had now removed itself lock, stock and barrel to India and therefore couldn't provide her with any references.

I overheard Mary Newling tell a visitor in the kitchen, 'Governess, my eye! That one earned her keep in the bedroom, not the schoolroom! Well, maybe she's lost those charms, but she's still got a silver tongue. The doctor is too good-hearted and listens to any tale of woe!'

I did mark her words though I didn't understand them. Poor Madame Leblanc had certainly fallen on hard times and was pathetically grateful to my father for rescuing her. She was about forty-five or -six, a real sparrow of a little woman with very dark reddish hair (I overheard Mary Newling declare this was the result of henna). She had deep-set dark eyes, tiny hands and feet, and moved with quick deft movements. Unfortunately her own education had been rather sketchy. She could teach me to read and write as well in French as in English and to speak the language fluently, but that was about it, apart from some simple arithmetic. Her idea of geography was vague and the only history she knew was French. It consisted entirely of wild romantic tales of knights and kings that I loved to hear. She was a royalist true to the *ancien régime*, who spoke with scorn of the upstart and former emperor Bonaparte and even more furiously of the rascally *Orléanistes*. When the uprising of 1848 drove Louis-Philippe from the throne he had usurped eighteen years before, her satisfaction was intense. 'Better a republic than that traitor, Orléans, *chère* Elizabeth!'

Sadly, when news reached us that in a further upset in French politics Louis-Napoleon, nephew of the old monster Boney, had declared himself emperor of the French, it was more than Madame Leblanc could bear. She consoled herself liberally with a bottle of brandy and passed out insensible on the drawing-room sofa. She was found there in the early morning, with the empty bottle alongside her, when Mary Newling went in to clear the hearth and set the fire. This lapse couldn't be ignored and she left us. I was sorry to see her go as I had become very fond of her. I lacked friends of my own age and Madame had been more than a governess: a companion who always had time to listen.

I was now fourteen and my father decided he would

take over my education himself. He never actually got round to doing this, because of his other commitments. I educated myself by reading voraciously any book I could lay my hands on.

Poor Madame; I thought about her now. Whatever had become of her after leaving our house? How similar my circumstances had become to hers, seeking a roof and employment! It was unlikely she had gone from us to another respectable situation. Perhaps she had finished up going from door to door selling little trinkets and items of stationery?

However, life went on. Mary Newling stayed with us until extreme age forced her to retire and live with a widowed sister. I became my father's housekeeper with the help of a maid. My father's death, when it came, was sudden but peaceful. He had said that he was tired and would go to bed early. He never awoke. His funeral was attended by almost the entire town. I was left to sort out his affairs.

They were in a terrible state. It was quickly obvious I could look forward to nothing but almost complete destitution. Many of my father's poorer patients had never paid him and he had never pressed them. He had also helped out many of them by giving them sums of money to tide them over while they were unable to work. This meant there was none left to settle his debts. Among the record of monies he had paid out over the years was a curious reference to regularly weekly sums paid out to two women named only as Mrs Ross and Mrs Lee but there was no evidence of his having treated them for any illness. Why he had paid them over so long a period was a mystery. If Mary Newling had still been alive I could have asked her about it, but she had died a couple of years earlier. That puzzle, at least, had been solved today by Inspector Ross.

At the time I'd had no leisure to worry about it, as it was obvious I would have to sell the house, pay the debts, and find myself lodgings. So I sold up and, having settled outstanding matters, gave a small sum to the maid together with a glowing reference. I told her I was sorry I couldn't do more for her.

She said, 'That's quite all right, miss!'

But I could see she thought the money very little and that I was very mean. Did she but know the truth of it, I needed every penny until I could find some means of supporting myself. In the meantime, I took a room in the house of a widowed neighbour, Mrs Neale, at a small weekly outlay, my food included. She had known me nearly all my life. I knew she had offered help partly out of her genuine concern for me and partly because it embarrassed her to think that Dr Martin's daughter had nowhere to go.

I could well imagine the gossip my circumstances occasioned in the town, the reproaches heaped on my poor father's head. I was sure he would not have left me in such dire straits out of thoughtlessness. He had simply been relatively young, only fifty-seven years old, and believed himself in good health. He had not expected Death to knock so early at the door with a summons that could not be refused. He had supposed there would be time to make some provision for me – or perhaps thought I might marry – but neither of these things had happened.

Now I did not need to imagine the looks of pity and concern directed towards me by all as I passed by. No one troubled to hide them. Nor did I think kindly Mrs Neale would want me under her roof indefinitely. She was already dropping hints. I must leave here, but where should I go? Owing to Madame Leblanc's erratic tutorial skills, I lacked all knowledge of those accomplishments reckoned necessary for young ladies. The post of governess, always a refuge for young women in my situation, was closed to me. The thought did cross my mind I might give lessons in the French language, if only there were any in our town who wanted to learn it. But enquiry soon showed me there were none.

In desperation I swallowed my pride and wrote to those few acquaintances of my father who might be in a position to help me find some employment. To my surprise and joy I received a positive response from the widow of my godfather, Josiah Parry. Mrs Parry wrote that she was sorry to hear of my father's passing and supposed that I was now in a pretty fix, since my father had never had any head for finance. If I wished to come to London and live with her I could do so. She was in need of a companion. She was in a position to offer me a home, bed and board, and a suitable salary could be discussed when we met. She would like me to start at once.

There was no question but that I'd accept, even though I had never met the lady and only latterly dimly remembered once meeting the sad gentleman who had given me a shilling.

It was a leap into the unknown, but I had no choice.

So it had come about that only a day or two after my twenty-ninth birthday, I set out for London, purchasing a railway ticket from my meagre resources. Here in London I had quite unexpectedly met a figure from my home and from the past.

I took the shale fern from the lacquer box and wondered if in some magical way it was responsible for this unexpected reunion and if anything, good or ill, would come of it.

Chapter Seven

Ben Ross

I KNEW her as soon as I saw her. She did not know me, of course, until I told her who I was. But then she remembered the boy at the pithead. In this teeming city I had seen dreadful things and my heart had often been heavy at the thought of the wretchedness suffered by so many. Now, when my mind was occupied with the violence done to one in particular and the difficulty of the task ahead of me, to find Lizzie Martin and know she remembered a moment twenty years before had lifted my spirits in a way nothing else could have done.

But I did not like her being in that house. From there Madeleine Hexham had walked out to her death. She had been companion to the owner, Mrs Parry. Now Lizzie had stepped into Miss Hexham's shoes. I remembered the little kid boots with the well-moulded uppers and little-worn soles. I hoped I would never hold a pair of Lizzie Martin's boots in my hand and speculate as I had done once before on the fate of their owner.

That we believed we might be lucky enough to identify the dead woman almost at once had been a great encouragement to us; although, as Morris had early observed, someone must have missed her. Enquiries at police stations in the central London area had revealed a young female of that general description had been reported missing from home at Marylebone Police Station by Mr Francis Carterton (whom I now knew his intimates to call Frank!). It was for Mr Carterton I was waiting in my office early that Wednesday evening. I hoped he would settle the matter of identification once and for all.

The day shift had departed and the night shift was arriving. The building was quiet. I sat at my desk and, to focus my concentration, sharpened pencils. I soon had a battalion of them set out on my desktop in a parade order but I was no further forward. Although Carterton might be able to confirm the identity of the deceased, the mystery of her unexplained disappearance had deepened. She had been reported missing some two months before. She had been dead at the most two weeks. Marylebone division had not exactly set the ground afire beneath their feet in looking for her. They had made some enquiries in the neighbourhood but no one seemed to remember her in any detail, let alone have any precise information. The superintendent of that division had noted that she would turn up sooner or later, alive or dead.

I was irritated by what appeared a casual attitude on the part of the officers concerned but I wasn't sure I could have done any better. People choose to disappear in great cities all the time. Not all of them are men. It was, in a sense, more difficult for a young female to do so, certainly one of Miss Hexham's background. But nevertheless they did it from time to time. The only significant detail in the police report was that she had taken no personal possessions or clothing with her. The Marylebone man's last note read, with a sense of weary resignation, 'Inform river police.'

Suicide. That's what he had suspected. But in the absence of a body, he could not be sure.

We now had a body: but not that of a suicide. She had not dashed out her own brains nor contrived to hide her remains under a rotted carpet in a house scheduled for demolition in Agar Town. But could we be haring off along a false trail? Was the dead woman Madeleine or someone whose appearance resembled hers? The clothes in which our corpse had been found were very similar to those Madeleine Hexham had been described as wearing at the time of her disappearance. Since my call in Dorset Square I had acquired some further information but instead of serving to clear the fog of incomprehension it had made it denser. There was the matter of the letter of which Mrs Parry had spoken. Had Madeleine Hexham written it herself or written it perhaps under duress? If only the letter had been kept! It might have told us so much. It began horribly to look as if I was right and the victim had been held somewhere against her will during the missing weeks. How much light Carterton would be able to shed on all of this was uncertain, if indeed he was able to shed any.

I had sent a note to the Foreign Office asking him to call at Scotland Yard. I thought he would prefer that to my calling at his place of work and arousing much curiosity. Even though I would not have been in uniform, I knew I'd be spotted as a policeman immediately, just as I had been when visiting the Agar Town site with Morris. Rich and poor, respectable and criminal, Foreign Office clerks, upper servants and navvies, all of them knew the Law when it hove into view – and none of them liked having it around.

I was curious to see Frank Carterton. When he eventually strode into my office he was very much what I had expected: a smart young gentleman about town. Women would find him handsome and probably appealing. There was a cultivated boyishness about him which would endear him to the gentle sex and aroused instant hostility in me. His clothing was from the hand of expert tailors and would have cost a pretty penny. I was not aware the Foreign Office paid its junior staff so generously but possibly he had some private income. His aunt, with whom he resided, obviously had no money worries. In the long term, he would have expectations of her estate, I didn't doubt. Murder had been committed more than once to preserve such hopes.

'See here,' he began, tossing down his cane and hat and seating himself uninvited. 'This is a foul business, Inspector. There is not the slightest doubt, I suppose, that the dead woman is Maddie Hexham?'

He and I were worried by the same doubt but came at it, if you like, from opposite directions. I feared the body might not be that of the missing companion. He feared that it was.

It is natural to hope and natural also to wish to avoid unpleasantness. I have brought similar bad news to people before and it's odd how their reaction is so often torn between despair and apprehension. They know now they will never see the missing loved one again, at least not this side of Jordan. But they fear the notoriety that will inevitably follow the grisly discovery.

'It is indeed a foul business,' I agreed. 'We are cautiously certain she is Miss Hexham.'

'Cautiously certain? You fellows are like lawyers. You never want to put your name to any statement without having a way to wriggle out of it.'

I was interested in Carterton's experience of lawyers. I didn't disagree with his view but I wondered where he had gained it.

'I don't mind telling you,' Carterton went on, 'that my superiors at the Foreign Office are taking a dim view of it.' He pushed back his dark hair and scowled down at my desk. 'I had to tell them. It will be in every newspaper and penny sheet.'

I wondered to what degree he was distressed to know Miss Hexham murdered and how much he was worried that the speculation and the undoubted interest of the newspapers would affect his own prospects. The impression I got at the moment was that the latter concerned him more. It made it easier to ask him what was in my mind. I no longer had to worry about his feelings. I even took a perverse satisfaction in anticipating the reaction to the request I was about to make.

'The clothing certainly tallies with hers and there is a pocket handkerchief with her initials on it. The general description fits her. We should appreciate it, however, if you could bring yourself to take a look at her, just to confirm the identification.'

He was, as I expected, horrified. He stared at me, open-mouthed and altogether aghast. 'Look at her?' he gasped. 'View the – the remains?'

Yes, my fine popinjay, I thought to myself. Aloud I expressed my regret at having to impose upon him in such an unpleasant way.

'I cannot force you to do it, sir. But in matters like this, well, we have to be certain and anyone may have come by her gown and be of similar build. I can hardly ask her employer, Mrs Parry, to do it. The young woman appears to have had no family and, if she did, they are a long way from here. I understand her to have hailed from an area near to Durham, very far north, and to first find someone and then bring them here . . .'

'Yes, yes!' he snapped. 'I understand your difficulty. You cannot ask such a thing of my aunt, naturally. I am the – the only man in the household. The job is mine. Is – is . . .' he faltered. 'Is she much disfigured?'

'Somewhat, sir, I'm afraid. She has been dead perhaps two weeks, perhaps a little less.'

'Two weeks? But she's been missing much longer than that! Look here, are you sure this poor woman can be Hexham? It doesn't make sense.'

His face had reddened in anger. I sympathised. If I was puzzled, so was he. His natural reaction was that we had made a mistake and he'd been hauled here needlessly. He'd been equally needlessly embarrassed at the Foreign Office. If all this turned out to be a mare's nest, it still wouldn't be forgotten in those hallowed halls of propriety. 'Ah, young Carterton,' the comment would go in years to come, 'wasn't there some fuss about a dead woman the police couldn't identify?'

Perhaps, I thought ruefully, it wasn't such an odd thing that no one liked having the police appear in their lives. We muddied waters which never quite cleared again.

'The doctor who examined the body gives two weeks as the maximum period since death,' I said, taking refuge in a known fact. He couldn't argue with that. 'We don't yet have an explanation for that but our object is to come up with one eventually. First, though, we have to be absolutely sure we have the right woman.'

Carterton passed a hand nervously over his mouth. 'I

see. Of course, if she had been dead eight weeks or more then to look at her would be useless, to say nothing of repulsive. Even at two weeks . . . Is there anything to be gained by my doing this? If she is unrecognisable . . .'

I ignored the appeal which had entered his voice and expression. 'Oh, I hope she is not that. I will say no more, sir. I must not influence you.'

'Has she – has the surgeon . . . ?'

'Yes, sir, but you won't see anything of his work, just her face, sir. The rest will be covered up.'

Carterton looked away, swallowed hard and rubbed his hand over his mouth again. 'Very well,' he muttered. 'When and where?'

'At a mortuary, sir. We can go there immediately. I anticipated that a gentleman like yourself would wish to help and I asked them to expect us.'

'Of course I want to help!' he almost snarled at me. 'But, oh dash it; let us be about it, then.'

He stood up and grasped his hat and cane, setting the hat on his head in a determined way, striking the crown of it with the flat of his hand.

'That's a fine cane, sir,' I observed.

It was, indeed, with a silver tip emblazoned with some crest or other.

He looked at me blankly and then at the cane. 'Oh, that, it belonged to my late father, the only thing he left me. This . . .' He indicated the crest. 'These are the arms of his regiment.'

He had given me valuable information about himself without realising it. He had not a penny of his own, only his meagre salary. He depended on his aunt's good will, then. Only she could have paid for the clothes, the quality boots and the linen. In such a situation he was vulnerable not only to the opinion of his Foreign Office superiors but to that of the kind relative who paid his bills.

He grew visibly more morose and nervous as we neared our destination. When we got inside, his mood turned to a mixture of belligerence which I guessed hid his fear, and an unconvincing swagger serving the same purpose.

'Come on, then, where is she?' He glanced around him with his mouth twisted in distaste. 'This place has a deuced unpleasant smell to it.'

'That will be the gas, sir,' I murmured.

Understandably this confused and alarmed him more before I pointed to the gas flame which hissed in the background and emitted an insidious odour.

'Oh, yes,' he said. 'Of course, quite . . .'

The daylight had been fading fast and on our journey over here we had passed the lamplighter who had been making his tour of the city's street lamps. Gaslight outdoors is a boon. Gaslight indoors, in my book, is a mixed blessing. The Parry household, I had noticed, was provided with gas jets. It was a wealthy home in the nation's capital. My own landlady could not afford to have the gas connected and relied on lamps and candles, which suited me. I consider gas jets in the home to be unhealthy and dangerous. But then, a pitman is only too aware of the danger posed by a naked flame.

Carmichael was not here but his eerie assistant awaited us. He still wore his butcher's apron and hovered by the sheeted body, casting malicious looks at Carterton. He avoided my eye. He knew I didn't care for him. I took a look at my companion. He had turned as white as the porcelain slab and dabbed sweat from his brow and upper lip.

I took pity on him. 'Now, sir, let us know when you are ready. Take a good look and if you are not sure, speak up and say so. We had rather you expressed doubt than you gave an opinion you didn't really hold.'

He nodded and gestured at the assistant to turn back the sheet. When the man did so with deft movements of his long thin fingers, the odour of death was released, that singular sweet rottenness which even the commercial gas could not disguise. Her face only was revealed, as I had promised Carterton. The sheet covered her body to the neck and the crown of her head was swathed in a white cloth which obscured the worst of the injury to the skull. Some flaxen hair escaped from beneath it. In this framework the bruised and mottled features with sunken cheeks, half-closed eyes and lips, all with the purplish grey tinge of encroaching decomposition, did not appear quite real. It was a grotesque mask. There was no life here of any nature; the spirit had fled. It was but a fast-deteriorating husk but none the less pathetic. I asked myself whether it had been realistic thinking to bring Carterton here and expect a positive identification. I cast an apprehensive look at him.

Carterton swayed and I was ready to catch him but he rallied and, to give the man his due, stood up to the ghastly duty well. He glanced at the ravaged features, looked briefly away, then turned back and stared long and carefully at them.

'That is Madeleine Hexham,' he said at last. 'At first I wasn't sure. She is not – she is not as she was. But now I am certain that is – I am certain of it.' He fumbled in his coat pocket for his handkerchief.

I nodded to the assistant to replace the sheet. Carterton turned aside, mopping at his mouth and suddenly retched. The assistant was ready for it and pushed under his chin a metal bowl which had been standing nearby for just such a purpose. Carterton vomited comprehensively into it.

The assistant spoke and it gave me a start for he was usually silent. Possibly, as representing Dr Carmichael, he felt obliged to comment.

'Very sad, gentlemen,' he said. His voice was as soft as his hands and as oily as his lank hair. 'Youth and beauty struck down. Very sad, sirs.'

He was enjoying it all. He enjoyed Carterton's discomfiture, my impotent resentment of him and the authority which these macabre surroundings and Carmichael's absence had temporarily invested in him.

'Will you be bringing others to view the deceased?' the man went on. He gestured towards the dead woman in a way which I found almost proprietorial, as if he were a showman and Madeleine his most prized exhibit.

'No!' I said curtly. 'I don't doubt the coroner will give his permission for her removal and burial.'

'Very well, sir,' he said softly.

We left him standing by her, watching us depart.

Carterton was silent until we got back to the Yard where he signed a statement to the effect that he had identified Madeleine Hexham. Putting pen to paper seemed to rally his spirits. Perhaps it was a familiar action.

He put down the pen and sniffed at the sleeve of his jacket. 'The smell of that place is sticking to me.' His tone was sullen.

'Yes, sir. We often find it so. But it will wear off by the time you get home. If not, have the servant hang your outer clothing in the fresh air tomorrow.'

He rose to his feet. 'I am sorry I made a fool of myself back there,' he said awkwardly. 'Puking like that.'

'Don't worry about it, sir, it's quite natural. Thank you for your help. It's much appreciated,' I told him.

'There is nothing else?' His voice rose hopefully.

'Only a couple of quick questions. Have you any idea why Miss Hexham left the house that day without warning and without luggage?'

'Why,' he said, surprised, 'at the time, no more than any of us. But then she wrote a letter to my aunt, as you know, telling us why.'

'You saw this letter?'

'I saw it, but if you are going to ask me if it was really her handwriting, then all I can say is, it looked like it. I was not well enough acquainted with her hand to say more.'

'And you were surprised that she had eloped?'

'Dash it, of course I was!' he snapped.

'She had not seemed distracted, as if planning something, or more than usually thoughtful?'

'No,' he said. 'Nor did she appear to be love-struck, if that's what you're driving at. As far as I could see, she was a woman of little or no emotion except at second-hand.'

There he had me foxed. 'At second-hand, sir?'

'She read novels. She got them from circulating libraries. Sentimental rubbish.'

So, I thought grimly, a girl without any personal experience of life and its passions, who had drawn all her ideas from the printed page of popular novelettes. Then real life had stepped in and, hard on its heels, an all-too-savage death.

Chapter Eight

Elizabeth Martin

A KNOCK at my bedroom door roused me from the memories of time past. I opened it to find Nugent who told me Mrs Parry needed my presence. I found her propped up, fully dressed, on her bed supported by a mound of pillows. The room reeked of cologne and sal volatile and I saw that the Madeira bottle had been called into use again as it stood, almost empty, with a stained glass on a side table.

Whatever the combination of treatments, Aunt Parry had rallied. She sounded brisk and appeared quite recovered. From her pillows she signalled at me with a small white podgy paw.

'Elizabeth, do write a note on my behalf to dear Dr Tibbett. Tell that I would be obliged if he would call – no, say if he could dine this evening. Don't tell him what happened to Madeleine, it's hardly the way to let him know of it. Just say, there is a matter I need to discuss with him urgently. Send one of the servants with it. Simms knows the address of Dr Tibbett's rooms.'

She paused. 'I shall ask him if he thinks we ought to go into mourning. In the circumstances I hardly think so. It would draw unnecessary attention and occasion questions. There will be gossip enough, I suppose, anyway. You are soberly dressed in any case, Elizabeth. What do you think?'

'Perhaps,' I suggested, 'some sign of the seriousness of the events . . . ?'

'But not mourning, yes, that's very sensible of you, my dear. Black is out of the question. Nugent! Lay out the dove-grey silk. I think that should do it.'

I went down to the library and penned a careful summons to Dr Tibbett as bid, sealed it and handed it to Simms. A little later I saw Wilkins in her bonnet and shawl, scurrying past the window on her way to deliver it.

I was sure Wilkins did not mind the errand. It not only gave her the chance to be out of the house and from under Mrs Simms's eagle eye, but it lent her a measure of importance. Excitement quivered in every line of her hurrying form. Simms would have told them all of Miss Hexham's fate. Wilkins would pass the news on to every acquaintance she met and, on the way back, take a moment to stop by each and every basement in the street to inform the staff of the house. Within the hour, every maidservant in Marylebone would know that there had been a horrible crime and, without a doubt, the mistress of the house in question would know of it soon after. The terrible event would be common knowledge: murder had struck at one of the most respectable and well-to-do households of the area. From drawing room to kitchen talk would be of nothing else.

But Dr Tibbett did not come to dine. Wilkins returned to tell us that a manservant had taken the note and informed her that his master had gone out. He did not know where and he did not know when he would be back. He was not expected to dine in his rooms.

Frank did not come back, either. Instead a note came to say he had been obliged to call at Scotland Yard and would thereafter dine in town. By the time this note arrived even the urchin who brought it had heard the news and demanded hopefully, when given the sixpence he had been promised by Frank would be his reward, 'Is this the 'ouse of the murder?'

So Aunt Parry and I dined alone together. My employer was fretful. She complained repeatedly of the absence of both Tibbett and Frank. I was perfectly happy to be without either of them that evening. I was particularly pleased to be spared Dr Tibbett's views, although no doubt we should hear them in due course. They would be both predictable and ill-informed. We did not know the circumstances of Madeleine's death. Whatever Tibbett had to say it would amount to declaring that it was all her own fault. I didn't believe Aunt Parry needed either of them there for advice. She needed them there for an audience but she had to make do with me.

'What do you think, Elizabeth?' she began almost every speculation, but then did not wait to hear what I thought. Well, that was what a paid companion was for. The requirement that I be a 'good conversationalist' was quickly proving itself little more than a formality.

Frank had not returned by the time we retired. I slept badly. This time, unlike the previous night when Frank had returned late, I did hear him come back. He stumbled up the stairs and was, I guessed, drunk. Simms had waited up for him and could be heard guiding him along the corridor.

I fell asleep eventually and was awoken by a clang of metal and sat up with a start to see Bessie edging into the room with the can of hot water. Her mob cap had slipped down over her face again and rested not far short of her snub nose.

'Thank you!' I called out.

She put down the can, pushed up the mob cap with both hands and turned to face me. Her little face was white and frightened.

'Is it true, miss? Is it true what Mr Simms has said about Miss Hexham being murdered?'

I got out of bed, threw a shawl over my nightgown and went to put an arm round her thin shoulders.

'Yes, I'm afraid it is true, Bessie. But you must not be frightened.'

'Did he cut her up, the murderer?' She stared at me fixedly.

'Cut her up?' I asked, startled.

'Yus, you know, slit her throat. Or strangle her or bash her head in or what?'

'I don't know,' I said faintly, taking my arm from her shoulders.

'Was it when she left here? Did she go and meet him?' Bessie's agitation was increasing.

'We shall find out eventually. I think a police officer may come to the house today and ask the staff if they saw anything that day, or know anything of the matter at all.'

'I don't know anything!' said Bessie immediately with unlooked-for ferocity. 'I didn't do anything!'

She grabbed the water can and scuttled out, leaving me thoughtful.

Unexpectedly Frank was up early, or perhaps had not been to bed at all. He looked a little rumpled and had cut himself shaving, but he was in his place at the breakfast table when I came down. He was not tucking in heartily as he had been the day before, but sat toying with a cup of cooling coffee and staring morosely at the toast-rack.

He nodded a greeting at me as I took my place. Simms came in and silently placed a glass on a saucer at Frank's elbow. It contained some strange yellowish-brown beverage.

Simms's imperturbable manner gave no hints of turmoil within. He asked if I required a hot dish and when informed I did not, simply retired.

'Have you noticed?' asked Frank a little hoarsely when the butler had gone. 'Old Simms seems to have found a way of floating above the carpet. His feet make no sound at all.' He picked up the yellow-brown drink and gave it a wary look before downing it in one long swallow. 'Oh, good Lord . . .' he muttered.

'What is that?' I asked.

'Beaten raw egg and sherry. It is Simms's cure for a – a headache.'

'You were drinking,' I said. 'I heard you return.'

'Wouldn't a man need a drink after what I had to do?' he returned sullenly.

I was not hungry, either. I had scraped butter across a piece of toast but it looked as desirable as a piece of cardboard.

'What had you to do, Frank?' I asked in a quiet voice, though I thought I could guess. If I was right, poor Frank had had a harrowing time of it.

'That confounded fellow, Ross the inspector, dragged me down to the— he insisted I go with him to see her. He wanted her identity confirmed.'

'I'm sorry,' I said. 'That must have been very unpleasant.'

'Oh well,' said Frank, rallying a little. 'It's over and done and we know what happened to her. Or, rather, we don't. We only know some villain beat her to death with an implement of some kind.'

'Is that how she died?' I asked awkwardly.

'So I gather. They had covered the wound. I was spared gazing on that.'

'She was found in Agar Town,' I said. 'Was it in one of Aunt Parry's properties?'

'No idea,' he returned moodily.

'You did not tell me, when you told me she had owned houses there, that they were slum dwellings.'

Frank brought his bloodshot gaze to bear on me for the first time. 'Well, they weren't palaces, I dare say. But poor people have to live somewhere and someone has to own the houses. They paid next to no rent so they couldn't expect much. I don't doubt they managed. Such people know no better.'

I opened my mouth to argue it out vigorously with him, but closed it again. Frank was in no fit state for debate and I decided to overlook his careless way of talking of the wretched inhabitants of Agar Town. He had gone through a dreadful experience and to expect him to expend sympathy on the hypothetical tenants of Aunt Parry's former properties was useless.

'Was Tibbett here last night?' Frank asked. 'I suppose he was. He will be in his element now.'

'He wasn't, as it happened,' I told him. 'A note was sent to him but he was out.'

Frank uttered a growl. 'Then he'll be here first thing this afternoon, you'll see. It's Thursday, too, and his day to dine, confound it. Well, I am off to work and hope that my superiors don't take the poor view of all of this they probably will. Her Majesty's Government does not like embarrassments of this sort among its minions!'

Simms glided in again and stopped by Frank's chair. 'I should inform you, sir, that two police officers have arrived, a sergeant and a constable. They are in the kitchen and wish to take statements from the staff. It will cause some disruption, I fear, to the smooth running of the house this morning.'

'Well, I shan't be here to experience it,' said Frank brusquely. 'And Mrs Parry probably won't come down before noon, as usual. They don't want to see her, do they?'

'No, sir, I gather their business is with the staff only.'

'How is Mrs Simms taking it?' I asked him. 'And Wilkins and – the other girl?' I had almost called her Perkins but that had been one of Frank's poor-taste jokes and I must find out the other maid's name. I asked Simms now what it was.

'Ellis, miss. Mrs Simms is bearing up well, thank you. So is Hester Nugent. Wilkins and Ellis . . .' Here emotion struggled to break through his glacial reserve. 'I regret, miss, that the two young persons in question appear to be enjoying themselves thoroughly.'

'There you are, then,' said Frank to me. 'It's an ill wind, isn't that what they say? An ill wind that blows no good to anyone?' He gave a sudden bitter laugh, before pushing back his chair and getting to his feet. 'I must be off. I have to persuade all those old fellows at the Foreign Office that I am not a louche type, the female members of whose household are apt to be foully done to death in disreputable surroundings. If panic and disorder break out in the kitchen you will have to deal with it, Lizzie. I'll see you this evening.'

I did not remember telling him he could call me Lizzie in that familiar way. I hadn't minded Inspector Ross using that version of my name. He was remembering me as a child. But with Frank it followed the pattern of his casual manner with others. Bessie was simply 'the mushroom'. All housemaids were called Wilkins or Perkins and all companions, although not exactly servants and in my case almost a relation, were called by some diminutive of their names. Maddie Hexham. Lizzie Martin. I glared but could say nothing in front of Simms.

Simms had something to say for himself. 'If there is an upset below stairs, sir, *I* shall take care of it.'

As Frank had foreseen, Dr Tibbett arrived that afternoon. He had by now heard the news. I think there were few left in London who hadn't. There had certainly been an increase in the number of people, total strangers, who wandered casually past the house, casting surreptitious looks at it and whispering together. Eventually Aunt Parry ordered the curtains drawn.

'We are, after all,' she said, as we settled down in the resultant gloom, '*almost* a house in mourning. With all her faults, Madeleine's memory should be paid the basic respects.'

Once Dr Tibbett arrived it quickly became obvious this respect for the memory of the deceased did not extend to speaking well of her.

'My dear friend,' he exclaimed on entering, striding across the carpet to take her hand. 'You must be quite devastated. But bear up, dear lady, bear up! Good afternoon to you, Miss Martin.' The last remark was an afterthought.

'Good afternoon, Dr Tibbett,' I replied. 'We are bearing up well, you will be pleased to know. Mrs Parry in particular is a splendid example to us all.'

He gave me a quick look and Aunt Parry's expression became nonplussed as she digested my words. On the one hand, she appreciated the vote of confidence. On the other, it meant that she could not now give way to unseemly laments, not if she was bearing up so well.

'I expected no less,' said Tibbett gravely. 'You have the heart of a lion, my dear friend. I feared something like this, you know. That girl always struck me as a dissembler. With my many years' experience as a schoolmaster, I am attuned, you might say, to spotting weakness of character, a *faiblesse* for shirking responsibility and a tendency to tell lies. That young person could never look me in the eye. Aha! I thought when I first saw her here. This is one to watch!'

With that he stared very hard at me.

'Well,' said Aunt Parry tentatively, 'Madeleine always seemed a nice enough young woman, that's why I was so shocked when we received the letter. As regards that letter, the police inspector seemed put out that I had not kept it.'

'Why should you keep it?' Tibbett retorted. 'It was a sordid document in which a declaration that she had fallen into sin was made with not the slightest sense of having done wrong. When a young person throws off the protection of her elders and betters and takes the potholed road to ruin, there are no depths into which it might not cause her to plunge, and no fate so dreadful that it can't be expected.'

Wilkins and Ellis the maids were not the only ones enjoying themselves thoroughly in the mayhem and misery, I thought.

'It was such a shock when a police inspector called yesterday, quite unexpectedly. Last night poor Frank had to go to Scotland Yard and from there . . . I cannot mention it. It was too dreadful.' Aunt Parry put her cologne-scented handkerchief to her nose.

'He was obliged to go to a mortuary and identify Miss Hexham,' I supplied.

Dr Tibbett tut-tutted and said it was dreadful indeed and Frank must bear up, too. A slight look of embarrassment then crossed his face. 'I am sorry I was not at home when your note came yesterday. I – ah – had been called to the bedside of a former scholastic colleague who is very ill, very ill indeed. At the request of his wife I sat with him for a while. I think it comforted him.'

Aunt Parry said she was sure it had and Dr Tibbett should not be dismayed that he had not been free to attend to her. She quite understood. But she looked a little annoyed. I wondered if she, as I did, suspected the scholastic colleague played a role similar to that of the constantly ailing grandmothers with whom junior clerks were famously well supplied.

'The – ah – police,' said Dr Tibbett with some unusual delicacy of manner, 'they have not – ah – returned?'

'The house has been full of them!' declared Aunt Parry vigorously, waving the handkerchief and filling the air with the scent of cologne. 'But they have not troubled me – or Elizabeth, although Elizabeth could tell them nothing, anyway. I can tell them nothing. I should think the servants can tell them nothing. Madeleine did not tell anyone here what she meant to do.'

'A sergeant and a constable came this morning to interview the servants,' I explained.

'Ah, the servants,' said Tibbett thoughtfully. 'They are sometimes tempted, in such circumstances, to let their imaginations run riot. A few grains of salt will be needed, I fear, with any statement any of them will have made.'

'I expect the police are well used to that sort of thing,' I said briskly. 'And will make sense of it all.'

By now the looks of disapproval Tibbett had been casting me were turning to those of dislike.

'No doubt,' he said. 'You seem well acquainted with situations of this kind, Miss Martin.'

'Well, not really,' I told him. 'But my father, besides his practice, acted as police surgeon in our town.'

'Oh, really?' was the dour reply.

At this juncture, Mrs Belling was announced.

She hurried into the room and embraced Aunt Parry before she had quite had time to rise from her chair in greeting.

'My dear! But this is all quite, quite dreadful! How do you do, Dr Tibbett? I am glad to see you here. Julia, whatever can I say to you? I feel such a responsibility for what has happened!'

Aunt Parry and Dr Tibbett began at once and together to assure her she bore no responsibility at all. As she had so far ignored me I did not feel obliged to say anything.

'I have written to my friend in Durham,' Mrs Belling went on when sufficient reassurances had been received. 'I have pointed out to her very frankly that she should have made far more rigorous enquiries about the girl before packing her off to London and us, that is to say, to you. I am most disappointed.'

I could not help then but observe as calmly as I could, 'It is terrible to think how frightened and helpless Miss Hexham must have been at the end when she found herself at the mercy of her murderer.'

There was a silence. Three pairs of eyes turned to me.

'I have thought about it,' said Aunt Parry with a gesture of the handkerchief in the general direction of her eyes.

'Well, yes,' said Mrs Belling, clearly annoyed. 'Quite so. But she put herself in that awful situation, did she not?'

'One hopes,' said Tibbett, 'that she found time before she died to ask her Maker for forgiveness.'

'Do ring for tea, Elizabeth!' said Aunt Parry sharply.

I gave the bell pull a savage jerk as if I had Dr Tibbett's neck at the other end of it.

When both visitors had left, my employer and I sat for some minutes in awkward silence.

'Elizabeth, my dear,' said Aunt Parry at last. 'You have a kind heart but I fear an impetuous tongue.'

'I did not mean to upset Dr Tibbett,' I said. 'I am sorry if I embarrassed you.'

'That is not quite what I meant,' she replied unexpectedly. 'In London, my dear, things are not as they would be in your own home town. There everyone knew you and knew your papa. Here in London people are very much judged by appearances. A word, a look, a smile or frown in the wrong place and a person's reputation may be fixed in an unfortunate way. I would not like you to gain a name for being, let us say, mischievous.'

'I am not that, Aunt Parry!' I exclaimed. 'I do speak my mind, I admit it. And although I did not know Miss Hexham, I feel very sorry for her.' Wryly, I added, 'I do, after all, sleep in her bed, do I not? I have to think about her.'

'My goodness,' said Aunt Parry, startled. 'So you do. Would you like to move to another room? Does it alarm you?'

I shook my head. 'No, ma'am, I am very well where I

am. Please don't worry on my account. I will keep everything you have said in mind.'

She patted my hand. 'There, there. You are a good girl. We shall do very well together.' She sighed. 'But these two days have been very trying. I think I will retire to my room for the rest of the day and have a supper tray sent up. Do write a note on my behalf to Dr Tibbett and say I regret I shall not be able to receive company at dinner tonight. It's Thursday and normally he would return this evening.'

I had forgotten it was Thursday. As I penned the note I wondered if this would mean I had to dine *tête-à-tête* with Frank. I really couldn't bear his conversation for an entire evening unsupported. But this was not to be. Together with a reply note from Tibbett saying he hoped his dear friend would soon recover from her low spirits and begging her to 'bear up', came a note from Frank saying he would again dine in town. In the circumstances, suggested Simms impassively, Miss Martin too might wish to have her supper on a tray in her room?

I acquiesced, having no great wish to sit in state in the dining room and have Simms and his wife telling one another downstairs that I was adopting airs above my station. The supper arrived, borne upstairs by Wilkins with sulky mien. It consisted of fish pie and rice pudding. I suspected it was the reheated remains of the main meal the staff had eaten earlier. I doubted the lady of the house had been served fish pie. However Aunt Parry might treat me, below stairs they knew my true status.

When I had eaten, I put the tray outside the door assuming that Wilkins would come back for it when she saw fit. The house seemed unnaturally quiet. There was no sound from Aunt Parry's room. I went downstairs and found the rooms there deserted. I decided I would fetch a book from the library.

The smell of cigar smoke still lingered in there. I searched among the tightly packed books, most of which were not to my taste, and found a volume of poetry. I took it down and went to one of the wing chairs. Light was fading now and Simms hadn't lit the gas jets in this room on his early evening tour. There were to be no gentlemen at dinner and the library would not be called into use as a smoking room. I did not need them. There was a stub of candle in a brass stick on the mantelshelf so I lit it with one of the safety matches and settled down.

I opened the book and found that the poem before me was one by Coleridge, 'Kubla Khan'. I whispered some of the lines aloud:

> 'In Xanadu did Kubla Khan
> A stately pleasure-dome decree;
> Where Alph, the sacred river, ran
> Through caverns measureless to man
> Down to a sunless sea.'

Why, I thought, Coleridge might be describing this great city of London. It is like a wonderful pleasure palace – but it is built above unseen and frightening things almost beyond imagination.

I closed the book and sat with it on my lap. Around me the fabric of this overheated house creaked as it cooled and settled in the night air. Occasionally footsteps would walk briskly past the window. Once I heard someone whistling a sad little tune in the distance before that too faded and was gone. Coleridge's words swirled around my head, but now they no longer applied to London but to the coal workings of my native county. I imagined them also as endless caverns in a sunless world where men and boys, some still children, toiled in semi-darkness as far above their heads the more fortunate walked heedlessly to and fro. After a while all these thoughts became muddled in my head and I drifted into uneasy sleep. In it I dreamed I walked alone through a long dark street until I reached a fork in the way and stopped, not knowing which branch to take. As I stood wondering, someone or something approached me and its warm breath brushed my cheek.

I gasped and awoke with a painful hop of my heart. My head had been crooked at an awkward angle against the wing of the chair and my neck was stiff. I raised my hand to rub it and, as I did so, became aware that the breathing I had heard in my dream could still be heard and was not mine but another's. My candle had burned out but a fresh one had been lit. I started forward in my seat as by its flickering flame I saw that I was no longer alone.

Frank Carterton sat in the companion wing chair

opposite to me and was watching me moodily, his legs stretched out before him, the fingers of his right hand caressing his chin. His shadow aped his form on the wall behind him so that it was as if two persons, not one, confronted me and in my muddled state I could not quite decide which one of them was real.

'What time is it?' I exclaimed, gripping the arms of the chair. The volume of verse tumbled from my lap to the carpet.

'A little after midnight,' he replied, letting his right hand drop to his side.

'How long have you been there?'

'Oh . . .' He and the shadow shrugged. 'Perhaps half an hour?'

'You startled me,' I said. 'I did not hear you return.'

One side of his mouth twitched as if he wanted to grin but thought it inappropriate. 'Forgive me. I told Simms I had a key and if he would leave the door unbolted there was no need to wait up for me. I would not be late and I would not be, well, I would not be rather the worse for wear as I was last night. And I am not, you see, not drunk.'

'What are you doing in here?' I still could not quite pull my wits together.

'I thought I would smoke a cigar before turning in. However when I came in here, there you were. I didn't like to wake you. But I didn't like to leave you, either.'

'Then I will leave you to your cigar,' I said, making to rise.

He leaned forward and gestured me back into my chair. 'Don't go, Lizzie. I want to talk to you.'

'You can talk to me at breakfast!' I retorted. My mind was functioning again as it should and I was annoyed with him.

'But then Simms will be gliding in and out and make no mistake, Simms has the hearing of a bat!'

'Is what you have to say so private?' I asked.

'Yes, it is. I want to talk to you about Madeleine. I am sure below stairs they talk of nothing else but they have the advantage that we do not hear them.'

'The police were here today to question all the staff,' I said.

Frank chuckled. 'I wager they got nothing out of them. Simms will have made sure of that. If, of course, there was anything any of them could tell our stout-hearted guardians of the law. But Simms holds the honour of this household very dear. His own reputation, too.'

'His reputation?' I asked.

'Why, yes. To have been the butler in a household where there was some scandal would not recommend him if he sought a position elsewhere. Not that he plans to leave as far as I know. He and Mrs Simms have it very comfortable here.' Frank stooped and picked up the volume of verse. He read the title on the spine and observed, 'I am no great reader of poetry.'

He placed the book carefully on a little table by his chair. 'Inspector Ross asked me if I had noticed anything in Miss Hexham's manner before she left us to indicate she was preoccupied or lovesick or anything of that nature. I told him, no. That is true. I paid very little attention to her. She was a whey-faced little provincial nonentity.'

'As am I!' I said sharply.

'Oh, no, no, Lizzie. You are quite a different kettle of fish. As I have said to you before, you are intelligent, independent of mind, observant I know, and handsome.'

'You flatter me,' I said drily.

'No, I do not do that,' was his sober reply. 'All I have said is true. I'd lay five guineas on it on the first three. The fourth I can see for myself.'

'Only five guineas?' I could not resist asking.

Frank pointed at me in triumph. 'You see? You're quick and you have a sense of humour. Madeleine wasn't quick, far from it, and she was utterly humourless. One couldn't tease Madeleine; she never saw the joke or even realised there was a joke. There was no sport in it and once I knew it I gave up and lost interest in her. But someone else had interest in her, didn't he? Or so we must now assume.'

I could see where this was leading but I chose to say nothing. It was he who had introduced the subject.

'We are left with two possibilities, are we not? What do you say, Lizzie? Either she met this unknown man in our circle, that is to say, she met him because she lived here in this house, or she met him elsewhere. But if elsewhere, where indeed? You are a young single lady newly arrived in London, as she was. You have the morning free since Aunt

Julia does not come down before noon. What might you choose to do with your time and where might you go?'

'So far,' I said, 'I have been nowhere. But didn't you say Madeleine read novels from a circulating library? Well, then, at the library. There she might have met someone.'

'You see? You are very clever, I knew it.' Frank nodded. 'But so is Inspector Ross a very clever fellow. I wonder if he has thought of that. I told him of Maddie's taste in literature. He has probably sent a plainclothes detective to each and every circulating library in the metropolitan area, there to watch and make note of anyone borrowing *A Romance of the Borders* or *The Corsair's Bride* or some such tosh.'

I still said nothing but this time because I had been struck by something I should have thought of at once and stupidly had not. I must tell Aunt Parry at the earliest opportunity that I had met Inspector Ross before and that my own father had paid for the detective's education. To keep the knowledge from her would not only be unfair but unwise, should it emerge later. But that did not mean I had to tell Frank, at least not before I had told his aunt.

'You understand,' said Frank, misinterpreting my silence, 'that I must be high on the worthy inspector's list of suspects? Moreover, he does not like me.'

'Perhaps you are being unfair on the inspector?' I suggested.

'Good Lord, Lizzie. I know when a fellow has taken a scunner to me, even if he is only a policeman, confound his impudence!' After a moment's silence he added, 'I hope you do not dislike me, Lizzie? I know you disapprove of me but that is not the same thing.'

He gave me no chance to answer, even though I had no answer. He said briskly, 'I am keeping you from retiring. Forgive me. Good night, Lizzie.' He stood up and bowed politely.

I got to my feet and said, 'Good night,' as politely.

As I closed the door I saw through the crack that he had opened the volume of verse and was leafing through it. I thought, He declares no interest in Madeleine but he had enough to take note of what she read. Now he is interested to learn what I read.

I felt uncomfortable with this piece of reasoning. But if, as Frank had gallantly declared, I was intelligent enough to puzzle things out, then I was also aware enough to know that the talent was an unsettling one. How much preferable it must be to content oneself with the pleasure palace and to be able to put entirely from one's mind the 'caverns measureless to man'. But I could not.

Chapter Nine

Ben Ross

IT IS my practice at the end of each day to write a detailed account of the observations I have made during working hours when I am pursuing an investigation. Call it a diary, if you like. Colleagues who have found out about this habit of mine have mocked me for it and called me pedantic. 'What, Ben? Do you think yourself still clerking?' But I find it useful to be able to look back and see not only where and when I have spoken to such an individual, but also to read I have recorded some little thing I noticed at the time but which later slipped my mind in the hurly-burly of events. It has proved useful on more than one occasion.

I suppose this of no interest to anyone but myself as I can imagine the mirth in any court where I might produce my little book. But I sincerely believe that the time is not far off when all officers investigating a crime will do as I do. If we do not act in an organised and scientific manner the detection of crime will never progress, and we shall for ever be tainted with the image of the bumbling village constable. Moreover, any clever lawyer will be able to muddle us in the witness box and make fools of us.

In the summer I generally take my notes home to my rooms and write there in peace. On dark evenings I stay at Scotland Yard and take advantage of the gaslight, ignoring its stink and the risk of interruption and mockery from my peers.

Looking back at my account of Thursday, the day following that on which I had taken news of Madeleine Hexham's murder to the Parry household, I see it was taken up both with asking questions and with fending them off. In between I thought a great deal about Lizzie Martin and in particular that part of our conversation in which I had revealed my link to her father. I had meant to sound grateful to him, as I was deeply so, and to tell how pleased I was to see her. But I feared I had sounded a pompous prig and she must have found me a sober dullard, especially when compared to a glittering fellow like Carterton.

I was in a fair way to dislike Carterton for reasons that had nothing to do with my investigation. I warned myself privately (not in my notes!) to beware of the temptation. No doubt he was an excellent fellow, devoted to his aunt and to his labours on behalf of Her Majesty and her business in foreign climes. It was my earnest wish they'd send him to oversee Britain's interests in somewhere like South America or Japan or an isolated island in the middle of the Pacific Ocean, where he would be out of Lizzie's way and she out of his.

But to return to my notes. I had ordered men to be sent back to the Agar Town site to finish questioning all the workers there. It was proving a slow and thankless business. A number of workmen had already quit the site. They did not wish to be quizzed by the police and their names entered in some official account. One or two may have had some minor offences already recorded against them. Others may have belonged to that shadowy fraternity of men who had slipped out of normal society and drifted on the outskirts of it or in London's teeming underbelly. They survived doing casual work here and there, enough to pay for a bed in a cheap lodging house and a meal. A building site offers plenty of such work. Not all were rogues and vagrants who knew nothing else. More likely they were the once respectable who had fallen from grace. There might be husbands among them who had abandoned wife and children. There might be bank clerks ruined through gambling or drink. Or again, pathetic one-time small businessmen whose stock had failed to sell and whose creditors had defaulted. London was a city in which a man might lose himself completely if he did not wish to be found. Our murderer counted on it. But he was out there somewhere and I would have him yet.

The task had to be done, though I knew very well what the results of my constables' labours would be. No one at

Agar Town would admit to having seen anything and I could expect to receive a visit from Mr Fletcher, the representative of the railway company, complaining bitterly that work was again held up.

He arrived in my office by half past nine on Friday morning. We were still organising the day ahead and I was anything but ready for him. But I received him, albeit with bad grace. He was perspiring profusely. The dull spring had unexpectedly taken a turn for the better and, on a whim, teased us with a sample of summer sunshine. I supposed Fletcher's brow was beaded because he had hurried over to the Yard from Agar Town but most of all he appeared to be in a lather of rage.

'This is outrageous!' he squawked. He took off his oval-lensed spectacles and blinked at me before pulling out his spotted handkerchief and mopping his damp brow. 'We are behind schedule! If the ground is not cleared by the due date, then the next stage of construction cannot begin. Everyone is waiting for the demolition work to be completed. All hangs on that! Have you any idea what that means? I see you do not. Can you put yourself in the place of the shareholders who become increasingly restless as they see the possibility that the return on their investment may be delayed? They badger the directors of the railway who in turn badger *me*!'

His voice rose in an aggrieved wail. 'Can you imagine the cost of the whole undertaking? Do you know what the wages of the labour force amount to?'

'Mr Fletcher!' I interrupted as civilly as I was able. 'I told you I was happy for work to restart clearing the site.'

'It is impossible to proceed at anything but a snail's pace,' he retorted, 'and that is due entirely to the presence of the police. No sooner a job is under way than a fellow in uniform appears and demands the men down tools so that he may quiz them. Every day a man or two decides he wants no more of working under the eye of a constable who regards everything he does with suspicion and pesters him with impertinent questions. It is bad enough that, although few of them have any formal religion, most of the navvies are superstitious so no one wants to work in the area where the body was discovered. Those who are God-fearing don't like being associated with a scene of crime. So each morning a few more don't appear for work and then new men must be found and taken on.'

'There are surely navvies a-plenty in London,' I snapped.

'And work a-plenty for them!' was Fletcher's reply. 'You may not have observed it, Inspector, but London has for some years now been in the process of being transformed above ground and below. Beneath our feet navvies are digging out Bazalgette's new sewers; they are tunnelling for a railway which will run underground; above and around us the railway companies build; the property speculators build; Her Majesty's government builds! If a navvy isn't happy at his place of work, why, he has but to pack his bag and take himself to the next site where they will be happy to hire him. The only ones who are always available are those who are shiftless, drunken or incapacitated. Do you understand now the difficulty of finding industrious and sober men to work on the new terminus? Do you understand now that such men will not stay if the whole place is crawling with police officers?'

I said nothing to this but raised my eyebrows and he seemed to realise that the last words were, to say the least, not tactful. He hastened to rephrase them. 'If their work is hindered by your investigations, I mean. Look, Inspector – er – Ross, I beg of you, recall your men. They are wasting their time and surely, in an investigation of this sort, time lost cannot be regained. It is certainly so in the construction business.'

There were men of his sort working in the coal-mining business, but I did not point it out to him. They looked only at profit and loss. Their aim was to sweat the maximum labour from each individual and they cared nothing for accidents and deaths. Remembering the men I had seen demolishing the upper walls with sledgehammers while perched on what structure remained, I wondered how many accidents there had been on the demolition site since work there had begun.

However, the police are public servants and it is our policy not to offend worthy citizens. They kick up such a devil of a fuss.

'I am sorry to hear it's disrupting your plans,' I said. 'But the quicker my officers can complete their enquiries, the sooner they will be out from under your feet and you can carry on knocking things down and clearing them away.'

I frowned as I spoke. He probably thought I was frowning at him as he looked a little nervous. But I was thinking that so much had indeed been carried away from that site that anything of interest to us would long have disappeared with the rest of it.

'I should like your officers off the site by midday,' he said, tucking the handkerchief into his pocket.

'That gives us hardly any time at all,' I pointed out.

'But they have been there since the body was found!' he exploded. 'And one of them has fallen into a cellar. His colleagues had to pull him out with a rope! He might have broken a leg.'

I wondered who it was had fallen into the cellar and was annoyed this had not been reported to me. I wondered also if Fletcher would have cared as much if one of his workmen broke a leg.

'So you see,' went on Fletcher, 'a building site is a dangerous place.'

'It certainly was for the dead woman, Madeleine Hexham,' I said.

'But, my dear man, you cannot imagine anyone there killed her!' he shouted.

I told him my mind was open at the moment. I had formed no theories. I thought he would choke.

'I shall take this further,' he promised, picking up his hat.

'As you wish, sir,' I said.

He was wasting my time and I was glad to see him leave. I little cared where he went.

When he had left, I went into the outer office and found Morris there.

'Who fell into the cellar?' I snapped.

'Biddle, sir,' returned Morris. 'A hole in the ground is powerfully attractive to the young and Biddle, being not much more than a boy and curious like boys are, went over to look in. It was unsafe, sir, of course and in he fell. Constable Jenkins and Adams the foreman got him out between them with a rope. I didn't trouble you with it as he wasn't much harmed. He ricked an ankle and sprained his wrist but he's young and they sort of bounce, sir, at that age. We strapped up both limbs and he is managing very well. He's a game lad.'

'He may be an excellent officer and all the other things you say, but hobbling round that site with a bandaged ankle he will be an object of mirth and derision. If he has sprained his wrist, how on earth is he to take notes? I hope he *is* taking notes!'

'It's his left wrist and he's right-handed,' said Morris promptly. 'Bit of luck, that. I did tell him and the others to write everything down, sir, just like you said.'

'Get him back here,' I ordered. 'Put him on office duties until he's fit. He is a representative of the Metropolitan Police and not the Chelsea Pensioners!'

* * *

I left the building before anyone else representing the Midland Railway could descend on me and take up my time with lamentations. They would not have believed me but there was a sense in which I was not unsympathetic towards them. I understood the problem they had very well. It was a vast undertaking: a whole new railway terminus and, so I gathered, a magnificent hotel to front it. There was some competition or other to find a design for the hotel, I had read in the newspapers.

But, at the same time, I thought, surely our murderer had taken account of all this? Had all gone according to his plans, that house should have tumbled down upon Madeleine's body. The crushed remains dragged from the ruins might well have been quite unidentifiable and certainly the cause of death would have been impossible to establish. We might easily have thought the body that of a drunken female vagrant who had been sleeping rough there. The need to continue with the demolition work would have meant that our enquiries were rushed and perfunctory. Dead vagrants, men or women and sometimes children, were discovered regularly in London. I could see how the murderer's mind had worked.

But Fate had played a hand. The two Irish navvies had entered the empty house prior to demolition, perhaps seeking any small item overlooked in the clearance to carry off and sell, perhaps hoping to take a drink on the quiet unseen by Adams the foreman. Madeleine had been found, identified and the cause of her death discovered. Not only that, but the time of her death. Only two weeks at the most had she been dead and two months had she been missing. Where had she been in the period between? Within ten days of leaving the Parry household, she had written the letter or been induced to write it. I thought it most likely she had written it herself. If it were faked then it had been faked by someone who had known her handwriting very well. But there were those who knew her handwriting and I was on the way to see one of them: Mrs Sinclair Belling of Dorset Square.

I had sent ahead to let her know I was coming as I knew she would not receive me in the presence of any of her society friends. As it was, she saw me in her drawing room, accompanied by her son whom she introduced to me.

'This is my son, James. My husband, Sinclair Belling, is away on business. He is in South America, and will not return before next month. His business is chiefly in banking but he has an interest in railway construction which is going on apace there. James is the man of the household in his absence.'

He might be the man of the household but he presented the appearance of a sullen youth. He was probably in his early twenties but he had a gangling frame and lank fair hair. He wore spectacles. He scowled at me and chewed nervously at his lower lip.

'What is it you wish to know?' demanded his mother briskly. 'You have come in connection with that wretched girl, Hexham. But I did not know her personally. She was recommended to me by a friend and, on the basis of that, I recommended her to my friend, Mrs Parry. It was a sorry day when I did it. But we were none of us to know.'

'Yes, ma'am, quite. After you were first put in touch with Miss Hexham by your friend in the North, I understand you had some correspondence with her?'

'With Hexham? Yes, I did receive a letter or two. I asked her to write to me with her details and the names of referees and to send any letters of recommendation she might have. She sent a letter from a bishop's widow to whom she had been companion. The letter praised her highly. One would have expected a bishop's widow to be possessed of common sense and judgement. I took the letter at face value. Madeleine herself wrote a sensible kind of letter. She gave me all the necessary information about herself. There was no reason, no reason at all, Inspector, to believe her anything but utterly trustworthy and responsible!'

'Do you have these letters still, ma'am?'

'Of course I don't!' she said irritably. 'I probably passed them all to my dear friend, Mrs Parry. I really don't remember. I may have destroyed them.'

Mrs Parry had mentioned the correspondence between Mrs Belling and the lady in Durham, but she had not spoken as if she had it in her possession.

'Did you see the letter Mrs Parry received from her following her mysterious departure from the house?' I asked next.

Mrs Belling reddened. 'I did see it. Julia Parry showed it to me. She was most upset and with good reason. The girl wrote she had eloped! There was no mention of who the man might be. There had clearly been a gross deception practised by the girl on her employer and upon me also. To run off with a man, what kind of girl does that? If he were respectable, why not ask her employer to meet him and give her opinion of him? Why did the man himself not come forward to explain himself and request Mrs Parry's permission to pay his attentions to her companion? The whole thing was completely irregular. Dr Tibbett, I understand, declares that the man's intentions could not have been honourable and I am inclined to agree. As for Hexham, the silly little goose, she may well have been gullible enough to believe he was offering marriage, but even so, it does not explain why she ran off with him. It was not the kind of behaviour one expected of someone who had been companion to a bishop's widow!'

Mrs Belling subsided into a glowering silence at the end of this speech. I ventured to rouse her from it.

'And did the handwriting in the letter Mrs Parry showed you, the one in which Miss Hexham wrote of her elopement, appear the same as that of the letters you had received?'

'Yes!' she returned crisply. 'If it had not, I should have remarked on it at the time.'

This I believed to be true. 'Tell me,' I said, 'if you remember, what her former circumstances were? What did she write to you of herself?'

Mrs Belling gestured with a thin white hand on which was an emerald ring of great beauty and no doubt corresponding value. I wondered if the stone had been bought in South America and thought unkindly that it was wasted on her. She was a sour-looking woman, in my view, and had never been handsome. She was, however, very fashionably turned out and formidably laced.

'She was a curate's daughter. I suppose that's why the bishop's widow took her on. One would expect a curate's daughter to have moral principles,' Mrs Belling added fretfully. 'If one can't rely on the clergy to bring up their children to set an example then moral decay can only spread among the lower orders to an even worse degree than it is exhibited among them already.'

'And her parents?' I prompted.

'Oh, both dead, also all her siblings. She had been one of five children, but was the only one of them to reach adult years. Very sad but these things are not uncommon. There had been no money. She was thrown on her own devices and we now know what those devices were!'

'We do, ma'am?' I enquired.

'She was looking for a husband,' said Mrs Belling sharply. 'Though she had nothing to recommend her.'

'I thought she seemed very pleasant,' said James unexpectedly.

He had been so silent I had almost forgotten he was there and so, I fancy, had his mother. Her head snapped round to look at him and she demanded, 'What should you know of it, James? You did not know her.'

He flushed. 'Well, no, but I met her, Mama.'

'When and where?'

I had been going to ask him that but his grim parent was ahead of me. It was better the question came from her so I was not displeased.

'I made up a four at whist on a couple of occasions when you and Mrs Parry played, and Madeleine. She also called here with Mrs Parry several times. I believe I went once with you to call on Mrs Parry and Madeleine was there.'

'Pah!' said his mother. 'How can you judge from so slight an acquaintance?' She turned to me. 'My son's opinion is of no consequence in this matter.'

'I am interested to hear it, all the same,' I said.

'Thank you,' said James briefly and, I thought, not without irony.

Perhaps his mother caught the ironic note. She said evenly, 'You know about nothing but those wretched fossils, James. You do better not to give an opinion on anything else.'

'Fossils, sir?' I asked him.

Some animation entered his pale face and he leaned forward eagerly. 'Yes, I collect fossils and am currently at work on a book I believe will contribute greatly to the recent debate. I have been on some very successful expeditions and my collection, I do believe, is amongst the best and most extensive in private hands in this country. Are you interested in fossils, Inspector?'

'I have seen some interesting impressions in pieces of shale, found in the area of coalfields,' I said.

'Then perhaps—'

But James was not allowed to finish. 'The inspector has not come here to discuss fossils, James.' Mrs Belling turned to me. 'Have you finished, Inspector? There is no more I can tell you and James can tell you nothing at all!'

'Yes, ma'am, thank you for your time.'

A butler materialised without his mistress having rung. He must have been lurking outside the door. He was much the same type as the Parry butler, Simms, and showed me out with the same efficient celerity.

I was not surprised, when I returned to the Yard, to receive a message from Superintendent Dunn to the effect that he would be pleased to see me in his office.

As I guessed, Mr Fletcher had been there before me.

'How long are you going to keep men at that site?' Dunn asked me as soon as I came through the door. 'I have had my ear bent by that fellow Fletcher who appears to think that all our enquiries are part of a plot to disrupt his schedule and undermine the plans of the Midland Railway company.'

'I hope to finish there today. I need the manpower. We are short-handed. But if those in charge there won't cooperate, it only slows down everything. I can't get Fletcher to see that.'

Dunn sighed and scratched his shock of iron-grey hair. In the morning when he arrived his thatch, well dampened down, lay fairly flat. But during the day it worked itself up into a veritable hayrick on his skull.

'Well, well, Mr Fletcher has those who snap at his heels so he snaps at ours! What is it they say? Great fleas have little fleas upon their backs to bite 'em?'

'And little fleas have smaller fleas and so ad infinitum!' I finished for him.

'It's never truer than it is for a policeman!' growled Dunn. 'Let's have it, then. Who are your candidates for murderer?'

'I can't say I have any, sir. There are one or two gentlemen who might bear investigation if, indeed, the girl did run off with a lover. There is one in the household, Francis Carterton. He has a career to make in the Foreign Office and I believe he must be the designated heir of his wealthy aunt, Mrs Julia Parry, who employed Madeleine. I can't think Mrs Parry would have approved a marriage between her nephew and her companion. I don't suppose it would have been the sort of socially advantageous match which would have furthered his career. If he had foolishly led the girl to expect otherwise, he would have been in a pretty pickle.'

'Carterton, hm . . .' mumbled Dunn. 'Any other?'

'There is Mr James Belling whose mother recommended

Madeleine Hexham to Mrs Parry. She didn't know her personally but had been recommended her by a third party, an acquaintance in Durham. Mr Belling certainly met Miss Hexham. He appears to be much under the thumb of his mother. He has an interest in fossils and likes to travel round collecting them. It's in my mind to try and find out if his travels ever took him to the North. He's writing a book on the subject. I fancy he has no other employment. His allowance will be strictly in his mother's control, I'm sure. The woman is a monster. She would not have approved a connection with Miss Hexham and would have made her son's life a misery if she had even suspected he had an interest in the young lady.'

'Hah!' said Dunn darkly, running his stubby fingers through his hair which now stood up like a house-painter's brush.

'Then there is the matter of the letters written by Miss Hexham to Mrs Belling from Durham, before she came to London. I am keen to know their whereabouts. Possibly they were destroyed. The lady suggested they may have been given to Mrs Parry, but Mrs Parry made no mention of having them though she knew of them. I feel it was a suggestion designed to dismiss my enquiry. Possibly they were overlooked somewhere in a desk drawer in the Belling house. Or, if indeed Mrs Parry was given them, they may have been forgotten somewhere in her house.'

Dunn leaned back in his chair and fixed his shrewd little eyes on me. 'So if anyone had a fancy to forge the girl's handwriting, then letters from her might be lying about in either house for the forger to copy?'

'Yes, sir. Although Mrs Parry did not keep the letter Miss Hexham wrote telling of her elopement. The girl's clothing was subsequently given to the servants. Miss Hexham was expunged from the record. That is a great pity, from our point of view.'

'Anything else?'

I hesitated. 'Yes, sir, but it is in the way of a personal matter of which I should tell you. Mrs Parry's present companion is a Miss Elizabeth Martin. Her father, the late Dr Martin, was my generous benefactor. He paid for my schooling and gave some small sum of money to my mother during that time when I was not at work.'

Dunn's bushy eyebrows twitched. 'Is Miss Martin involved in this somehow?'

'I don't see how she can be, sir. She only arrived in London on Tuesday, the day the body was found. She was a stranger to Mrs Parry and her nephew. She was offered the post of companion to the lady because the late Mr Parry had been her godfather.'

'Will it get in your way?' demanded Dunn.

'No, sir, though I confess I don't like her being in that house.'

'Don't let it influence you, although you are sensible enough not to let it do so. Well, well, carry on, then. Concentrate on finding the culprit and I will keep the railway company off your back. Let 'em bite at me!' He gave his forest of spiky grey hair a last run-through with his stubby fingers. 'But if they get no joy from me, they will go above me. We have not so much time to solve this one.'

'There is one thing, sir,' I said, 'with regard to the railway company. It seems that Mr Sinclair Belling, James Belling's father, is a banker with an interest in railways. He is at present in South America looking into some railway development there. I just wondered whether, by any chance, Mr Sinclair Belling might be a shareholder in the Midlands Railway Company. There may be no connection but I should like to know where everyone's interest lies in this.'

Dunn stared at me, then scribbled the name of Sinclair Belling on a piece of paper. 'I'll enquire into it.' He tapped the pencil on the desktop. 'This is turning into a dashed complicated business,' he said, 'a regular cat's-cradle of possible motives.' His little eyes suddenly peered up at me. 'And that is assuming, of course, that the murderer is a man. The victim was of slight build, you say?'

'Yes, sir, and Carmichael also thinks showed signs of poor nutrition in the period before her death, although not generally. If she was starved, it was in the last two months.'

'So a woman might easily have overcome her?'

'With no trouble at all, sir. But she would need an accomplice to move the body.'

'Confound it,' said Dunn softly. 'Miss Hexham appears

to have made herself a nuisance to them all. They could all of them have had a hand in it!'

Chapter Ten

Elizabeth Martin

A PEREMPTORY knock was followed by a hearty shove and my bedroom door flew open at a little before eight on Friday morning. Bessie appeared, lugging the heavy hot-water can and puffing noisily. It might have been with effort but it struck me this display had its origin in annoyance. She certainly gave the impression of being somewhat out of sorts. She returned my greeting gruffly without meeting my eye.

As I got out of bed and threw a shawl round my shoulders she took the pottery jug from the wash-stand and stood it on the carpet. I watched her as she tipped the water from her can into it. Her little face was set in concentration lest she spill any.

'Do leave it there, Bessie,' I said when she had completed the task and made to lift the filled jug up to the wash-stand. 'I'll do it.'

'All right, then, miss.' She grabbed her empty can and made for the bedroom door like a beetle disturbed when a stone is overturned and it rushes for another bolthole.

'Bessie!' I called.

She was already half out into the passage beyond but she could not pretend she hadn't heard me. She returned unwillingly and hovered in the open doorway.

'Yes, miss?'

'What happened yesterday below stairs when the sergeant and police constable came to question the staff? Do you know if they learned anything of interest?'

'No,' said Bessie. 'Nobody don't tell me nothing. Anyway, Mr Simms said we were not to gossip.' This was uttered in a tone of lofty virtue and accompanied by a meaningful look at me.

'Mr Simms did not mean you were not to talk to me, Bessie. Nor did he mean you were not to give any information to the police which might help them.'

Bessie gave me another look, this one suggesting she knew Simms rather better than I did. But I wished to make it clear that whatever authority the butler had over her, he had none over me.

'Did one of the police officers talk to you, Bessie?' I asked pleasantly.

Bessie shifted the empty water can from one hand to the other and hesitated. But, as I had guessed, some grievance festered in her heart. Now it bubbled over and finally the words tumbled out.

'They came to me last. I mean, I'm just nobody, not as far as any of 'em think. They questioned everyone else all proper and writing it down and everything. Then the constable, a great lump sweating away in that blue uniform, he says to me, grinning, "Well, then, half-pint! Have you got anything to tell us?"'

Bessie scowled ferociously and the mob cap slipped down over her furrowed brow. '"No,"' I snaps right back at him. "And you don't have any right to be free with me. I'm a member of the public, I am, and you're supposed to be polite." He near laughed himself silly. So the sergeant came over then to see what it was all about and ordered him away. Then I got in trouble with Mrs Simms for being impertinent with an officer of the law. But I wasn't the one taking liberties, he was!'

'Perhaps he only wanted to put you at your ease, Bessie, in case you should be frightened,' I suggested.

'Nah,' sniffed Bessie. 'He fancied himself. He was trying to give the eye to Wilkins on the sly, when his sergeant wasn't looking, but it didn't do him no good. Wilkins is walking out with the footman from number sixteen. He might have done better if he'd tried his luck with Ellis, mind you. But she's not as pretty as Wilkins. If I don't go right back downstairs now, miss, I'll be in trouble with Mrs Simms again.'

With that she whisked away. I reflected that below stairs there existed a world which, in true Darwinian fashion, had evolved quite differently to society above. Had the great naturalist set himself to study it, he might have found as much of interest there as he had in Tierra del Fuego. Bessie, for all her youth, understood the world about her very well. She had sharp eyes and had observed what motivated adults. Perhaps the police officers should have spoken to her first, not last. When one of them did so, he made a mistake in insulting her dignity. Whatever Bessie knew, and I was sure she knew something, she would now keep it to herself on principle.

'Or,' I said softly to myself, 'because she fears retribution.'

I was a little later going downstairs than on previous days and Frank had already left the house. I was pleased about this. The memory of our encounter in the library had left me with mixed feelings. He should not have sat there watching me as I dozed. He held me quite at a disadvantage when I awoke and I felt I had answered him foolishly. On the other hand, I appreciated the delicate situation in which he found himself with regard to Madeleine's disappearance and subsequent fate. He must, as he himself had said, be at the top of Inspector Ross's list – if Ross had a list.

But I had my own programme in mind. To this end I first set about getting on the right side of Simms. Annoying though it was to need to do this, a butler is a person whose goodwill is forfeited at peril and I required his approval of the plan I had in mind.

'Shall I cut you some ham, miss?' he enquired as he put down the coffee pot.

'Well, Simms,' I said. 'I don't want to put anyone to any trouble, but Mr Carterton tells me Mrs Simms makes a truly delicious omelette. Would she have time, do you think, to make a small one for me?'

Simms considered the matter. 'Well, miss, I'm sure she would. I'll go and ask.'

In due course the omelette arrived. Frank had been right and it was excellent. When Simms returned for the plate, I said honestly, 'Please thank Mrs Simms. I enjoyed that so much.'

'Not at all, Miss Martin,' he returned quite graciously.

'I hope you were not too much disturbed yesterday by the activities of the police officers,' I went on. 'That must have been quite a nuisance for Mrs Simms.'

'Mrs Simms Coped,' said Simms. 'Mrs Simms is a remarkable Coper. I believe there is not an emergency of a household nature which Mrs Simms could not take a good grip on and knock into shape in no time.'

'Indeed, I'm sure she must be. She is clearly an excellent cook and the house appears to run like clockwork.'

I warned myself to be careful not to overdo this. But I didn't think Frank was one for expressing thanks to the staff, nor was Mrs Parry, and rain which falls on parched soil is quickly soaked up.

'Thank you, miss,' said Simms and almost smiled.

'I hesitate,' I said, 'to impose on Mrs Simms's goodwill further. But, as you know, I am a newcomer in London. There has been such a to-do since my arrival here that I have had no time to explore. I have it in mind to make good the omission today but I confess I am more than a little afraid of becoming lost. I was wondering if Mrs Simms could spare Bessie for an hour or two this morning. Bessie is sure to know every road and alley and if I took her with me, there would be no fear of setting foot in the wrong area. I had thought of asking if Mrs Simms could spare either Wilkins or Ellis. But I feared I might sow dissension between them. If either of the maids thought the other had been given a morning free from her duties, which must of necessity be done by the other one in addition to her own, that might not be a good thing. What do you think?'

Simms gave me a shrewd look. He appreciated my argument with regard to the maids. He pursed his lips. I waited. The decision had to come from him and must not be a demand by me.

'I will have a word with Mrs Simms, miss,' he said at last to my great relief.

He returned later to say that Bessie would be ready at half past ten and he would send her up to the small sitting room.

Bessie arrived promptly as the ormolu clock on the mantelshelf struck the half-hour. She was well scrubbed and wearing a clean dress without her usual pinafore. Her boots were polished. Instead of her overlarge mob cap she wore a bonnet of a style fashionable many years before with a deep brim shading the face and a frill at the nape of the neck, quite unlike the currently fashionable small bonnets designed to sit on the back of the head.

'Where are we going, then, miss?' she enquired.

'To explore,' I said. 'All this is new to me. I was never in London before Tuesday last, the day I arrived.'

'What, never?' asked Bessie, amazed.

As we set out across Dorset Square Bessie took it upon herself straight away to act as my guide. 'Mr Simms says there used to be a cricket pitch here, only they moved it when they built all the houses and turned this space, what was left, into a nice little park. I come here on a Sunday afternoon sometimes and sit watching the people. The nursemaids come with the babies and little ones just toddling in their petticoats. It's nice.'

She pointed out a house of imposing frontage on the side of the square facing Mrs Parry's. 'Mrs Belling lives there. She comes visiting the mistress.'

I was surprised because although I knew Mrs Belling must live nearby, I had not realised that she lived almost directly opposite across the square. I looked with interest at the house and, as I did, the front door opened and a young man came out. He was tall and lanky with fair hair escaping from beneath his silk hat and, as we watched, he pulled out a gold pocket watch, consulted it, and began to walk briskly in the direction of the Marylebone Road. I wondered idly where he might be going and calculated that as we were walking towards him and he approaching us rapidly from the left, there was a strong possibility our paths would collide.

'That's 'er son,' observed Bessie.

'That gentleman? He is Mrs Belling's son?'

'Yes, miss, but I don't know his Christian name. He's come to our house sometimes with his mother. They play cards. The mistress likes a game of cards.'

I wondered if Mrs Parry knew as much about Bessie as the kitchen maid knew about those who came and went above stairs, and doubted it. But I at least knew the name of Mrs Belling's elder son from his mother's extensive account of her children's extraordinary abilities and recent achievements.

We had reached that point at which I had expected our steps and those of Mr James Belling to intersect. Self-preservation caused both of us to stop. He took off his hat and bowed.

'I do hope you will excuse me, ma'am,' he said to me. 'But I believe you have come from Mrs Parry's residence and the little maid there works for her. So I venture to introduce myself. I am James Belling. I think you are probably Miss Martin of whom my mother has spoken.'

Viewed closer to hand he presented an amiable but undistinguished appearance. His face was long, his nose rather pointed; his very pale blue eyes blinked at us myopically. I wondered if he normally wore spectacles but had put them aside to walk in the street.

I also wondered what his mother had said of me. I thought I could hazard a fair guess.

'I am Miss Martin,' I agreed. 'I have come to replace poor Miss Hexham.'

A slight flush darkened his pale cheeks. 'Oh, yes, Miss Hexham. I was very sorry to hear the sad news.'

That was an improvement on his mother's reaction, at least.

'Yes, it is very sad,' I agreed. 'I did not know her, of course, but I cannot condemn her as some have done. She must have suffered greatly.'

'Indeed,' he said, looking flustered. 'I suppose she did. That is to say, yes, she must have done. I knew her only slightly but I must say she struck me as a most respectable young woman, not unlike you.'

'Thank you,' I said, I confess a little drily.

The pink stain on his cheeks darkened to red. 'Forgive me. I spoke clumsily. I am not a fellow with a great turn of phrase when speaking to ladies . . .' He gestured with his outstretched arm and silk hat.

'Please, Mr Belling,' I said, at once feeling that I had been wrong to tease the poor man, 'I am not offended. I am glad to hear you speak well of my predecessor. I am sure you share my hope that the police will find her murderer soon.'

'Oh, yes, the police!' he exclaimed. 'I, that is to say we, my mother and I, understand from Mrs Parry that an inspector by the name of Ross is in charge. Mrs Parry declared that he appeared rather young for such responsibility. My mother also expressed surprise at that news.' Here James allowed himself a faint smile. 'My mother has great faith in the advantages of experience.'

'Really?' I said. 'I have met Inspector Ross. I am sure he's very efficient and, if he is young, then perhaps he will have fresh ideas and be keen to achieve success in the investigation.'

'We understand, Mother and I, from Mrs Parry that the inspector took notes during his conversation with her. I fancy Mrs Parry was taken aback at having her words written down. She felt almost that she was being asked to make a legally binding statement. She is strongly of the opinion it wasn't a thing a gentleman would have done. A lady should be free to change her mind.'

'I dare say it was to guard against slips in his memory,' I said.

'Well, well . . .' He gestured vaguely at the surrounding houses as if they might have something to contribute. As they did not, there was a silence during which he seemed to seek something further to say and failed to find it. 'Perhaps we shall meet again, Miss Martin!' he blurted suddenly and with another half-bow clapped his hat on his head and hurried away.

'What a nice gentleman,' said Bessie approvingly, 'he remembered who I was. Not many do that.'

A nice gentleman indeed and one whom Madeleine

might well have met frequently in the square just as I had done, by chance – or by design.

I was interested to hear my employer had complained of her words being written down by Ross. I could see his purpose, but if he took to doing that a great deal, he'd find people a lot less willing to chat to him.

We walked on a little. 'Tell me,' I said, 'did Miss Hexham go out very much of a morning, walking like this?'

'I think so,' Bessie said cautiously. 'I saw her from the basement a few times, going past.'

'You didn't happen to see her on the day she disappeared? Leaving the house and walking past the basement, I mean.'

'No!' said Bessie a little too firmly.

There was also a note of relief in her voice. I realised that somehow I had phrased my question wrongly. Another way I might have got a different answer, I was sure of it. Bessie had seen something. I did not think she would willingly tell me an untruth, hence the relief in her voice that she was not put in a position to make the choice. She had not seen Madeleine walk past the house as on several previous occasions. Where then and in what circumstances had she seen her? Bessie herself never left the basement of a morning except to buy the milk or, possibly, she might be sent on some other errand by Mrs Simms. When else would Bessie see Madeleine? Only in the early morning when she brought the hot water to her bedroom.

'Something wrong, miss?' enquired Bessie.

I had stopped short, struck by a thought. I hastened to move on. 'No, Bessie, I only stubbed my toe.'

'You want to be careful,' said Bessie. 'Turn your ankle really easy on these stones.'

I murmured agreement but I was trying to think of a way of broaching the subject which had entered my mind with such force. A way was offered by the approach of one of the nursemaids Bessie had mentioned. A smartly-turned-out girl in a starched cap with lace ribbons, she was pushing a wicker bassinet containing a very small infant.

'That is a nice baby,' I said to Bessie, as the girl passed by with her charge.

'I wouldn't mind being a nursemaid,' confided Bessie. 'In the orphanage I used to mind the little 'uns. I fed them their gruel and kept them clean. I liked doing that. I always cried heaps when one of 'em died.'

Her tone was philosophical; nonetheless I thought her affection for her small charges had been sincere.

'Did many die, Bessie?'

She hunched her thin shoulders. 'You're going to lose a few, stands to reason. If one of them catches something, they all catch it. Although if a child was sickly, the orphanage wouldn't take it in, for fear of the infection. Some of them was like me when I went there, just babies, and they didn't stand much chance. Most was abandoned. Mother couldn't keep 'em, not married most likely or already got more kids than she could feed. She'd leave it somewhere like my mother left me in a church. She took trouble, my mother.

She put me somewhere dry and out of the weather and where she knew I'd be found. I'd got a little knitted coat and a bit of blanket wrapped round me, so I was told, and a note pinned on me asking that I be looked after and not given to the parish. So the parson what found me, he gave me to the orphanage the church ran. Some of them just get left in the street. They'd often find one on the orphanage doorstep. Sometimes they was so new they wasn't even properly tidied up, still got the cord attached to their bellies. The orphanage wouldn't keep them when they come in like that and passed them on to the parish. The parish puts 'em out to nurse if they're not yet weaned and that's pot luck, that is. Some of 'em is lucky and gets well cared for and some of 'em don't. I was about four months old when I was found in that church so my mother tried to keep me, I reckon, but couldn't manage it.'

It had been a harsh introduction to life and death but I guessed Bessie was well aware of what were sometimes called 'the facts of life'. I wondered about Bessie's desperate mother, who had been literate enough to leave a note with her baby begging she be cared for, and aware enough of the shortcomings of the parish system to beg her child not be left to its Spartan regime. Perhaps she had been a girl of 'good' family who had been betrayed. Perhaps she had been a young woman in service who had been seduced. If so, perhaps she had paid someone to care for the infant for the first four months, but with her meagre wages had been unable to keep up the financial outlay.

'Bessie,' I said carefully, 'in the weeks before she disappeared, when you took hot water up to Miss Hexham of a morning, was she ever ill?'

There was no reply. I glanced sideways at my companion. She was looking down at the cobbles and the bonnet hid her face.

'Was she being sick or had she been sick? I don't ask you this in order to tell Mrs Parry. I ask you because I want to know what happened to Miss Hexham. First I need to know the circumstances in which she left the house.'

'Sometimes,' Bessie mumbled so quietly I could barely catch the word.

'Sometimes she had been sick?'

'Yes, miss. I helped her clear it up. I managed to get it done without Mrs Simms knowing, or Wilkins or Ellis.'

'You must have liked Miss Hexham, to have helped her so and to have kept her secret.'

'I did like her!' said Bessie with sudden energy. 'She was a nice lady. I hoped that when she went off she was going to get married. I was that upset when I heard she was dead.'

'Tell me,' I invited. 'Tell me about Miss Hexham leaving to get married.'

There was another mumble in which I only distinguished the word, 'Can't!'

'Why not, Bessie? You wouldn't be betraying her. She is dead now. You only betray her memory if you refuse to help catch the man who did that to her.'

Bessie looked up, her small face furious. 'I hope they do catch him and they scrag him!' She put her hands round her thin neck and made a movement of an upward and sideways jerk, afterwards letting her head loll sideways in a realistic mime of a man on the gallows. The bonnet fell to the back of her head and was held there at the nape of her neck by its ribbons.

'Well, then,' I encouraged her. 'If you would see justice done by her, tell me what you know about that day when she disappeared.'

I thought Bessie wanted to tell me but there was still some matter troubling her. She pulled the bonnet back to its rightful position and said nothing.

I went on, 'I am a doctor's daughter, Bessie. I lived in a small town. I knew very well what went on. Miss Hexham was expecting a child, was she not?'

'It was beginning to show,' Bessie said abruptly. 'Her dresses were getting tight round the waist and her face was a bit puffy. I'd go in her room – your room now, miss – and there she'd be with her head over the basin, brought up everything and was just retching with nothing more to lose, and crying. I was so sorry for her. I tried to help by clearing it all away, like I told you. But I knew she would have to go to Mrs Parry soon. Besides, there were others. Wilkins and Ellis, they gossip terrible and are awful ones for knowing everyone's business. And nothing, not nothing, gets past Mrs Simms!'

Bessie and I walked on a little. I said nothing.

Bessie had decided to tell it all and would do so in her own way.

'I was afraid what she was going to do,' she said now very quietly. She cast a sly glance up at me from beneath the brim of her bonnet. 'You being a doctor's daughter and that, you know what I mean, most likely.'

'I think I do,' I said.

They did such foolish things, those poor girls, and then my father would be called in to save their lives. They drank all manner of liquids they believed would induce a miscarriage. Generally it did not. Sometimes they went to visit a 'wise woman', some old hag who either sold them herbal 'cures' or did far, far worse. Then the mother often did die from loss of blood or morbidity.

As for the families, they often disowned the girl, and yet they were sometimes also very quick and ingenious to hide the truth. Many a child grew up calling its natural mother 'sister' or 'aunt', and remained unaware of the real relationship until adult – and occasionally even not then. Mary Newling had informed me of such cases in our town, when I was grown up and we peeled vegetables together in our kitchen. She told me willingly, knowing that I observed the same confidentiality my father showed his patients. But I think it was her way of warning me by example and reminding me I had no female relatives to step forward to the rescue.

'Why should they not pretend that the child belongs to a married sister or the grandmother, if the grandam is still young enough to be bearing children?' Mary asked when I expressed my shock. 'It seems natural. Older women sometimes have a late baby. If it means the girl will not lose the chance of marrying a decent young fellow one day, where is the harm?'

She went on to observe, 'This crinoline fashion, it leads to that sort of thing, if you ask me. Who is to see a natural bump under so much false swelling?'

It served to make me wonder just what went on behind the respectable façades of 'decent' homes. It certainly added to the worldly wisdom that I had begun to acquire as a child. Like me, Madeleine had no mother or sister to claim the child as her own and shield her reputation. So Bessie, with her own unchildlike awareness of life's harsh ways, had feared the worst.

'And that is why you hoped, when she left the house that day, that she was going to be married?' I prompted.

'Yes, miss!' said Bessie eagerly. 'And I do believe she was or she thought so, anyway! She was happy. It was the first time I'd seen her smile in weeks. She was waiting for me that morning, when I came with the water. She was all dressed and ready to go out and seemed really excited. "Bessie," she says, "will you help me with a plan I have?" I told her I would, of course. "Well, then," she says, "I want you to keep an eye open for an empty cab going past, if possible a growler. They go slowly because they're hoping a fare will stop them. If you can, run up the basement stair and hail him. Ask him to wait round the corner and a lady will come directly. Only the lady does not wish to be seen." So I did that. I heard a cab coming, really slow. I looked out quick and saw it was a growler. Mrs Simms was busy ordering Wilkins about, and Ellis was upstairs doing the beds. Mr Simms had gone out to the wine merchant. So I slipped up the basement stairwell and run out. Mind you, when I saw the cabbie, I near changed my mind!'

She gave a short bark of laughter and I asked, 'Why was that?'

'He had a face like someone had done a clog dance on it,' said Bessie, 'all squashed and twisted. It'd give anyone a fright, especially if you was to meet him on a dark night.'

I stopped on the spot and Bessie nearly fell over as I grasped her arm.

'What's wrong, miss?' She peered up at me.

'Nothing, nothing at all. I believe I may know the man, the cabbie. What did he say to you, when you told him what was wanted?'

'I told him to wait round the corner for a lady, like Miss Hexham asked. Then the cabbie, he says, "Ho! Like that is it? And where am I to take this lady?" I said, that the lady would tell him herself. "How do I know," he says, "that I won't be getting into trouble?" How can you get into trouble, I asked him, just taking a fare? It's not your business what the fare gets up to, is it? You're just the cabbie. Anyway, I said to him, by the looks of you, you've had trouble enough yourself! I said that to let him know I wouldn't stand any of his lip. He pointed at his squashed mug and he said, "I wear these scars as a badge of honour. I come by 'em fair and square in the prize ring."'

Bessie snorted. 'I never heard of anything being fair and square in the prize ring. But I wasn't going to spend more time with him in case Mrs Simms came back. I made sure he'd do as I asked, and I ran inside to tell Miss Hexham. She came running with her bonnet and shawl and off down the street to where the cab was waiting and that was the last I saw of her.'

Her voice broke on the last words and she snuffled. I handed her my handkerchief. She said, 'Thank you, miss,' and blew her nose.

'Come along!' I said to her briskly. 'We must put our best foot forward. We have not so much time. We can't waste a moment.'

'Where are we going?' Bessie asked as we hastened along.

'Why, to King's Cross cabstand. I believe it is this way, or do you know a quicker? I know the cabman you spoke of. We must find him. I do hope he returns to the stand and he remembers Miss Hexham and where he took her!'

Bessie thought she did know a quicker way, if I would but trust her and not take fright. She plunged ahead of me into a maze of narrow streets in which I had soon lost all sense of direction and my chief fear was that I would also lose my guide. Here houses crowded one upon another and small businesses of all kinds pressed their wares on passers-by from displays set out in the street itself. Rolls of cheap cloth gave way to woven baskets and racks of umbrellas, kitchen pots and pans and sacks of rice and tapioca. From the butchers' shops issued the sickly odour of dried blood and dead flesh, and the buzzing of clouds of flies. Other shops traded in live animals, canaries in tiny cages and fancy mice, barely weaned puppies huddled in a pathetic tangle and goldfish in murky bowls of water. Three balls hanging from a metal arm above a door signified a pawnbroker who lurked, like a spider in the centre of its web, in the darkness behind. Here were shops which not only sold but bought: old clothes, jewellery, books and household goods so dented and battered and well used that it was a puzzle to know who would want them.

'You can't buy new if you're poor!' replied Bessie to my innocently expressed observation.

People of all descriptions pushed their way back and forth. Voices filled the air; some speaking tongues which were foreign to me, some speaking an English so guttural and distorted it might as well have been an alien language. Mangy dogs and scrawny children swarmed around us. We skipped over or bent our paths to avoid puddles of dubious origins. From time to time we passed a public house from which came a stench of beer and tobacco; unshaven men and slatternly women sat slumped on benches before the doors, pints of ale before them, and small children crawled in the dirt at their feet with the inevitable flea-bitten mongrels.

I was glad when we left these by-ways to re-emerge into the main roads although the crush there was scarcely less, even if it was better dressed. As on the day I'd arrived I was amazed by the hurly-burly and the sheer number of vehicles of all kinds which rattled by us. I knew we must be near the site of the Agar Town demolition work because, among all the others, the familiar wagonloads of debris rumbled past, filling our nostrils with brick dust.

We had drawn level with an organ-grinder, a tattered individual accompanied by a sad little shrivelled monkey in a red jacket. Suddenly Bessie stopped and pointed ahead of us. 'Look, miss, it's the reverend gentleman!'

The monkey had been taught to react to passers-by who slowed their step or halted. It hopped forward holding in its tiny paws a little cloth-covered beaker. The expression in its eyes was the most mournful I had ever seen in any animal's. I did not like the look of the musician and liked his discordant playing even less, but I could not refuse the monkey. That, of course, was the purpose of the poor beast's use. So I searched for a penny as I tried to follow the direction of Bessie's pointing finger at the same time.

I dropped the penny in the beaker and the monkey leapt up on to the barrel-organ. The man had stopped playing and removed the penny, putting it in his pocket before picking up the little animal by the back of the red jacket and dropping it carelessly down to the ground.

I wanted to advise him to use the creature more gently, though it would have done little use. But just then I saw the object of Bessie's interest. A little way ahead of us a tall and stately form in a black frock coat, with silvery grey hair falling from beneath his hat brim to his collar, proceeded through the mob with the confident ease with which the Israelites must have crossed the Red Sea. As the crowd parted before him and re-formed behind, he simply swung his walking stick to encourage a small boy or dog out of his path, but might otherwise have been proceeding down an empty street. Even from the rear it was impossible to mistake him.

'Why, it's Dr Tibbett!' I exclaimed.

As I spoke I saw, coming towards us and Dr Tibbett ahead of us, two young women. They were well dressed, if in gaudy colours, and as they progressed they chatted animatedly together, putting me in mind of a pair of parakeets. Neither was more than nineteen years of age and both, although ostensibly engaged in what the other was saying, kept a weather eye open for any single man whose attention they were adept at engaging. At the same time, though they leaned their pretty heads close together, their smiles appeared directed towards these chance encounters.

I had already noticed, on our progress so far, that London's streets seemed well supplied with women of this sort. In the poorer streets they had been scruffier and more brazen; here they attempted a certain style. Dr

Tibbett must have noticed them. They were almost level with him. Then, to my surprise, all three stopped and some conversation between them began. Having heard his oft-expressed opinion of moral laxity, especially where young persons were concerned, I wondered what he was saying. Upbraiding them, perhaps? Begging them to reform? But no, the young women's smiles were broader than ever and any attempt to pretend they were not meant for the gentleman abandoned. A discussion was taking place. I took Bessie's shoulder and guided her into a shop doorway from where we might watch unobserved. I did not think Dr Tibbett would be pleased to see either of us.

An agreement was reached. Dr Tibbett turned to raise his walking stick and hail an approaching growler. He handed one of the young women up into it, first speaking briefly to the driver, who nodded. Tibbett hopped up into the growler in quite a sprightly manner; the driver shook the reins and the horse and cab clip-clopped towards us bearing its two passengers.

'Look at that!' said Bessie beside me in some admiration. 'The reverend gentleman is going off with a ladybird!'

As she spoke, the growler rumbled past us and I just glimpsed, through its window, the ladybird in question lean forward and affectionately pinch the whiskered cheek of her companion. It may have been her normal action but it struck me as having something of a return welcome about it, as if this was an old and valued friend (and customer).

They had disappeared from sight. I was unable to restrain myself and burst out furiously, 'The miserable old hypocrite!'

'It's all right, miss,' soothed Bessie. 'It's what gentlemen do, isn't it?'

An image flashed into my head at her words: that of Frank Carterton on the first night I had spent in London, leaving the house late after his aunt and I had retired, swinging his silver-topped cane and stepping out cheerfully. At the same moment the barrel-organ started up again, its sudden cacophony of tinny sounds seeming to mock me.

I thrust aside the image, and the sound of the music, and was recalled to where I was and with whom. I was also aware that the shopkeeper had observed us lurking in his doorway and was about to descend and urge us to come in and inspect the wares.

'Bessie!' I said firmly. 'You must on no account speak of seeing Dr Tibbett today, ever! Do you understand me? You must not tell anyone below stairs or any friend you may have. It is most important.'

'That's all right,' said Bessie, unperturbed. 'I won't say anything. Mrs Simms thinks the reverend gentleman is a walking miracle and if I was to say a word she'd beat me round the head with a soup ladle.'

The other young woman had reached us but we were of no interest to her and she strolled on. Viewed closer to hand I could see, despite her years and prettiness, there was a hardness to her features and eyes which betrayed a young spirit both corrupted and crushed. I felt a great sadness on her behalf, wondering at what tender age she had been introduced to such a life and what possible future, if any, she had.

We carried on, the jingle-jangle of the barrel-organ fading in our ears. At last we reached our destination. Here the traffic seemed even more frantic, if that were possible. Cabs and private carriages arrived and decanted passengers of both sexes and all ages, boxes, portmanteaux and the occasional pet dog. Porters ran from inside the station to capture the new business. Other passengers accompanied by laden porters staggered out of the station and stood in bewilderment gazing at the scene before them as I had done. Around them wandered the customary idlers: louche young men and yet more women, sisters to the pair to whom Tibbett had spoken; beggars and ragamuffin children.

'You watch out for your purse, miss!' ordered Bessie. 'There will be any number of dips working this place.'

But I was scanning the cab rank. 'Keep your eyes open, Bessie, and if you see the cabbie who took Miss Hexham that day, tell me immediately before he takes another fare and we lose him!'

I was afraid we would have a long wait or even be unsuccessful, for there was no guarantee that Mr Slater would return. He might be hailed en route and find business a-plenty to keep him away. After twenty minutes I began to think I had brought us both on a fool's errand.

I was gaining some strange looks. One or two men smiled at me and one tipped his hat and bid me 'Good morning, my dear.' At this my small duenna piped up with a fierce, 'Here! Don't you go calling my lady your dear, which she ain't nor likely to be!'

Eventually one of the cabmen approached and asked if I wanted a cab. I told him no, but that I hoped to see Wally Slater.

He turned and called to his colleagues: 'Anyone seen Wally out and about?'

'I passed him in Oxford Street,' called back one.

'Anyone who sees him, tell him there's a young female waiting here for him, along with a little girl!'

This well-meant instruction might only serve to confuse Wally, I thought, and make him stay away.

We waited for another ten minutes and I began to be worried that time was not in our favour. I could not keep Bessie from her duties in the kitchen for too long or I should not be able to ask for her to come with me again. Besides, Mrs Parry would be rising and getting ready for the first event of her day: the light luncheon. She would be surprised not to see me there. But if I found Wally, then I must persuade him to come with me to Scotland Yard. That would take more time and, I suspected, a good deal of effort.

At that moment a nearby cabman called out to me. 'Here comes Wally now!'

Sure enough, a familiar growler and horse were coming

our way. Bessie left my side and ran towards it waving her hands. The horse threw up its head and snorted. On the driver's perch, Wally hauled on the reins and looked down at the bobbing bonnet by his feet.

'What's all this, then?' he enquired.

'Miss Martin wants to speak to you!' Bessie shouted up at him.

'Oh? Does she now? And who might she be and where might she be, then?' he enquired.

I hurried to join them. 'I'm Miss Martin. Oh, Mr Slater, do you remember me? Do say you do!'

'Ah,' said the cabbie, tilting his hat to the back of his head. 'Now, how could I forget you? You're the young lady what has a peculiar interest in the deceased.'

He hitched the reins and clambered down to join us.

'Now then, what's happened, eh?' He looked from one to the other of us. 'What's it all about?'

'You did say, Mr Slater, that if I needed help, I should seek you out,' I reminded him.

'I did say so,' said the cabbie. 'And I'm a man of my word. You may ask anyone here . . .' His meaty paw swept through the air to indicate his fellow cabmen. 'Wally Slater is a man of his word.'

'Mr Slater,' I began, 'you took me to that address in Dorset Square, you do remember the house?'

He sucked his yellowed teeth and observed, 'I might. Not but what I drive a lot of fares to a lot of houses. Not all in Dorset Square maybe.'

'When I gave you that address, here at the station,' I went on, 'you didn't remark on it apart from saying it was very nice. But when we got there, I believe you recognised the house because you asked me again, was it the right one? I thought it was only your manner of speaking at the time, but it wasn't, was it? You remembered the house and it was after that you offered your help, should I need it.'

'It may be,' said Mr Slater. 'I ain't saying it is, but it may be. What's gone wrong, then?'

The horse tossed its head up and down and snickered.

'Just a moment,' said the cabman. He went to the rear of the growler and unhooked a nosebag which he took to the horse and hitched over its head. I had been in London long enough to notice that, compared with some of the horses drawing other growlers, Wally's horse appeared well cared for. I had seen some sad sights of poor overworked beasts stumbling along, hardly able to haul their load, although horses hitched to the hansom cabs, on the other hand, appeared of better type and better turned out.

'Since it seems we're taking a rest, the 'orse might as well 'ave his dinner. I don't say I wouldn't mind mine,' he observed.

'Mr Slater, I will buy you dinner, if you will only listen!' I begged. I pushed Bessie forward. 'Do you remember this young girl?'

'Oh, I don't know about that,' said the cabman promptly. 'I can't be remembering scraps of little 'uns like her. Ten to a penny, her sort.'

'Yus, you do!' snapped my valiant little companion. 'You remember me. I see it in your face. I remember your face, all right. There ain't another like it.'

The cabbie stared down at her. 'Like as not, there isn't. This face is a record of my career in the prize ring.'

'You told me that before and all. I asked you to wait round the corner for a young lady,' said Bessie. 'And you did, didn't you? Don't go saying you don't remember.'

'Hush, Bessie,' I ordered because I feared her peremptory tone might upset the man. 'Mr Slater, that young lady was my predecessor as companion to the lady of that house and she is now dead. I mean the young lady is dead.'

Mr Slater solemnly removed his hat and held it against his broad chest. 'I am sorry to hear it, miss. God rest her soul.' He glanced piously skywards and replaced the hat on his head.

'Do you remember, as we drove to Dorset Square, we passed by several wagons taking rubble from the Agar Town site for the new railway terminus? One of the wagons carried a dead body found there. That body, Mr Slater, was of the young lady in question.'

Mr Slater blinked and observed, 'Lord, lumme. Are you sure about that, miss?'

'I am more than certain, Mr Slater. I wish it were not so, but it is. Do you see why it is so important that you try and remember where you drove her to that day? Please say you remember!'

There was a silence broken only by the horse chomping

221

its feed. Behind us cabs clattered past and the drivers whistled.

'Murder,' said the cabman at last with a thoughtful air. 'I'm not getting involved in any murder.' He shook his head.

'Mr Slater, I put to you, it is your duty as an honest man, which I believe you to be, to help. Please help us, if for no other reason than that I now live in that house.'

'Miss Martin,' said Wally earnestly. 'Believe me, I wish you safe and sound. I do remember that young lady and very uneasy I was about that fare, I can tell you. But my advice to you would be, leave the house and find a situation elsewhere. There, that's good advice that is. Take it.'

'I want to know how she died!' I said firmly.

'I dare say you do,' he returned, 'what with your interest in corpses and such.'

'I am interested in justice, Mr Slater, justice for those who cannot obtain it for themselves.'

'Ah,' said Mr Slater. 'That sounds your mark, that does. And how are you going to do it, then? Get justice for the poor young lady?'

'By going directly, all three of us, to Scotland Yard and telling Inspector Ross there the whole story. He is in charge of the investigation.'

'No!' said Wally immediately. 'I'm not going near no police station, much less Scotland Yard. The police is all very well in their way, but they give no end of trouble to an honest cabbie. They are always accusing cabmen of passing bad coin. I don't say I never had bad coin passed to *me*, mind you! But I myself, Walter Slater, cabman of Kentish Town, have never knowingly passed a bad sovereign nor a dud sixpence and so help me Gawd. But I have been accused of it, more than once I have! Accused by wet-eared lads in blue uniforms, nowadays wearing them silly helmets. When they wore proper hats it was bad enough; but to be made to listen to a lot of nonsense from a fellow with a flowerpot on his head, that's the last straw.'

'I am very sorry, Mr Slater, if you have recently had some – some contretemps with the law, but please, that should not affect this matter!' I begged.

'Contretemps, is it?' he repeated thoughtfully. '*Con-tree-tomp* . . . that's a very fine word and I'm obliged to you for it. But I'm not going to Scotland Yard with you. I beg your pardon, but there it is. I can't oblige you in that. I have a reputation to keep up. Hobnobbing with peelers won't do it any good.'

I gazed at him in despair because he sounded so adamant. But I had reckoned without Bessie, who had been listening intently and now jumped between us. She reached up and grasped the cabbie by the lapels of his greatcoat.

'Oh, can't you oblige Miss Martin? Well then, I, Bessie Newman, kitchen maid of Dorset Square, will be obliged to go with my lady to Scotland Yard without you. Once we're there, I'll tell my story to the inspector AND I'll tell him that we asked you to come and you wouldn't. That's obstructing an inquiry, that is. That'll cost you your cabman's licence, Mr Wally Slater of Kentish Town, so there!'

'Oh, Bessie . . .' I exclaimed, trying to silence her in vain. 'Please believe me, Mr Slater, I would not do that to you.'

'No,' said Bessie, 'Miss Martin wouldn't. But I would. So what are you going to do?'

Slater heaved a deep sigh and looked at us both, first me, then Bessie, and then back to me. 'Well, it looks like I'm driving you to Scotland Yard, don't it? I'll never live it down,' he added mournfully with a furtive glance across to his colleagues at the cabstand. 'Don't you go telling any of them fellers now, will you?'

I took his callused paw and exclaimed, 'Oh, thank you!' at which he turned beetroot red.

'You're a rare one,' he mumbled. 'I said it before and I say it again.'

He then turned a ferocious stare on Bessie.

'As for you,' he said, 'you are going to make some poor devil a hard-working, reliable wife some day, and whoever he may be, he has my sympathy.'

Chapter Eleven

'WHAT? ALL of you? All at once?' demanded the sergeant at the desk.

'Yes, please,' I said firmly. 'To see Inspector Ross if he is here.'

It had occurred to me as we rumbled towards our destination that the inspector might not be there and it would be far more difficult to explain ourselves to some other officer. But I did not think I would be able to persuade Wally Slater to return to Scotland Yard if this visit failed. I held my breath.

'He's not long come back,' admitted the sergeant unwillingly. 'He did go in to see the superintendent but I fancy he's back in his own office now. I'll go and ask him if he'll see one of you.' His eye travelled over us, lingered doubtfully on Wally, dismissed Bessie and returned to me. 'You, ma'am, perhaps?'

'All of us!' I repeated. 'Please tell the inspector it is Miss Martin and I have brought with me a member of the domestic staff from Dorset Square – and another witness.'

'I'll tell him,' said the sergeant, 'but I hope you are not here to waste his time. May I know the nature of your business, ma'am?'

'I've just told you, I have come from Dorset Square – from the house where Miss Hexham lived, the murder victim.'

'Ah, that one,' said the sergeant rubbing his chin. 'Just wait a bit, will you?'

Wally had been shuffling his feet and glancing nervously around him during this conversation. Had it gone on much longer, I think he would have cut and run. As for Bessie, she was now in high good spirits. She had enjoyed the cab ride, sitting bolt upright on the seat with her feet stuck out in front of her and peering eagerly from the window. I wondered where Ross had been that he had just 'come back'. Perhaps to Agar Town?

The sergeant returned and said the inspector would see us. We followed him up some stairs and through an anteroom office in which a pink-faced young constable with his left wrist bandaged sat scribbling at a desk. Eventually we were ushered into Inspector Ross's presence.

He had risen from his desk to come and greet us and looked understandably startled at the sight of us. We lined up in front of him in descending order of height: Wally, then me and finally Bessie. It occurred to me we resembled the three bears of childhood story fame.

'Thank you,' I said to him, 'for agreeing to see us. I

would not have bothered you but I believe it very important.'

'I'm sure you would not have come on any trivial matter, Miss Martin,' he replied. He looked around him and pulled forward the one free chair. 'Please sit down.'

I sat down. Wally took up a position behind me, putting an obstacle between himself and the inspector, and Bessie stood protectively beside me. A photographer could not have arranged us better.

'You are lucky to find me here,' he went on. 'I have just come from Dorset Square.'

'From our house?' demanded Bessie.

Ross assessed her gravely and replied, 'No, I called upon another resident of Dorset Square.'

'It wasn't Mrs Belling, was it?' I asked. 'We met her son James as we left home.'

Ross raised his eyebrows. 'Indeed? The gentleman was in attendance on his mamma when I called there.'

I frowned as the import of his words struck me. James had returned to his mother's house by the time Ross had arrived there. He could scarcely have had time after speaking to me to do more than walk round the block!

Another idea occurred to me and I didn't like it. Had James Belling seen me leave Mrs Parry's house opposite with Bessie and hurried down to the square to engineer a 'chance' meeting? The play with the pocket watch and the hurried air had been just that: a piece of theatre. Having spoken to me he had walked only a block or so and then returned, in time for Ross's arrival. I calculated that Ross must have been at the Bellings' about the time I was waiting at King's Cross for Wally Slater.

'Ah, yes, Mr James Belling,' said Ross. 'He has an interest in fossils.'

Ross was also looking thoughtful as if mentally composing a timetable of Mr Belling's movements that morning. I recalled Frank had spoken of James Belling's interest in fossils but I couldn't imagine what had brought up the subject during Ross's visit on police business. The inspector did not oblige by explaining so I was left in the dark.

Ross was also still in the dark with regard to our joint visit. 'Well,' he urged, still looking bemusedly at our group. 'What may I do for you?'

'We shall begin with Bessie Newman,' I said hastily, indicating my small companion who was occupying the time with a thorough study of her surroundings. 'And the day on which Madeleine Hexham left the house in Dorset Square never to be seen alive again. Bessie is the kitchen maid. Tell the inspector what happened that morning, Bessie.'

Bessie obliged, taking the story to the point where Madeleine hurried away to find Wally's cab.

When she fell silent, I felt I should give a word of explanation. 'Bessie would have told the constable this, the one who came to the house to talk to the staff. But she was worried for Miss Hexham's reputation and also that she would be in trouble with Mrs Parry for having facilitated Miss Hexham's secret departure. Bessie is an orphan and Dorset Square the only home she has.'

'I quite understand,' said Ross gravely.

'So now Mr Slater will tell you what happened next. He has not told me so I know no more than you,' I added.

Ross looked enquiringly at the cabman.

Wally cleared his throat and drew himself up. 'I'm here because the young lady brought me. The young lady there is a rare one and you should know it.'

'I think I do know it,' said Ross unexpectedly. 'But who are you?'

'Walter Slater, licensed hackney carriage driver, of Kentish Town,' the cabman introduced himself hoarsely. 'I'm an honest man. But one who has been unjustly accused by the police on more than one occasion of passing bad coin. I have never done such a thing and I want it put on record.'

'Has this to do with Miss Hexham?' asked Ross.

Wally scowled at him. 'No, it's on my own account.'

'I am not interested in whether or not you passed bad coin,' Ross said tersely. 'I am investigating a murder. Get on with it, will you?'

'All right, keep your hair on,' advised Wally. 'Now, as you'll know, a licensed cabbie is required to take a fare. That's the law. Of course, should the fare be roaring drunk and abusive or suffering some dreadful disease, I might have cause to refuse. But the young lady on the day in question was none of these. I was therefore required to take her where she wanted to go, even though it seemed rum to me.'

He paused but as none of us spoke and Ross merely gestured with his hand as a sign to continue, Wally went on, 'She was a nice young lady, very well turned out and neat.'

Here Ross did speak to ask, 'Do you remember her clothing in any detail? The colour of her dress or shawl?'

'Do I look,' returned Wally, 'like a man what studies fashion plates of ladies' dresses? She was very tidy, that's all I know.' He frowned. 'Her skirt may have been some striped material. Don't ask me what colour, blue or pink or something. I'm a cabbie and what I remember is where people ask to be took. "To St Luke's Church," she says. "In Agar Town, if you know it." I told her, I knew it well enough, but was she sure that was the church she wanted? Because it was to be pulled down and, to my way of thinking, there might not be any services held there any more. But she would have it she wanted to be taken to St Luke's. So that's where we went. I wasn't easy in my mind, not just because Agar Town isn't the kind of place I'd have expected her to want to go, but because of the way I'd been asked to wait round the corner. I mean, I've been asked it before, but it's generally meant a *rendy-voo* of a romantic nature. Why should she go creeping out of the house just to go to church?'

'And did you take her there?' asked Ross.

'I did. When we arrived I said to her again that it didn't

look to me as if there was any service going to be held there. There was no one else about, not a living soul, just a churchyard full of dead ones.'

'There were no workmen there? No one pulling down any houses?' Ross asked.

Wally shook his head. 'They hadn't got that far then. They were just starting to clear the area for the railway terminus and goods yards but some distance off and that bit by the church wasn't touched. They hadn't managed to find a way to get over or under or round the graves, as I heard, so I suppose they left it until they thought one up. Anyway, she says to me, "I want to visit a grave!" Now then!' Wally shook a large and distorted finger at us. The knuckles of his hand appeared to have suffered greatly and were much scarred.

'I reckon she said that to put me off. People who visit graves generally take flowers. At least they look a bit mournful, sob a bit even if they're only putting it on, and she didn't. She looked pretty pleased with herself, if you ask me! So I asked her, if she was visiting a grave, did she want me to wait? Because I didn't like leaving her there all alone. But she said no, she would be some little while. "You will not get another cab, miss," I said to her. "Not here in Agar Town. You will have to walk some way towards the main streets." It did no good; she just told me everything was arranged. So what could I do but believe her?' A note of appeal entered the cabman's voice. 'I didn't know I was leaving her to be murdered.'

'Of course you did not, Mr Slater,' I said.

'No, I don't suppose you did,' said Ross.

'The murderer was waiting for her,' opined Bessie. 'I reckon he was waiting for her hid behind one of them gravestones or monuments. I hope they hang him.'

'They don't much hang anyone for anything these days,' remarked Wally. 'They'd string you up for nothing until a few years ago. My late grandfather was a cabman. We're a family of cabmen. After I quit the prize ring at the request of the lady what is now Mrs Slater, I returned to the business. Not that I regret it, mind, for all being a cabbie and out in all weathers is no great pleasure. But then, to be honest, neither is getting your head knocked in. Although as a fighter you get to mix with some real swells and the purse money can be very good and to hear the crowd cheer you on is something special. But as I was saying, in his day, my grandfather's day, honest cabmen what had done nothing more than pass a bad coin in all innocence . . .'

Here he became aware that everyone else was showing signs of impatience. Ross in particular looked as if he was wondering if there was some offence with which he could charge Wally.

'Times change, that's all,' the cabman finished.

Ross got to his feet and went to the door. He called into the outer office, 'Biddle! Come and take care of these people, would you?'

'Here!' demanded Bessie in alarm, 'are we being arrested?'

'No, no, Miss Newman!' Ross soothed her. 'But you will be asked to repeat your stories for Constable Biddle here who will write it all down and then you will be asked to sign it. Can you write your name?'

Bessie, who had been looking much pleased at being called 'Miss Newman', reverted to her normal combative self. 'Of course I can! They taught us reading and writing at the orphanage.'

The constable with the bandaged wrist had entered the room and could be seen to be limping.

Bessie looked him up and down. 'You've been in the wars, haven't you?' she observed.

'Statements, Biddle!' ordered Ross crisply. 'From Mr Slater and Miss Newman. Not you, Miss Martin. Perhaps you'd wait a moment?'

My companions left the room and Constable Biddle closed the door. Ross heaved a sigh.

'Would you care for tea, Miss Martin? I dare say some can be procured. I should have asked you before.'

I thanked him but refused. 'I can't stay much longer. I must get back to Dorset Square and take Bessie with me, or there will be so many questions asked it will not be possible to find answers to them all.'

At this Ross permitted himself a brief smile. 'I have confidence in your ingenuity, Miss Martin.'

He returned to his chair and sat down with his hands resting on the wooden arms. 'Well,' he said, 'you seem to have been making rather better progress in this matter than I have. I, too, have a great many questions to which I haven't yet found answers.'

'It was chance,' I told him, 'that I was able to recognise the cabman from Bessie's description.' I hesitated a little before plunging on, 'Madeleine Hexham was with child, wasn't she? You did not mention this when you came to tell Mrs Parry of her death, but Bessie took hot water to her room every morning and several times found her very ill and vomiting.'

Ross contemplated me for a moment then replied quietly, 'Yes, she was almost four months gone with child, possibly the reason she was murdered. However, I am not keen to see the information passed around at the moment. It is difficult enough to get any one to talk about her. If they knew of her condition I dare say they would refuse completely. We – I am dealing with highly respectable people here. I must tread carefully lest I offend their sensibilities.'

I thought of Dr Tibbett departing merrily with his ladybird at his side, but only said, 'I understand that and no one will learn of it from me nor yet from Bessie.'

'Tell me, Lizzie Martin,' he said suddenly and I looked up in surprise. He was smiling but the smile did not reach his dark eyes. 'Tell me what you think of this matter.'

'What I think?' I faltered. 'I only think her murderer should be brought to justice.'

'You are like your father,' he said. 'You wish to protect the weak. Sometimes, in so doing, one risks upsetting the powerful.'

'My father never let that stop him and I hope neither should I.'

'Forgive me, but your father was a man and one of some importance in his community. Everyone needs a doctor sooner or later. Even if he has offended you, you still take care not to fall out with him too much. Your situation, if you will excuse me pointing it out, would seem to be very different. You cannot afford enemies.'

'I am a woman and alone, but I know my duty,' I said quietly. After a moment I added, 'That sounds quite horribly priggish. Let's just say, I cannot let poor Madeleine Hexham's memory be washed away like a stain on a carpet. It isn't right.'

'Very well then!' Ross said briskly. 'Let us put our heads together and see what we can do. Tell me, what do you think happened to her? I cannot put myself into the head of a young woman, so I ask you. Why did she leave the house that morning in secrecy and why ask to be taken to a deserted church?'

I had been working out my theory of that since listening to Wally Slater's evidence. I leaned forward and began earnestly, 'Mr Slater is both observant and shrewd. He has a comical way of expressing himself sometimes and tends to run on somewhat, but that does not mean what he says is not serious. He warned me when he took me to Dorset Square that I might need a friend. He had already guessed that some mischief was afoot and was connected with that house. What I think is this: Madeleine was seduced by some man of good standing who would not or could not marry her. He persuaded her to keep their affair secret. That could easily be done. He might have said, for example, that he had to persuade an elderly relative, of whom he had expectations, that a marriage to a penniless girl was acceptable. He might have told her Mrs Parry did not approve of him and would deny Madeleine any opportunity for them to meet. Whatever it was he told her, she believed it.'

Ross was nodding but said nothing, only watched my face closely as I spoke.

'I don't know,' I said, 'but I am guessing when Madeleine told him of her condition he agreed they should be married but in secrecy. Bessie told me that on the morning she left the house Madeleine was happy. It was the first time she had been so in weeks. Mr Slater also saw that she was optimistic and had no fears about being left alone at St Luke's church. She told him it was because everything was "arranged". I believe that her seducer had persuaded her he had obtained a special licence for their marriage. I think he suggested that, in order to avoid it becoming known, their marriage should take place somewhere very private. St Luke's was already as good as abandoned. But he told her he had persuaded or bribed a parson to come there and marry the two of them. Who would see the ceremony? Even the navvies working on the site were not in that vicinity.'

'The marriage would require two witnesses,' Ross interpolated.

'Then he told her he had two good friends who were utterly reliable and whose discretion was absolute. She was in love with him. She believed everything he told her. I don't think she was a very intelligent girl. I do know she had a romantic heart because I believe she read a great many novels about love affairs and elopements and so forth.'

'Who told you that?' asked Ross softly.

'Why, Frank, Frank Carterton did. Frank and I think it possible she met this man at a circulating library. She frequented such libraries. Well, let's see, where was I?'

'Miss Hexham went to St Luke's to be married, or so she believed,' Ross prompted.

I realised at this point that I had come to the end of my conjectures. 'I don't know what happened next,' I said. 'I fully realise I cannot prove any of it.'

'You know she was missing some two months but had only been dead two weeks or less,' Ross said.

In some ways that was the worst knowledge of all and I said, 'It does not bear thinking of. He kept her prisoner. He was afraid to let her go. In the end he killed her. I think he had left himself with nothing else he felt he could do.'

Ross's eyebrows shot up enquiringly. 'He had a choice?'

'No! Of course not! Not morally. But we are not talking of a moral man. We are talking of a monster.'

'Oh, monsters,' said Ross. 'Yes, I have met a monster or two in my time in the police force. I have also met a lot of very frightened people who have done dreadful things out of fear. Murderers are not always born to evil, they are sometimes made.'

'To keep her hidden away for so long?' I countered. 'That to my mind is the action only of someone quite unnatural.'

'Where did he keep her hidden?' asked Ross.

'Why,' I said, 'in one of the condemned houses in Agar Town. Everyone knows of them. Any observer might see where the navvies were working. At night there was no one there and by day the noise from the demolitions was such that who would have heard her cries for help?'

Ross drummed his fingers on the top of his desk. 'If what you say is right – and let us say it more or less tallies with my own thinking – there is still a problem. Why did he not kill her at once? Every day she remained alive there was a possibility she would be found. We must assume he made her his prisoner on that first day when Slater took her to St Luke's church.'

'He had some other plan,' I suggested, 'but it didn't work.' I racked my brains for another explanation and realised belatedly I was chewing my lower lip as I did when I was a child and puzzling over something. 'He first kept her elsewhere?' I suggested. 'He moved her later to Agar Town?'

Ross murmured something but I couldn't catch what it was. More loudly he said, 'Well, I know what I must do next but you, you must go back now to Dorset Square. I will arrange some conveyance for you and Bessie.'

'I'm sure Mr Slater will drive us,' I said, rising to my feet.

He came round his desk to stand before me and said very seriously, 'I am mightily obliged to you, Miss Martin. I am also very concerned for you.'

He certainly looked worried. His forehead was creased in a frown beneath a tumbled lock of black hair. This touch of untidiness brought to mind the boy at the pithead. Perhaps he had not changed so much as I'd first thought.

'Don't worry about me,' I said gently. 'You have troubles enough.'

'And I don't want you to become one of them!' was his unexpected reply. 'Don't misunderstand me, Miss Martin. Of course I am concerned about your welfare for your own sake. But I am concerned as a police officer, too. You must take great care. We are dealing here with a man who has killed once. He probably feels now that he has taken a step along a path from which he cannot turn back. He will, if he finds it necessary, kill again. Do not let anyone see how interested you are in this matter. It would not be prudent.'

He smiled unexpectedly. 'Dr Martin took good care of me,' he said. 'Should I not take good care of his daughter?'

I opened my mouth, swallowed, mumbled something, I have no idea what, and withdrew in a little confusion – but with his warning well lodged in my mind.

Chapter Twelve

WE WERE late returning to Dorset Square, even though Wally Slater drove us there at such a fast clip the growler rocked from side to side and I was more than a little alarmed, although Bessie enjoyed it tremendously.

I sent her scurrying down to the basement and went indoors where I apologised to Simms.

'The mistress is lunching,' Simms informed me. 'Will you go in directly, miss? Or shall I tell her you are here and will join her later?'

'I had better go straight in,' I told him, 'if I don't look too dishevelled.'

Simms studied me thoughtfully from head to toe and observed, 'You have a smut on your chin, miss. It looks very like soot.'

My wait at the railway station had probably left this mark. I wished one of my companions had told me of it before I tackled Inspector Ross! I peered into a convenient mirror and rubbed the offending smudge away. Then I surrendered my bonnet to Simms, straightened my skirts and took myself to the dining room. As I reached the door Simms called after me, 'There is a gentleman lunching with the mistress, Miss Martin.'

I had no time to enquire who it was. It could not be Tibbett, whom I knew to be otherwise engaged, and it ought not to be Frank, toiling or otherwise at the Foreign Office. Anyway, Simms would have said if the man were Mr Carterton.

I opened the door. A lively conversation had evidently been in progress but it broke off immediately the participants realised I had joined them.

Aunt Parry looked up with an animated and flushed face and exclaimed, 'Oh, Elizabeth, there you are!'

I could have sworn she sounded quite disappointed. Had I interrupted a tête-à-tête? I looked with some curiosity at the other person present.

He had pushed back his chair and risen to his feet, his crumpled napkin in his left hand. He was a youngish man with oval-lensed spectacles and a dark blue coat. His straight brown hair was well brushed back from his high forehead and glued in place by a liberal application of some gentleman's hair oil. I thought he had the look of a banker's chief clerk. For his part, he looked surprised and somewhat put out at the sight of me.

'This is Mr Fletcher, Elizabeth.' Mrs Parry gestured at him to sit down again. 'It is only my companion, Miss Martin, Mr Fletcher. Please go on with what you were saying. Elizabeth, do sit down. I will have Simms bring back the chicken.'

'Oh no,' I said. 'I am so sorry to be late but I am not hungry.'

That at least caught Aunt Parry's attention. 'Not hungry? Oh, nonsense. At least have some cold shape.'

This drew my attention to a fawn-coloured mound, the ingredients of which were mainly milk and cornflour with a cupful of strong sweet coffee to lend flavour and possibly an egg or two for substance. I have never been a lover of cold shape of this sort, whatever the flavour.

I had once, as a child, wandered into Mary Newling's kitchen to find her skinning a rabbit. I had been surprised at the ease with which she stripped away the entire furry coat with no more difficulty than one might have taking off a glove. It just sloughed away leaving a brightly shining but not bloody body with all its musculature and sinews displayed. I have never fancied rabbit since and the 'shape' bore an unpleasant resemblance to that small skinned beast. It being surrounded by a garland of green leaves like a funeral wreath did not help matters.

'Thank you,' I said and, in the absence of Simms, helped myself to a small portion.

I was seated opposite Mr Fletcher and Aunt Parry, between us, was at the head of the table. Although she had urged him to continue, he seemed loath to do so and only fidgeted with his napkin, studying me all the while with doubt written all over his face. At last, catching my eye, he blurted, 'Pleased to meet you, Miss Martin.'

'Sir,' I replied politely, or as politely as possible through a mouthful of coffee shape.

'I wasn't aware, ma'am,' Fletcher went on to Aunt Parry with a nervous sideways glance at me, 'that you had engaged a new companion.'

'Oh, Elizabeth is the late Mr Parry's god-daughter,' she explained. 'Her father died not long ago and she was in need of a roof over her head so it suited us both very well that she should come here. We are doing handsomely together, are we not, Elizabeth?'

'You are most kind, Aunt Parry,' I replied.

'Mr Fletcher,' said Aunt Parry, as if suddenly recalling that I should be given some explanation of the visitor's identity, 'represents the Midland Railway Company. He is here on some business.'

'Would you rather I left you, Aunt Parry?' I asked, putting down my spoon. 'I've no wish to intrude on a private business discussion.'

'There's no reason why you shouldn't stay. In fact, you might as well hear this. Go on, Mr Fletcher.' She nodded at him.

I thought Mr Fletcher anything but content to have an unexpected third party present at the conversation but there was nothing he could do about it once she had given her blessing.

He released his grip on his napkin but instead began to fiddle with the silver ring which had held it. 'As I was saying, ma'am, delay causes any number of inconveniences. Costs rise with every working hour lost. The navvies grow restive. They don't like having policemen about the place asking questions.'

'There I sympathise,' said Aunt Parry with some feeling. 'We have had such an experience ourselves, here in this house. Even the servants were quizzed. I found the whole situation extraordinary. It's not the sort of thing to which a respectable householder expects to be subjected. I thought the police existed to keep the lower orders from crime and make sure the better-off were not troubled.'

'What is worse, we are now also getting sightseers,' Fletcher went on, apparently little worried by any inconvenience Aunt Parry might have suffered and completely taken up with that to himself. 'They come in family parties with elderly aunts in tow and demand to be shown the spot where the body was found!' His voice rose plaintively. 'They are dressed in best bib and tucker. They squawk and chatter like a parliament of magpies. Their children swarm over heaps of bricks and beneath the wheels of the wagons at risk to life and limb. I declare that for some it is the best entertainment on offer since the Great Exhibition. It is beyond description.'

'I can't understand what motivates them, but I can well believe they have bothered you,' said Aunt Parry with a sigh. 'They walk up and down before this house, some of them quite respectable-looking people, too. They whisper together and point. It's most disagreeable and quite beyond my comprehension.'

'The British public is by nature ghoulish, ma'am,' observed Fletcher. 'What is worse, far worse, is the press.'

'The press?' asked Aunt Parry, startled. 'But surely the Royal Navy doesn't recruit in that way any longer? My father used to speak of its activities when he was a young curate. They appeared on several occasions in his parish of that time during the French wars and obliged young men to go with them. It was the cause of great distress.'

'No, ma'am, forgive me, you misunderstand. I meant the newspapers. Journalists, ma'am. Sightseers of the common sort can be chased away. To get rid of a journalist is well-nigh impossible. Not only that but they come like the Greeks, bearing gifts, in their case money. Offer a navvy a few shillings and he will remember having seen almost anything you want him to. As I said, ma'am, the public likes to have its blood chilled and journalists pander to its cravings.'

'Disgusting,' said Aunt Parry.

'Quite, ma'am. I am relieved that I have not yet seen a man from *The Times* there, but there has certainly been one from the *Morning Post* which I had previously thought a respectable publication. All the penny dreadfuls have sent their hacks and as for the evening sheets, why, they are the worst of all! Their fellows are desperate to inform the readers of a snippet of news ahead of the next morning's dailies and they are like terriers after a rat!'

'Who would have thought it?' murmured Aunt Parry, a wistful eye resting on the partly demolished coffee shape amid its greenery.

'So, you see, I am almost at my wits' end as to what to do about these investigations being held by the police. I have spoken to the inspector in charge, Ross, and got nowhere. He is a surly, impudent fellow.'

My mouth flew open at this but I managed to shut it again before any protest escaped, not without difficulty. I glared my thoughts at Fletcher across the table instead, although he was intent on Aunt Parry and didn't notice. How dare he speak that way of a hard-working and dedicated police officer? Did poor Ben Ross not have enough obstacles in his path without also having to contend with this pettifogging fellow obsessed with building his railway terminus? Was investigation into the death of an innocent young woman to be hurried over and cleared away in the same way her body had been done, removed from the site with all the other rubble? The inspector is worth any two or three of your kind, Mr Fletcher! I wanted to tell him.

'That is the one!' cried Aunt Parry. 'That is the inspector who called here, was it not that one, Elizabeth? I found his manner brash and ill-suited to the conversation of ladies. He wrote down what I said, every single word of it.'

I seethed with the desire to point out Ross had, in fact, only written down what she remembered as written in Madeleine's letter, but I realised it would be unwise to correct her. So again I swallowed my protest and took out my frustration on my serving of cold shape which I mashed into a horrid mess with my spoon.

Fletcher, encouraged at hearing Mrs Parry had shared his experience of the Law, surged on with his litany of complaint with renewed vigour. 'I have spoken to his superior, Superintendent Dunn, who is nearly as bad. They take no account of our problems or our timetable at all. The work threatens to lag behind; labourers down tools or quit. The directors of the company seem to feel I should be able to do more, but what *can* I do?' His voice rose in despair.

Aunt Parry soothed him with, 'Now, now, Mr Fletcher. In the quite some time that I have known you, I know you to have been dedicated always to your responsibilities.'

'You are too kind, ma'am. But still Ross's constables clamber all over the place and get in everyone's way with their prying and questions. And to no avail, ma'am! Do they think someone among our workforce killed the unfortunate young woman? It is my opinion they have no other leads and so wish it to look as if they are doing something.' Fletcher's tone had been becoming steadily more bitter as he spoke and by the time he finished he sounded like a man announcing the end of the world.

'I do understand,' said Aunt Parry thoughtfully, drumming her plump little fingers on the tablecloth.

'As a shareholder in the company, and as the employer of the deceased,' Fletcher went on, leaning across the table towards her, 'you will naturally want to see things put to rights. You want to see the police concentrate their activities in the proper area, wherever that may be, and the work resume at its normal pace.'

His tone had become confidential. I realised that whatever was to be suggested, Ross wouldn't like it. But I didn't like what I'd already heard. I had pushed aside my now inedible pudding and sat almost unable to believe my ears. Aunt Parry had not only sold houses in Agar Town to the railway company. She was a shareholder in it!

'I am sure,' I ventured now in defence of Scotland Yard's activities, 'Inspector Ross is determined to do things correctly and will leave nothing to chance.'

Fletcher turned his jaundiced gaze on me. 'You are not acquainted with building sites, I think, Miss Martin?'

'Well, no . . .'

'If you were,' Fletcher informed me, 'you wouldn't speak of having police constables roaming all over the place as leaving nothing to chance. One of them has already fallen into an excavation.'

'Was he injured?' asked Aunt Parry.

'Not badly, I understand, ma'am.' Fletcher's tone clearly indicated he meant 'not badly enough'. 'But it is only a matter of time before a lump of brickwork falls on one of them and dashes out his brains.'

'Oh, my goodness!' exclaimed Aunt Parry faintly.

Fletcher leaned forward again to address her in that coaxing tone. 'So, ma'am, any influence you can bring to bear on Scotland Yard to hasten their enquiries and be finished there would be of the greatest assistance to us all.'

'But I don't see how I can influence them,' she protested.

'You were the girl's employer. If you make it clear that you consider everything necessary has been done and you expect no more of the police, well, they would not feel so obliged to keep messing around as they are doing. They wish to prove themselves, ma'am, to the public but above all to you.'

'I will give it some thought,' said Aunt Parry and sounded as if she meant it.

Fletcher obviously decided he had achieved his purpose. He rose to his feet. 'I thank you for an excellent luncheon, ma'am, and now, ladies, I must go back to see what is happening at the workplace.'

'You won't have a little cheese?' asked Aunt Parry, but absently, her mind elsewhere.

'No, ma'am, thank you. Miss Martin!' He gave me a perfunctory nod of the head. 'Dear lady,' he added, turning to Aunt Parry and bowing low.

'Ring for Simms!' Aunt Parry ordered me in the same absent-minded way.

I rose and went to the bell. Simms appeared with his usual alacrity and the visitor left.

I returned to the table but instead of taking my seat again stood behind the chair with my hands resting on the frame. Before me lay the dish bearing what remained of the shape which, in the manner of its species, had collapsed into an unsightly ruin amid its surrounding vegetation and succeeded in looking even worse than before. I thought I might safely abandon my helping. Besides, there was something more important than food and when Mrs Parry heard what I had to say, she would have more to think about than my loss of appetite.

She was staring thoughtfully at the tablecloth. Eventually, in a voice which trembled with emotion, she said, 'If I had had the slightest suspicion of the trouble that would be caused by bringing Madeleine Hexham into this house, she would never have set foot over the doorstep. It seems I am to have no peace while the police continue their investigations.'

'They may conclude them soon,' I pointed out. 'Then both you and Mr Fletcher will be at ease.'

'He may be. I shall not!' retorted Aunt Parry sharply. 'The railway company will see its work resume at a normal pace. But any criminal trial will redouble the number of curious sightseers outside this house. Oh, it's enough to put one out of all patience!'

It wasn't the best moment for my news but it had to be now. It couldn't be delayed further.

'Aunt Parry, there is something I should tell you, and should have told you before. I think I should tell you now, immediately, in view of everything Mr Fletcher was saying.'

She looked mildly surprised and then apprehensive. 'Elizabeth, I hope I am not going to hear you have – have got yourself into any kind of scrape?' Her voice rose to a plaintive wail. 'Is it possible? Surely not? My dear child, you have only been in London a matter of days—'

'Oh no, Aunt Parry, nothing like that!' I hastened to assure her.

'What then?' she demanded resentfully.

I explained, as best I could, that although I had not realised it when he first called, I had some previous acquaintance with Inspector Ross and my father had been his benefactor all those years ago.

'Good heavens!' exclaimed Aunt Parry, who had listened goggle-eyed. She grew thoughtful and her podgy fingers again drummed out that rhythm on the damask cloth. Without warning she turned to me and released on me a smile of devastating goodwill. Before it, I felt myself wilt.

'Dear Elizabeth,' she said, 'what an extraordinary thing and really, what an extraordinary piece of good luck. I am sure the inspector will be sensible of his obligation towards you and your family – and your friends.' I hadn't thought the smile could broaden but it did. It was not reflected in her eyes, however, which were as sharp as a jackdaw's when it has spotted some shiny treasure.

I could only gaze at her in dismay. I had imagined various reactions to my news but not this. She saw my tenuous link with Ross as an advantage to be exploited. I had forgotten Frank telling me she was a businesswoman although seeing her with Fletcher I should have remembered.

'Aunt Parry,' I faltered. 'I can't ask the inspector for – for favours in the matter of his investigations.'

The sharp look had been wiped from her eyes and only benevolence beamed from them. 'Of course not, Elizabeth,' she said hastily. She rose to her feet and patted my arm. 'Of course not. You must not mistake my meaning. But it is always better to have the ear of a friend than to deal with a total stranger, mm?'

Chapter Thirteen

Ben Ross

ON SATURDAY morning Dunn summoned Morris and me to a council of war, or that was what it felt like. I could not rid myself of the notion that we formed part of two battalions of lead soldiers lined up on a playroom table. The Midland Railway Company had hoisted its colours on one side of the divide and Scotland Yard on the other. Between us lay, figuratively but perhaps also physically, the corpse of Madeleine Hexham. The remains of the unfortunate young woman had now been committed to a pauper's grave. There was no one who might be asked to pay for any better interment. In the circumstances, asking Madeleine's employer would have been a waste of time. Her mortal remains might now rest with thieves and vagabonds, but I was determined that her spirit should be better respected. I would find who killed her . . . were I allowed to do so.

'I have another letter from them,' said Dunn, indicating a sheet of paper on his desk with an irritable jab of his stubby forefinger.

I had already made out the official heading of the railway company from where I stood and although I could not read the letter, I could guess what it contained.

'They hope we shall conclude our enquiries at the site of the new terminus very soon. They have just about finished clearing the area and the new building work must begin on schedule. I have to admit that, as a letter, it's not unreasonable. They simply cannot understand why we keep constables at the site bothering, as they see it, their employees. I'm beginning to wonder myself why we do. Have we gained *anything* from our questioning of these labourers?'

Dunn pushed away the company's letter, ran his hand through his brush of hair, and directed a sudden and very direct look at me.

I have always thought that Mrs Dunn must stand at the door every morning and check that her husband left the house with his hair well flattened with the aid of water or hair oil as he generally arrived with it quite neat. It was seldom long before it was disturbed. At the moment it looked like the erect quills of a defensive hedgehog. The impression was heightened by the fact that the superintendent was a burly man with a fondness for tweed suiting which gave him a countrified air.

His question wasn't easy to answer. We had gained as

good as nothing from our enquiries at the Agar Town site. Beside me, I saw from the corner of my eye that Morris was shifting uneasily in his chair. He probably thought the lack of progress would be laid at his door.

'There are many labourers there and few constables,' I said rather feebly and thought at once with annoyance that my words had come out sounding like a misquotation from some sermon. I attempted a brisker tone. 'It takes time. The navvies are not easy to question. They don't like us – the police. They are a mixed bunch. Some are honest workmen, others casual labour employed more or less on a daily basis. Some may have something to hide which has nothing to do with the murder of Madeleine Hexham. Others, I suspect, take a perverse pleasure in thwarting us. Sergeant?'

I turned to Morris who said stolidly, 'Yes, sir, exactly. It's as the inspector says. They are awkward b— they are inclined to be difficult, Mr Dunn.'

'So have you gained any information of use?' Dunn persisted.

'At the site, no,' I confessed. 'But we have gained information of great interest from Miss Martin, from the servant girl she brought with her and the cabman, er, Slater.'

'Ah, yes, that,' said Dunn. 'We have to be grateful to Miss Martin and her efforts on our behalf. Without them, we should have little to show.' He glowered at us both. 'I am not happy at having the only progress in this matter being due to the quick thinking of a lady's companion! We are supposed to be professionals, or so I thought. Come on, Ross! What the dickens are your men doing?'

I thought of Biddle and refrained from replying, 'Falling into holes in the ground.' I said, 'Their best, sir. We are short-handed.'

'Their best ain't good enough!' retorted Dunn bluntly. 'I am afraid that I shall soon have to oblige the railway company and pull men off that site. In view of our lack of progress there, I can hardly refuse. I can stall them for a little longer, but I don't know how long.'

'Let me go back there myself!' I begged. 'I'll go this morning. There is the foreman, Adams. He's a surly fellow but he may know more than he is saying.'

'A downy bird, that one,' offered Morris in a dire tone.

'Downy bird he may be, but if he can't be persuaded to sing – or has nothing to squawk about – we cannot go on questioning him indefinitely. Go down there this morning by all means, but I want some results, Inspector! And I don't want them courtesy of young women. I want them from my officers!'

Morris and I took this as dismissal. Morris got to his feet with alacrity and was out of the door like a hound after a hare. I dragged my feet a little.

'I don't think we are looking for a murderer among the workmen at the site, sir. Whoever killed Miss Hexham, he is what is generally known as a "gentleman".'

I couldn't help the sourness in my voice. I had dealt

with enough so-called gentlemen in the past to lose any general respect for the type. Give me an honest working man any day.

'Hum,' said Dunn. 'I dare say you are right. But that's where the girl's body was found and that, if our thinking is correct, is where she was imprisoned for at least part of the time. Don't tell me no one there saw a damn thing!'

'Yes, that is, no, sir.'

Perhaps like Morris I should get out of the room while the going was good. But I was not to do so without Biddle's invisible presence being evoked.

'What's the matter with that young constable in the outer office? He appears to be a mass of bandages.' Dunn's tone was exasperated.

'Superficial injuries, sir, gained in the pursuit of his duty.'

'Some ruffian knock him down?'

'No, sir. He fell.'

'Fell, *fell*? Can't they stand on their own two feet nowadays? Something wrong with his boots?'

'No, sir, purely an accident.'

Dunn growled and I made good my escape.

The brief foretaste of summer had been replaced by a return of the unsettled weather we had grown accustomed to. Perhaps at this time of year we ought not to expect any other although April and its showers were well behind us. Yet during the previous night there had been quite a heavy downpour. I had lain awake at my lodgings listening to its insistent beat on the window-panes. It had not been the only thing keeping me from slumber. Dunn was right to complain of our lack of progress. Lizzie Martin and her oddly matched companions had been extremely useful, of course. I had smiled to myself in the darkness at the memory of the three of them lined up before my desk.

The sight of Lizzie and her little band had called up other memories of the past. I began, as I lay sleepless, to think about Joe Lee, the other pit boy Dr Martin had taken under his wing and for whose education he had provided. I did not know what had become of Joe and found myself wishing I did. He had been quite a leader of the other boys in the colliery village and I had a vivid image of him leading his troop of ragamuffins through its narrow lanes. Joe had been afraid of nothing, or never showed it. No one liked going down the pit. None of the adult pitmen ever went down without a nagging question at the back of their minds as to whether they would ever come up alive, or at all. Some of the very young boys burst into tears as they walked to the start of their shift thinking what lay ahead of them. But Joe never seemed afraid and whistled cheerfully as we clambered down into the darkness dotted here and there by the guttering pinpoints of light belonging to the candles of the men already working. Because he showed no fear, I would never let myself show any. It was bravado, I suppose, on Joe's part.

The only time I detected any nervousness in Joe was

the day the pair of us, thanks to Dr Martin's generosity, started our studies at the town's ancient grammar school, a place through whose portals we should never normally have passed. I shared his trepidation. The other boys were waiting for us. They knew of our coming and who we were. I suspected the masters had told them of it. We were taunted and pushed about and stood for it as long as we could – which was not long. No one insults a pitman and stays on his own two feet for many minutes afterwards. After we had handed out a fair sprinkling of black eyes and puffed lips to our tormentors, the harrying ceased.

After that we were accepted by the sons of wealthy townsmen in the line of business or the professions who formed the bulk of the other pupils. The masters followed the boys in this. We had no more trouble. On one occasion near the beginning the headmaster accosted us as we left morning prayers and advised us mildly that if we must fight then at least we should try and fight 'like gentlemen'. I never found out what that meant as neither Joe nor I had any pretensions to be or become gentlemen.

I remember my mother weeping the day the doctor came and explained that I should go to school. It was not fear or sorrow but joy which called up her tears. My father had been a collier and it had killed him, not in an accident but from the coal dust which had seeped into his lungs and clogged them. I had been fortunate but I did wish I knew what had happened to Joe.

Morning came and with it the old memories melted

away. Those difficulties were long gone and I faced new ones. It had been an embarrassment to the force to have the only discoveries of any value so far made by members of the public. But, in the end, did not we as detectives depend on the public for our information? I set off for Agar Town after quitting Dunn's office, determined this time to come back with something.

I was quite surprised when I reached my destination. For all of Fletcher's laments that we held up the work, somehow the remaining houses had come down and the bulk of the rubble been carted away. What was left now was a weird blighted tract of man-made desert. The rain had served to clear away the dust but instead a thin layer of mud covered the site, formed puddles on the uneven ground, and soon spattered my boots. I enquired for Adams but only received the reply, 'Not seen him!'

I was thinking over what to do next when I heard my name and turned to see I was being hailed by my bugbear, Fletcher. He was making his way cautiously towards me. I saw as he neared that he had taken the precaution of covering his footwear with rubber galoshes. He carried a furled umbrella as a barrier against further rain showers. If he had not been such an irritant the sight of him would have caused me to smile. He looked for all the world like an elderly lady on her way to church on a wet morning.

'What are you doing here again, Inspector?' he greeted me with scant civility. 'Are you not finished yet?'

'I would be pleased if we had made as much progress as you have!' I retorted, indicating our surroundings.

'I have a timetable!' he said testily. 'I am answerable to those above me if I fall behind.'

I thought of the recent interview in Dunn's office and felt like asking him if he imagined I was answerable to no one. But there was no point in arguing with the fellow. Instead I merely told him I had come in search of Adams but failed to find him.

'Both of us have done that!' snapped Fletcher. 'He has failed to appear for work and sent no word. He was all right yesterday, not sick. It is bad enough when the navvies disappear without warning but to have Adams do it is extremely annoying. It's also very odd since today is Saturday and this afternoon at close of work they are paid their wages. They turn up of a Saturday without fail.'

Something within me, a mental warning bell, sounded a distant but urgent alarm. 'Where does he live?' I asked. 'Can you find it out for me?'

'As it happens,' returned Fletcher, 'I have just consulted the pay clerk's roll to find it out for myself. I intend to send someone to enquire after him. He lives in Limehouse. He has worked for the company for quite some time, since the beginning of this project, and it's not like the man at all to be absent. Were I a betting man, which I am not, I would have put my money on Adams. I am most disappointed. He will be difficult to replace if he has decided to quit. But, like everyone else, I dare say he has been pestered out of all patience by the questions of your constables!'

'Give me the address,' I said tersely. 'I will seek him out. I like his failure to appear for work no more than you.'

Fletcher blinked and stared at me. 'Very well,' he said. 'Then I will come with you myself. Have you a conveyance?'

'No,' I said, 'but we can find a cab.'

'We do not need one,' he said and pointed.

I saw then, at some little distance, a small closed carriage waiting. I was surprised that he had private transport but followed him to the carriage. He gave some instructions to the coachman and we set off.

As we rumbled away from Agar Town, I expressed my curiosity about our vehicle.

'It is not mine!' he said quickly, flushing. 'I am hardly in a position to maintain a private carriage. It has been put at my disposal by one of the major shareholders in the railway company.'

'That is very generous of him,' I observed.

Fletcher's flush deepened. 'I have the honour to be engaged to his daughter,' he said stiffly.

'My congratulations, sir,' I said politely.

He mumbled, 'Yes!' but then turned his head to look out of the window and obviously wished no further conversation.

It occurred to me that Fletcher's prospective father-in-law was probably making life very difficult for him and it was hardly surprising he had responded by harassing the police. The master kicks the valet who kicks the footman who kicks the kitchen boy who kicks the dog. I wasn't sure where, in this order, the police came. I still had no sympathy for the fellow.

Our arrival in Limehouse caused some stir. It is not an area where many private carriages venture. As we progressed at a snail's pace through the busy streets we were soon accompanied by a gaggle of urchins who ran alongside us whistling and shouting. Numerous mongrel dogs joined in and snapped at the horses' hooves. They took exception and the carriage rocked and lurched as they tossed their heads, snorting and bucking in the traces. The coachman's language was fit to turn the air blue.

The lane in which Adams's lodgings were to be found was too narrow to allow our vehicle to pass without completely blocking it so the driver stopped at the top of it to allow us to descend and Fletcher and I continued on our way on foot. In a poor area this street was one of the poorest, all the buildings old and dilapidated, naked of paint or outer plaster. There was a creeping mist swirling about us as the day's sun dried the damp air. A washing line had been strung from one side to the other above our heads and from it dangled a pair of men's woollen combinations which dripped on to the heads of passers-by beneath and probably still wouldn't be dry by the end of the following week. Over all hung a stench compounded of boiling bones, sewage and Thames river mud. The tide must have been going out.

'I don't like this at all,' moaned Fletcher, rolling his eyes as he gazed about him.

'Come, come, Mr Fletcher,' I encouraged him. 'Take heart. You are accompanied by an officer of the law.'

'But do they know it?' he wailed. 'You are not in uniform.'

'You may depend upon it that they know it,' I returned briskly. 'They have an unerring instinct in such matters.'

Our motley array of camp-followers came with us as we made our way down the lane, their ranks growing by the second until the whole narrow thoroughfare was blocked with a surging sea of unwashed humanity: not only the urchins and the dogs that had chased the carriage, together with some new ones, but various idlers with nothing else to do. There was a drunken seaman or two, a crippled beggar who hopped along on his crutch shouting out that he had lost his leg in the service of Queen and Country and would we be so good as to give him a shilling apiece, and a sprinkling of slatternly girls who shouted out invitations to us, couched in the most explicit terms, causing Fletcher to splutter indignant protest. An elderly Chinaman, his sparse hair plaited into a long thin pigtail, completed the array of bystanders. He seemed to believe us some kind of street entertainment and clapped politely. Perhaps he had judged it right, at that. Entertainment we most certainly provided. People came to their doors as we passed and shouted out, 'What's to do?'

'Someone's died!' shouted back one fellow. 'And here's the undertaker!' He pointed at Fletcher whose face contorted in anger.

I must admit it caused me to smile but the smile was soon wiped from my face by another lout who called out, 'Hah, the other one is the law in plain clothes, all done up like a gent! Someone must have tried to rob the Bank of England!'

This witticism was greeted with great merriment and repeated throughout the growing crowd so that by the time it reached the outer fringes of it, people there were informed of it as a fact. The news that an attempt had been made to rob the Bank and the perpetrators were hiding out in Limehouse now generally accepted, it would spread like wildfire and probably appear in that evening's newspapers.

I could see that Fletcher was becoming increasingly nervous and more than regretting his offer to accompany me. The boisterous crowd alarmed him. He grasped his umbrella as he would have done a cudgel.

'We may be robbed; assaulted and stripped of everything we carry. Let us go back!' he begged.

I ignored him and continued. As he feared to forgo the insurance of my company and return to the carriage alone, he was obliged to do the same, whimpering beside me. At last he grabbed my arm, halting us before a cheap lodging house outside of which hung a creaking sign announcing that rooms were available, payment strictly one week in advance, no exceptions.

'Here it is,' panted Fletcher, taking off his silk hat and mopping his brow. 'Inspector, cannot you use your official capacity to disperse the crowd? This is most unpleasant.'

'They wouldn't go,' I said simply. 'And alone I can't make them. Ignore them.'

'That is easier said than done!' he muttered.

I rapped on the door and we waited. Behind us the crowd waited too in anticipation. Someone chuckled.

The door flew open and there appeared in the frame a fearsome virago wearing a dirty apron over a grubby dress with the sleeves rolled up to reveal forearms which would not have disgraced a coal-heaver. With her issued a strong odour compounded of sweat, cabbage water and burnt fat. It completed Fletcher's discomfort. He muttered, 'Faugh!' and pressed his handkerchief to his nose and mouth.

The woman's sharp little black eyes in her doughy face made her visage look like nothing so much as an unbaked Chelsea bun. She stared at one and then the other of us and clearly had no trouble identifying my calling.

'What is it?' she demanded. 'I've got no trouble here.'

'I'm pleased to hear it,' I said. 'I am Inspector Ross. Who might you be?'

'I'm Mrs Riley and I run a decent establishment what is well spoken of by all. Ain't that right?' She appealed to the bystanders who obediently chorused agreement.

One wit at the back ventured, 'She's got the healthiest bedbugs between here and Buckingham Palace!'

This inspired a drunk, who had staggered from an alehouse tankard in hand to see what was going on, to cry, 'God save the Queen!'

His loyalty was ignored. As for the others, such was their awe of the lodging-house keeper that few had laughed at the sally. I wouldn't have given much for the chances of the joker if Mrs Riley had got her muscular hands on him, if the evil look thrown by her glittering black eyes in his direction was anything to go by.

'We are seeking a man by the name of Adams . . .' I turned to Fletcher. 'What's his first name?'

'Jem,' came from beneath the handkerchief. 'But I don't know whether it is Jeremiah or Jeremy.'

'Jem Adams, then. We understand he lodges here.'

'He does,' said Mrs Riley. 'But he ain't here.'

'Did he leave at his usual time this morning?'

'No,' said Mrs Riley.

'What time did he leave, then?'

'He didn't.'

Getting information from Mrs Riley was akin to drawing the proverbial teeth. 'Does he or does he not lodge here?' I demanded sharply. 'You say he does, but isn't here and hasn't left. Be so good as to make sense.'

'He's paid till Sunday,' said Mrs Riley. 'I only accept those who pay one week in advance on a Monday morning. So today being Saturday he still lodges here. Come

Monday morning if he's not come back he won't be lodging here no longer and I shall be free to let the room, there!'

My heart was sinking fast. Confound it! Had I left it too late to speak to Adams? What could have become of the fellow?

'May we come in?' I asked.

Beside me Fletcher moaned a protest which I ignored.

Mrs Riley stepped back to allow us into her cramped dingy hallway. We entered and she slammed the door in the face of the audience which, robbed of its entertainment, raised a derisive jeer.

'When did you see him last?' I demanded sharply.

'Last night. He come home as usual and he went out as usual.'

'Do you know where he went?'

'To an alehouse, I suppose. He's a working man and a working man likes a pint of an evening. He never came back drunk, mind! I don't stand for it. No drunkenness, no dogs and no loose women.'

'Can we see his room?'

She turned and led us up the creaking uncarpeted stair to the top floor where she flung open a door and stood aside to allow us to enter.

The floorboards here were also uncarpeted and dusty. It was a small room with one window which looked out over the street below and had a torn scrap of net curtain hanging from a rail above it. The furnishings consisted of a single chair, a bed with grimy linen on it, a rickety marble-topped wash-stand bearing a cracked basin and jug and a piece of cheap soap in an odd saucer. Also upon it was an enamelled mug painted with forget-me-nots and holding a shaving brush. Alongside it, neatly sheathed, lay a cut-throat razor. The remaining piece of furniture was a chest of drawers topped with a mirror in a wooden frame and a candlestick. Only the top drawer contained anything and that but a pair of socks, a spare shirt and some woollen underwear felted with much use and washing. I pushed the drawer in with some effort, as the wood had swollen and warped in the damp atmosphere, and turned to the landlady.

'How long has he lodged here?'

'Six months,' she said promptly. 'He's been a good tenant, has Jemmy Adams.'

'He has not taken his personal possessions,' I pointed out. 'That means he left intending to return.'

Fletcher, the handkerchief still well pressed to his nose against the evil miasma of his surroundings, had sidled to the window and was peering from it down to the street below and the heads of the crowd. They glimpsed him and raised a cheer which sent him scuttling back into the room again.

'So he may have done,' Mrs Riley said. 'But if he don't return by Sunday night, I let the room. If he don't claim his belongings, then I'll sell 'em to old Jones the rag man. Not that he's left me anything much to sell.' She stared round her discontentedly. Then her eye lit on the razor and her expression brightened momentarily.

I too had made note of the razor. I surmised that if Adams had anything of value he would not have left it here when he quitted the house, even for a normal working day. Anything in the way of a pocket watch, say, or any money, he would have carried on him at all times. He might leave his shaving equipment here of an evening against his return from the alehouse, but if he had decided to bolt permanently for whatever reason, he would have taken the razor. It was a relatively expensive item and it had more uses than skimming whiskers from his chin.

'If he returns, tell him Inspector Ross wishes to speak to him immediately at Scotland Yard!' I told her.

From behind Fletcher's handkerchief his voice said indistinctly, 'Tell him his employers are also desirous of a word!'

'What's Jemmy done?' demanded Mrs Riley.

'Nothing that I know of,' I told her. 'He may be able to help in some enquiries.'

'I don't like having the p'lice in my house,' she said. 'It lowers the tone. Neighbours talk. But you're not in your uniform, at least. I suppose that means you're important and these enquiries of yours are important, too.'

'Give her two shillings,' I muttered to Fletcher.

Fletcher spluttered but dug one-handed in his pocket and handed over the coins.

'I'm obliged,' said Mrs Riley, secreting the coins safely

in a pocket in her skirts. 'I'll tell him. You may depend on it.'

Her manner had cheered up somewhat on payment but turned sour again in an instant when I picked up the razor and slipped it into my pocket. 'You may also tell him I have taken possession of the razor. I'll give you a receipt.'

I tore a sheet from my notebook and wrote on it, 'Received of Mrs Riley, landlady, one cut-throat razor in leather case and property of Jem Adams.' I signed and dated it and handed it to her. She stared at it with blank incomprehension, turned it the other way up and frowned. Clearly she could not read.

We found the crowd still waiting patiently outside the house. It sent up another cheer as we emerged.

'Wot?' shouted someone, 'no prisoner?'

Despite this disappointment they trailed behind us back to where we had left the carriage. When we reached the spot we found the coachman in conversation with the one-legged beggar who had preceded us and was awaiting our return. Unable to get near to us in the crowd, he had astutely placed himself between us and our escape.

'What are you doing, Mullins?' demanded Fletcher furiously of the coachman. 'Why are you encouraging this wretch?'

The beggar spoke up. 'I was telling him my sad story, sirs.'

'Well, don't tell it to us,' I advised him. 'I am a police

officer and to importune people on the highway and demand money of them is against the law.'

'Gawd bless you, sir, I ain't a common beggar man!' he replied, unoffended and also unabashed. 'I'm an old soldier. I lost this leg when I was nothing but a boy at the great battle of Waterloo, serving under the Iron Duke himself.'

There was no way of telling whether this story was true. He certainly looked old enough to have served in the army as a boy. But as he was ill-washed, unshaven and his hair uncombed and straggling, he might have looked older than he was. I climbed up into the carriage but he grasped the sleeve of Fletcher who followed me.

'You're a fine gentleman, ain't you, sir? You ain't a peeler. I'm only trying to keep body and soul together. You understand, sir, don't you?'

'Let go of me!' snapped the goaded Fletcher, snatching his sleeve from the other's grimy grip. 'Oh, very well, then!' He dug in his pocket again and some coins changed hands. 'Now, do go away!'

'Hooray!' cried some of the crowd in approval. Others laughed and informed us that would keep the ale running.

The beggar raised a forefinger to his brow in salute. 'Bless you, sir, the angels has a book where they writes the names of all those who show charity to the unfortunate. And the devil has probably got a book where he puts the names of all the peelers!'

With that he hobbled away towards a nearby tavern.

The crowd, appreciating the last sally, applauded him as he went.

'It has proved an expensive morning for you, Mr Fletcher,' I said, trying not to laugh as we rolled away to a last rousing cheer from the crowd and a deep bow from the elderly Chinese man.

'I don't know what Mullins was doing, allowing the fellow to hang about waiting for us,' Fletcher grumbled, wiping sweat from his brow. 'I don't know why you couldn't have arrested him.'

'And put him in this carriage with us to take him to the nearest police station? I didn't think you'd want it. Come now, I applaud your generosity.'

Fletcher positively glowered at me. 'As for my generosity, you were happy to make free with it and spend on my behalf back there. I don't see why it should have cost *me* two shillings at the boarding house to buy the cooperation of that frightful harridan! She told us nothing.'

'Really? She told us quite a lot to my mind. However, if we were to be sure she'd pass on the message, the two shillings were necessary. It compensates her also for the loss of the razor.'

'Then I don't see why you couldn't have paid it!' he retorted sulkily.

'You are his employer. Besides it is not police policy to disburse monies to witnesses.'

Fletcher subsided and only muttered, 'I don't see she told us anything. Adams is probably lying stone drunk somewhere.'

'Has he failed to turn up for work before on account of drink?'

Fletcher admitted the man had not.

'And the landlady said he was not a drunkard,' I reminded him.

Fletcher made no reply to this. 'Why do you want the razor, anyway?' he asked in a plaintive tone.

'Because the landlady will sell it and it is not hers to sell. Adams paid his rent in advance and owes her nothing. Next week, if he hasn't returned, she will let the room to a fresh tenant, as you heard her say. Adams may yet turn up, and I can return his property to him. Besides, it's a fearsome weapon and I don't like it lying around ownerless in such a place. Anyone may get their hands on it.'

'What if he doesn't come back?' Fletcher asked miserably. 'How am I to replace him?'

'I have no idea!' I snapped. I had had quite enough of Fletcher for one morning. I requested him to set me down at the first convenient spot and returned to my office. Luckily Morris was there.

'We've lost him!' I said briefly to the sergeant as I entered. 'I'll go back to the demolition site and see if he's turned up again, but to my mind he's gone for good.'

Morris looked glum. 'Done a runner, has he, sir?'

'Possibly, but I doubt it.'

I gave him a brief account of my morning's experiences, adding, 'If Adams is lying anywhere it is not stone drunk, I'd put my last penny on that. It is far more likely to be stone dead. I don't like it when, in the middle of a murder investigation, a man who may have valuable information, who has been as regular as clockwork in turning up for work and in paying for his lodging, suddenly goes out of an evening and doesn't come back. We shall be lucky to speak to him now and so will anyone else.'

I took out the razor in its leather sheath and put it on the table. 'He would not have left this razor, Morris, if he fled of his own free will. Also, as Mr Fletcher informed us, today is pay day for the navvies and Adams would need a powerful reason to prevent him collecting his beer money. Contact Thames Division at Wapping. Send them a description of the man. I am dreadfully afraid this will prove a job for Thames Division, and Adams will be pulled from the river.'

Chapter Fourteen

Elizabeth Martin

I WASN'T sure what action Aunt Parry would take with regard to her new information but I felt in my bones she would take some. The first thing she did utterly surprised me, however.

I was in my room the following morning, Saturday, when a knock at the door heralded Nugent, who came in bearing laid across her outstretched forearms a shimmering froth of Indian tussore silk in the palest shade of gold like a ripening exotic fruit.

'The mistress is wondering, Miss Martin, if you could make use of this gown? It was one made for the mistress when she and the late master went on their wedding journey. It would need some altering to bring into modern fashion but Mrs Parry's usual dressmaker could do it.' Nugent shook out the gown and held it up. The folds of silk billowed to the floor with a soft seductive rustle. 'Or if there wasn't much to do, I could probably do it, miss. I'm good with a needle.'

I hardly knew what to say but Nugent was standing there, still holding up the gown, and waiting for a reply.

'It is very kind of Mrs Parry,' I managed at last. 'I'll go and thank her immediately if she's able to see me.'

The gown looked about my size. Aunt Parry had once been somewhat slimmer! The main alteration would need to be in the sleeves which were set rather low in a previous fashion.

I took the gown from Nugent. It weighed almost nothing in comparison to my other dresses. The fine wild silk crumpled in my hand like thinnest tissue paper. 'I sew a little,' I said. 'If you would help me, I'm sure we could manage something without troubling the dressmaker.'

I could not refuse the gift, but I was determined not to expose myself to the slightly pitying look of the seamstress called in to alter a second-hand gown for the impecunious companion of a rich woman.

'Right you are, miss!' said Nugent, sounding quite cheerful. It occurred to me she was looking forward to tackling the beautiful material. 'I'll tell the mistress. I've already had a look at it, miss. It won't take that long. We'll unstitch the sleeves; see here, where they are set into the yoke. Then we can take a small panel from the skirt, there is plenty, and use it to make puff sleeves which we can sew on to the top of the narrow sleeves and then reattach the whole lot to the bodice, just reshaping the holes for the sleeves first.'

'Are you sure, Nugent?' I asked doubtfully.

'Bless you, miss, I've done more difficult sewing than that. When the mistress – I shouldn't say this – but when she began to put on a little weight, I had to let out all her gowns and some of them, it wasn't easy. In the end, she had a new lot made, fashions changing and that.' Nugent patted the tussore gown complacently. 'I always did like this one. The master's business imported all kinds of beautiful materials from the East and this was some of it. The only thing is, I don't have any matching silk thread in my sewing box.'

'That is no problem,' I said quickly. 'I'll go and buy some today.'

She left me alone. I spread the gown out on the bed and stared down at it, trying to order my emotions.

It was not merely wounded pride I felt. Obviously my lack of wardrobe had been noted. It would be wrong of me to take offence, despite the embarrassment. I told myself I ought not to be ungrateful for a gift kindly meant. But had kindness alone played a part in it? Aunt Parry did not want me appearing night after night at the dinner table in the same dress. That would be disagreeable to her. I realised this and understood it. It was not that which made me suspicious: there was something else, another explanation, and I didn't like it.

Since my conversation yesterday with Aunt Parry I no

longer trusted her motives. She had been quick enough to see that her worldly reaction to my news of my childhood acquaintance with the inspector had gone down badly with me. She wished to erase any unfavourable impression she might have made. She also wanted me on her side. If she was to use my connection with Ross it would be necessary. In that light, the beautiful gown took on the appearance of a bribe.

I went at once to Aunt Parry's room to thank her for her gift. Delay would only make me more confused and my speech of gratitude more halting. I found her propped up in bed on a mound of feather pillows. She wore a frilled nightgown and a lace nightcap, and was sipping tea from a delicate china cup patterned with roses. She had been examining her morning post, but put it aside and received me and my thanks graciously, before waving me away and saying I should return later to discuss it. I left, but not before I had noticed that one of the letters had the heading of the railway company.

I supposed this meant I wouldn't be free to go and do my shopping until much later. Sure enough, Nugent reappeared towards eleven to say Mrs Parry wished to give her opinion on what we should do with the tussore silk and so we repaired once more to her boudoir. Matters had progressed and now I found Aunt Parry seated before her dressing table, her hair neatly coiled and pinned leaving only a couple of lovelocks to curl either side of her plump cheeks. Instead of a peignoir she was wearing a silk kimono embroidered with chrysanthemums ('From the East, too!' whispered Nugent in my ear).

As for the dressing table, I don't think I'd ever seen so many aids to feminine toilette in one small area. Glass perfume sprays jostled jars of hand creams and bottles of skin tonic, little pots of rouge, brushes, combs, pins and a pair of curling tongs. Nowhere was there any sign of the correspondence I'd seen her reading earlier.

Nugent and I explained our dress-altering intentions and Aunt Parry said she supposed that would do it, but would it not be possible . . . ? Then followed a long list of suggestions, none of which were very practical. I suspected that if Aunt Parry had done some sewing in her youth then, other than the obligatory sampler, it had been restricted to hemming handkerchiefs and darning stockings. Nugent and I listened attentively and thanked her but exchanged glances signifying we would stick to our original plans.

'Sit down, my dear,' said Aunt Parry, when Nugent had carried away the tussore silk.

I sat down on a small velvet-covered stool.

'I have had more on my mind than your wardrobe, my dear. I have been giving matters in general a lot of thought,' began Aunt Parry. She paused to sigh and went on, 'Although with the sad affair of poor Madeleine's death hanging over us it's a wonder I can think of anything else. I've really become quite melancholy about it and I do wish an end could be put to the whole thing.'

She paused for the barest moment to ascertain that I had taken heed of her viewpoint and would remember it when I next saw my old acquaintance, Inspector Ross. She then began again briskly, Madeleine apparently relegated to some other area of her consciousness dedicated to mourning.

'There comes a time when one must adopt a worldly approach and speak frankly. I hope you will allow me to do so and understand that I have nothing but your best interests at heart.' She patted my hand.

Hand-patting as a gesture I have always treated with misgivings; generally it is a prelude to bad news.

'Yes, Aunt Parry,' I said as she had paused and a reply was obviously expected. I wondered just what was coming next.

'You are not a bad-looking young woman, Elizabeth,' she informed me in a kindly tone, 'although no beauty and of course you have no personal fortune. Nor are you, shall we say, a girl.'

'I shall be thirty on my next birthday, Aunt Parry.'

'You certainly don't look thirty,' she said, eyeing me dispassionately, rather as though I had been an article of furniture. 'You have kept yourself together very well.'

I thought I detected a slight note of resentment in her voice. Her attention was distracted from me for a second or two while she leaned forward over her dressing table to peer into the mirror. Something about her hair wasn't to her liking and she fiddled with a chestnut lovelock.

'Thank you, Aunt Parry,' I said. I was doing my utmost not to laugh. Some people might have been insulted by this address but she looked so serious, sitting there in her extravagantly embroidered kimono, intended for the slender form of some Japanese lady. It was tightly wrapped round her and well secured with a silk cord, so that she resembled a sofa cushion of the bolster sort. A tray stood on a little table nearby and on it, in addition to the tea things I had noticed earlier, lay a plate with cake crumbs.

'There are many older gentlemen,' Aunt Parry said now, leaning forward in a confidential manner, 'who find themselves either bachelors or widowers and desire to remedy the situation. They require a life's companion who will be agreeable, good company, look presentable, preside over their table and entertain their guests, run their household . . . in short they are looking for a wife who will not vex them in the way a younger woman would. She wouldn't want to be gallivanting around all the time, for example. Someone who will be, in time perhaps, a nurse-companion. There your being a doctor's daughter might stand you in very good stead. As for your lack of fortune, I speak of gentlemen who are well established in life. They are not looking for a wealthy wife. Nor do they seek sophistication. That you are, dear child, a penniless girl from the provinces would not be held against you.'

I pressed my lips together in order not to be caught gaping like a landed fish. What? Did this plump little woman, so ridiculous in her Japanese finery, imagine she

looked sophisticated? As for the husband she proposed
she should find for me . . .

Here I frowned and wondered whether she was describing my late godfather, Josiah Parry, at the time he had
married her. Had not Aunt Parry then been a penniless
parson's daughter from the provinces, if Frank was to be
believed? She certainly seemed to have it all well thought
out. I was listening to the voice of experience.

'I am, of course, delighted to have you as a companion
and should be more than sorry to lose you, dear Elizabeth!
But I believe you are deserving of your own household
and place in the world. Josiah would have wished me to do
my very best for you, and so I shall.' She suddenly turned
on me that smile of goodwill which I had already experienced and which I realised she could conjure up whenever
she felt the moment required it. 'I shall keep an eye open
for you, Elizabeth.'

'Really, Aunt Parry,' I faltered, 'I am more than grateful
for your kind interest but I wouldn't wish anyone to think
I was husband-hunting, because I am not.'

'Naturally!' she said approvingly with a nod of her
head. 'You would not do anything so vulgar. But you're
sensible and I'm sure you know where your own best
interests lie. Now, I need Nugent to help me dress, so run
along, my dear. I'm driving out to Hampstead today with
my dear friend, Mrs Belling, so you will be left to your
own devices.'

I was more than happy to be left to my own devices and

my own thoughts. She wanted me out of the house, so much was clear. Once all this distressing business of Madeleine's murder was dealt with, and my link with Inspector Ross no longer of any potential use, I would become a liability. I had observed too much already; my eye was too critical and my tongue too impetuous. I was not the meek, self-effacing companion required. I was, as the naval saying went, a loose cannon sliding dangerously about the deck in a rolling sea.

However, she could not dismiss me without good cause. I was her late husband's godchild. Nor did she want me taking up a situation in another household where I might be tempted to talk about the goings-on in Dorset Square. Safely married! That was the answer. Safely locked into the bonds of matrimony with some elderly curmudgeon who wouldn't let me out of his sight. An unpaid nursemaid to a valetudinarian in a bath chair! Pah!

A spurt of anger overcame me at that moment and caused me to throw a few cushions around my room. Never! Never, in any circumstances, would I take a husband of Aunt Parry's choosing.

Mrs Belling, it seemed, kept a carriage. It drew up before the house at a quarter past twelve and bore Aunt Parry away to the delights of Hampstead.

'What would you like for your luncheon, miss?' asked Simms. 'Mrs Simms has galantine of cold chicken.'

Concocted from the remains of the fowl which had

supplied the previous day's luncheon, no doubt, and followed by a close relative of the cold shape.

'Tell Mrs Simms I thank her kindly, but really she needn't bother about me. I have several errands to run and don't require any luncheon. Mrs Simms provides a generous breakfast table!'

In truth I had only the silk thread to buy. I obtained a few strands from the seams of the tussore gown to provide a match and set out. I'm a good walker and by proceeding in more or less a straight line I found myself just below Marble Arch at the beginning of Oxford Street in no more than twenty minutes and set out along the famed street. Although I'd been so little time in the city I was already beginning to feel myself a Londoner, having quite lost my awe of its bustle and crowds, although not my prudence. There were beggars and ragamuffin children a-plenty and some sharp-looking fellows who loitered with apparently nothing to do. One of them, I noticed, contrived to bump into an elderly gentleman walking ahead of me. The offender expressed his apologies, anxiously taking the other by the arm to steady him and hoping he was not hurt? He then hurried away and was soon lost in the crowd. The old gentleman walked on a little before a thought seemed to occur to him. He stopped, apparently searched for his wallet, and failed to find it.

'I say, there!' he cried, turning in the direction the other had gone and waving his stick in the air. But the pickpocket had long made good his escape.

I obtained the silk thread with little difficulty and had turned to make my way homeward when I heard my name shouted above the hubbub.

I looked round in surprise and saw Inspector Ross dodging vehicles to cross the road and waving a hand to hail me as he did so.

'Well, Inspector!' I greeted him, as he avoided the last flashing hooves and rumbling wheels and arrived beside me, breathless but thankfully uninjured. 'I'm surprised to see you here.'

He took off his hat and panted, 'Good afternoon, Miss Martin.' A bead of sweat trickled down his brow from his black hair.

'You look,' I observed, 'as if you have been out and about.'

Not only perspiring but distinctly dishevelled and not merely from his dash across the thoroughfare. His boots and trousers below the knees were plentifully splattered with mud.

He glanced down at himself and I saw an expression of almost comical dismay spread across his features as if he had only now realised what a sight he presented.

'I look a mess,' he said ruefully and rubbed one jacket cuff ineffectually against the other. 'I apologise for that. I have been out and about, as you say, and I'm only now returning to my office. I was first at the site in Agar Town and later in Limehouse where it's dirty underfoot and you don't find any crossing sweepers. I've just been a second time to Agar Town although to call it that now is meaningless. There's nothing left standing at all. The place is quite levelled and they hope to start building the new yards and terminus soon. I must say, things there progress at a tremendous rate. The board meetings of the railway company must be more cheerful affairs than they have been of late.' He pulled a wry face.

This was somewhat at odds with the picture painted by Mr Fletcher during lunch the previous day. But I supposed that if they were ready to move on to the next stage of the construction of the new terminus, then it must be doubly annoying to have the police still poking about the place. Building materials needed to be delivered, foundations to be dug. The architects would be arriving with their plans. There would be feverish activity on all sides with Fletcher no doubt buzzing from one spot to another exhorting everyone to greater efforts.

'How do things go at Scotland Yard?' I asked. 'Or shouldn't I enquire?'

'You, of all people, Miss Martin, have a right to enquire,' he returned with a brief grin. He then grew serious again and shook his head. 'They go very badly. I make little or no progress and sometimes feel I'm slipping backwards. There is a man called Adams, a foreman at the demolition site, with whom I was very anxious to speak, but he seems to have disappeared. I've been seeking him, in company with a man called Fletcher who is employed by the railway and whose chief goal in life seems to be to make mine a misery.'

'I can believe it,' I said. 'I have met Mr Fletcher.' Ross looked surprised so I hastened to explain that on my return to Dorset Square the day before, after leaving Scotland Yard, I had found Mr Fletcher at table with Mrs Parry.

'Indeed?' said Ross thoughtfully at this news. 'I wonder what the devil – excuse me – he was doing there?'

'Mrs Parry is apparently a shareholder in the company,' I said. 'She and Fletcher appeared old acquaintances. What with that and her having sold some houses in Agar Town to the company, she has a keen interest in what goes on there even without being poor Madeleine's employer.'

I wondered how much I might reveal of the conversation at which I had assisted without betraying my employer's confidences, or her subsequent gift. I thought of the thread I'd only just purchased to sew the alterations to the tussore gown and almost had an impulse to take it out and throw it away. The whole thing put me in an embarrassing position with regard to Inspector Ross. If I told him of Aunt Parry's present he would probably see it, as I increasingly did, as a bribe to me to use my slender acquaintance with him to the advantage of my employer and her co-conspirator, Mr Fletcher. As if I'd meddle in his investigations! Taking him the valuable information given by Bessie and Wally Slater wasn't meddling, of course. That had been my duty as a citizen. But how much more could I tell him? Aside from any embarrassment to myself in the matter of the tussore silk, I owed a loyalty of discretion to my employer, however much it irked me.

I owed nothing, however, to the Midland Railway Company and certainly not to its representative Mr Fletcher. I could quite fairly report his words. 'He spoke of his frustration at the interruption to the work caused by your enquiries and also at the number of curious sightseers the place is now attracting. I must say, I find that quite horrible,' I added honestly.

'Horrible perhaps, but natural,' was Ross's blunt reply. 'Have you never witnessed a carriage accident? Or seen some poor soul run down in the street by a cart, or a workman fall from a high place? Perhaps not, but believe me, all those things attract sightseers like wasps round a jam pot. If you had seen Fletcher and myself in Limehouse an hour or two ago, you would have learned that it doesn't need disaster to attract them. Any kind of unusual sight will do it. Although I dare say in Limehouse they had high hopes of witnessing me make an arrest. A chance would be a fine thing!' he added forlornly.

'You will do,' I said encouragingly. 'I am sure of it.'

Ross shook his head to dismiss his gloom. 'You are very kind and I could only wish Superintendent Dunn had your confidence in me. Yes, I suppose Mrs Parry, as a shareholder, doesn't want matters held up. She is torn two ways, eh? She wants us to find out who killed Miss Hexham and she wants us off the site so that her investment may be realised in good time. It's quite a normal reaction. The public invariably wants the police to sort matters out but as quickly and with as little inconvenience to the law-abiding as possible. I suppose Fletcher was there to enlist her support? Don't reply to that if you'd rather not!'

'I won't,' I told him, 'but I will warn you that she may try to enlist *my* support. I was obliged to tell her that my father was your benefactor.'

He took this information in his stride. 'I'd supposed you had already done so, just as I had to tell Superintendent Dunn. It would have been unwise for either of us to keep it a secret.'

I was relieved to have told him. It had been weighing on my mind. 'As a matter of fact,' I found myself saying more frankly than I'd intended, 'I am not altogether sure how anxious Mrs Parry is to see Madeleine's murderer caught. She's a law-abiding citizen, of course, though she'd certainly prefer enquiries over and done with. The notoriety is unpleasant to her. A trial would add to the general curiosity, wouldn't it? The newspapers would be full of it. I'm not unsympathetic to her fears, even though to have her constantly putting herself first—'

I checked myself but I'd already said too much and had to continue. 'My impression is, if anything, that she is annoyed and embarrassed by Madeleine's disappearance and death rather than feeling any grief or desire for justice. We have had spectators in Dorset Square, too, just as at Agar Town, although not yet in such numbers. It would be that much worse with lurid details of a trial filling the popular press daily. The address would be referred to and it would draw more people. Her name must be mentioned as Madeleine's employer. She'd hate that.'

'Indeed?' Ross murmured. He eyed me sharply. 'And what do others in Dorset Square think of Miss Hexham's violent death?'

I realised that my imprudent tongue had again led me, in a conversational sense, down a dangerous path. 'I'm not sure I should give an opinion,' I said. 'I hardly know any of them. I only arrived in London Tuesday last, after all.'

'So you did,' he said in wonder. 'You've had a baptism of fire, all right. But you are bearing up well, if you'll allow me to say so. I'd expect nothing less of Dr Martin's daughter, of course. And I have a great respect for the opinions of the doctor's daughter, whom I know to be sharp-eyed and sharp-witted.'

'I don't know that I quite care to be described like that,' I told him ruefully. 'I am beginning to think I am far too outspoken for my own good. But very well, for what it's worth, my impression is that the domestic staff have mixed views. Bessie you have met. She was fond of Miss Hexham. I believe she is sincerely upset. Simms the butler feels the whole business reflects badly on the dignity of the household. The maids are enjoying themselves tremendously because they are no doubt the centre of attention in their own world. Mrs Simms is a dragon who lurks in her basement lair and I don't know what she thinks but probably the same as her husband. Nugent, Mrs Parry's maid, has expressed no opinion. I think looking after Aunt Parry is enough for Nugent without having to worry about anything else!' I broke off and put my hand guiltily to my mouth. 'I should not have said that. Anyway, Nugent is kindly helping me with some sewing. She is very busy, that is all I meant.'

'So much for below stairs,' said Ross. 'And above stairs? You have told me what you think Mrs Parry's attitude is. What of others?'

But this time he had put his question too bluntly. I was not, after all, a witness to the events he was investigating. Nor had I been in London long enough to form any opinion based on knowledge, only on first impressions. First Mrs Parry and her ally Fletcher tried to recruit me to their cause; now Ross was doing so.

'I think,' I told him seriously, 'that in some ways you are without scruple. You flatter me, artfully refer to my father, and then expect me to tell you things I ought to keep well to myself. You are as bad as Mrs Parry or Mr Fletcher in seeking to enlist my support.'

That was unfair and I knew it – too late – the moment the words had left my lips. If Ross was seeking to use my knowledge it was at least in the cause of discovering Madeleine's murderer. But I was upset and too obstinate to apologise.

There was a silence. Ross made no reference to my last remark, though I didn't doubt he'd made a mental note of it, just as he made written notes of everything else. Instead he said quietly, 'Believe me, I am not without scruple. But I am a man investigating a murder and no one is disposed to help me. Whatever their reasons, they frustrate me at every turn. You are living in the house, Lizzie, and you do care for justice.'

It wasn't the first time he had called me 'Lizzie' and it was becoming all too much of a habit. I supposed I ought to ask him not to, but I found I really didn't mind, even though I was annoyed with him. If anything, however, the awareness that I didn't mind his familiarity made me even more cross, this time with myself.

'All I can tell you,' I retorted, 'is that I have already said more than enough about Mrs Parry and I won't say a word more. Mrs Belling, on the other hand, is someone to whom I owe no loyalty. I find her an unpleasant woman and her only concern, as far as I can see, is that she shall not be blamed for bringing Madeleine to London in the first place.'

'Is that her only concern?' Ross asked unexpectedly. 'She has a son.'

'I know. I've met him only once, very briefly. He seemed a nice enough person and spoke decently of Madeleine. I've nothing against him and nothing more I can say of him!' I was even more feeling I was being quizzed unfairly. It was one thing to be asked about people with whom I shared a roof, but to expect me to be able to talk of the state of mind of strangers was ridiculous. I said something of this to Ross, who looked suitably abashed.

'Don't misunderstand me, please, Miss Martin. I don't expect you to do anything but give me a general impression of what you've been able to observe and I'm sorry, really, if you feel I'm taking liberties.'

That made me even angrier because I felt he wasn't really sorry.

'There is nothing else I can tell you about anyone,' I concluded.

'But you have left out one very important person with whom you share a roof,' Ross said gently but firmly.

I gave an exclamation of annoyance and glared at him. 'You mean Frank,' I said.

'I mean Mr Carterton, indeed. Does he wish to see Miss Hexham's killer caught?'

'Of course he does! If only because he fears he is at the top of your list.'

'At the top of my list?' Ross asked with a quizzical twitch of his eyebrows.

I felt myself reddening. 'That's his expression, not mine.'

'Ah, so you have been talking it over with Mr Carterton. Well, that's not surprising. Does Mr Carterton know that your father sponsored my education?'

'I haven't told him,' I said uneasily. 'His aunt may do so, I suppose.'

I was by now wishing myself out of this conversation and was about to tell Ross I had to hurry home at once when the conversation was interrupted for me.

'Miss Martin!' boomed through the air, causing several passers-by to stop and turn.

Both Ross and I turned, startled, in the direction of the

voice. I saw bearing down on us the imposing and extremely irate form of Dr Tibbett. Brow furrowed, silver hair flying and black coat-tails flapping, it was as if Jove had decided to quit Olympus for the day to give mankind the benefit of his opinions.

'Who is this?' whispered Ross, sounding incredulous.

'A friend of Mrs Parry,' I just had time to reply. Tibbett was upon us.

'Good afternoon to you, Dr Tibbett,' I said politely, despite my private scorn for the hypocritical old reprobate.

He stared at me very hard and I remembered that he had been a schoolmaster for many years and was not easily deceived as to what people were thinking. I noticed for the first time that he had very clear bright blue eyes. I supposed that in his youth he had been a handsome man and was so, still.

Tibbett had turned his gaze to Ross. 'And this?' he asked icily. He pointed with a long slender kid-gloved finger. I was a little surprised not to see lightning issue from the tip of it. 'Perhaps you'd be so good as to introduce me to this gentleman?'

'Certainly,' I said. 'This is Inspector Ross of Scotland Yard. He is investigating Miss Hexham's death and you must have heard about him from my Aunt Parry.'

'I have indeed,' said Tibbett, looking and sounding completely unimpressed.

'And I have heard your name mentioned by Mrs Parry, sir,' said Ross.

Tibbett was not mollified by this statement but looked even more suspiciously at Ross. 'And do matters progress satisfactorily, Inspector?'

'As well as can be expected at this stage, sir,' replied Ross.

'Indeed?' said Tibbett. 'What stage would that be, I wonder? What clues do you hope to find in Oxford Street on a Saturday afternoon? However, I see you are not letting grass grow beneath your feet in at least one respect. You have finished your conversation with the young lady? I assume it to have concerned a professional matter although I am puzzled as to what its nature could be. Miss Martin was not a member of Mrs Parry's household at the time of Miss Hexham's regrettable disappearance. She did not know her.'

I caught a glint in Ross's eye. 'I conduct my enquiries how and wherever I see it necessary, sir.'

'Then we shall not detain you! You must be a busy man and anxious to be about your public duties,' retorted Tibbett. 'Good day to you, Inspector.'

I thought for one awful moment that Ross would at last crack and his cool manner give way to an explosion of rage. Instead he slowly and quite deliberately turned his back on Tibbett and, ignoring his farewell words, said to me, 'I hope I have not held you up, Miss Martin. Thank you for talking to me.'

He touched his hat, bowed to me and, still ignoring Tibbett, walked off.

'An impertinent fellow!' snapped Dr Tibbett.

Having already been obliged to listen to Fletcher's criticism of Ben Ross, this was altogether too much. Perhaps I had myself just reproached the inspector but that didn't mean I intended to go on letting others do it.

'Dr Tibbett,' I burst out, unable to contain myself any longer. 'Inspector Ross, in my view, is not the one showing impertinence. How dare you interrupt a private conversation in which I was engaged, and in such a manner?'

I won't say Tibbett reeled back in amazement but his jaw did drop momentarily and he did take half a step back, if only better to behold the source of the unexpected attack. 'Do I believe my ears, young woman?'

'I suppose you do,' I said calmly. 'You appear to have excellent hearing.'

Tibbett did not reply at once. He raised his walking stick and tapped his chin thoughtfully with the silver pommel.

'You have a quick tongue, miss,' he said at last.

But I knew I had wrong-footed him and followed up my advantage. It would not last long. 'I believe, Dr Tibbett, you owe me an apology.'

'I owe you no such thing!' he spluttered. His face had reddened alarmingly.

I remembered that he was an elderly man and thought I should take care. I had no wish for him to have an apoplectic fit at my feet in the middle of Oxford Street.

I said nothing and held his gaze steadily.

His colour, much to my relief, returned to something more normal. With it, his manner gained its usual calm though I suspected turbulence below.

'My dear friend, Mrs Parry,' he said, 'has suffered greatly from the improper behaviour of her last companion and its sad but predictable results. I would not have her embarrassed a second time. You arrived in London only Tuesday last, I believe. We understood you to know no one in town. Yet I find you this afternoon, chatting in a friendly manner with a young man, here in Oxford Street.'

'Quite,' I said, 'in the middle of this crowd. Hardly a tête-à-tête! I am not behaving like a maid on her afternoon off, flirting with any young man, which your manner suggests.'

'You express yourself with some want of delicacy,' he said with distaste. 'I did not know the young man was the police inspector. He seems to have gained preferment at an unsuitably young age. The sight, as I beheld it, did not bode well for the future. I have my good friend's interests at heart. One might say, in the circumstances, yours, too. No doubt the inspector is a handsome fellow and a police inspector might appear to some, though not to me, a dashing occupation. Remember the fate of Miss Hexham!'

If he thought he was getting away with that grudging admission, he was wrong. He was trying to reclaim the moral high ground. I was determined he should not have it. We were like children playing 'King of the Castle'.

'I express myself frankly,' I told him. 'As it happens, I

301

have some slight acquaintance with Inspector Ross dating from childhood. Mrs Parry will be happy to explain it to you. I still await your apology, Dr Tibbett.'

'Wait and be damned!' he burst out, crimson flaring in his cheeks again. He bit off the words and pursed his lips together.

'Well, well,' I said. 'Now you express yourself with some lack of delicacy, sir.'

His mouth twisted in a sneer. 'You are a clever girl,' he said quietly, 'and a bold one. I am sorry to say I find increasingly that there is a type of modern young woman who fancies she may speak as freely as a man. I am an old-fashioned fellow who believes that woman is the greatest ornament to her sex when she realises the boundaries Nature has set for her. Perhaps your hero Darwin should have given some thought to that when he was drawing up his ideas on natural selection. If you imagine that I shall apologise to you, you are very much mistaken. Moreover, I strongly advise you to curb your tongue. The opinions of a provincial doctor's daughter might carry some weight in the limited society of your home town but not here. You are dependent upon charity and should remember it and conduct yourself accordingly. Most of all, I should warn you that you act unwisely in making an enemy of me!'

I opened my mouth to advise him that people who lived in glass houses shouldn't throw stones. But it would be unwise to reveal that I had seen him recently in the company of a common prostitute. I had angered him but he did not fear me. If he ever thought he had reason to do that, he would act swiftly and ruthlessly to eliminate the threat, persuading his dear friend Mrs Parry to turn me out forthwith.

'Good day, sir,' I said, turned on my heel and walked off.

I found by the time I had left him too far behind to be any longer in his sight that I was shaking. It was not fear but anger which caused my emotion. To be honest, some of the annoyance was directed at myself. Perhaps I'd been foolish to lose my temper so obviously. He would complain to Aunt Parry, I thought. Perhaps I'd be dismissed? No, for the time being she needed me and my link to Ross.

But perhaps he wouldn't say anything of this meeting to his friend Julia Parry? He had not come off the best in our duel, or so I fancied. He had not apologised but neither had he forced me to back down or pretend a respect for him I didn't feel. He would not wish, I decided, to let anyone know that a young woman, a mere lady's companion at that, had criticised his behaviour to his face . . . and got away with it. He was my enemy now; that was clear. Henceforth he'd seek to undermine my position with Aunt Parry whenever he could, but he would be subtle in how he went about it. He was a bully. Bullies hate those who face up to them. But they take care not to offend them again openly. Like a Chinese Mandarin, a bully cannot afford to lose face.

Chapter Fifteen

I WAS still in an unsettled state when I reached Dorset Square. It seemed a good idea not to go into the house straight away and let Simms see that I was upset. He couldn't fail to notice it and might well mention it to Mrs Parry on her return; she in turn might tell her suitor. I certainly didn't wish Dr Tibbett to know I'd returned home in any distress. He would take the greatest satisfaction from it.

I decided to take a leaf from Bessie's book: sit here in the square for a little while and watch the children and their nursemaids until I had calmed down and my face was no longer – as I suspected it was at the moment – beetroot red.

I took a seat on a bench which had dried off. It was cool but pleasant enough in the watery sunshine and the previous night's heavy rain shower had freshened up the grass and leaves. As my breath returned to its normal pace my cheeks stopped burning. Two little boys ran past bowling hoops with great expertise on the gravel path and shouting merrily.

'Master Harry!' cried one nursemaid despairingly. 'Do watch out for the puddles and your boots!'

But the little boys careered on and I remembered with what pleasure I had splashed through puddles when their age, and how cross it had made Molly Darby who had to clean my boots. I was beginning to feel at peace and ready to go home – as Aunt Parry's house was for me, at least for the time being – when I heard myself hailed for the third time that afternoon.

'Good afternoon, Miss Martin.'

This time the voice was polite and slightly nervous. I looked up and saw James Belling with his hat in his hand, bowing.

I returned his greeting.

'Are you waiting here for someone or may I join you for a moment?' he asked next.

I indicated that he might sit down if he wished. I wondered what inspired this desire for conversation with me and whether I might use it to learn something. I was now convinced his first meeting with me had been contrived. This time, however, he had not come from his house but appeared to have been returning there.

'You weren't called upon to escort your mother and Mrs Parry to Hampstead?' I asked.

'No, fortunately. They have gone to some tea party or

other where it will be all sponge cake and gossip. I have been spared.'

He really sounded as though he meant it. I saw that a book protruded from his pocket and asked him what he was reading.

He flushed, took out the book and showed it to me. 'It is Mr Darwin's account of his voyage as a young man in the ship, the *Beagle*. It is not a new book now but one I have read and reread.' His tone grew wistful. 'I wish I could do as he did when young and travel in unknown parts to take note of all the various natural life. But even if such a chance were offered to me, my father would never cough up the money.'

'Your father is in London?' Mrs Belling had spoken a great deal of her children but not mentioned their father, yet I hadn't received the impression she was a widow.

'He is away on business. He is in South America. I asked if I might go with him but he wouldn't have it.' James sounded resentful. 'I might have retraced some of Darwin's own steps! However my father made it plain that I should not be allowed to do so. He said I might come if I'd take an interest in his work, but then it was my turn to refuse.'

'And what business is he in?' I asked.

'Railways,' said James gloomily.

Another one!

'So you don't intend to follow him into the same career?' I prompted.

'Not if I can help it!' he retorted with some energy. 'I have no desire whatsoever to cover this country and every other in the world with lines of metal track carrying smoke-belching monsters and huge numbers of people from one place to another at such speed that all they see from the carriage windows as they go along is a scenery changing at such a rate, there is no chance to spot anything of real interest.'

'You would travel slowly and stop to turn over stones and study plants and animals.'

'Yes,' he said defiantly. 'I should and, indeed, I do, whenever I can.'

'Please don't think I am criticising you!' I begged. 'I quite understand. I have also read that book you have there and I've read *The Origin of Species*, too.'

His pale face turned pink with enthusiasm and he leaned forward. 'You have? My dear Miss Martin, you can't imagine what pleasure it gives me to hear you say that. There are so few ladies who take a real interest in natural studies – other than pressing flowers and painting insipid watercolours, which passes for an accomplishment with them.'

'I am largely self-educated,' I confessed. 'I never went to any school. I had a governess for a few years, but she wasn't greatly educated herself, and after that my father took over my schooling. But he was busy so I'm afraid it was left to me to gather scraps of learning wherever I found them. He did keep a good library and I read every book I could lay my hands on.'

'That is splendid!' said James fervently. 'I believe girls should be permitted access to serious books and be encouraged to think deeply. My sister, who has a perfectly good brain, has never been allowed to use it. My mother seems to think that somehow it would impair Dora's chances in the marriage market.'

By now I was beaming at him. After Dr Tibbett's lecture on a woman's place this was music to my ears. 'Frank Carterton has told me of your interest in fossils.' I said.

'Frank is a good fellow,' James told me earnestly. 'He and I were at school together. That is, he is a year older than I am and so a year above me. But he was very kind and took me under his wing. Boys' schools can be brutal places, believe me, particularly if a boy is bookish and no good at sports. I shall always be grateful to Frank.'

An idea struck me. 'Were you both, by any chance, pupils of Dr Tibbett?'

'No, thank God! ' cried James immediately and then apologised. 'I should have said "thank goodness!" or perhaps nothing at all.'

We both burst out laughing.

'Dr Tibbett has a poor opinion of ladies who read serious books,' I said.

'Dr Tibbett has a poor opinion of mankind in general,' returned James. 'Apart from himself and a few chosen mortals, that is.'

We had thus disposed of Dr Tibbett.

'Tell me,' James went on, 'what do you think of Mr Darwin's arguments?'

'Ah,' I said, 'there I am hardly qualified to give an opinion. I'm not sure I followed all of his explanations, to be honest. I am full of admiration for the depth of his scholarship and the extent of his observations. Sometimes it seems to me there are gaps in his reasoning. I think he is aware of it himself.'

'For example?'

'Oh, he arrives at a conclusion that all the horses, donkeys and zebras in the world are descended from a common ancestor but he finds that all the dogs in the world cannot be. Why not? There can hardly be more difference between a drayhorse and a zebra than there is between a greyhound and a King Charles spaniel. But then, I am neither a naturalist nor an animal breeder. I do find Mr Darwin to be singularly obsessed by pigeons.'

A city pigeon landed at my feet as if on cue and began to strut back and forth.

James laughed. 'His findings are not complete. How can they be? We are only just beginning to understand the world about us. I am only sorry,' he added suddenly, 'that Frank has no interest in natural history. I have tried to persuade him but it is useless. If he were interested I could have asked him to come with me on my field trips. I go all over the country, you know.'

'Frank told me you had been to Dorset, fossil-hunting,' I said carefully. 'Do you travel north, as well?'

'Oh yes, I go wherever I can. It's fascinating to observe the change in flora and fauna from south to north and the effect of the seasons, which come earlier or later depending where you live, and varying climates.'

The nursemaid had gathered up the little boys with the hoops and led them away. Other children and the adults with them had also disappeared and James and I were alone in Dorset Square. It must be teatime. I should go myself or someone might see us sitting here alone and report it either to Mrs Parry or, more dangerously to James, to his mother.

I got up and he rose somewhat reluctantly.

'I must go now,' I said. 'It has been very interesting talking to you, Mr Belling.'

'Believe me,' he said earnestly, 'it has been a very great pleasure.'

'To find a lady who reads?' I said, daring to tease him.

'Oh, they read,' he said dismissively. 'My sister *reads*; but utter rubbish. If ever I give her a more serious book, my mother takes it out of her hands immediately. Madeleine was the same. She read a great many books but they were all badly written romantic tosh.'

It was as if a shower of cold water had suddenly drenched me. I felt myself freeze and I forced my voice to sound light and casual.

'You discussed books with my predecessor?'

He flushed. 'Yes, she—' James hesitated. 'Look here, Miss Martin,' he said awkwardly. 'Can you keep a secret?'

Now he had put me on the spot. Yes, of course I could keep a secret. But my recent conversation with Ross was fresh in my mind. If James was about to tell me something that shed light on Madeleine's disappearance and death, I should have to pass it on. On the other hand, James wouldn't tell me a thing more if he doubted my discretion. Besides, my word once given, I couldn't break it.

I compromised. 'I hope you don't think I'd be indiscreet?' I said.

He looked relieved and I felt a monster of duplicity.

'Of course you would not,' he said. 'Well then, the fact is I had met Madeleine before, before she came here to London, I mean. I accompanied my mother on a visit to her friend in Durham. I was very keen to go and hoped to add to my studies. I had, of course, to put in a certain number of appearances at my mother's side. I met Madeleine while I was there. She was companion at the time to some crotchety old lady and I felt very sorry for her. I engaged her in some conversation because everyone else was ignoring her. I am sure my mother doesn't remember seeing Madeleine at that time. If, indeed, she did physically see her at all. That Madeleine was in the room doesn't mean my mother took in her presence. She certainly didn't speak to her. I'm sorry to say that, for my mother, people like Madeleine don't exist.'

'And I am sorry to say I can well believe it!' I heard myself say before I could prevent it.

He gave an apologetic smile. 'She has slighted you,'

he said. 'Don't take it personally. She takes a rather grand attitude. Anyway, when Madeleine arrived here in London she remembered me at once. She was delighted to find an acquaintance and especially that it was me. I was somewhat alarmed, to be honest, because of my mother, you understand . . . I couldn't have Madeleine greeting me like an old friend every time we were in the same room.'

His expression begged my understanding. I nodded encouragingly.

'I persuaded Madeline she ought not to let it slip that we had met before, so we cultivated a certain distance when we were in company. But I used to see her here from time to time, sitting in the square as you were doing. She was usually reading. I think she liked to get out of the house. She was very unhappy and lonely. I would stop and exchange a few words with her, generally about the book she had in her hands. It was invariably the same sort of thing.' He sighed. 'I was appalled to hear the news of her death. She was harmless, you know, but rather—'

'Foolish?' I suggested.

'I was going to say stupid,' James said with unexpected frankness. 'Because of that I was always a little scared, you know, that she would reveal we'd met in Durham and both of us remembered the meeting. My mother would have insisted Mrs Parry turn Madeleine away at once. She would have been convinced we were on the verge of an understanding, which is ridiculous. But when my mother takes an idea in her head there is no shifting it. I should never have heard the last of it.'

I could well believe that, too. But Madeleine *was* stupid, I thought. James could not be sure of her. And as for Madeleine, had she seen James's interest as a simple act of kindness or something more? For her had the idea of an understanding been so ridiculous? Would it not have been just the kind of Cinderella tale she was so fond of reading? Alas, for Madeleine there would be no happy ever after.

'I must go indoors,' I said. 'It wouldn't do for us to be seen gossiping here together.'

For all I knew, Dr Tibbett might pop up again. At the very least, some servant either from Mrs Parry's house or the Belling residence might spot us and report the matter. Among the servants in any household of substance there is generally one spy.

The thought struck me with a sudden force. Yes, but who in the Parry household was the spy? Nugent, who was closeted daily with her mistress and had time to impart the latest news as she curled her hair? I didn't think so. Nugent appeared a woman singularly unlikely to gossip. No, it would be Simms, I decided. Simms who glided about so noiselessly, as Frank had pointed out. His employer might not be the only one to whom he passed snippets of tittle-tattle. I hadn't forgotten how I'd seen him in private conversation with Dr Tibbett at the front door on my first evening in that house. Frank had remarked that the butler and his wife had it 'very comfortable' in their present situation. They had ample opportunity to observe Dr Tibbett's visits and speculate on his intentions. Simms would ensure that whatever happened, he and his wife would not be the losers by it. I was doubly glad I'd waited here in the square until I'd regained my composure and not gone straight home.

James Belling was talking, taking his farewell and begging my pardon for delaying me.

I made some appropriate reply and crossed to the Parry house where the door was opened to me not by Simms but by Wilkins, very smart in a crisply starched lace cap and apron.

I asked about the butler's absence and received a somewhat startling reply.

'The mistress not being at home, miss, and you not wanting any luncheon, Mr Simms and Mrs Simms have taken the afternoon off and gone to visit their son at Highbury.'

'Oh?' I said. 'I didn't know they had children.' Though, of course, there was no reason why they should not.

'Only the one boy,' said Wilkins. 'Really proud of him, they are. He's clerk to a solicitor.'

'My goodness,' I said. 'They must be very gratified that he's done so well.'

'Mrs Simms does give herself airs on his account,' said Wilkins rather waspishly. 'But I suppose I would too, if I was her.'

We live in a fast-changing society, I thought, as I climbed

the stairs. Ben Ross, whose father was a pitman, had schooling thanks to my father and has risen to be an inspector of police. Young Simms, whose parents would reckon they had done well in rising to be upper servants, aspires to be a professional man one day. They and those like them are already snapping at the heels of the Frank Cartertons and James Bellings and in another generation or two, I was sure, would overtake them. And women? I wondered. When would we break free of the shackles society placed on us, strike out for new shores – and fulfil Dr Tibbett's deepest fears?

I paused by Aunt Parry's bedroom door. I thought I could hear movement on the other side of it and knocked.

Nugent, as I'd expected, opened the door.

'I don't want to disturb you at your work,' I told her. 'I only wanted to say I've obtained thread of just the right colour for our dress alterations.' I showed her what I'd purchased.

Nugent's dour features cracked into a smile. 'Why, it's perfect, miss. I've already unpicked the sleeves. Come and see.'

She stood aside and I went into the room to inspect her work so far on the tussore gown.

'I brought it in to Mrs Parry's bedroom, miss,' she confided, 'as the mistress has gone out for the afternoon and the sun shines in nice and warm. I like working here.'

I told her I appreciated her giving up what might have been seen by her as the luxury of free time.

'Oh no, I like sewing,' she said.

I sat down on the velvet stool where I'd sat earlier that day to listen to Aunt Parry map out my future.

'Wilkins told me,' I said, 'that Mrs Parry gave Miss Hexham's dresses to the staff.'

A shadow passed over Nugent's brow. I saw an inner struggle reflected on her face. She did not want to say anything critical of her mistress but her honesty wanted to speak out. I was sorry to be putting her in this fix but the disposal of Madeleine's wardrobe had worried me from the moment I'd heard of it.

'It didn't seem right to me!' Nugent burst out. 'I wouldn't say it to anyone but to you, Miss Martin. But I couldn't help thinking Miss Hexham might have changed her mind and sent for her clothes. I didn't expect to see her come back, not once the mistress told me she'd eloped.' Nugent clicked her tongue disapprovingly. 'Who'd have thought it? She seemed such a respectable young lady. But I understood she wouldn't want to face the mistress, not after letting her down so badly. I did think she might send a message, though, to say what she wanted done with her things.'

'I believe she put something in her letter about that, the one in which she told Mrs Parry of her elopement,' I said.

Nugent shook her head. 'So she may've done. But it still seemed all wrong to me.'

'How so?' I probed gently.

Nugent looked a little embarrassed. 'You won't mind

me speaking frankly, miss? I mean no disrespect. Miss Hexham didn't have very much by way of a wardrobe, a little like yourself, miss. What she had was good quality and she mended and darned everything very nicely. But there had never been any extra money for frivolities in her life, you could see that. That's the way with most people, I'm thinking. Now then . . .' Nugent took a deep breath. 'Someone who has a wardrobe full of dresses and money to replace the lot if she's a fancy, she might go off and leave every stitch of spare clothing behind her and not send for it, but someone like Miss Hexham wouldn't, there, that's my mind.'

It was a shrewd observation and it encapsulated perfectly what had been niggling at the back of my brain. 'Perhaps,' I suggested, 'the gentleman concerned had promised to replace everything.'

'It's a matter of pride,' said Nugent quietly. 'A young woman doesn't go off and take not a thing with her, not a pair of stockings or any underthings, having to ask for everything right from the start, even those articles. It would be downright indecent!' With that Nugent nodded and pressed her lips together. She would say no more on the subject. But she had said enough.

Madeleine might have written the letter, but the words in it had not been hers. She wasn't free to return for her clothes nor could she be allowed to give a forwarding address. The man who'd stood at her shoulder and directed her pen had no doubt thought himself clever in thinking of every detail, right down to what should be done with her possessions. But he'd betrayed himself and his dreadful intentions. The only reason Madeleine would not need her clothes was because she would soon be dead.

Ben Ross

I was called to Superintendent Dunn's office on my return to Scotland Yard and I am afraid it was not a happy interview.

'I hear you lost a witness this morning!' he began it in characteristically brusque manner.

'The foreman, Adams,' I said. 'He's disappeared and I think something may have happened to him. I hope I'm wrong but, to be on the safe side, I've sent word and his description to the river police.'

'Like that, is it?' Dunn scratched his wiry shock of hair.

'Yes, sir. There's no evidence to show he won't return but I feel it's unlikely. Why on earth should the fellow disappear *now*? I did go back to the demolition site to see if by any chance he'd turned up there since my visit this morning, but no luck. On my way back I made something of a detour via Oxford Street, only walking really to clear my head and think out my next move. I chanced to see Miss Martin there.'

'Oh, did you, indeed?' Superintendent Dunn's tone might be a little different to Dr Tibbett's but I could see his suspicions were the same.

'I assure you it was entirely by chance, sir.'

'I don't doubt your word, Inspector. What had Miss Martin to say of interest?'

'That our friend Mr Fletcher has been to Dorset Square, calling on Mrs Parry.'

'The devil he has!' muttered Dunn. 'What took him there?'

'Mrs Parry, it turns out, is a shareholder in the railway company engaged on building the new terminus. Miss Martin thinks Mrs Parry, for all she is sorry that Madeleine Hexham came to such a violent end, would like our enquiries wound up. She doesn't care for the notoriety the case is attracting to her household. She fears the publicity of a murder trial more than she cares for justice. Fletcher and his employers fear the same. He was almost certainly there to enlist Mrs Parry's support and we may expect to hear from the lady, I fancy. She will probably also try to enlist Miss Martin's support because Lizzie, I mean Miss Martin—'

Dunn's bushy eyebrows twitched alarmingly.

'Miss Martin was obliged to tell her that the late Dr Martin was my benefactor and Mrs Parry is the sort of woman who'd imagine that gave his daughter some hold over me. Put me under an obligation to her, I mean.'

'And I mean to make it clear that it does not,' growled Dunn. 'Although it seems to me too that Miss Martin has some hold over you.'

I felt myself redden and could find no reply.

Mercifully Dunn let me off the hook. 'Is that all she had to tell you?'

'We were interrupted, sir, by an agitated old fellow by the name of Dr Tibbett. He is a good friend of Mrs Parry and a visitor to the house. I would be curious to know more about him. I don't know if his title is medical or clerical, or he may be a doctor of philosophy. If I had to guess, I'd lay a pound to a penny he is a schoolmaster, or was. He must be sixty if he's a day.'

'I'll look into that,' said Dunn, scribbling the name on a sheet of paper. 'You get on with finding this man Adams.'

I was glad to escape. Lizzie did have a hold over me, Dunn was right. But then, she had occupied my mind since I first saw her as a boy. To me, a child of the pit accustomed to the company of the stunted, half-wild and coal-grimed children surrounding me, the doctor's daughter had appeared like a creature from another world. I had pressed my lucky piece of shale into her hand with its clean nails and soft skin, and sent up a prayer to a God I was not sure listened to the requests of pit boys that she would remember me. Perhaps he did listen because she had, something I could only believe miraculous.

When Lizzie had accused me of being without scruple in seeking to use her, it had hurt me deeply and I was still brooding about it. I really hadn't wanted it to appear that way to her. Of course, she had been right today to say I had been using her position in the Parry household to obtain information. But she had come to me in the first place with her two supporters to bring me what she'd discovered herself. Mrs Parry and the wretched Fletcher were not the only ones wishing this business over and done with. For as long as Lizzie remained in that house, I felt she was not safe.

Chapter Sixteen

Elizabeth Martin

IT WAS Sunday morning and Mrs Parry had announced the evening before on her return from her visit to Hampstead that she would attend divine service in the morning and I should go with her.

I did wonder whether I would be the only person to accompany her. My fear was that Dr Tibbett would offer his services. I really felt I couldn't face Dr Tibbett again so soon. It was possible he felt the same way about me. At any rate, there was no mention of him and instead it appeared Frank would escort the ladies.

I suspected Frank hadn't actually volunteered to do this, but that his aunt had let it be seen it was expected of him. He put a very good face on it and we set off for St Mary's church, Mrs Parry on her nephew's arm and me following behind. The weather had turned cool so I wore a little cape. On my expedition to the haberdasher's to buy

the silk thread, I'd also bought some satin ribbon and
painstakingly trimmed the cape with three rows of it. This
was London; in my own small way I must try and cut a
little more dash. I am sure Frank noticed. Several times he
glanced back at me and once, I could have sworn, he
winked.

It turned out there was a procedure to be followed
when Mr Carterton took his aunt to matins. He sat with
us through the earlier part of the service until the parson
gathered up his skirts and began to ascend the pulpit. At
this moment, Frank got up and with an all-but-inaudible
murmur which might or might not have been an excuse,
slipped out of the building. Mrs Parry showed no surprise,
nor indeed any curiosity, but sat listening attentively,
apparently blind to his defection.

After about thirty minutes the parson concluded his
address and began to make his way down the pulpit steps
again. At that moment, Frank Carterton, as if by some
magic, reappeared at the end of the pew and took his seat
again, eyes fixed ahead of him and expression bland. Again,
I observed no reaction of any sort from Mrs Parry.

I thought I understood what was going on. It was a tacit
bargain between aunt and nephew. Frank gave up his
Sunday morning to attend his aunt on condition he had
not to sit through the sermon.

Mrs Belling was in church accompanied by her son
James and a young woman who bore a striking resemblance
to her and must be her daughter, Dora. Dora Belling had

the same sharp features and discontented mouth but nevertheless looked to my eye a pale and insipid female. James bowed politely to me but gave no sign we had met. I returned his acknowledgment of my presence with a dignified nod of the head. Mrs Belling ignored me and Miss Belling, after giving me one good long stare, turned her attention to Frank, bestowing winsome smiles on him. She had a way of pressing her lips together when doing so which made me suspect irregular or bad teeth.

Poor little Madeleine, I thought, had day after day been subjected to this ruthless dismissal, even her kind friend James behaving as if they did not know one another. It must have left her feeling that she was of no more consequence than the beggar woman who stood at the church door as we came out, and vainly held out a grimy hand for alms. I gave her threepence, which was all the small change I had left, for which she blessed me.

Mrs Parry saw me do it and a slight frown crossed her brow. I expected to be told later I ought not to encourage the feckless.

Outside, the Bellings departed *en famille*. Miss Belling cast a last regretful glance at Frank but he was doing very well pretending not to notice it. Other acquaintances claimed Aunt Parry. After some animated chatter, she turned to me and told me I might go on home ahead of her, Frank also. Accordingly, we set out.

'Where do you go during the sermon?' I asked frankly. 'It cannot be very far.'

'It isn't,' he returned. He pointed to an establishment which looked like an inexpensive eating house.

'Isn't that risky?' I asked. I had to admit I was shocked. We had already breakfasted and so I supposed he had gone to that place to obtain a glass of wine at least. I knew Frank to be unpredictable but I hadn't thought him so brazen. I was astonished Aunt Parry allowed it.

'No, no,' said Frank carelessly, 'the sermon is always thirty minutes by the clock together with three minutes for the parson to get up into the pulpit and find his place in his notes and another two for him to get down again. Thirty-five minutes in all, plenty of time.'

'Suppose Aunt Parry smelled drink on you?'

Frank burst out laughing and turned an amused look on me. 'Well, now! How censorious you are, Lizzie. And suspecting the worst, too! She wouldn't smell drink because I have not been drinking: at least, not alcohol. A fellow I work with, who lodges in the area, is accustomed to make a late breakfast there every Sunday and read his newspaper. I join him, have a cup of coffee at his expense, and am back in my place in the pew, as you saw, promptly.'

I felt myself redden. 'I'm sorry, I suspected you unfairly.'

'Oh, don't apologise, Lizzie. Why should you not think the worst of me? Your friend Ross does,' he added moodily.

'He isn't my friend!' I said quickly.

'Isn't he?' Frank darted a quick glance at me. 'But I thought you and he were old acquaintances?'

'Only in the sense that we met on one occasion only

when children. I suppose your aunt told you that. I had to tell her about my father and his kind interest in the two boys. There was another boy, besides Ross, you know. But I don't know what became of him.'

'Yes, she did tell me and seemed mightily impressed by it.' Frank raised his cane to salute an acquaintance across the street who, in reply, tipped his hat. The stranger also gave me an interested look.

'Your host at the chop house, perhaps?' I asked.

'Yes, as it happens, Norton, a very good fellow even if his sense of humour can be a little tedious at times. He will rag me now that he has seen me with you. He saw me with Madeleine once and I heard of nothing but that for a week. When I convinced him I had no understanding of any kind with her and we were absolutely NOT walking out, then he pestered me to introduce him to her.'

'And did you?'

'Certainly not!' said Frank crisply. 'It is not my habit to put young women living in my aunt's household in the way of young men. But then, Madeleine did not need me to act as her sponsor in that regard, or so it seems. So you and Ross are childhood playmates, eh? It's a strange world.'

'We were *not* playmates. Haven't I made that clear enough? Or do you not believe me?'

'Oh, I believe you, Lizzie,' he said earnestly. 'Your acquaintance with him is slight.'

'Yes, and like your friend Mr Norton, you read too much into a simple acquaintanceship.'

Frank accepted my strictures with good mien. I wasn't surprised Aunt Parry had told him of my father's sponsor-ship of Ross years ago but I did wonder what else she had said. Was Frank going to enlist my help as she had tried to do? Frank had his own reasons for wanting Ross's investi-gation directed away from Dorset Square, believing as he did that he was at the top of some list he imagined Ross to have. At any rate, he was not about to let the subject of Ross drop.

Frank stopped and turned to me. 'See here, Lizzie, has he said anything to you – about me or about anything to do with this wretched affair?'

'He has not expressed any suspicion of anyone to me,' I said firmly.

'And nothing else?' A sharp note had entered his voice.

'There has hardly been the opportunity,' I said.

'Lizzie, you should be a diplomat. You have a talent for answering questions in a way which seems completely satisfactory and actually says nothing at all.'

'Oh, for goodness' sake!' I exclaimed. 'If you must know, I did meet Inspector Ross very briefly in Oxford Street, completely by chance, yesterday afternoon. We were interrupted by Dr Tibbett before we had exchanged many words. I then, after Ross had left us, had some words of my own with Dr Tibbett. We had a fair exchange of home truths! I might as well tell you this. He will probably go complaining to Aunt Parry about me.'

'Oh dear,' said Frank slowly. 'That wasn't a good idea,

Lizzie, to go upsetting the good doctor. He is a vicious old fellow in his way if anyone crosses him.'

'I can believe it,' I said. 'I think I am not quite the companion Aunt Parry was hoping for.'

'That might be her opinion,' he said unexpectedly. 'But it isn't mine.'

I wasn't sure what he meant by this and felt uneasy. We walked on a little way in silence.

'I've been seeking an opportunity to speak to you, Lizzie,' he said.

'You have plenty of opportunities to speak to me,' I replied.

'No, not seriously nor at any length. I see you at the breakfast table but that's hardly the place with Simms floating in and out. On all other occasions we risk interruption either from Aunt Julia or from Simms. He sneaks around the place in such a way. I'm sure he's Aunt Julia's spy,' Frank finished his speech discontentedly.

So Frank thought it too! I wondered what he had to say that his Aunt Julia mustn't learn of.

'We spoke alone the other evening in the library, when you returned late,' I reminded him, not willingly because that memory was an unsatisfactory one.

'You were half asleep,' he returned bluntly.

I was tired of this fencing. I stopped at the entry to Dorset Square and turned to face him. 'Well, then, what is it that you want to say?' I demanded.

'Oh, Lizzie,' he replied, half rueful and half laughing.

'You have an accomplished way of pouring cold water on a fellow.'

'I don't mean to be rude, Frank,' I apologised. 'But I really don't know what you mean.'

'Don't you?' he asked. 'Well, then, I must speak more clearly. You know I am off to St Petersburg soon?'

'Of course I know that. Have you a date for your journey?'

'I shall be leaving in about a month's time, no more. I know Aunt Julia will be upset but she's always known and accepted that I would not be staying indefinitely in Dorset Square. I want to ask you, Lizzie, if you would consider coming with me.'

I'm afraid his question quite took the wind from my sails and I gaped at him. Eventually I croaked, 'How can I come with you?'

'Why, I mean that we should be married, of course. I didn't mean any other arrangement.'

'Frank,' I began, 'this is nonsense . . .'

He reddened angrily. 'Why should it be nonsense? Oh, I know my manner offends you quite often but I can be perfectly sensible. When I get to Russia I shall have to be, representing Her Majesty's government and all the rest of it. See here, I should offer you a comfortable home and a very entertaining life. There will be parties and balls and we should have a fine time. Do consider it, Lizzie.'

'There are plenty of young women who could be your dancing partner!' I said sharply.

'But none I have ever met with whom I could embark on an adventure,' he said soberly. 'You are intelligent and resourceful and, well, there is no one else I would want as my wife.'

He was turning the brim of his hat in his hand as he spoke and watching me very seriously. I realised that he meant it. I had no idea how to respond. That is to say, I knew I must refuse, but how to phrase it? What explanation should I give or was I obliged to give any?

'I am honoured,' I began, 'and deeply appreciative, but I cannot accept your offer. You must know that, Frank. Think how your aunt would react!'

I could imagine the hysterical recriminations. She was planning to marry me off to some elderly widower. She didn't have Frank in mind for me. She probably had her own plans for Frank; Miss Belling, perhaps?

'Why should she object? You are Uncle Josiah's god-daughter. Anyway, although she might make a fuss, she'd come round.'

I couldn't agree with this sanguine statement. 'I can't see it,' I said. 'Anyway Frank, you hardly know me. I have not yet been in London a week.'

'Oh, I knew it the first evening you arrived,' he said. 'Or let's say, I half made up my mind then and made it up completely the next morning at breakfast. I am not a fool, Lizzie. Perhaps, however, you think I am?'

'No, of course I don't! But I can't marry you, Frank.'

'Because you've only known me such a short time? Or

331

because you're afraid of Aunt Julia? I don't believe that. You fear no one, I'll wager.'

'I can't marry you,' I said, 'for several reasons. We have known each other less than a week. Despite what you say, your aunt would be furious and it would be a bad start to any marriage for it to cause a serious quarrel between you and her. I suspect, though you hide it, you are not without ambition and I'm not the wife for an ambitious man and certainly not for one in the diplomatic corps. I am too freely spoken for one thing. I should bring nothing to the marriage but myself and before you gallantly protest that doesn't matter, I fancy that in our circumstances eventually it would. You will be expected to keep up a certain standard of dress and so forth in your position in St Petersburg. So would your wife. Who would pay for it all? Would your salary be so generous? You have no private money of your own, other than what your Aunt Julia may give you and that allowance would stop the moment you told her of an engagement between us. Even if all of that could be overcome we simply shouldn't suit one another. We'd be miserable.'

'Why?' he asked.

The plainest questions are often the most difficult to answer. 'I think,' I heard myself say, 'it is to do with the true price of coal.'

'What?' Frank was staring at me incredulously as well he might. 'Is that some Derbyshire saying?'

'No, it's something my father once said to me about – about something else. I meant by it, we don't look at the world around us in the same way. We value different things in others. Matters which would cause me concern are as nothing to you.'

'Look here,' he said awkwardly, the hat brim positively spinning in his fingers by now. 'I don't expect you to say you love me. But do you think, if I tried hard to be sensible and you put aside your worries about Aunt Julia and your lack of fortune, we couldn't still be happy and you might even come to love me?'

'No, Frank,' I said gently. 'I don't think it. I am sorry but perhaps it's as well. If we were imprudent enough to marry for love it would the height of foolishness. No marriage could survive long on such a basis. Love would fly out of the window as the bills arrived in the post. Just imagine the pair of us, miles away from here in Russia, with snow up to the windowsills and nothing to do but scowl at one another.' I smiled at him.

After a moment he smiled back. ' "A soft answer turneth away wrath," eh? You see, I am not irreligious though I object to sitting through sermons.'

'They say the devil can quote scripture,' I retorted.

'Phew! I was right and it's a pity it cannot be you who goes daily to the Foreign Office in place of me. Oh, Lizzie, do come to Russia with me. We should never bore one another and I do believe boredom must be the greatest enemy to married bliss. No, don't reply. I must accept your refusal though I am disappointed. I hope you will reconsider.'

'I don't think I shall, Frank. Please don't wait for me to do that.'

By common accord we walked on and made the rest of our short journey in silence. Indoors, I went upstairs to take off my bonnet and catching sight of myself in the looking glass murmured, 'There are those who would say you are a fool, Lizzie Martin. You turn down the offer of a young man with prospects, you who are almost thirty years of age and have neither beauty nor money.'

I turned and saw the tussore silk was hanging from the picture rail. If Aunt Parry knew what had happened this morning she would probably demand it back again. It was at that moment that two thoughts popped into my head and I wished very much they hadn't.

I wondered again about Frank's eagerness to quit London for Russia . . . and whether, despite his denials to his friend Norton, he had ever asked Madeleine Hexham to marry him.

Chapter Seventeen

Ben Ross

ADAMS WAS not dragged from the river but discovered beside it, sprawled on the evil-smelling greenish mud. He had been washed up with all the other flotsam and jetsam and found by the mudlarks who scavenged along the river's edge at low tide.

Though there was no immediate sign of foul play and such drownings were not so uncommon, Adams had been sought by the police as possibly having information in the matter of a murder inquiry and a postmortem was requested of the coroner with some urgency.

Morris and I made our way towards the river and Wapping Station in this connection on Monday morning.

'Why,' said Morris. 'Who'd believe it will soon be June? Look there, you mark my words, sir, we shall have fog before the day is out.'

The air around was indeed already thickening and we

put our best foot forward, hoping to have finished our business and be back home before it got worse. There was no telling how much time we had before it closed in as a dense yellow veil. The London fog is like that. It lurks about the place, showing itself as a mist above the river or a swirl of vapour across parkland, and then, before you realise it, it has oozed from its lair and is everywhere like a hunting octopus stretching out its many arms.

We were greeted by a sergeant of the river police, a real grizzled, mahogany-tanned, weather-beaten waterman who looked as if he had been built of ship's timbers. The atmosphere here was an unpleasant mixture of odorous vapour rising from the river's surface to mingle with the smoky city sky, the ingredients of a London pea-souper. The return of the chilly weather had led to more house-holders lighting fires the previous evening. The air carried on it an odour of tar and bilge water and a hint of salt spray, telling us the open sea was not so very far away and asking why we landlubbers were loitering ashore when we could be heading out to distant lands. Seagulls circled overhead, some seen and some already invisible. They added their cries to the message of the wind. I wondered what had driven them so far up the estuary. Rough weather out at sea, perhaps.

'A poor morning, gentlemen!' said our guide, rubbing his hands together. He did not appear too put out and was probably used to being out and about on the river in all weathers. His cheerful humour was in no way impaired by the fact that he led us to the mortuary maintained by the river police for reception of those unfortunates dragged from a watery grave. It was here where the examination had already been carried out.

I wished it had been conducted by good reliable Carmichael, but it had been done by a surgeon new to me. At least we were spared the presence of Carmichael's unpleasant assistant. The surgeon was a short, stout, irascible fellow who gave the impression of perpetual anger with the world about him and punctuated his conversation with belligerent cries of 'Hey? Hey?' as if someone had offended him.

'Drowned!' he announced tersely in reply to my question as to cause of death.

'No doubt about that?' I asked unwisely.

'Doubt? Doubt?' he barked. 'Lungs full of river water. How can there be any doubt?'

'I meant,' I said hastily, 'that perhaps there were other injuries?'

'None inconsistent with having fallen in the water and the body bumping up against moored craft or flotsam.'

'Ah, so none inflicted before death? He hadn't been in a fight, say?'

'Hey? Hey?' cried the surgeon, his eyes popping from his head in rage. 'No, sir, none!'

I refused to be faced down and persisted, 'No bruises to the face? No damage to the knuckles?'

'Are you deaf, sir?' shouted the surgeon. 'I said none

and there are none. The fellow had been drinking heavily, a mixture of spirits and ale. He was weaving his way home and fell in the river. It happens all the time, is that not so, Sergeant?'

This appeal was to the river man beside me who nodded and said, 'Aye, it does. No sign he was a jumper, sir. No note upon the body. Doesn't look the type, anyway. In my experience most jumpers are poor women who can face no more, or girls who've been seduced and abandoned, and ruined businessmen or unlucky gamblers.'

'Quite!' snapped the surgeon. 'A labouring man, honest fellow no doubt in his way, but given to drink as they all are. As for his knuckles, look for yourself!' He held up one of the corpse's hands for my inspection. 'Skin like leather but unbroken over the knuckles. No fist fight. Nails bitten,' he added casually. With that he let the dead man's hand drop.

'Nails bitten?' I asked, startled.

'Must I say everything twice?' howled the surgeon. 'Hey? Hey? Some people bite 'em. Nerves. Bad habit. Should be corrected of it as children.'

I opened my mouth to comment but thought better of it in this company. I turned to the Thames Division man. 'Who identified the body?'

'A gentleman by the name of Fletcher, sir, from his employers, I gather. He took it very bad. We had to take him into the other room and give him a drop of brandy to steady his nerves.'

'Fellow was a fool!' snapped the surgeon. ' "Come, come," I said to him, "this is only a labourer you employed and not a close relative. Have you never seen a dead body before? Hey?" '

'He said he had,' put in the river man, 'but not one that had been in the river.'

'So it was in the river!' said the surgeon, determined to show the miserable Fletcher no sympathy. 'It had not been there very long, as I pointed out to him. "It's in good condition, hardly deteriorated at all. Why," I said and I took the trouble to show him, "the crabs have not yet had a chance to nibble at it much, only part of the left eyeball gone." At that the fellow turned quite green.'

'We had to give him another shot of brandy,' said the river sergeant.

'So,' I asked the surgeon, 'how long do you calculate he was in the water? He was missed on Saturday morning last when he failed to appear at work and, according to his landlady, he had gone out the night before, Friday, and not returned.'

'The body was found at low tide, early this morning,' said the river man. 'The rats hadn't got to it so I reckon it had not been ashore above an hour. Beached, by a bit of luck, or you would have had to wait until the gases brought it to the surface. That can take time especially if a body gets wedged up against some underwater obstacle.'

'He went in during Friday night, by my reckoning,' said the surgeon. 'On his way home, as I said.'

'How was the weather over the river on Friday night?' I asked the river man. 'I seem to remember it rained in the early hours.'

'So it did, sir. But before that we had heavy mist then too. It was lying across the river like a blanket until the rain came down and dispersed it. You had to be careful walking along the wharves. Step to one side and you step into nothing until splash, down into old Father Thames waiting for you. Fall into his embrace and he don't let you go easy.'

'You see?' said the surgeon. 'That satisfy you? Hey, hey?'

'Well,' I said to Morris as we wended our way back to our base. 'That does not satisfy *me*. What do you make of it, hey? Hey?' I added sourly.

Morris chuckled. 'It was what we expected, sir. Lucky the body washed up so soon. Sometimes it takes a while, as the sergeant back there said. Then it's sometimes a problem identifying it.'

'Do you bite your nails, Morris?'

'No, sir. I did when I was a little child. But the school I went to was run by an elderly widowed lady, what they used to call a dame school. She was a holy terror when it came to nail-biting. If she caught you at it, boy or girl, you had to hold out your hand and crack! Down came the ruler good and hard across the palm. That cured it.'

A large and unfriendly looking seagull landed to perch on a post nearby and fix us with a malevolent eye. Morris appeared not to care for its company.

'Don't seamen believe those things to carry the souls of

seafarers?' he asked, indicating it. 'Or is that some other bird?'

'I fancy it is the storm petrel which they believe does that,' I replied, 'although I am no great authority. Certainly if a bird as humdrum as that one harbours any dead soul,' and I pointed at our wicked-eyed observer, 'it's that of a pirate, and one who was hanged. Mind your hat when it takes flight. It probably has a crack aim.'

The gull opened its vicious beak and uttered a discordant croak.

'Tell me, Sergeant,' I asked Morris, 'would you describe our late friend, Jem Adams, as a nervous man?'

'I should say not, sir. All the sensitivity of an ox, I'd say.'

'Exactly. Yet he had been biting his nails. That suggests to me that he was recently under some particular and unusual stress which caused him to return to a childhood habit. Not something he normally encountered and could manage. Something quite new and beyond his scope.'

'Well, now,' said Morris. 'There had been the finding of the body at the demolition site and the delay to the work there.'

The seagull rose from its post with a sudden flap of wings and instinctively both Morris and I ducked as it soared over our heads. Afterwards we both attempted to look as if we hadn't.

'The delay to the work there was not his to worry over,' I said, 'unless it was caused by any of the workforce in his charge. It wasn't. It was caused by a matter outside his responsibility. Fletcher is clerk of the works and while it may cause *him* sleepless nights, from the point of view of Adams it would be an excuse for any other failing. He could blame any problem among the navvies on the finding of that body. Nor did he seem very upset on that first morning we went there. No, he had been mulling over something since, or something had occurred since, which bothered him and caused him to start to chew at his fingernails, a long-abandoned habit.

'There is another thing. That surgeon spoke of a mixture of spirits and ale drunk by the deceased. We know Adams frequented the alehouses of an evening because Mrs Riley told us so. But she also said he never returned to his lodgings drunk. That suggests to me he did not normally drink spirits. But, if we are asked to believe what we have just been told at Wapping, he had drunk so freely of both ale and spirits on Friday evening that he was rolling drunk, so drunk he couldn't find his way home safely and fell into the Thames. Does that sound like Adams's normal habit?'

'No.' Morris shook his head. 'Think he was drinking with someone, sir, who was paying the bill? It was Friday night and the end of the working week. I dare say he hadn't much money left and was waiting for pay day, the next day. He wouldn't say no if anyone was offering to buy. So someone plies him with spirits which he didn't normally take, and gets him drunk.'

'Offers to escort him home and, at a quiet spot hidden

by the fog, pushes him into the water,' I continued.

'Grabs a spar or anything handy and pushes him back in if he tries to climb out,' suggested Morris, growing enthusiastic as the picture was painted. 'Kneels down and grabs him by the hair and holds his head under? The man's rolling drunk. It wouldn't take much effort.' Morris was now performing a pantomime of one man drowning another.

'But why? Why?'

'He lied to us, sir, or let's say he didn't come forward with any information he had. But he did have some. Whatever it was, he thought about it, chewed his nails over it, before he decided what to do.'

'And then,' I said softly, 'like a fool he went to the murderer with it in the hope of some financial gain. It may have been no more, as you remarked, than that it was the end of the week and he had spent up all his pay and hadn't the money for a pint. But our murderer has already killed once and you can only be hanged once. There is nothing to stop him killing again. Blackmail, Morris. There's our motive, I'll swear to it, although we can prove none of this. I wish I had cause enough to request a second postmortem, conducted by Carmichael. But I don't, confound it.'

The seagull, or one exactly like it, had returned and flapped down to settle a short distance off. I thought there was something familiar about its surly expression and wondered briefly, if it sheltered any soul in its fishy-smelling breast, whether it were that of Adams.

* * *

I returned to Scotland Yard and knocked on Dunn's door.

'Ah, Ross,' he said, shuffling papers on his desk. 'You may wish to speak with – er –' He picked up a scribbled note. 'Inspector Watkins at St James's Division. He has some information about your Dr Tibbett which may be of interest.'

'Tibbett?' I exclaimed. 'I'll go at once. Only first I should tell you that I've just come from Wapping and I'm afraid the witness Adams is finally lost completely to us.'

'Recovered the body?' Dunn knew exactly what I meant.

'Yes, sir, the surgeon says he drowned. He was found on the shore at low tide. He was apparently drunk when he went in. No other injuries.'

'Pity,' said Dunn. 'Still, couldn't be helped, I suppose.'

'With respect, sir, I think it could – be helped, I mean, or rather, he was helped. I am sure someone was drinking with him, picking up the tab, began to walk home with him and caused him to fall into the river. I have no evidence at all.'

'Then you'd better find some,' was Dunn's comment.

I went to find Morris and told him to organise some men to go around the taverns near the stretch of river where the body had been found and ask if anyone had seen Adams there on Friday night and, if so, in what company.

'Needle in a haystack,' observed Morris dolefully.

'I know it. If they saw him they won't say, most probably.

But we can only ask. There is just a chance. Of course, it's possible our killer went there in some disguise to meet with Adams. Indeed it's very likely. So if we do get a description it may only serve to lead us further astray. But at least we could be sure that he was drinking in company and if it was with a total stranger to all who saw them that indicates foul play no matter what that surgeon had to say. So do your best.'

With that I set off for the area of Piccadilly.

They were busy in Vine Street. The entrance to the police station was abuzz with shrill chatter, most of it from females of dubious character protesting they were respectable women unjustly apprehended by the constable while walking home or out on some errand. Among them were two little girls whom I would have placed at scarcely more than ten years of age. But that was old enough to bring them here. They were decked out in grubby finery and had sharp little faces atop their ill-nourished bodies. They stood close together watching the proceedings with apprehensive eyes. I was angry to see them there, not only because of the way they were being used by the families who were content to sell them and the men who were eager to buy, but because this was not the place where such unhappy victims of society should be dealt with or, indeed, how they *should* be dealt with.

Watkins was a man of about forty with a sallow complexion and world-weary air. He received me as though

Ann Granger

my visit were one more burden placed on his overtaxed shoulders. He listened dispassionately as I explained my purpose and said I understood he could give me some information about Dr Tibbett.

'I can tell you something about *a* Dr Tibbett,' he said. 'Whether it is the same one you'll have to establish. It was two years ago. There are several expensive houses of ill repute hereabouts. On this particular evening, a new client to one of these establishments wandering about unfamiliar corridors happened upon the murdered body of one of the women working there. It was half-clothed and partly hidden behind some curtains. The unfortunate client was something of a novice visitor to such establishments. If he'd been more experienced and kept a clearer head he would have got out of there as soon as he could. Instead, and fortunately for us, he panicked and rushed yelling into the street before the madam of the house could stop him. There, by chance, he ran straight into a police patrol. They came at once and prevented anyone leaving the place. You can imagine the scene!'

Watkins allowed himself a faint dry smile.

I could indeed. There would have been outwardly respectable men in all walks of life scared out of their wits and trying by any means possible to leave the place without giving their names and addresses.

'Tibbett was there?' I guessed.

'Yes, he was. I was called to the scene and I spoke to him myself. I remember him well. I never heard so much

346

high-flown rhetoric and bombast. He denied he was there as a client and objected strongly to his details being taken. He said he was only there to conduct research into organised immorality in London with a view to a campaign directed to the reform and redemption of the young women involved. I tell you, Mr Ross, you hear almost any kind of excuse in those circumstances but that one took my breath away.'

'Did you find the murderer?'

'We did. A fellow named Phelps. He'd been a regular customer there and always asked for that same girl. As sometimes happens when a man's a regular client of the same prostitute, he had become somewhat possessive and jealous. Phelps was a tradesman, reasonably successful in his line of business, but awkward in the company of the ladies. He had begun to imagine the girl liked him above her other clients and interpreted her professional words of delight at seeing him as being a genuine regard for him. He wanted her to leave there and let him set her up somewhere under his protection. She refused. She had told other girls before the fatal evening that she didn't like him and found his manner odd, persistent and a little threatening. When he finally saw that she wouldn't agree, he flew into a rage and strangled her.'

'Strangled her?' I asked quickly.

'Yes, strangled,' repeated Watkins, a little irritated. 'He was only too anxious to tell us all about it. Later, of course, he regretted his willingness to confess and tried to retract it. The judge and the jury would have none of it and he went to the gallows. It was something of a sad case. He was a lonely man and the company of those girls the only female company he ever had.'

Watkins showed a spark of interest. 'Is Tibbett involved in this case of yours?'

'I don't know. All I can say is that I have plenty of suspects and no evidence. But what you tell me about Tibbett is very interesting.'

'Let me know if Tibbett's your man,' Watkins replied. 'I found him a ghastly old humbug.'

I found when I left Vine Street that the fog had thickened as I had feared it would. The swirling tendrils were dyed a virulent yellow as if soaked in nicotine and they enveloped everyone, choking the breath from one's lungs, numbing one's senses. Pedestrians hurried past me, muffled in scarves and coughing, some with handkerchiefs held to their mouths in a vain attempt to keep the intruding miasma at bay. Cabs plodded past at the same slow pace as brewers' drays. The air smelled foul. Distorted sounds floated in it in disembodied fashion, divested of their sources. It was as if I were surrounded by ghosts.

In the midst of this, as I struggled to make what speed I could, I heard my name called. I stopped, sought about me vainly for the source of the greeting and eventually was obliged to call out, asking, 'Who is it? Where are you?'

'Why, here, Inspector Ross,' returned a voice which

although not familiar yet I felt I had heard recently. A figure materialised in the gloom and I saw it was Carmichael's assistant, of all people.

'It's Scully, sir,' he said when I didn't return his greeting. 'You know me, sir, I help Dr Carmichael.'

The fog crawled down the back of my overcoat between collar and neck and caressed my spine with damp cold fingers. Or was it only Scully's presence that did that? I hadn't even known his name before but of course I knew his pasty face and the way he held himself, as if hovering. What the devil was he doing out and about and how had he recognised me? How could he see me so clearly when I couldn't see him? Had his eyes some gift of piercing the gloom which mine had not?

'What brings you out on such a day?' I asked testily.

'Believe me, I wouldn't be out if I hadn't some business to attend to,' he returned. 'I dare say it is the same for you, sir.'

'Yes, yes, forgive me, I am in a hurry,' I said and stepped away from him.

'Perhaps it will keep evil-doers indoors, eh, Inspector Ross?' Scully's voice floated after me.

And perhaps it won't, I thought sourly. The fog provided cover for those who sought anonymity.

Anonymity veiled secrets. What business had brought Scully out into the fog? But even the most upright pillar of the community might guard his secrets. Like that old scoundrel, Dr Tibbett, who saw fit to dismiss me when he found me talking to Lizzie, but who prowled the brothels by night indulging who knew what perverted preferences. Watkins's information had been by way of a revelation, I thought as I continued my return journey to Scotland Yard. Even so I must be careful not to let a personal dislike lead me into chasing off down a blind alley. Watkins's account of the murder in the brothel and Dr Tibbett's presence on the scene had shaken me. Yet the unfortunate prostitute had been strangled, not bludgeoned. A multiple murderer does not necessarily always kill in the same way but often he will. He has found a means which works and he sticks to it. In the earlier killing, however, circumstances might have played a part. If the girl had been savagely beaten she might still have found time to cry out loudly enough to attract enquiry. With strangulation that would not be so. But then, why not strangle poor Miss Hexham?

However tempting it was to try and fit this sordid but not uncommon (and in its own way pathetic) tale of the seamier side of London life into the murder I was currently investigating, to do so might only stir up needless complications. However, Tibbett appeared to be a common link and in my line of work a common link is always to be followed up.

What if I put aside both the death of the prostitute and the murder of Madeleine Hexham and concentrated on the unexplained death of Jem Adams? How would Tibbett fit into that? Would Tibbett have risked drinking with

Adams in low taverns where he must be an obvious stranger and cut an unusual figure even in some disguise? That impressive figure and manner and the head of silver hair would be remembered. No, it hardly seemed possible. But a desperate man is ingenious and a man with all to lose takes risks . . . and there are such things as wigs.

Chapter Eighteen

Elizabeth Martin

I LEANED from my bedroom window on Monday morning and saw the sky above Dorset Square was a dull dirty white and the air unpleasant to breathe. The sun could not break through and the cloud cover served to keep low the accumulated smoke and smells of the city which could not escape into the higher atmosphere.

Bessie, bustling in with her jug of hot water, observed: 'We'll have a proper fog by tonight, miss; you can put your money on it. A real pea-souper, that's what. Keep your window closed or it will come in and choke you.'

Aunt Parry, I was told by Nugent whom I met on my way down to breakfast, was unlikely to make an appearance, at least not until the evening.

'It's the low pressure, miss, gives madam migraines. The moment the barometer falls she has to take to her bed.'

The thought of the entire day to myself should have cheered me, but if it turned too unpleasant to go out, I should be shut indoors all day with only my own company.

There was other company, Frank's, at breakfast. Since our conversation on the walk back from church the previous day we hadn't been alone together. I'd been rather dreading our next encounter without others to carry the conversation. There must be some little awkwardness in the circumstances.

But Frank was eating his way through a hearty breakfast in his usual manner and bid me good morning as if nothing had happened. I wondered if, having had time to think, he had decided perhaps he'd been rash to make his offer and was now relieved I hadn't accepted it.

I, too, was relieved to find he'd put the matter out of his mind. But, as when I'd been slighted by the prowler at the railway station on my arrival, I felt a little put out. One didn't expect to find a rejected suitor demolishing a plate of bacon and kidneys with quite such gusto.

'Bessie tells me she expects fog before tonight,' I said, determined to show that I was equally at my ease – even if I wasn't.

'Bound to be,' said Frank, cutting energetically through a thick slice of fat fried bacon. 'You've not seen it yet but London fogs are notorious. Very bad for the chest. You should stay indoors if you don't want to be wheezing and coughing like a grampus for the rest of the week.'

This unattractive picture ought to be enough to make

anyone decide to stay home but it served to make me more restless, wanting to be out and about. When Frank had taken himself off to his Foreign Office desk I felt even more fidgety. I wished I had some employment which offered me more of a daily challenge than playing cards with Aunt Parry and listening to her chat. Even that would be denied me today. I was imprisoned indoors in a solitary confinement and the hours stretched out ahead of me filling me with frustration and despair.

I returned upstairs to my room, pausing to tap at Aunt Parry's door. Nugent opened it.

'I'm sorry to hear Mrs Parry is unwell and I've come to ask if there is anything I can do for her?'

Nugent glanced over her shoulder. The room behind her was in darkness behind drawn curtains. An early-morning stuffiness seeped out into the corridor where I stood. I heard a faint moan.

'It's all right, miss,' said Nugent. 'I'll take care of her. She sees nobody but me when she's like this. Why don't you get on with that sewing? It's the sort of day to stay in and sit by the fire, that's a fact.'

I did my best to follow her advice. I took the tussore silk down to the first-floor sitting room and settled myself there. But the light had grown too poor, even by the window, for such fine work and I soon saw I would have to light a lamp if I wished to continue. The thrift bred in me rebelled against this. Eventually I took the sewing back upstairs and put it away.

My next attempt was to read and the same problem arose with the poor light. Besides, I was not in the mood for it. Simms came to ask what I would like for my luncheon and I replied that just some soup would do me very well.

He raised no objection to this and a tray with the soup arrived in the sitting room. The dining-room fire, said Simms, had not yet been lit, it being unlikely that Mrs Parry would come down at all that day.

My soup soon finished, I went back to my room and sat at the rococo dressing table to think out what on earth I could do. I could write letters. Mrs Neale would be glad of my news. But how to explain to her all that had been happening here? She had been concerned about my departure for London with all its attendant dangers and unpredictable ways of its inhabitants. It would only confirm her worst fears to write: 'I've discovered my predecessor was kidnapped and murdered.' To pen: 'I have received a very good offer of marriage and turned it down' was equally impossible. I didn't know which of the two would have shocked Mrs Neale more. So, no letter-writing.

But if I couldn't justify to Mrs Neale why I'd turned down Frank, then could I fully justify it to myself? There were all the excellent and true reasons I'd given Frank at the time. Mrs Parry would have hysterics and cut her nephew off without a shilling. Frank would have no glittering career with a penniless provincial wife in tow.

There would be petty quarrels and finally bitterness. Frank might not see it now but I could.

Was this, however, all my reasoning? I liked to think it was and yet there was something more, something harder to put into words, which lurked unspoken and unadmitted at the back of my mind. There was nothing wrong with Frank other than that he was the wrong man. I could not spend my life with him. It was as simple as that. I heaved a sigh of dissatisfaction.

'At this rate, Lizzie Martin, you will end up frequenting the circulating library like poor Madeleine!' I said aloud.

I ran my finger along the dressing-table edge and traced the outline of the marquetry garlands of flowers. How pretty this piece of furniture must once have been. I envisaged the Georgian lady who would have sat here while her maid powdered her hair.

There was the faintest click from the table. It was not due to the movement of a weakened joint or the loosening of another fragment of marquetry. I repeated the action I had just made with my finger but there was nothing. Nevertheless, something I had done had dislodged or released some mechanism.

I began to run my hands systematically over the table top, around the edges and beneath the rim. There! A little drawer slid out. Its presence had been disguised by a cunning piece of design in the pattern and the layers of ancient polish and grime.

It was a shallow drawer, somewhere for my Georgian

lady to have hidden correspondence away from prying eyes of servant or, indeed, of husband. It now contained a flat, silk-covered book. I took it out and opened it.

It was a diary but not an old one. The dates began in June of the previous year. It must be Madeleine's. Most diaries run on an annual basis and to start a diary in June seemed a trifle odd but perhaps she had not long arrived in London and was beginning a fresh account for that reason.

It has never been my habit to keep a diary, although I know it to be the recognised thing for a young woman to do. What should I have written in mine, if ever I had kept one? I went to no parties or balls. The only theatre in our town was a dubious music hall on the stage of which, so I had been informed by Mary Newling, women wearing flesh-coloured tights and satin stays sang bawdy songs, and red-nosed men in loud jackets told ribald jokes. I might have been curious to see this for myself, but could hardly have done so. I met no interesting people, no travellers returned from exotic locations. Flirtations were absent from my life.

So what did I do? Before my poor father's death, as soon as I was old enough, I had taken charge of the household accounts and the management of the house in general. The ageing Mary Newling ruled over her kitchen to the end. I worried over the accounts rendered by butcher and grocer. I sought out a man to climb on the roof and mend the tiles blown loose in the winter's storms. I mended, darned and repaired any small damage to the furnishings. I dealt with would-be patients who called when my father was out or otherwise engaged. I took their messages and delivered any from him to them. Tired out at the end of every day, did I have the inclination to commit all that to a diary? Hardly!

Between my father's death and my arrival in Dorset Square, keeping a diary had been further from my thoughts than the necessity of keeping myself from the workhouse. But Madeleine had kept a diary and it was here, in my hands. In it I might read her innermost thoughts, her wishes and dreams. I'd learn how she passed her days and whom she met and talked with.

Excitement caused my heart to thud; even so, there was a natural repugnance at the thought of reading another's most intimate revelations. But here, surely, there must be some clue as to her murderer? I opened it out flat.

The handwriting was tiny but regular, each letter carefully formed, as if it had been laboured over in the schoolroom. The early entries were dull enough. Mrs Parry had been suffering from migraines and Madeleine, when not ministering to her, had fallen back on her favoured reading material to while away the days. There were therefore a number of accounts of the plots of the latest books she had brought from the circulating library. Not that these were in themselves dull. What with noble ladies falling in love with highwaymen who held up their coaches but inevitably turned out to be gentlemen; and poor girls of admirable character refusing the advances of dreadful rakes, until finally rescued by a gallant admirer of good character . . . That is, if the dreadful rake didn't reform under the influence of the poor but respectable girl and offer marriage, a country and a town house and a carriage. Indeed, life hadn't been dull in Madeleine's imagination. But it quickly became obvious that the line between imagination and reality in the reader's mind was blurred. Poor Madeleine, she had remained a schoolgirl in more ways than in her childish handwriting.

For Madeleine believed these things really happened. She longed for such a happy adventure to befall her. Worse, a hero appeared in the closely written (and, it must be said, somewhat ill-spelled) pages.

He was not named, that was the frustrating thing. With exasperating coyness he was referred to only as He! Generally the pronoun was underlined.

<u>He</u> sat across the table from me at whist this afternoon and his eyes were constantly upon me.

Probably he was wondering what mistake his fellow player was going to make next.

There was company this afternoon and the conversation very busy although dominated by Mrs B for the most part. I sat silent in my corner but <u>He</u> was watching me all the while.

I was returning from the library this morning and when by the happiest chance I met <u>Him</u> . . .

Mrs B? Mrs Belling, almost certainly, a lady much given to dominating any conversation. The 'chance' meeting? Who was clever at faking 'chance' meetings? The 'he' could only be James, I thought with dismay. It was what I had secretly feared. Madeleine had mistaken James's kindly meant interest. She had shown interest of her own, reciprocating what she had believed to be serious advances. Had James fallen into the temptation of accepting what this infatuated young woman was so clearly offering, and then panicked?

I sat with the book in my hands for a few moments. Ross must see this diary and I must take it to him immediately. Fortunately, as it now turned out, Aunt Parry was shut away in her bedroom and couldn't be disturbed so I had an excellent excuse for not telling her beforehand what I meant to do. She would insist on seeing the diary and if she deduced from it what I had done, then I wouldn't put it past her to take possession of it and neither I nor Ross would ever have the chance to read it. Aunt Parry would seek above all to protect her friend, Mrs Belling, and also to keep police enquiries from returning to the house in Dorset Square and her close circle. I knew her now to be quite ruthless about this. She cared nothing for Madeleine's murderer being brought to justice, or at least, not if it meant a scandal which would touch her.

I quickly pinned on a hat and took a light wool jacket in view of the cool weather and, without any of the servants observing, slipped out of the house. I was carrying a drawstring purse but the diary was well hidden in a pocket in my gown. I had remembered the episode of the old gentleman who had lost his wallet in Oxford Street, and I couldn't risk it being snatched from me by some fleet-footed thief.

I hadn't realised, intent on my reading, how the weather outside had deteriorated. It seemed the fog had descended much earlier than Bessie had predicted. Already visibility was restricted and I could only dimly see across Dorset Square to the houses on the far side. No children and nursemaids had ventured into the little garden today. No one would be about who was not obliged to be. The swirling vapour struck cold against my cheeks. It carried an odour of coal-fire smoke and sulphur. I hurried on. Little spots of dirt began to stain my clothes, precipitated from the atmosphere. Other intrepid pedestrians and a few horse-drawn vehicles emerged from the yellow veil in a ghostly fashion. The clip-clop of the hooves had a curious muffled sound to it.

The poor visibility led to an encounter I would have done almost anything to avoid had I been forewarned in time. In the gloom a dark shape appeared approaching me and, despite the difficulties presented to all pedestrians, walking with confidence. To my horror and dismay it gradually resolved itself into the tall, stately outline of Dr

Tibbett. My heart sank but it was too late. He had seen me. I stopped and waited as he grew ever nearer until he stood before me.

'Well, Miss Martin,' he said unpleasantly, 'another unexpected encounter. You wander about at will and at whim, it seems. Might I ask what brings you out on such an inclement day?'

'I am seeking a haberdasher's shop,' I said, remembering the reason for my being in Oxford Street when last I'd met him. 'There is one nearby, I fancy.'

I was fairly sure Dr Tibbett was not well enough acquainted with haberdashers' shops to contradict me.

As it was, he didn't try though he obviously didn't believe me. He sniffed disapprovingly. 'Very unwise,' he said. 'The fog settles on the lungs and gives rise to serious congestion.'

'Then I'm surprised to see you out!' I said boldly. 'A gentleman of your years should take great care in conditions such as these.'

He gave me a look of the purest dislike. 'I am on my way to visit my dear friend, Mrs Parry. I am surprised to see you have deserted your benefactress on such a day.'

'I haven't deserted her,' I retaliated. 'She is sick with a bad headache and keeping to her room. So you will be disappointed if you call in Dorset Square. What a good thing I met you, Dr Tibbett,' I had the effrontery to add, but I was so angry with him I couldn't resist it, 'I have been able to save you a needless journey.'

'On the contrary,' he returned immediately. 'My journey is far from needless, Miss Martin, because I can now escort you home.'

'I told you—' I began indignantly.

He held up a majestic hand and I found myself silenced. 'No ifs or buts, Miss Martin! I won't hear of you risking your health out of doors on such a day. No visit to a haberdasher's premises can be that urgent. Will you take my arm?'

He accompanied the words with an appropriate gesture.

'No, sir, I will not,' I said firmly. 'It may be unpleasant walking but I am quite able to look after myself. You have made your opinion of me quite clear. I won't burden you with my company! Good day, sir.'

With that I dived across the road, trusting that in the poor visibility traffic would be progressing at a snail's pace. I thought he called after me but I ran on as fast as I could, turned the first corner I came to, scurried down this side street, turned again and then again, hoping that the general direction was still my original one, and left him far behind me.

Sadly, after I'd gone a little further along my new path I was no longer quite sure where I was. The thickening fog meant there were no landmarks I could take my bearings from. I still believed, however, I was heading in the right direction and continued. Soon, however, my confidence began to ebb away. I was forced to realise my sense of direction was deserting me. The fog had closed round me, wrapping me up as securely as a newborn babe. I found I shared that babe's bewilderment at finding myself in an alien world. I could not tell north from south, east from west, and hardly knew up from down. Was I climbing a slight incline? Was I descending some back alley? I thought I must be in the vicinity of Oxford Street but I might well have been walking away from it. I could hear no noise of traffic but the fog deadened all sound and reduced all progress whether on two feet or in a wheeled vehicle to a crawl.

I put out my hand and felt on my right side the rough surface of a wall. After that I tried to keep in constant contact with this one solid object.

Then, without warning, I bumped into someone.

'I'm sorry,' I gasped.

'Don't apologise, my dear,' said a man's voice. 'You aren't hurt, I hope?'

'No, no,' I returned, but uneasily. There was something in the voice I didn't like. The speaker wasn't Tibbett, for that at least I had to be grateful. But who was he?

He had moved closer, looming over me as a dark shape in the swirling fog. A new odour invaded my nostrils in addition to the smell of the smoky vapour. This smell was sweet yet rotten, like that rising from the wet earth in rain-sodden graveyards.

He placed his mouth close to my ear. I felt his horrid breath on my skin. The odour was stronger but was it his breath or his clothing which was imbued with that smell of corpses?

'This is no weather to be out and about alone,' he almost whispered. 'Can I help you, my dear? Why don't you come with me?'

To my horror, a hand came out of the gloom and took my elbow.

I tried to shake it off but he gripped me the tighter. 'No!' I almost shouted. 'No, thank you. I am almost home!'

He chuckled very softly. I acted instinctively. I swung round and thrust out my free hand with the fingers outstretched rigid in the direction I guessed his face to be. I was in luck. At least one of my fingers stabbed his eye.

He swore but released me. I plunged forward into the stifling fog, not knowing what lay before me or beneath my feet, whether I would trip over an obstacle or plunge into a cellar. My only purpose was to escape him.

When I at last slowed my reckless pace and dared to stop, my heart beating painfully, I could hear nothing. There was no footstep, no sound of breathing except my own ragged breaths. He had not managed to follow me – or had he? Was my grisly interlocutor closer than I imagined? Did he stand motionless in the fog, as I did, straining his ears for the sound of my hurrying footsteps?

And where, oh where, was I now? In a mad world full of dangers on all sides. I could never find my way myself out of it and I prayed desperately I'd be rescued. I would almost have been willing to greet Dr Tibbett with pleasure if he'd reappeared.

There was a rumble of wheels and the clip-clop of

hooves; some vehicle approached at walking pace. The black shape of a closed carriage emerged, pursuing a line which must bring it very close to me. I pressed myself against a wall behind me, not wishing to be run down. The carriage rumbled level with me in terrifying proximity. There was a shout from within it and another which caused the coachman to pull up. The carriage door had opened and a figure was leaning out.

'Miss Martin? Is that not you?'

The voice was not immediately familiar and I couldn't make out the caller. But he knew my name. It was not some unknown prowler. I approached cautiously.

'I thought it was,' he said. 'Whatever are you doing out on this dreadful day?'

'Oh, Mr Fletcher,' I said in some relief, now close enough to see who it was. I had been afraid it might be James because I knew Mrs Belling kept a carriage.

'Whatever are you doing out on such a day?' he said again. 'May I not take you where you are going? You will become lost.'

'Oh, yes, please,' I gasped. 'I hadn't realised it would thicken so fast.'

'Oh, when it comes down it does so at a great rate and it's easy to be caught out. Here, I'll let down the step. Allow me to give you a hand up. Where is it I should tell Mullins to take us?'

'Oh, anywhere near to Scotland Yard, if that's convenient.'

Ann Granger

'Scotland Yard, eh?' Fletcher went to speak to his coachman. I climbed gratefully into the interior.

Chapter Nineteen

Ben Ross

ALL THE way back to Scotland Yard I found I was straining my ears for the scrape of a boot on cobble. My eyes peered into the murk. To what purpose? Because I had the nonsensical idea that Scully was out there, even following me as a mangy ownerless dog will sometimes attach itself to a passer-by. But why would he do that? Fog is a disorienting thing; it plays games with the mind. I would not let Scully haunt me. I thrust away his unseen presence.

When I reached my destination I found the place unusually quiet and all the gas jets burning merrily away. Morris had gone out to organise the trawl of waterside drinking dens, hoping to find someone who had seen Adams on Friday night with a companion. I wished him luck. I hoped he watched where he put his feet and didn't do as Adams had done and fall into the Thames. Only

Biddle was in the outer office, crouched over his desk. He was laboriously copying out some report. The tip of his tongue protruded between his lips in concentration and his breathing was heavy with the effort of his task.

As I took off my hat and slapped it heartily to rid it of the moisture clinging to the nap, I asked him, more by habit than by any real wish to know, how he was.

'A lot better, sir!' he said eagerly. He seized the opportunity to put down his pen and scrambled to his feet. 'Look!' he begged.

He began to walk up and down to demonstrate that the ankle was improved.

'Excellent, Biddle,' I said, making for the door of my office.

'Might I return to normal duty, sir?' He had intercepted me and his round boyish face gazed imploringly at mine. 'Anything, Mr Ross, so long as it's out and about. I mean, Sergeant Morris says you are short of men to conduct enquiries in Limehouse. I don't mind going to Limehouse, sir.'

Anything and anywhere to get away from that desk and the wearisome job he had there. I sympathised. I had, in any case, no time to waste words discussing it.

'Oh, I suppose so. Have a word with Sergeant Morris when he gets back.'

He beamed gratitude at me. I could have wished every constable as enthusiastic as young Biddle.

I went into my office and sat at my desk to review all I

knew about this case. The more I thought, the more convinced I became that if I were to get to the murderer, it would be via the death of Adams. Every murderer made a mistake sooner or later. The murder of Adams would be just such an error.

But if Adams were the key, it took us back to the demolition site at Agar Town. Let us suppose, I thought, that Madeleine was kept a prisoner there for the last part of the time she was missing. Let us suppose she was in one of the houses, the one in which her body was found. Where in that house? In the cellar, almost certainly. There were mould stains on her gown such as would have come from the damp walls of an underground chamber. In a cellar her cries would not be heard.

A cellar!

I jumped to my feet and dashed into the outer office. Biddle, alarmed, dropped his pen and gazed at me open-mouthed.

'Constable!' I exclaimed. 'Tell me in detail about this accident you had.'

'It really wasn't my fault, sir,' he began.

'I'm not saying it was! Just tell me what happened, boy!'

'Well, sir . . .' Biddle gulped and furrowed his brow. 'I didn't make a note of it, sir, as you like to do, I'm afraid.'

'Then let it be a lesson to you,' I said sternly. 'If you would be a detective you must learn to write down everything you observe and everything that happens to you or to others. Nothing is too trivial!'

'Yes, sir, right . . .' Biddle began a slow, painstaking account but I controlled my impatience. No matter how long he took, provided he left nothing out.

'We'd gone back to those houses. You know, sir, where the body was found. But they'd been knocked flat as pancakes by then, sir, and there were navvies taking away the rubble in great cartloads. With all that removed, well, it left the cellars open to the sky. I went over just curious, sir, and looked in. I was particularly interested to look into the one belonging to the house where she was found. We'd searched the whole place attic to cellar, of course, using our lamps. But now daylight was shining in and I could see it was really only a damp sort of cave under the house, not a proper-built cellar at all . . .' Biddle sounded censorious of the shoddy building standards which had thrown up the Agar Town houses at speed.

'The walls were rough brick with gaps in the mortar between them. I reckon I could've built better myself and that's a fact. But being so poorly finished, they offered plenty of toe- and fingerholds. So I thought I would climb down and look round. I'm a good climber, sir. I could always scramble up any tree. Once I climbed out of an upper window of our house on to the branch of a big old tree outside and made my way down and off. Mother had locked me in on that occasion, sir, for something I'd done wrong. Well, I thought I'd get down into that cellar with no trouble at all so I took off my boots . . .'

I hadn't intended to interrupt Biddle but at that point I couldn't help exclaiming, 'Took your boots off?'

'Yessir. I reckoned I could work my toes into a crevice but not my police boots. They're on the clumsy side, sir. Well, I'd just started my descent when from above me comes a great shout of "What do you think you are doing?" I looked up to see a man's face above me, red and angry but looking really frightened, too. I told him he shouldn't fear. I was quite safe and wouldn't fall but he just shouted more that I should come back up. "Here!" he said and he stretched down his hand to me to help me up. I called back that he must not try and take my hand, sir, or I would lose my grip. But it was too late and he knocked my hand from where I held on fast and there was nothing I could do. I fell backwards and down. Not wearing my boots, I damaged the ankle, sir. I damaged the wrist, too. But I suppose I was lucky. But I wouldn't have fallen, honestly, Mr Ross! I wouldn't have fallen if he hadn't come interfering!' Biddle's round eyes fixed me earnestly.

I believed him. 'Who was it?' I demanded. 'Who caused you to fall? Did you know him? Was it Adams?'

'Oh, no, sir,' said Biddle. 'It was the gentleman, Mr Fletcher. He scuttled off afterwards like he didn't want to take the blame for it, what I'd call cowardly. But either he sent Constable Jenkins and the foreman feller, or they heard me shout and came over. Either way they got me out. I didn't tell Sergeant Morris it was the gentleman's fault because I knew there was already some bad feeling between Mr Fletcher and us, the police, I mean. I didn't want to make things worse.'

Elizabeth Martin

'Well,' Fletcher said, when he had rejoined me and we moved forward. 'Might I be so bold as to ask, Miss Martin, what takes you to Scotland Yard on a day when I'd have thought you'd much prefer to stay at home?'

I reflected with some annoyance that although it was nice to have been rescued, this encounter could yet prove a nuisance. I was not well disposed towards him. He was kind enough to help me, however, and I could not but be civil to him.

'I wanted to consult Inspector Ross and I took the opportunity because Mrs Parry is indisposed and doesn't need me.'

'I see,' he said. 'It is to do with the investigation into the death of the unfortunate Miss Hexham, I suppose?' Fletcher leaned forward eagerly. 'Do you have any news? I have a great interest in how matters progress, as you know.'

'I can't say I have any news,' I said awkwardly.

He leaned back with a sigh. 'You can't imagine what this terrible business has meant to me,' he said. 'My employers worry me out of my senses. If I thought Ross was making progress and it would all be settled soon, at least I could tell them that. But whenever the directors enquire I can only tell them it is in the hands of the police. They tell me to find out what the police are doing, but the police don't tell me!' His tone grew dissatisfied. 'One would think I had no reason at all to ask! So I am pestered on all sides. It's beyond bearing.'

I felt a little badly at my critical feelings towards him. The poor man had his job to do, after all.

'I am so sorry,' I said although that wouldn't do anything to cheer him. 'At least,' I added, 'you won't get sightseers at the site on a day like this.'

It was too gloomy in the carriage to make out his features but I felt the discontentment which must show in his face as it sounded in his voice. 'Neither can much work be done on such a day. Delays are now threatening serious disruption of the entire timetable of works. You say you are on your way to see the inspector? I hope you will beg him, on Mrs Parry's behalf, to hasten his efforts.'

'I can't do that!' I retorted. 'Anyway, Mrs Parry has not asked me, at least, not directly,' I was forced to add in honesty. He heaved such a deep sigh at this that I went on impetuously, 'But, without wishing to offer you any false hope, I am about to hand something to Inspector Ross which will possibly yield a clue or two.'

'Oh?' He leaned forward in renewed eagerness. 'May I know what it is?'

I immediately regretted my imprudent tongue which

always jumped in of its own accord and uttered words my brain, if I had used it, would have kept silent. I wished we might arrive at Scotland Yard and I'd be released from this conversation, but it seemed to be taking an age to get there. The fog had slowed our progress as was to be expected but it also had a curious effect of suspending time. I found I could not be sure now just how long I had been in this carriage. Moreover, the swaddling of fog isolated us and placed Fletcher and me in a strange intimacy, travellers through a vaporous world.

'Well,' I said, 'I have found a diary which I think might have been kept by Miss Hexham.'

He was silent a moment then asked, 'You have read it?' His voice was tense.

'No, only glanced at it enough to see what it was.' I had no intention of telling him of my suspicions regarding James Belling.

'And Mrs Parry, she has also seen this diary?'

I told him she had not.

'Hum,' he said thoughtfully. 'Well, let us hope it proves helpful.'

The carriage at last rocked to a standstill and the coachman came to let down the step. Fletcher followed me out of the carriage and we stood in the now opaque, yellowish and foul-smelling atmosphere of the street. Fletcher called out, 'Off you go, then, Mullins!' and, to my surprise, the carriage clattered away.

'Why have you dismissed him?' I asked.

'Because I think I should come with you to see the inspector. Now, watch your step . . .' So saying, he took hold of my arm in a firm grip.

By now my senses were returning and the fog, although still around me, had got itself, metaphorically, out of my head. There were no lights in the solid frontage before us. A busy building full of people at work with paper and pen and with visitors passing constantly in and out would not be left in darkness on this dismal day when all natural light was obliterated. Nor would there be a complete absence of the movement and chatter of other people.

'This is not Scotland Yard,' I said tightly.

My heart had begun to pound violently. I knew I was in great danger. I had made a series of serious mistakes. My greatest error was to jump to a conclusion in the identity of 'he', Madeleine's admirer. I'd forgotten so soon what I had recently learned: Fletcher was also a visitor to Dorset Square.

His suspicions must have been aroused the moment I had told him I was bound for Scotland Yard. What could take me out on foot on such a dreadful afternoon but the discovery of some information I felt it so necessary to tell Ross at once, that I risked my health and some accident by plunging into the fog? He had to know what it was and had directed his coachman immediately to bring us to some other destination. And now he also knew what that information was: the existence of the diary.

'You see,' he said in a calm but expressionless voice which seemed curiously at one with the surrounding blanket, 'I think you should give me the diary.'

My brain thudded as I tried to think of a stratagem to distract him and, in the fog, make my escape. He would be more persistent than the man who had smelled of grave-clothes. It was Fletcher's own life which now hung in the balance. It would be no use telling him I had not brought the diary with me. I would hardly have been making my hazardous way to Ross without it. There was only one hope. He wished to keep me from seeing Ross, but he wanted the diary itself more.

My father, as a young man, had been a keen cricketer. When I was a little girl, if he had no visits to make, he would sometimes take me into the yard on a sunny afternoon and having provided me with the miniature bat he had himself used as a boy, bowl gentle overs to me. Sometimes he allowed me to bowl to him and had showed me how to do so properly. Mary Newling would come to the kitchen door during this and call out crossly, 'Doctor! That is no accomplishment for a young lady!'

Now it was an accomplishment this young lady was about to put to good use. Fletcher fortunately held me by my left arm. I twisted away from him and, bringing up and over my right arm, hurled my purse as far as it would go into the fog. I heard the stitching of the shoulder seam of my gown give way in protest, but my father would have complimented me on that throw. The little purse flew out of my hand and was lost in the murk. I didn't even hear it fall to the ground.

'Well,' I panted to Fletcher, 'if you want the diary, you will have to go and search for it. It is in that purse.'

He swore and hesitated. I realised his dilemma. In the obscurity, he could hardly hope to find the purse quickly, if he were lucky enough to find it at all before the fog lifted. Then there would be a chance another might get there before him: a lost purse soon acquires a finder in a London street.

But my plan for escape had failed. He did not rush off into the gloom but held me even more tightly by the arm.

'That was foolish, Miss Martin,' he said. 'I shall have to go and hunt for it, of course. But I cannot allow you to wander around in this weather until someone finds you and directs you to your friend, Ross. Come!'

He hauled me forward and I stumbled beside him up some steps. He was searching in his pocket and produced some keys. Still keeping his tight and painful grip on my arm, he began to unlock the door before us.

I let out a cry for help but he only said brusquely, 'There is no one to hear you. They are all waiting for the fog to lift and keeping well indoors.'

His own door was open now – I assumed this to be his house – and he pushed me ahead of him and slammed the door behind us.

'Go on!' he commanded, propelling me ahead of him down the dark hallway.

I stumbled along as best I could, colliding with pieces of furniture, until we went through a doorway. Fletcher closed the door behind us and I heard a key turn in the lock.

'One moment,' he said.

I waited as he moved away from me in the gloom. There was a rasp of a safety match and a soft light glowed, bathing the room. He had lit an oil lamp. I saw that we were in what appeared to be a dining room, though not one much in use. A smell of undisturbed dust hung in the air and the room had a forlorn appearance. There was furniture by way of a table and a set of chairs but apart from that only a single small cupboard. I noticed no pictures or ornaments nor any sign of tableware.

Fletcher turned towards me and I could now see that he had lost his hat somewhere between the street and here. His hair tumbled untidily over his forehead. His face was white and strained and the lenses of his spectacles did not disguise the wildness in his eyes. If anything, their glitter made it worse. I realised with sinking heart that I could never reason with him.

'You killed poor Madeleine,' I accused him. There was nothing to be gained now by anything but bluntness. I was afraid but I told myself it would be a mistake to show it. He too, I guessed, was afraid. I had seen a cornered rat in Mary Newling's kitchen long ago. Its terror had made it all the more dangerous. Mary had despatched it with a blow from an iron saucepan. There wasn't a single thing in this desolate room that I could seize as a weapon.

Fletcher, faced with my air of resolve, looked shifty and momentarily uncertain.

'She brought it about herself!' he defended himself at last in a sulky tone.

'She carried your child. In killing her you killed your child too! And you blame her, the victim? You are not only a common murderer but a coward. How could she have brought it about herself?'

'I would have paid her to go away and give birth to the child somewhere. It would have been placed in an orphanage and she could have returned to the world with no one the wiser. Not to Dorset Square, of course. But I would have helped her find another situation.' His tone was still sullen as if he knew the flaws in his reasoning were obvious.

'How could she return to ordinary life? The gap of some months must be accounted for. And what of her feelings? She was in love with you!'

'She was a stupid little nonentity with her mind full of ridiculous nonsense culled from the books she read,' he retorted.

'But you didn't hesitate to take advantage of that!' I flung back at him.

'She was willing,' he said coldly.

'She thought you would marry her.'

'Pah!' he turned his head away, as if to avoid the scorn on my face. His voice when he spoke next had gained a wheedling tone as if he begged me to believe his excuses – which he had no doubt been telling himself to justify his unspeakable actions. 'How could I do that? I am an ambitious man. What kind of a wife would she have made me? Besides, I am already engaged to a young lady who will be exactly the kind of wife I require and I don't mean to let anything come in the way of it.'

'Perhaps you should have thought of that before you started your sordid affair with Madeleine.'

He paused for a moment and then said simply, 'It was so easy.'

I had once described Madeleine's killer to Ross as a 'monster'. Ross had replied that although he had met some monsters in his career, he had met more frightened men driven to murder. I could see now that Fletcher was such a man, but that did not make what he had done less horrible or inexcusable or the threat to me less real.

'Marriage?' he said now thoughtfully, almost as if to himself. 'She would have nothing but marriage.' He sounded puzzled. 'Even when I made it clear I'd never marry her, she held to it. Even at the very end . . .' His voice tailed away.

Even at the very end, when starved exhausted Madeleine had been his prisoner, bullied and threatened, perhaps part of the time drugged to keep her quiet when Fletcher wasn't there, she had clung to her dream.

'She had nothing else,' I told him. 'She was without family or friends; she had no money and no prospects. Her life was one of bravely borne despair. But then you opened a window for her into the world of her daydreams in which she was happy. How could you expect her to close it again? To what would she have returned?'

He shook his head violently as if he would shake my words from his hearing. When he looked at me again I saw his expression was calmer but no less frightening. It had gained a resolve in it which struck a chill into me. Madeleine had looked into those eyes and seen her death there. I was doing the same. Madeleine, by that time more than half driven out of her mind by his ill treatment, had retreated into her private world of the imagination in which she had both marriage and happiness and refused to leave it. But I was not Madeleine.

'You cannot leave my body in Agar Town,' I said to him, I hoped in a controlled tone.

'I am aware of that!' His voice cracked on the last word. 'I shall leave it here.'

'In this house?' Prepared for almost anything as I was, that took me aback.

'I cannot move you out of it, alive or dead.' He paused, frowned and seemed to be considering his problem. 'I shall bury you here,' he said at last in the tone of one who has solved a conundrum. 'Damn it, it will be a difficult task but not impossible. But first I need to retrieve the diary you threw into the street. Come along!'

He strode towards me and dragged me to the door which he unlocked with one hand, still holding my arm in a painful grip with the other. Together we stumbled out into the hall again. Beneath the stairs there was a narrow wooden door. Fletcher yanked it open and hauled me forward.

I saw the top of a flight of wooden steps going downwards and realised it was a cellar. I could not escape from a living tomb – and tomb it would be. My body would be concealed in a hole hacked in the floor or bricked up into a wall. He was a man who spent his career on building sites. He could obtain the bricks. He probably had a fair knowledge of how it was done from watching the labourers at work.

All this churned through my head as I struggled. He thrust me through the door and I was forced to fling out both hands to try and save myself from flying head first down the stair into the darkness below.

Chapter Twenty

Ben Ross

I BURST into Dunn's office in such a manner that he leapt to his feet in some alarm.

'Good heavens, Ross!' he exclaimed. 'Whatever is the matter, man?'

'Fletcher, sir!' I told him. 'I must have a warrant for the arrest of Fletcher!'

'Fletcher? What's he done now?' Dunn scowled at me. 'See here, Inspector, the man has been as much a nuisance to me as to you but I hardly think he has done enough to get himself arrested.'

'He has killed Madeleine Hexham,' I retorted, 'I am sure of it. And Adams too, yes, yes, he killed Adams.'

At this Dunn opened his mouth, closed it again, sat down in his chair, put his broad countryman's hands flat on the top of his desk and finally said, 'Explain yourself.'

I sat down on the very edge of the chair facing the desk

and leaned forward, the words pouring from me. 'From the start he has obstructed us and tried to persuade us to leave that demolition site. He organised the removal of the body before I got there. All of this he did ostensibly in the name of the railway company, but I believe it was done for his sake and not for the sake of any delay to the work. To be able to say it was done in the name of his employers has been very convenient for him. There are so many things now which should have roused my suspicion that I am embarrassed to think I didn't consider him seriously before. Of course, I knew it must be someone with some knowledge of the site. But Fletcher, by his very visibility if I may so describe it, by his constant presence and the noise he made, somehow deflected me from considering him as a murderer who normally would be seeking anonymity and to hide himself from us.

'I suppose it was when Lizzie, I mean Miss Martin—'

Dunn's bushy eyebrows twitched but he said nothing.

'When she told me that Fletcher and Mrs Parry were known to one another and that he had visited that house, it was then I began to see him differently, if you like. It drew him into the picture and it worried me that he hadn't even mentioned it, let alone the possibility that he might have met Madeleine there on previous visits. He was gambling it wouldn't come out. He reckoned Mrs Parry wouldn't talk much about how close she was to the building going on at Agar Town. No one wants to be known as a slum landlord and after Madeleine's body was found there, she liked even less the idea that people would associate her with the place. So he was pretty sure his name wouldn't come up via her. But he didn't know about Miss Martin and it must have given him a shock when she walked in that day and found him at lunch with her employer. He didn't know she'd tell me, but he realised she might mention it somewhere and someone would pass it on.

'I believe that at first he had Madeleine hidden somewhere other than Agar Town, some private house most likely. His own, perhaps. He is a man of some substance, with plans to marry well, and I dare say he has thought about buying a property. After a while it became dangerous to keep her there any longer and he moved her to Agar Town. I believe he had decided by then that she must die. But he could not do this without some help and the person whose help he sought was the foreman, Adams.'

I had been hurrying my explanation fearing Dunn would stop me; but he showed no sign of doing so and I was able to slow my speech and take the points more calmly.

'Fletcher probably knew Adams of old and knew him to be without scruple, if the money were right. From Adams's point of view, to help Fletcher would stand him in good stead, should difficulties arise at his place of work. Whatever he did in the future, Fletcher would protect him. There would be no fear he would ever be dismissed from his job, for as long as Fletcher remained clerk of the works. They would be bound to one another, obliged to protect one another. So somehow Madeleine was moved, probably in a drugged state, to Agar Town. That would explain why she had taken no food during the last days of her life. I know I cannot prove it, Mr Dunn, yet I think I am more or less right.'

'More or less is not good enough,' growled Dunn.

'I have been speaking to Constable Biddle, sir,' I said. I repeated what Biddle had told me. 'Fletcher saw Biddle climbing down into that cellar where, I believe, he had Madeleine hidden prior to her death and, indeed, murdered her. He could not be sure there might not be some clue revealed by daylight flooding into it. Something he might have dropped, perhaps. He couldn't risk it. He hurried over there, hoping to persuade Biddle to abandon his descent. But Biddle was set on exploring the cellar and Fletcher panicked, reacting instinctively and causing the lad to fall. It was foolish but if Biddle were injured and forced to retire from the scene it is likely blame would fall on the constable and Fletcher would get away with it.'

'Panic,' said Dunn thoughtfully. 'It would be a foolish thing for him to do, but if he panicked, he might do it.'

'Yes, sir, but it was his behaviour at Limehouse,' I repeated, 'which should have alerted me. I think Adams became greedy, suggested in some way that Fletcher should remember he was beholden to him and should show his gratitude with some tangible gift. Or Fletcher may simply have decided that he couldn't trust Adams and the foreman must die. He arranged to meet the man in Limehouse on Friday evening. Fletcher went there disguised. They drank,

Fletcher moderately but ensuring his companion drank freely. He may even have dropped some drug into his ale. I wish it had been Carmichael who conducted the post-mortem!

'However, Adams was pushed or tripped or somehow caused to fall into the river and either in his drunken state could not save himself, or Fletcher stood by with a stave to push him back in or hold him under. He then went home, trusting to his disguise, to the protection of the fog which shrouded the waterside at night, and the natural inclination of the local inhabitants to turn a blind eye to anything which might bring the police to the area.

'He thought he'd got rid of the man. But when he went to the site the following morning to his horror he found me there asking for Adams. When I told him I intended to go to Adams's lodgings to try and find out what had happened to explain the foreman's disappearance, Fletcher was faced with a dilemma. He didn't want to return to Limehouse so soon. But if he didn't go with me, he would not know what I discovered. So he came. His behaviour, in retrospect, was odd. He fussed a great deal over his safety yet he led me down the street and stopped before that lodging house in a way which should have suggested to me he had been there before. He covered his face with his handkerchief as soon as the landlady opened the door to us. He kept it covered the whole time we were there, supposedly against the evil odours of the place but in reality because he feared recognition, for all his disguise on his previous visit. But most of all it was his attitude to the beggar.'

'Beggar?' asked Dunn. 'Which beggar was this?'

'A cripple, a self-proclaimed old soldier. He waited for us by the carriage and intercepted Fletcher, asking for alms. Fletcher had previously with clear reluctance given two shillings to Mrs Riley the landlady at my request. He continued to grumble about that on the way home. But yet, he gave money to the beggar. Why such generosity? I then remembered the beggar's words.' I cleared my throat and recited them as I recalled them. ' "You're a fine gentleman, ain't you, sir? You ain't a peeler. I'm only trying to keep body and soul together. You understand, sir, don't you?" '

'Ah,' said Dunn softly. 'You think that either the beggar had recognised Fletcher or Fletcher, having a bad conscience, believed he did!'

'Yes, sir, I do think it.'

Dunn leaned back in his chair and steepled his fingers. I waited impatiently. At last Dunn spoke.

'We can't arrest him on conjectures without evidence. You may well be right. But he is the sort of fellow who will have a good lawyer and if we cannot make the charges stick, we shall be not only in trouble, we shall be made objects of ridicule.' He ran a hand through his thatch of hair. 'Think of the gentlemen of the press!' he said grimly.

'But, sir—'

'Now, now,' said Dunn gently but in a manner which

stopped me in my tracks. 'You are a young man of great promise, Ross, and I don't want to see you blight what might be an excellent career by a foolish and very public mistake. You have reached your present rank at an early age and I am one who would like to see you go further. So, listen to me. There is more than one way to skin a cat. From what you tell me of the incident with Biddle, Mr Fletcher is panicked by any unexpected development. Go and find Fletcher and ask him politely to come at once with you to the Yard as we wish to discuss the case with him. He may be suspicious but he will not refuse. After all, he has been here of his own free will almost daily making our lives a misery. It would look very odd in him to refuse now. When we get him here we'll begin by discussing Adams and asking Fletcher questions about the man and his habits, and above all about his relationship with Fletcher. How long had Fletcher known him? Had he ever met with him other than at work? When we have him well and truly nervous we'll turn to his acquaintance with Mrs Parry and enquire how familiar he is with Dorset Square. Why has he never mentioned any of this to us? Is he sure he never met the deceased girl? He'll know we are in a position to check that with Mrs Parry. If he admits he did meet her, we shall ask him why, then, he has not spoken up to say so. Did he not recognise her body? She was not so disfigured as to be unrecognisable. Did he know that Mrs Parry's companion had been reported to the police as missing? Either he will bluster, become confused and crack

– or he will hold firm, may even threaten us with his lawyer, and oblige us to let him walk out of here. We shall have men ready to follow him because, mark my words . . .'

Dunn leaned forward with a wolfish grin. 'By now he will be in a fine state and my belief is that if he's guilty, he will cut and run. Then we'll have him!'

'It's risky, sir,' I dared to protest.

Dunn shook his tousled head. 'No, no, he will run. I'm an old hand, Ross, and I've seen it before. He has gambled that we would never even think he might be our murderer. But just as he interpreted the words of the Limehouse cripple to mean he'd been recognised, and Constable Biddle's curiosity to mean the lad had actually spotted something below in the cellar, so he'll interpret our words to mean we are on to him. He'll seek to save his skin. I believe it's the only way we'll get him; if we frighten him enough to break his nerve and make him bolt.'

Dunn leaned back in his chair again. 'Well, well, why are you waiting here? You had better go out and find him,' he advised me. 'And issue a pressing invitation to him to join us.'

Elizabeth Martin

I would have fallen headlong and might well have broken some bones or even my neck but my hand, flailing in the empty air, struck against a rickety rail. I grasped it with the desperation of a drowning man grabbing a floating spar and it saved me. Behind and above me the door was slammed shut. I heard the key turn. I was plunged into darkness, hanging awkwardly from the rail. My sweating fingers slowly released their grip and I sank down on to the steps beneath me where I sat panting, knowing that I had very little time to live.

Fletcher would be on his way to search in the fog for my purse. With luck that would take him some while. But he might be lucky and stumble across it and then he'd see the diary was not in it and realise I'd lied to him. I had the diary but it was still on my person. He would hasten back, furious at being deceived, and my fate would be sealed.

My eyes were becoming accustomed to the dark and I saw that it was not as complete as I'd thought. There was a glimmer of light which just made it possible to make out the outline of the cellar below me. I made my way cautiously down the rest of the steps and saw that the light came from an opening of horizontal oblong shape which was high above my head and must be at pavement level. But how to reach it? And if I reached it, could I possibly squeeze through it? I moved forward and immediately stumbled over something and fell forward, throwing out my hands to save myself.

I landed awkwardly and painfully but at a slight upwards angle. My fall had been broken by what felt like a heap of rocks. I sprawled across it and my searching fingers felt the outline of a variety of shapes, some larger, some smaller, irregular in form but with a glossy surface. Dust had been disturbed and rose to fill my nostrils with a familiar odour. Coal!

Now I knew what that opening was up there. It was the access to the coal chute by which the fuel was delivered to the house. If I could only climb up there I might not be able to get through it but I could hope to attract the attention of a passer-by with my cries. But would there be any pedestrians in this awful weather? Would Fletcher be the only one out there, casting back and forth across the street in his search for the purse? If there were others, would they be able to hear me in the muffling fog or locate my voice if they did?

Those were the odds against which I had to gamble. But first there was the diary to think about. Fletcher must not get his hands on it.

I took it from my pocket and, making my way to the wall against which the cascade of coal rested, pushed the diary well in among the lumps towards the back of the heap. I then began to prepare for my climb.

Dressed as I was I'd be hopelessly impeded by skirts. This was no time for modesty. As quickly as was possible I got out of my dress, petticoat and corset, my fingers tugging roughly at buttons making them fly off and be lost, and ripping hooks from the stitching. Now I was down to my drawers and chemise and ready to start the ascent.

At first I had no success, as each time I tried to go higher the coal beneath my feet gave way and I slid back down to the floor. I was soon hot, sweating and almost crying with frustration. The coal dust was rising in clouds, filling my nose and lungs. I coughed and spluttered and when, in gasping for air, my mouth filled with the grit, I spat it out until my mouth was so dry I could not even do that. I was bruised from lumps of coal bouncing off me. I was faced with failure; time and my strength were running out.

After my third ignominious slither to the ground, I sat on the floor and forced myself to devise some other stratagem. What if I crawled up crab-wise and at a diagonal? Would my weight not be better distributed? Accordingly I began again, but not directly below the pavement opening. Instead I began at the side of the heap and worked my way round and up. The smaller pieces of coal rained down on the floor below and some of the larger lumps were dislodged and rolled to earth with a terrifying clatter, but I found the interior of the heap stayed firm.

Even so, my progress was agonisingly slow. Surely Fletcher would be back at any moment! The light drew nearer. Besides coal I could also smell the fog. The air was damp. I had reached the top! Or as near to the top as I could get and still have enough coal beneath me to support me. The aperture was a kind of trough in the ground above. It was open to the air but, to my dismay, covered at pavement level with a stout metal lattice.

I pushed at it but it would not move. So I grasped it and

used it to haul myself up into the trough. Holding on with one hand, I pushed the other through a square hole in the lattice. But what chance was there that anyone would see my palm waving weakly down near their feet and in that awful murk?

I sat there in despair, clutching at the lattice to prevent myself sliding back down the coal heap to the bottom. Should Fletcher return having found the purse but no diary, he would try and force me to tell him where it was. Perhaps I could persuade him after all it was back at the house? Or would he guess it was hidden amongst the coal lumps? Either way, he'd be in a furious state of mind.

My ear caught the scrape of a footstep above my head in the street. He was coming back!

But no, surely more than one pair of feet walked towards the house? There were others out and about up there, despite the weather.

'Help!' I shouted with all my force up at the lattice. 'Help me! I'm locked in the cellar!'

The footsteps paused. A man's voice, distorted and muffled by fog, asked some question of his companion.

Another man replied, 'Yes, sir . . .' and then some words I couldn't catch.

I bellowed out my plea for help again. My throat was hoarse with the strain of it and I dissolved into spluttering and coughing.

The footsteps were on the move again. They were above me.

'I'm here!' I croaked and pushed my hand through the square hole in the lattice.

To my immeasurable relief the man, whoever he was, both heard me and located where my voice came from.

He must have been kneeling on the pavement by the lattice and pressing his face close to it because his voice suddenly sounded very close to mine, echoing in my ear.

'Who are you?'

It sounded familiar but I hadn't time to identify it. 'Oh, sir,' I gasped. 'My name is Elizabeth Martin and I am prisoner in this cellar. The house-owner will return shortly—'

'Oh, my God, Lizzie! Is it really you?' exclaimed the voice and I knew it to belong to Ross. 'How the devil have you got here? Are you hurt?'

My chilled hand poking through the lattice was gripped by a strong warm one which sent new life pulsing through my veins.

'Oh, Ben!' I cried out, 'you aren't imagining things, it's really me!' A feeling of relief swept over me as into my head leapt the thought: Ben is here and now everything will be all right. But in an instant the relief gave way to apprehension. Ben was out there ... but so was the desperate and murderous Fletcher. To my fear for myself was added that of what might happen to Ross. Perhaps even now Fletcher crept towards him in the fog ...

Ben was rattling at the lattice vigorously with his free hand and I heard him exclaim to his companion, 'Give me a hand here, Morris! Damn it, the thing is locked down.'

'He's out there, Ben!' I shouted up at the lattice. 'There's no time to rescue me now or explain how I got here. You must watch out! It's Fletcher! He's your murderer!'

'I know it is,' his voice returned grimly. 'Lizzie, has that devil harmed you? If he has, I swear I—'

'No, no! He has only locked me in.'

Beneath me the coal heap rattled and compacted. I slid away and had he not gripped my hand I should have gone further backwards. His fingers tightened on mine and hauled me up again to the grating. My arm ached as his must do by now and soon I would not be able to keep my grip on his or he continue to bear my weight.

I gasped. 'He's seeking Madeleine's diary which I found and was bringing to you. He won't find it because it isn't in my purse. I told him it was and threw the purse away from me. It's safe; I've hidden it here in the coal heap. Ben, whatever happens, you must search the coal heap for the diary.'

'Lizzie, keep heart! We'll have you out in no time,' was his reply. 'Sergeant Morris is here with me and we'll break down the door.'

'I can wait!' I cried back, 'now that you know I'm here. You must catch Fletcher, he's dangerous. Do be careful, Ben!'

'I know, I should have known it from the start. Where is he, searching the street, you say? I can't see a thing for this confounded fog.'

'He'll be back soon!' I called.

'Lizzie!' Ross's voice became even more urgent. 'Morris and I will hide ourselves here near the front door and catch him on his return to the house. Wait!'

His hand gave mine a last encouraging squeeze and then he released me. I heard him scramble to his feet and he and Morris moved away.

I knew they wouldn't abandon me but I still felt a return of my former despair as they left. But my strength was out. I could not hold on to the lattice now. The coal beneath me gave way. I uttered an involuntary shriek and slithered in a cascade of rocks to the floor of the cellar, nuggets striking my body and head, dust filling my nostrils and mouth. I reached the floor half stunned.

I had barely pulled my wits together and found my feet when I heard some noise above in the street. Voices entered into violent dispute. There was some scuffling and then the piercing note of a police whistle blown, no doubt, by good Sergeant Morris.

There was more scuffling and then Ross's voice floated down to me through the grating above.

'Lizzie? Are you safe? Where are you?'

'Down here!' I yelled up at him. 'I slipped down to the ground. Have you caught him?'

'Oh, yes,' said Ross in a matter-of-fact way, 'we have him. Just wait a few minutes and we'll get you out of there.'

I sank to the floor of the cellar, my knees giving way as

relief swept over me. After a short while a series of hefty thumps at the top of the cellar steps preceded the door flying open. A man's form was outlined in the opening and he came clattering down the steps.

'Lizzie! Lizzie! Where the devil are you? Are you hurt?' Ross arrived panting in my prison cell.

I managed to scramble upright and ran towards him. 'I am quite all right, but, oh, so glad to see you!'

I held out my hands to him and he seized them in his and grasped them tightly, pulling me towards him so that I found myself pressed against his chest.

'You can't imagine how overjoyed I am to find you, Lizzie! To think I might not have been in time and you were in the hands of that devil! But for the purest chance and Biddle's tale . . . No, it doesn't bear thinking of. You are safe and that is what matters.'

'Oh, Ben . . .' I mumbled into his coat.

'Sir?' cried Morris's voice from above. 'Everything all right down there? Is the lady safe?'

'Yes, thank God!' Ross shouted back.

Our joint response to the arrival of a third party on the scene was to spring apart. Ross glanced over his shoulder towards the sound of the sergeant's voice, hesitated and threw a rapid look over me. 'Look here, Lizzie, might I suggest that before anyone else comes down here, you put on your dress?'

Chapter Twenty-One

'I AM very glad to find Miss Martin so well recovered,' said Inspector Ross courteously. 'You are suffering no ill effects, ma'am, I hope?' He looked across the room at me and raised his eyebrows.

We were quite a party seated in Aunt Parry's first-floor sitting room. Frank was there, having taken time from his Foreign Office duties and the preparations for his impending departure for Russia. He sat with his back to the window, one ankle propped on the other knee, staring very hard at Ross. Dr Tibbett was also there, as might be expected, placed before the mantelpiece with his hands behind his back. He looked very much, I fancied, as if he were practising being master of the house. I hoped Frank was right and Aunt Parry wouldn't be so foolish as to entrust herself to such an old rogue. However, once Frank had left for Russia my employer might well miss a man about the place and be tempted to listen favourably to Tibbett's proposal, should he make one.

At Ross's enquiry directed at me, Tibbett cleared his throat in a disapproving way. Mrs Belling sat by Aunt Parry, bolt upright in a plaid walking dress and another of those casquette hats she liked so much perched atop her false chignon. Behind her stood James in attendance on his mamma and looking miserable.

Miss Belling was not present, even though it would have been another opportunity to put her in Frank's line of sight, but probably her mother didn't consider it quite decent for Dora to be here listening to details of such a shocking adventure.

Ross sat before us all, rather as though he were presenting himself to a committee for interview. I thought him particularly smartly turned out and his boots – which had occasioned Mrs Parry some doubts on his first visit – shone like mirrors. He puts them all to shame! I thought proudly. And shame is what they all ought to feel. But they don't. They haven't enough sensitivity in them. He is a capable, intelligent, brave and successful man who has stuck to his enquiries despite all their best efforts to hinder him. What a sorry crowd they are!

'Thank you, Inspector,' I replied politely. I ignored Tibbett and inclined my head graciously in the questioner's direction. I was, as it happened, black and blue from my encounters with the lumps of coal but it wouldn't do to say so. 'I'm quite all right.' To Tibbett's visibly increased ire I added, 'Thanks to you, and to good Sergeant Morris, of course. How grateful we must *all* be to you!'

Tibbett scowled and fiddled with his watch chain. Mrs Belling simply looked uncomprehending. Frank had the grace to mutter, 'Yes!'

'When I think of the danger Elizabeth was in!' exclaimed Aunt Parry. 'What a piece of great good fortune that you arrived in time to rescue her.'

'A piece of good fortune indeed!' snapped Frank now. 'Seeing as the police hadn't considered Fletcher at all as a suspect. It was purest chance you got there in time.'

'I began to suspect him,' returned Ross mildly, 'once Miss Martin had informed me he was a familiar visitor to this house, something I hadn't known before.'

There was an embarrassed silence. Dr Tibbett ceased fiddling with the watch chain and took it upon himself to reply.

'He was not that familiar a visitor, Inspector. He came purely in the line of business. He could by no means be described as a friend.'

'Indeed not!' confirmed Aunt Parry hastily. 'Why, when Elizabeth came home and found him here that day, he had come on business. It was purely by chance that he stayed to lunch with me.'

'No doubt,' said Ross still in that mild way, 'he hoped to persuade you to use your good offices to encourage us to abandon our enquiries.'

Aunt Parry turned brick red. Frank glowered and Dr Tibbett's brow took on that Olympian frown. 'Sir!' he boomed. 'My dear friend, Mrs Parry, would never have done anything so improper. I hope you are not suggesting that she would.'

'Of course not,' said Ross immediately. 'Forgive me, ma'am. I merely observed that no doubt it was in Fletcher's mind.'

Aunt Parry looked even more disconcerted and Frank thunderous.

'My aunt can't be expected to have read the scoundrel's mind!' he snapped.

'No, Mr Carterton, of course not.'

'*I* wasn't aware he was still calling at the house,' Frank went on, turning to his aunt.

'Well, Frank, dear . . .' began Aunt Parry.

Dr Tibbett cleared his throat warningly.

Frank flushed and said stiffly, 'I seek only to defend my aunt's reputation.'

'Has he confessed?' demanded Mrs Belling, cutting across the threatened embarrassment of a family dispute breaking out before witnesses.

She had been out of the conversation for longer than was her wont and growing visibly restless. Her sharp eyes glowed with an almost hungry look. It occurred to me there was no difference between her attitude and that of the blatant seekers after thrills who had turned up at the place where the body was found or paraded up and down outside this house in the square. I'd never liked her but now decided she was an odious woman. I hoped that Frank never found himself with Mrs Belling as a mother-in-law.

'Yes, madam,' Ross told her politely. 'Mr Fletcher seems quite anxious to talk about it and has told us all. He has lost everything now and there is no reason to hide any of it. His fiancée has broken off their engagement and her father insisted the railway company dismiss him. Even if he continued to deny his guilt – which would in any case be difficult – his reputation is destroyed. His world has crumbled about him.'

'As poor Madeleine's did when he rejected her,' I said.

They all looked at me.

'I have not changed my opinion of that young woman!' said Dr Tibbett.

'No, sir, I don't suppose you have,' Ross murmured.

'Evil breeds evil,' declared Tibbett. 'Sin opens the door to yet more of its hideous kind. Her want of moral character and duplicity were the start of all this. It cannot be denied.'

'She was deceived,' James put in unexpectedly and with some vigour. 'That is not her fault. Rather you might say it was because she was an innocent she was led astray by Fletcher. She can't be held responsible for anything he did later.'

'Nonsense, James!' interrupted his parent. 'You know nothing about it. Be quiet.'

James opened his mouth and for one moment I thought he might answer back. Even Frank looked surprised and sat up straight ready for the unbelievable to happen.

It didn't. James closed his mouth again and fell silent.

'We are all very grateful to you, anyway, Inspector Ross,'

declared Aunt Parry suddenly in a clear firm voice.

Ross recognised his dismissal. He stood up. 'I'm glad to have been of service, ma'am. Now, if you'll excuse me, I must be off.'

'Yes, yes,' said Tibbett testily, 'you will have your duties. We mustn't keep you from them.'

At this I could take no more. They were intolerable. I stood up, saying loudly, 'There is no need to trouble Simms. I'll see the inspector out.'

I won't attempt to describe the sneer with which Dr Tibbett greeted this. Mrs Belling looked disapproving. Frank glowered even more ferociously. Aunt Parry murmured, 'Yes, of course,' and looked at me a little nervously.

I led Ross down to the entrance hall in silence. There was no sign of Simms or any of the other servants. The long-case clock in the corner ticked and dust danced in the shaft of sunlight entering through the transom light above the front door. I remembered standing here waiting with my modest baggage at my feet while Simms paid off Wally Slater, so very recently and yet, somehow, seeming an age ago.

Although Simms was not to be seen there was no saying he wouldn't suddenly and silently appear. I opened the door to the library and Ross and I went in without a word and I closed the door behind us. Dr Tibbett would place his own interpretation on that. But I knew the schoolmaster for what he was. He had no call to criticise me and if he did so again to my face I would let him know it.

I turned to face Ross. 'I wanted to thank you myself,' I said, 'not only for saving me but for seeing justice will be done by poor Madeleine. I also want to apologise because they were all so rude to you upstairs.' My indignation vibrated in my voice.

He looked slightly amused. 'I'm accustomed to having brickbats thrown at my head. The scorn of Dr Tibbett and the others hardly makes an impact.' He shrugged.

'You may be generous enough to forgive them, I don't!' I burst out. 'They are hypocrites, the whole lot of them, except possibly Frank, and Frank is not among them only because he is content to believe everyone will love him as he loves himself and he need make no further effort to gain approval. Mrs Parry knew that Madeleine was a stranger in London and it was her responsibility to take good care of her. She has no business to speak or allow others to speak of Madeleine with such scorn. Aunt Parry herself was a country parson's daughter, just like Madeleine. If my godfather Josiah, in that portrait up there –' I flung out my hand to point to it – 'if he had not met her and married her, she would have been in just such a position as Madeleine, a governess or companion. It puts me out of all patience!'

I was so cross at the thought of them all that I stamped my foot in exasperation, which seemed to amuse Ross the more. But he grew serious almost at once.

'They are not the only ones with a heavy responsibility

to bear. Perhaps Mr Carterton is right and I should have had my eye on Fletcher sooner. Then you wouldn't have run into such danger. I do blame myself for that. Yes, yes, that's my fault. I don't know now how I could have been so stupid as not to see him at once for what he was. Oh, dear Lizzie, when I think what he might have done – I mean, dear Miss Martin . . .' He stammered to a halt.

'Why ever should you suspect him?' I comforted him. 'You didn't know Fletcher had been in this house. It's not surprising he didn't tell you, but one of the others, either Mrs Parry or Frank, should have done so. One of them should have realised what Fletcher was like.'

'Mrs Parry, I think, does not discuss her business matters with police officers. As for Mr Carterton, it probably didn't cross his mind.' Ross permitted himself a slight smile.

I felt impelled to defend Frank, although I had criticised him earlier. 'You mustn't think Mr Carterton a fool,' I said. 'He can be quite sensible and I hope, when he gets to St Petersburg, he'll acquit himself creditably.'

'You will miss him?' Ross asked, watching my face.

'No,' I said quietly. 'I shall not miss him. Don't mis-understand me. I have no interest of a personal nature in Mr Carterton.'

A small sigh as of relief escaped Ross. 'Will you stay in this house, Lizzie?'

I shook my head. 'No. For the time being I must do so but I mean to start looking for an alternative situation at once. I don't think Aunt Parry will seek to dissuade me. She won't want me to go at once because that might suggest something is amiss here and she has a mortal fear of gossip. But she knows I've seen through her, seen through all of them.'

Besides, once Frank was gone, Tibbett would eventually persuade her to dismiss me, I was sure of it. I would go on my own two feet of my own free will first and deprive him of his petty triumph.

'You know,' Ross began looking unaccustomedly ill at ease, 'it's been a great – well, I'd say it's been a great pleasure although that's too feeble a phrase – it's brought me great happiness to see you again.'

'And I you,' I said earnestly. I had a brief memory of burying my face in his coat in the cellar of Fletcher's house and felt my cheeks burn.

'Ah.' He half grinned, scratched his mop of curling black hair and, I swear, also blushed. 'When I came down to London as a youngster, as I told you, I dreamed of making my fortune.' He smiled again awkwardly. 'I haven't exactly done that. But I have not done so badly, either. I had an engine driving my dream. You were not aware of me. But as I grew up I watched you grow up, too. I saw you walking about in our town. First of all you would be with that French governess the doctor employed. What a strange female she was. The boys at the grammar school were wont to make jokes about her, I'm sorry to say, but not about you. All of them respected Dr Martin. I should never have allowed them to say anything disrespectful, anyway. In later years I saw you shopping with that elderly housekeeper of yours or setting off in best bib and tucker to visit a friend or to go to church of a Sunday. You never saw me. I kept out of the way. But my dream was that if I made a fortune in London, I should be able to return home and claim Lizzie Martin – if she would have me and no one else had claimed her first.'

I couldn't meet his gaze. Since the moment he had called down into my cellar prison I had had time to reflect on the emotions I'd felt on hearing his voice. Relief at the prospect of rescue, certainly; but there had been – and still was – something more: a new and strange uncertainty which both exhilarated and alarmed me. It caused me to lose my usual confidence.

I stared down hard at the Turkey carpet and heard myself whisper, 'No one else claimed her first.'

'Do you think,' he went on hesitantly, 'that Mrs Parry would object if I called on you, while you're still living here?'

I shook my head and managed to retort with something of my usual briskness, 'Whether she minds or not, she is in no position to object!'

'Ah then,' said Ben sounding more confident, 'Would you object? To us walking out, I mean?'

I looked up then, full in his face. 'No, Ben,' I said, 'I shouldn't object. I think I should like it very much.'